PRAISE FOR ALISON BLISS

More to Love

"Fresh, fun, adorable!"

—Lori Wilde, *New York Times* best-selling author

"Romance novels with heroines who are not model thin are hard to find and valuable. Fans of Jennifer Weiner will enjoy Alison Bliss."

—*Booklist*

On the Plus Side

"Bliss's second installment to this fun series will convince readers that sexy comes in all shapes and sizes. Valerie is a confident heroine and the kind of cheeky role model women of all ages need in their life." —RTBookReviews.com

Size Matters

"*Size Matters* pulls at your heartstrings and your belly will be hurting from the amount of laughs you'll have while reading."

—HeroesandHeartbreakers.com

"This book was so entertaining that, once I started, I couldn't put it down. I loved everything about it. Ms. Bliss gave us a story that was full of life, laughter, and felt so real."

—Romancing-the-Book.com

OUT
of the
BLUE

ALISON BLISS

FOREVER

New York   Boston

Forever
Hachette Book Group
1290 Avenue of the Americas, New York, NY 10104
read-forever.com
twitter.com/readforeverpub

First Edition: February 2022

Forever is an imprint of Grand Central Publishing. The Forever name and logo are trademarks of Hachette Book Group, Inc.

The publisher is not responsible for websites (or their content) that are not owned by the publisher.

The Hachette Speakers Bureau provides a wide range of authors for speaking events. To find out more, go to www.hachettespeakersbureau.com or call (866) 376-6591.

Print book interior design by Abby Reilly

Library of Congress Cataloging-in-Publication Data

Names: Bliss, Alison, author.
Title: Out of the blue / Alison Bliss.
Description: First edition. | New York : Forever, 2022. | Series: A perfect fit
Identifiers: LCCN 2021041295 | ISBN 9781538764589 (trade paperback) |
    ISBN 9781538764572 (ebook)
Subjects: LCSH: Single women--Fiction. | Overweight women--Fiction |
Personal trainers--Fiction. | LCGFT: Romance fiction. | Humorous fiction. |
    Novels.
Classification: LCC PS3602.L574 O98 2022 | DDC 813/.6--dc23
LC record available at https://lccn.loc.gov/2021041295

ISBNs: 978-1-5387-6458-9 (trade paperback), 978-1-5387-6457-2 (ebook)

Printed in the United States of America

LSC-C

Printing 1, 2021

To my aunt Annie Ruth,
thank you for all the love and support.

It means a lot!

AUTHOR'S NOTE

Dear Readers,

Thank you so much for picking up a copy of *Out of the Blue*! Before the story begins, I want to share with you what prompted my interest in writing a novel featuring a plus-size heroine and her oh-so-hot personal trainer.

A few years ago, I was in the same situation as Preslee. I was prediabetic and needed to make some lifestyle changes. So I hired a personal trainer to help me protect my health. Now, keep in mind that I'm a happily married woman, and I assure you that this story is not autobiographical in any other way. But with my personal trainer's help, I was able to improve my fitness and repair the damage I had done to my health.

That's why this story matters. That's why this story is so personal to me. But Preslee's story is not a weight loss journey. It's a wellness journey about how Preslee took action to achieve her goals and grew in confidence along the way. And since I'm a romance author, the situation was undoubtedly destined to become a love story. I hope you enjoy it!

Alison Bliss

OUT
of the
BLUE

CHAPTER ONE

Preslee Owens sat in her green Honda Accord outside the Body Shop, daring herself to go inside. If her vehicle had needed repairs, she wouldn't have hesitated to stroll through the doors and ask someone for help. But since it was her plus-size figure that needed the overhaul, she couldn't help but feel self-conscious about doing so.

After all, it was like a bad joke. *Preslee Owens walks into a gym...*

Only she also happened to be the punch line.

At twenty-eight, she had never once set foot inside a gym before. She realized how ridiculous that sounded since most people had probably played sports at some point in their life or, at the very least, taken a physical education class during their school years.

But not Preslee. She'd been homeschooled all of her life and had never had any interest in sports. Not only because she was clumsy but because most sports took place outdoors and she couldn't fathom the idea of standing out in the Texas heat any longer than necessary. Who in their right mind likes to sweat?

Okay, she guessed some people did. But not her.

The only physical activity she'd participated in on a regular basis as a child consisted of her taking out the trash or washing the dishes. Neither of which had ever gotten her heart rate up high enough to be considered exercise.

Well, unless she counted the time she'd burned a pan of lasagna in the oven until it was completely black. Even after soaking the pan in hot, soapy water overnight, she'd scrubbed it so long and hard the next day that she'd nearly passed out from the effort.

That's what I get for adding a ridiculous amount of cheese.

Preslee sighed. Clearly, her diet hadn't helped matters either. She'd always eaten whatever she wanted, whenever she wanted. She'd never paid any attention to the number of calories in each serving, much less considered the negative impact that her poor choices might have on her health. Well, until now.

She glanced sullenly at the untouched cream-filled snack cake she'd tossed into her center console on her way to work. Though it was still calling her name, she hadn't eaten it at lunch like she'd planned. She couldn't. Not after what her doctor had said when he'd called this morning with her test results.

Last week's appointment with Dr. Fowler had started out as a routine annual physical. But when he'd noticed that Preslee's blood pressure was a little high and that she had gained weight, he asked about her family's medical history with diabetes, high blood pressure, low HDL cholesterol and high triglycerides, and even gestational diabetes. None of which she had an answer for.

At three weeks old, Preslee had been adopted by a childless couple who'd been unable to conceive on their own. Because they weren't blood relatives, she had zero knowledge of her biological family's medical history. Therefore, Dr. Fowler's preliminary screening hadn't been able to produce any helpful information to adequately gauge her health risks.

So he'd done the only thing he could. He'd ordered some lab tests of her fasting glucose level, oral glucose tolerance level, and A1C. All of which determined whether or not she had impaired glucose levels.

At the time, Preslee hadn't been concerned. After all, she was young and hadn't experienced any health issues that would indicate anything was wrong. Sure, she'd gained some extra weight and her blood pressure was a little high, but neither seemed like much to worry about on their own.

Still, the determined Dr. Fowler had refused to take no for an answer. Although she loved having the elderly man as her doctor, the persistent grump glowered when he didn't get his way. Without a doubt, he would've harped on her until the end of time—or at least until his death—if she hadn't conceded and taken the damn tests.

Maybe that wouldn't have bothered most people since they probably never ran into their doctors outside of their offices. Unfortunately, Preslee didn't have that luxury. Her father lived next door to the man. Besides that, Granite, Texas, was a small town, and it wasn't unusual for her to run into Dr. Fowler several times a week. Often at the post office, occasionally at the grocery store, sometimes in the bakery, and he even knew where she worked. Jeez. Nowhere was safe.

So Preslee had sucked it up and agreed to the tests. She'd stopped eating at eight o'clock the night before and woke up early the next morning to drive herself to the nearest lab in the next town over to have her blood drawn. All the while feeling like she'd been starving for weeks and had sand trickling down her dry, scratchy throat.

Yeah, fasting sucked.

Thank goodness she didn't know any top-secret government intelligence. If anyone ever wanted to torture her for information, all they'd have to do was refuse her food or water for about twelve hours. She'd tell them everything they ever wanted to know. And probably then some.

Over the past week, however, Preslee had forgotten all about those dang tests and—thankfully—her horrible fasting experience. That was, until the doctor had called this morning to give her the upsetting results. As he spoke, only one word had stood out to her. *Prediabetic.*

Although the medical term sounded ominous, Dr. Fowler had assured her that it wasn't the worst thing he could've found and it was completely reversible if she took action now. Then he'd urged her to change her crappy diet and become more physically active in order to lose some weight and get her glucose levels back to normal.

Right. Because it was just that simple.

Maybe the optimistic doctor hadn't realized that he'd just asked her to change her entire lifestyle, but he had. And whether she liked it or not, that was going to take some seriously hard work on her part. But she didn't have a choice. Her health was at stake, and she wanted—no, *needed*—to take this seriously. Otherwise, it wouldn't be long before she dropped the *pre* and was left with only *diabetic.*

Preslee cringed and then hauled in a deep breath. "Better go inside and get this over with."

She waited purposely for two young guys to enter the gym before sliding out of her car and adjusting her tight outfit. She'd purchased her workout attire at a local shop during her lunch hour without trying it on, and the clothing was more fitted to her body than she normally preferred. Like *a lot* more fitted. But it couldn't be helped. She'd bought the items in the largest size available and had hoped for the best. It wasn't like small towns had many options when it came to clothing stores. Especially for a plus-size woman.

She was only a respectable C cup at best, so at least the blue sports bra kept her boobs in place. Even if the straps dug uncomfortably into her shoulders. And the black calf-length leggings? Yeah, those had gifted her with an unpleasant wedgie that constantly needed to be picked.

Still, the workout clothes seemed somehow necessary... though she'd hidden both articles under a loose, oversize T-shirt. The idea was that looking—or rather *feeling*—the part would help motivate her. Or, at the very least, keep her from standing out in the gym like a brick in a pile of pennies.

Yeah, right. Good luck with that. She'd been sitting outside in her car for almost thirty minutes, and everyone she'd seen entering or leaving the gym had all been way more physically fit than her. Some of her workout clothes may have matched theirs, but the shape of her full-figured body didn't.

Preslee glanced back at the gym doors, and nervous energy raced through her veins once more. She swiped the back of her hand over her brow. God, she was already sweating profusely, and she hadn't even started working out yet. Maybe she could just do *that* for a daily workout instead. Park outside the gym and panic for half an hour at the terrifying thought of going inside.

Hell, at that rate, I'd be skinny by the end of the month.

Preslee fought back a grin at the silly thought and then shook her head. Okay, enough. She couldn't allow herself to stall any longer. She was going through those gym doors, whether she liked it or not. *Woman the hell up.*

With another frustrated sigh, she heaved herself in the direction of the Body Shop's entrance, her sheer determination forcing one foot in front of the other.

Too bad she didn't get far.

Preslee had been so focused on the doors and talking herself into walking through them that she misjudged the curb and caught the toe of her sneaker on the edge of it. She tripped, stumbling forward with arms flailing, before landing on all fours onto the hard concrete sidewalk. Pain ripped through her as the metal car keys in her right hand stabbed into her palm and rough cement scraped both knees.

Ouch! Dang it.

Wincing, she rolled over to sit on her butt and checked her palm first. A purplish indention marred her right hand, and while it hurt a little, at least the skin wasn't broken. So she dusted off her dirty palms and then rolled up her leggings to check her knees. Angry red patches glared back at her where the concrete had skinned them, and a small cut marked her left knee where a sharp rock must've bitten into the skin.

She was bleeding too. Great.

As if it wasn't embarrassing enough, a truck chose that moment to rumble into the parking lot and pull into a nearby space. The last thing she wanted was for someone to walk up and find her sitting on the ground looking like an idiot. So Preslee quickly hobbled to her feet and limped toward the gym's entrance. She probably should've gone home to clean her bleeding knee, but dang it, there was no way she was going to give herself an out. If she did, she had no doubt that she would take it and never come back.

Uh-uh. No way. She was going to do this even if it killed her. And, at this rate, chances were good that it probably would...since she hadn't even made it *into* the building without hurting herself.

She shook her head. *Gym, one. Preslee, zero.*

As she opened the glass door and stepped inside, a rush of cool air wafted over her, and she let out a contented sigh. Thank God. She hadn't been entirely sure whether the gym would have air-conditioning or not. But now that she thought about it, any building that wasn't climate-controlled in the South Texas heat would probably be a death trap for everyone inside.

Preslee glanced around and took in the unfamiliar surroundings. The large one-room space was of substantial size and had a warehouse feel with high ceilings and black rubber floors. Mirrors lined the back wall, and there were rows of machines and other equipment available for use toward the front of the gym. While the place wasn't exactly packed, there were a dozen or so people scattered throughout.

Her gaze landed on the check-in desk to her left, and she moved toward it, trying not to limp. A blond male stood behind the counter. He looked to be in maybe his late twenties or early thirties, and his large biceps bulged against the tight sleeves of his black T-shirt that sported a white Body Shop logo.

He glanced up from a clipboard as she approached, and

surprise registered in his eyes before he managed to mask it with a good-natured smile and a friendly hello. She might've been insulted if it hadn't been for the fact that she was just as surprised as he was that she was inside a gym. "Uh, hi. Is this where I sign up for a new membership?"

He nodded and leaned on the counter with one hand. "Yes, ma'am. Are you looking for monthly or yearly?"

"Um, monthly, I guess." Jeez. That almost sounded like a question.

His smile widened. "All right," he said, reaching for a paper and sliding it across the counter with a pen. "Here's a form you'll need to fill out. The monthly rates are at the bottom, and the gym rules and other helpful information are on the back. But feel free to let me know if you have any questions. My name's Kurt, and I'm the manager."

Preslee nodded. "Great, thanks. By the way, you don't happen to have a Band-Aid back there, do you?" She held up her knee to show the small amount of blood oozing from it. "I scuffed it in the parking lot on my way in."

"Let me check." He pulled a first aid kit from beneath the counter, popped it open, and rifled through the contents. "Hmm, we should probably restock this kit. Looks like this is the only thing we have left," he said, holding up a long white bandage. Then he shrugged. "It might work."

She accepted it. "It'll do. Thank you."

After applying the bandage to the small cut, she realized she couldn't cover it with her leggings without the stretchy fabric pulling tight across her sore knee. And that hurt too much. So instead she left her legging up over her kneecap and hoped that no one would notice how dumb it looked.

She glanced back up at Kurt, who wore an amused grin on his face. Well, no one else anyway.

The gym manager continued to smile as she moved off to the side and read over the information on the form he'd given her. She couldn't really blame him. Although he didn't say as much, she looked like she was wearing a panty liner on her knee.

When she was done filling out the form, she slid it back across the counter along with his pen. He asked for photo identification, which she provided, and then she paid him her first monthly fee.

Once they completed the entire transaction, Kurt handed her a black, plastic membership card with the Body Shop logo on it. "You're all set. Any questions?"

Yes, but she was too embarrassed to ask them. "Nope."

His smile weakened, and his voice softened, as if he knew she was lying. "All right. Well, I'm here if you change your mind."

"Thanks." Preslee gave the good-looking man a polite smile and then walked away from the check-in desk, although she wasn't really sure in which direction to go. How did anyone know where to start?

She traipsed up and down each aisle, looking for a machine labeled for beginners, but apparently they didn't make those. The more she glanced over the equipment, the more uncertain and self-conscious she started to feel. Especially when her slow progression around the room began drawing unwanted attention.

Two buff guys lifting and clanging weights on the other side of the room both wore smirks as they followed her movements with their eyes. Maybe they were fascinated by her inability to choose a machine due to her lack of knowledge. Or maybe they weren't used to seeing a newcomer who didn't know what the hell she was doing. Or maybe they were just riveted by the fact that a plus-size girl was going to actually work out. Who knew? But it only made being inside the gym that much more intimidating.

Determined to ignore their beady eyes staring her down, Preslee glanced to the next row over and spotted a stair-climbing machine. Oh, that one looked simple enough. Who couldn't climb stairs? And she'd probably be great at it given how she ran up and down a set of stairs at work all the time. Her dad's antique shop had only one storeroom, and it just so happened to be located in the basement. Lucky her.

Excited that she'd finally found a machine to try out, one that even looked like fun, she hustled down the aisle toward it. But just as she careened around the corner, a man stepped out of a doorway and landed directly in her path. She tried to skid to a stop but pitched too far forward and barreled face-first into him, her cheek smacking into a rock-hard chest.

Two strong hands shot up and grasped her shoulders, holding her with a firm yet gentle grip until she steadied herself. "Whoa. You okay, miss?"

Dazed, she shook her head to clear her blurry vision and then nodded. Sure, she was okay. She'd only collided with a brick wall like one of those crash-test dummies from the TV commercials. No biggie.

Man. Now her face hurt. *Gym, two. Preslee, zero.*

She rubbed at her sore cheek. "Um, yeah, I'm good," she said, her gaze lifting to his. "Sorry about . . ."

Preslee's mouth went dry, and the ability to form words

vanished from her tongue as quickly and as quietly as disappearing ink dries on paper.

His unblinking, deep-set brown eyes, the color of warm bourbon, swept lazily over her face and sent an involuntary shiver spiraling through her. His dark brown hair stood on end in different directions, giving him a tousled, bed-head look, and his broad, powerful body towered over her by at least six inches. Yet he appeared relaxed and unimposing, confidence oozing from him in spades.

Even through his tight black athletic shirt, Preslee could plainly see huge biceps and a thick ridge of hard muscle that rode his wide shoulders. And that only made her wonder what he looked like without his shirt on. No doubt more of that smooth, tanned skin and, if she had to guess, perfect pecs and a chiseled set of abs.

He cleared his throat, and her eyes lifted back to his face. And what a handsome face it was. In fact, he was one of the most striking men she'd ever seen. Not in a *GQ* model kind of way though. Rather in more of a rugged, manly, *I would screw you until you scream my name* kind of way. And she couldn't imagine many women disagreeing with her. Scratch that. *Any* women disagreeing with her.

He gently released her shoulders. "Sorry. I should've watched where I was going."

Preslee swayed. "I, uh..." What the hell was he talking about? It had been her fault that they'd bumped into each other. Okay, fine, crashed into each other. Whatever. Either way, the sly smile spreading across his face told her that he knew but was polite enough not to point it out. "Um, sorry about that."

"No need to apologize." He charmed her with a wink. "I work here. Can I help you find anything?"

Yeah, her breath. Because he'd taken it the moment she'd glanced up at him. Gosh, he was pretty to look at. And he worked at the gym? Had she known that earlier, she might've come in sooner or at the very least signed up for the yearly membership. "No. I'm good. Thank you though."

"All right," he said, stepping aside and sweeping one arm out. "Ladies first."

Preslee couldn't help but smile. He'd probably only done that so there was zero chance of her mowing him down for a second time, but she strolled past him without another word. Once she moved farther away, she glanced over her shoulder to see if he was still standing there and blew out a relieved breath that he'd continued on his way in the opposite direction.

So she did the same. And tripped over air, her feet stumbling a little before she caught herself. Oh man. Thankfully, he hadn't seen *that*. Sadly, it was a common, everyday occurrence for her, one her clumsy self had grown accustomed to. Unfazed, she carried on her way.

Reaching the huge, black stair-climbing machine, she stepped up onto it and climbed the several steps to the top. She gazed at the machine's buttons for a second before finding a green quick-start button and pressing it. The stairs slowly began to move, descending beneath her, and she stepped up onto the next step. She alternated each foot as she gradually climbed each step. Right. Left. Right. Left.

Yep, definitely easy.

Actually, probably too easy. Because it didn't take long for the routine stepping to become boring. She walked faster than this through the grocery store, for goodness' sake. Shouldn't it be more of a challenge?

As she continued to idly climb the stairs, she let her mind wander, going over her long day at work. She recalled how busy she'd been taking inventory, how many orders she'd received, and how the phone hadn't stopped ringing. Then she remembered something else that had her groaning. She had promised to do an update for her followers on her antiquing vlog before leaving work—something she'd failed to do. Crap.

Preslee wasn't all that great at social media. Sadly, the antique shop's online presence consisted only of a fairly basic website and an Instagram account with a small number of followers. Still, Preslee hated disappointing anyone, especially when it came to the loyal customers who were supporting her father's store. When she made them a promise, she always did her best to keep it. But with the upsetting phone call from the doctor this morning, the rush to find workout clothes at lunchtime, and the angst that came along with joining the gym, she'd forgotten all about it.

Maybe she could do a short video update from here. After all, it was just some information she was sharing about some new antique pieces that would be arriving next week. And lots of other vloggers made videos while doing mundane things, such as driving, shopping, or cooking. Why couldn't she? It would be . . . very twenty-first century of her.

So Preslee propped her phone on the stair-climber's dashboard to stabilize it and began making a short video via a live feed, keeping her voice low so as to not disturb the other patrons. Within minutes, she'd finished her quick update. But as she reached to end the livestream, her hand accidentally brushed across a random button on the stair-climber...and the machine instantly sped up.

Oh crap.

&

Adam Caldwell rounded the counter at the check-in desk and clapped Kurt on the back. "Hey, buddy. How are things today?"

Kurt shrugged. "Same as always. Where have you been? You were supposed to be here an hour ago."

"Sorry. Got tied up. My dad called...again."

Kurt's brow rose slightly. "Are they still lecturing you about quitting medical school? Man. That was forever ago. Get over it."

Adam ran a frustrated hand through his unruly hair. "Tell me about it. But I guess me quitting school to open a gym is apparently always going to be a sore spot between us. I can thank Michael for that."

"Your older brother? Why?"

"He followed in my parents' footsteps and got a medical degree, that's why. If he hadn't become a doctor like both of them, then they probably wouldn't be so persistent about me going back to med school. But it's never going to happen. Whether they like it or not, I am exactly where I want to be."

Kurt nodded. "You would think they'd be happy that you found your dream job. Especially while you're still in your early thirties. Not everyone does."

"They don't care that this is something I enjoy. To them, it's the equivalent of working in a fast-food restaurant."

Kurt shook his head. "There's nothing wrong with working in a fast-food place."

"I agree," he said with a nod. "But that's not the way *they* see it. As far as they're concerned, if I don't become a doctor like them, then I'm wasting my life."

"I'm sorry, but your parents are pretentious assholes."

Adam grinned with amusement. "Maybe so. But I don't think the gym manager is supposed to say something like that to his boss."

Kurt rolled his eyes. "You're not my boss, moron. You're my best friend. I've known you and your family for years. Hell, as close as we are, they're practically like family to me now. I can call them whatever I want." He leaned back against the counter and crossed one sneaker over the other. "And just because I work here and you sign my checks doesn't mean I'm going to let you order me around. You should know that by now."

Adam gave a one-shoulder, noncommittal shrug. "I could always fire you, ya know?"

"Yeah, you could. But then you'd have to run the place yourself, and I know how much you hate paperwork." Kurt chuckled, clearly amused by the idea of Adam running the gym himself. "Besides that, it wouldn't leave you any time to train your clients. And like you said, it's your dream job. You wouldn't want to give that up for anything. It's why you hired me to begin with."

"Doesn't mean I still won't fire you."

A slow smile stretched Kurt's mouth. He obviously wasn't the least bit worried about Adam's threat. "That road runs both ways, buddy. I could just as easily up and quit on you too."

Laughing, Adam shook his head. "Give me a break. You

threaten to quit on me at least once a week. We both know you're not going anywhere. You love working here as much as I do."

"Yeah, maybe. But that's only because I get to work out for free."

It was Adam's turn to roll his eyes. "Yeah, right. You had a free membership even before you started working here. The perks of being best friends with the owner."

Kurt grinned. "I know."

"Okay, now that we've established that neither of us is going anywhere, we still need to solve our biggest problem. If we don't figure out how to bring in some new gym members, both of us will be out of a job...whether we like it or not."

Kurt tapped a pen on the counter. "Speaking of which, I signed up a new member just before you arrived. A woman by the name of"—he glanced at a form lying on the desk—"Preslee Owens. She apparently lives here in Granite. Do you know her?"

"No, why? Did she ask for me personally?"

"Nope, I was just wondering. She didn't list anyone as a referral on the form so I was trying to figure out how she'd heard about us. Thought it might be a good way to determine where to put our advertising dollars."

"What advertising dollars?" Adam asked seriously. "It's not like we have much in reserve to spend on marketing. Besides, everyone knows the best form of advertising is word of mouth. And that's all we can afford right now."

"True. But this woman found us and she wasn't referred to us by anyone in particular. Or at least not anyone she wanted to admit to knowing. That's why I figured she must know you." Kurt offered him another grin.

Adam laughed. "She could've seen the sign out front as she drove past. It doesn't take a genius to figure out that we're a gym and not an auto shop with the two huge dumbbells on the logo."

Kurt shrugged. "Yeah, probably."

Adam glanced in the direction he'd come from. Wait a minute. Were they talking about the pretty woman with the bright blue eyes who had just plowed into him? "Is that her over there on the stair-climber?"

Kurt nodded. "Yep. She came in alone."

"What did you say her name was?"

"Preslee. Why? Does she look familiar?"

"Not really." Adam watched her for a moment before his gaze lowered to her leg. He blinked. "Uh, why does she have a woman's feminine product strapped to her knee? Is that supposed to be padding or is there some new trend going on that I haven't heard about yet?"

Kurt chuckled. "Neither. It's a bandage. She was bleeding a little."

Adam's eyes widened. "A little? Judging from the size of that bandage, she might as well have been bitten by a shark."

Kurt laughed. "It was the only one I had. We apparently need to restock the first aid kit. I'll pick up some more bandages on my way to work tomorrow. Our marketing fund should have enough money in it to cover them."

"Doubtful," Adam replied with a smirk.

He glanced back to Preslee and recalled how she nearly ran him down moments before. Then after walking past him, she had tripped over...well, nothing. Thankfully, she'd caught herself before hitting the ground. Although when she'd glanced

back at him, Adam had pretended not to notice. But he'd noticed, all right. With her around, they might need a more comprehensive first aid kit. Or an EMT on hand.

He glanced back at her injured knee, and concern trickled through him. "What happened to her? Did she get hurt on a machine?"

"No, she walked in like that. Not sure what happened, but it was just a small scrape. Trust me, the Band-Aid makes it look a lot worse than it is. If she wasn't bleeding, I doubt she would've asked me for anything."

"Why do you say that?"

"I don't know. She seems a bit skittish about being here. In the gym, I mean."

Confusion spiked through Adam. "Why?"

Kurt shrugged. "Not sure." He motioned to the back of the room where two regular members were lifting weights. "Though, earlier, those two creeps were watching her and making comments. Nothing too obnoxious, but their remarks probably didn't help any. I'm keeping an eye on them just in case I need to intervene. I don't want them running her off."

Adam glared at the two men pumping iron. He had never trained with them before, but he was familiar with them. They were notorious for not putting the weights back on the racks and never wiping their sweat off the equipment after using it, even if it was a machine next to one of the sanitizing stations. The inconsiderate jerks.

While Adam eyed them, the bigger of the two men began chuckling and nudged an elbow into the other guy's ribs as he pointed in the direction of the woman across the room. Then they both burst out laughing.

Adam's eyes narrowed. He wasn't sure what was so funny, but they were acting like complete nimrods, and he didn't like it one bit. But when he twisted his head to glance at the newcomer across the room to see if she had noticed their offensive behavior, Adam sucked in an audible breath.

The last thing he expected was to see this Preslee woman sprinting as fast as she could—on a stair-climber no less—with a look of sheer panic lighting her eyes. Man. He'd never seen anyone move on a stair-climber at that pace before. Her shoes barely had time to slap against one stair tread before the next one immediately took its place, requiring her to double-time it to keep from tripping over her feet. But no matter how fast she climbed, she couldn't seem to reach the top of the stairs to turn the machine off. Probably why she was holding on to the side bars with a white-knuckled death grip.

Why doesn't she just step off the damn thing?

Kurt raised a brow. "You going over there to help, or do you want me to?"

Adam was already moving in her direction. "I've got it. I'll go turn it off before she hurts herself."

Hustling across the room, Adam made it to the aisle behind the machine and came around the opposite side of the stair-climber. The machine was tall, but he jumped onto the front easily enough, grasping the bars to pull himself the rest of the way up. Then he quickly reached over the railing and punched the red emergency-shutoff button. As the stairs immediately slowed to a complete stop, he leaped off the machine and hurried around to the other side to see if she was okay.

Panting heavily, the exhausted woman leaned against the rails and rested her head on her forearms. Her long auburn hair was pulled back in a ponytail, but a few loose wisps had fallen around her face and were now soaked with sweat. As was most of her shirt. *How long was she running like that anyway?*

Her head slowly lifted. Although he thought her face couldn't possibly get any redder than it already was, the moment her gorgeous blue eyes landed on him, the color in her cheeks deepened immensely. "Uh, thanks," she muttered awkwardly, her eyes darting away.

"No problem," Adam replied. "You okay?"

"Yes." She nodded as she took another deep breath and exhaled slower, her breath trying hard to return to a normal state. "Thank God you have fast reflexes." She blew out another breath. "That's twice you kept me from hurting myself." Then she murmured something low to herself that he almost didn't catch.

Confusion spiraled through him, and he cocked his head. "What does *gym three* mean?"

She visibly cringed. "Uh, sorry. It's nothing. Just me talking to myself. I...uh, do that sometimes."

He didn't like that he'd made her cringe but shrugged nonchalantly. "Don't we all?"

"Well, yeah. I guess most people do." The sincere smile she gave him was so genuine, pure, and unexpected that it warmed him from the inside out.

An underlying current began to hum slowly through his veins, and he swallowed hard. "What were you, uh, trying to do?"

She laughed nervously. "I wasn't really *trying* to do anything. Well, at least not to the machine. I was doing a video update on my antiquing vlog. But when I ended the live feed,

I accidentally touched one of the buttons on the stair-climber. The machine went crazy, and it was going way too fast for me to stop it. I didn't know what to do."

"Can I give you some assistance with it?"

She tensed and darted a glance at the back of the room where the two smirking idiots were still watching her. Her face grew somber. "Um, no. I don't think I should try it again. Seems a bit more dangerous than what I was aiming for."

"I can help with that." He offered his hand to keep her full attention on him and off the two guys who needed to leave her alone and mind their own business. "I'm Adam Caldwell, the owner of the gym."

Her eyes widened. "Oh. Um, Preslee Owens," she said, timidly sliding her soft hand into his. "I didn't realize you were the owner. I just joined your gym today."

"Good. Glad to hear it. We love having new members." He gestured to the stair-climber. "If you'll let me, I'd like to give you some pointers on how best to use this machine. It's in my job description, after all. I'm not only the owner but also the gym's only certified personal trainer. Even if you don't want to use the machine right now, you might want to try it again in the future. I'd really like for you to know how to use it, just in case. It'll only take a minute."

"Okay."

Adam motioned for her to climb the stairs and followed behind her until they reached the top and were standing in front of the machine's console. Even with him standing one step lower than her, he was tall enough that he could still see the screen over her shoulder. Her ponytail dangled somewhat in his face, and the faint scent of fresh coconuts and sweet pineapple lingered in her hair. He couldn't help but turn his nose toward it and take a deeper breath to capture the delicious scent in his lungs.

Don't sniff the woman! What the hell is wrong with you?

He mentally slapped himself and then reached around her to lift a reddish-orange clip attached to the machine by a black cord. "This is a safety key," he said, holding it up in front of her. "Most of the machines here have one, and you clip it onto yourself like this. Pardon me," he said, wrapping his free hand around her waist and pulling the hem of her shirt slightly away from her body as he fastened the clip to the edge.

She stiffened at his slight touch. "Oh, okay."

"That way, if you fall off a machine or it's going too fast and you need to step off it, the clip will pull out and automatically shut it off. It's a safety feature that can keep you from getting into a situation like you did a minute ago and possibly injuring yourself."

Preslee turned her head to gaze at him over her shoulder and offered him a teasing grin. "Is this your gentle way of saying you don't want me bleeding to death on your gym floor?"

He returned her smile. "Yeah, I'd prefer that didn't happen."

"Well, you're no fun."

Adam's smile widened. "You *did* sign the waiver saying that if you injure yourself, it's not the gym's fault, right? Because I'm thinking about having you sign another."

She giggled. "Don't worry. You're covered. I signed it. Besides, if I sued someone every time I got hurt, I'd be a billionaire by now."

His brow rose. "Let me guess. Accident prone?"

Her shoulder lifted in a quick shrug. "Well, I would've

said klutz, but the way you put it sounds much kinder. Let's just say I'm the only person I know who can cut myself with a spoon."

Adam chuckled. The woman obviously had a good sense of humor and could laugh at herself. He admired that. He also liked that she hadn't given up after the mishap she'd had on the machine. Though he'd make damn sure that didn't happen next time.

He continued giving her tips on how to use the stair-climber successfully, as well as the proper form she should maintain while doing so. Once he finished going over everything at the top of the machine, she grabbed her phone, and they moved to the bottom. "See those metal footholds on both sides? Those are there for you to step on or off the machine."

"I didn't even notice them before. That makes sense."

He nodded. "Use them next time. And after you use this machine a few more times and get used to it, I can show you a variety of exercises you can do on it that will work whichever muscles you want to focus on."

"Well, I'm here to lose weight so that's pretty much all of them," she said, then winced as if she hadn't meant to say the words out loud.

He leaned toward her and lowered his voice, hoping to put her at ease. "Preslee, don't be shy about asking questions. Between Kurt and me, one of us is always available and happy to help."

"Thanks," she said, smiling. "I appreciate that."

Just as Adam opened his mouth to tell her it wasn't a problem, the tip of her tongue darted out to lick her full pink lips, and his own lips froze on the words. Because it would've been a blatant lie. There was a problem. And it mostly had to do with how one little sensual gesture on her part had caused something warm and insistent to move through him, low and deep, at the speed of a rocket.

He tried his best to ignore it by clearing his throat. "Uh, so let me know if you need anything else."

She hesitated, as if she picked up on the weird vibe coming from him. "Yes. Will do," she said, turning to move away.

Feeling foolish about the awkward exchange, Adam let his head fall forward and noticed that her left shoe had come untied. "Uh, Preslee?"

She turned back to face him, stepping on the loose string and effectively tripping herself again. Her eyes widened as her arms shot outward, searching for something to grab on to. Having seen it coming, Adam rushed forward and allowed her to tumble directly into his arms.

The two weight lifters at the back of the room must've seen the whole thing because they both erupted in laughter once again. It set Adam's teeth on edge. He shot them a contemptuous glare that stifled the sound coming from their direction before focusing back on Preslee. He steadied her and pushed the loose strands of hair away from her face. "You all right?"

"Yeah, sorry. I told you I was a klutz." A delicate pink blush bloomed on her cheeks as she bent to tie her shoelace.

"No, that was my fault. I shouldn't have called out your name like that when I saw your shoelace was untied."

Preslee straightened and gave him a *yeah, right* look. "That's nice of you, but you don't have to take the blame for me being clumsy."

"I'm not."

She sighed and gazed up at him with those big beautiful eyes, framed with long, dark lashes. Her voice softened. "You're sweet, Adam. And kind too. Unfortunately, not all men are. Your...uh, wife or girlfriend is very lucky." Then she turned to walk away once again.

"Preslee."

She stopped in place and glanced down before carefully turning back to him. "Yeah?"

He smirked. "What makes you think I have a wife or girlfriend?"

Her assessing gaze flickered over his entire body before landing back on his face. "Because guys like you never stay single long." Before he could respond, she spun on her heels and strolled...right into the nearest treadmill. Thankfully, she managed to keep herself upright and continued on her way down the aisle mumbling something about *gym five*. He wasn't sure what any of that meant, but he no longer cared when he heard the two men in the back snickering again.

Fire burned through him, and his nostrils flared. He hated guys like that. Bullies who got off on mocking others or laughing at someone else's misfortune. Well, enough was enough. He'd given both of them a cautionary glare earlier that had promised retribution if they didn't knock it off. They should've heeded his warning, because it was the last one they were going to get.

He marched back to the check-in desk, steam building in his veins, as if he were a human pressure cooker ready to explode. It took everything he had to keep himself from going over there and punching both of those jerks in the face. But instead, he planned on hitting them where it would hurt most.

Kurt saw him coming and stepped out of his way. Smart man. Then his friend nodded toward the two men in the back of the room. "I take it we're going to do something about that."

"Damn straight," Adam said, heat rolling through his gut. "Cancel both of their memberships. Assholes like them don't belong in my gym."

CHAPTER TWO

Preslee wanted to smack herself.

In the forehead.

With a chair.

While she was happy to finally be off the devil machine and back on solid ground, she couldn't believe the stuff that had come out of her mouth. It was embarrassing enough that she'd needed help with the possessed stair-climber. Did she really have to blurt out stupid stuff on top of it?

She hadn't meant to tell Adam that she joined the gym to lose weight. Then she had to go and make an even bigger fool out of herself by accidentally flirting with the man. What had she been thinking? She didn't know what had come over her. She wasn't the forward type. Maybe it was a little old-fashioned of her, but she normally preferred for a guy to make the first move. Probably because she was scared to death of rejection. She'd already had enough of that to last her a lifetime.

But the moment he'd told her to let him know if she needed anything else, a sexy image of him slowly removing his shirt from that hard body of his had flashed through her mind—apparently her brain really liked the idea of him being shirtless—and she'd involuntarily licked her lips. Like it was an invitation or something.

Preslee sighed. Okay, so maybe it was.

Not that it mattered. Adam had looked directly at her mouth while her tongue slid across her lips and had no reaction. Zero. As if she hadn't even done it. If anything, he probably just thought her lips were chapped.

She should've taken Adam's clear disinterest at face value. But she hadn't. Instead, she'd carried her inept flirting one step further and used the oldest trick in the book to ask if he had a significant other. Like that wasn't being obvious.

And he hadn't even really answered her question. His reply had only hinted that he might not have someone in his life. But he'd never actually confirmed it. As if she hadn't heard that tired line before. It didn't matter though. She already knew any guy with a body like Adam's was way out of her league anyway.

Though, for a second there, Adam had been so overly friendly and encouraging that she'd almost thought he had been flirting with her. She'd even managed to convince herself that he'd casually sniffed her hair while standing behind her on the stairclimber earlier.

Now that she was away from him and had control of her faculties again, reality had come crashing back, bringing with it an unsettling realization. There was one huge problem with the whole Adam-flirting-with-her scenario that her mind had conjured up. The gorgeous guy was as fit as they come while she was . . . well, not.

Hard-bodied men like him probably don't date women my size.

Sighing, she refocused her efforts and went over to try out one of the spin cycles against the wall. Surely she couldn't screw that up or hurt herself on a stationary bike. Unless, of course, the darn thing broke off its stand and rolled her right out the front door...which, at this point, she almost hoped would happen. At least then she wouldn't have to endure the other gym patrons staring at her anymore.

Preslee took stock of the entire building. Not counting her, there were still about a dozen people in the gym. Adam and Kurt. The two jerks in the back. A toned blond woman who was running on a treadmill as if it were a racetrack and she were a sleek Thoroughbred. And at least seven other buff males who were participating in various weight-lifting activities.

Not a single one of them had an ounce of fat on them that she could detect, and that alone made Preslee uncomfortable. She was completely out of her element and surrounded by fit individuals who looked more like dedicated athletes.

She clearly didn't belong here, and they probably all felt sorry for her. Including Adam. He kept glancing back at her as if he was fascinated. Only not in a good way.

Either he was seriously concerned that she would injure herself in his gym and try to sue the pants off him—jeez, there she goes, trying to get his pants off—or he was keeping an eye on her to make sure she didn't get stuck on another machine that required him to come to her rescue again.

Feeling defeated, Preslee tinkered around unsuccessfully on a few other machines before finally throwing in the proverbial white towel. A sweaty one at that. She didn't know what she was thinking by coming here. It was obvious to her that working out wasn't her forte. Even if Adam had been polite enough not to say so to her face.

As if on cue, he looked over again.

Dang it. Why does he keep doing that?

Embarrassed, Preslee turned away from him. She wanted nothing more than to slink away from all the prying eyes that were making her extremely uncomfortable and self-conscious. She didn't normally feel this bad about herself in her day-to-day life, but somehow being surrounded by so many hard bodies was bringing out all of her insecurities. She didn't like it one bit.

Unfortunately, she also didn't want Adam to watch her give up and go home. Not after he'd gone out of his way to help her. The least she could do was wait until he wasn't paying attention before she faded into the background and ducked out the door.

Her heart sped up, and her stomach churned. For some strange reason, she hated the thought of him being disappointed in her. She didn't want him to think she was incapable of making it through one workout by herself... which apparently was the truth.

Oh well. None of that mattered. Because once she finally made it out that door, she was never setting foot in his gym again anyway.

❧

Adam gripped the counter so hard that his knuckles turned stark white as he glared at his gym manager. "Tell me again why I shouldn't cancel their memberships."

Kurt scrubbed a hand over his face. "You heard me the

first time. We can't afford to lose any paying customers at the moment. Even if those two are slimeballs."

Adam shook his head. "I don't care. I'd rather have no clients than them in my gym. You know how I feel about bullies."

Kurt nodded solemnly. "I know. But you're not that same kid who got picked on by guys twice your size."

"Everyone was twice my size back then," Adam said, gritting his teeth. "I was always the smallest guy in the room."

"Now you're the biggest."

Yeah, maybe. "But I still remember how it felt when others made fun of me. I'm not going to let that kind of crap go down in my gym. Especially when it comes to two men doing it to a woman." He pointed one accusatory finger into Kurt's chest. "Frankly, I'm surprised *you* aren't more ticked off about this. You normally would be right there on the front lines with me when it comes to this kind of stuff."

"I *do* agree with you. Of course. But it's also my responsibility to look out for your best interests. Not only because I'm your friend but because it's my job as manager. That's what you hired me for."

Adam crossed his arms. "What does any of this have to do with my best interests?"

Kurt groaned in frustration. "Look, if you want me to cancel their memberships, I will. But you better come up with a way to get more business in here soon. I ran the numbers while you were over there helping that woman. You're running out of options, buddy. If you're lucky, you can keep the Body Shop running for another four or five months before you'll have to close down. Six, if you're really lucky. And that's only if you don't lose any more customers. Unfortunately, that includes those two idiots."

Damn it. Although Adam knew this was coming, he didn't think it would be this soon. But when he gazed back at Preslee across the room, his jaw clenched tightly. While he didn't know her, she came across as sweet and innocent and didn't deserve to be made fun of. By anyone.

He glanced back at Kurt. "Cancel their memberships. Those jerks deserve to be taught a lesson. We're the only gym within a thirty-mile radius of Granite. Maybe the inconvenience of those two having to find a new one and drive a good distance to work out will teach them some manners."

His friend nodded. "All right. Done. Now what are we going to do about keeping the gym open?"

"I'm not sure. Any ideas?"

Kurt smirked. "Yeah, you could ask your wealthy parents for a loan."

Adam snorted. "I'm thirty-one. What kind of grown man runs to Mommy and Daddy for a handout at the first sign of trouble?"

"The desperate kind."

Adam scowled, remembering the way his dad had chastised him this afternoon about returning to med school. "I'll never be that desperate. It's bad enough that they already think I won't be successful. All because it's not the career they would've chosen for me. But I'm going to prove them wrong by making this gym profitable." Even if he didn't yet know how.

He glanced over his shoulder to check on Preslee again and make sure she was still alive and well. So far, so good. She was on a spin cycle, legs pumping up and down as fast as they would go. At least she couldn't hurt herself on that particular machine. Well, probably.

Adam watched as her legs came to a slow stop and then she slid off the spin cycle with pinched lips. She didn't look happy. Then she did something that he hadn't expected. Glancing up, she noticed him peering in her direction and quickly turned away. His gut clenched as unease settled over him. He didn't know why her reaction bothered him, but...well, it did.

Kurt stepped up beside him, gazing over at Preslee. "Did you give her some advice on using the equipment? Like how to use the safety clips?"

Adam nodded. "Yeah, I was thorough."

His friend smirked. "I'm sure you were. I bet all the female clients love that about you."

Adam cocked his head, annoyance coursing through him. "I showed her how to use the stair-climber, idiot. It wasn't anything sexual."

Kurt shrugged one shoulder. "Really? Because I was watching, and it looked like you were over there smelling her hair." His mouth curved. "If you play your cards right, she might take you home and let you sniff the rest of her."

"You know, if you worried more about your own sex life instead of mine, you might actually get some once in a while."

"I get plenty."

"Your hand doesn't count."

Kurt snorted. "Touché." Then he nodded toward Preslee as she moved on to a rowing machine. "You know, she's like a rubber ball, bouncing from one machine to the next. She's all over the place and doesn't seem to stay on one machine long enough to get a good workout. That isn't helping. Even if she's circuit training, she's moving around too fast."

Adam didn't know why, but he felt the need to defend her. "I think she's just trying to feel them out."

"Or maybe she's never exercised a day in her life."

Adam frowned. "Why do you say that? Because she's got curves?"

"What? No. Of course not." Kurt shook his head adamantly. "That isn't what I meant. I can just tell she's inexperienced, that's all. She's skittish of being here and doesn't know what to do with any of the machines. She's clearly never used them before."

"Maybe, but she can learn. And we'll probably be seeing a lot more of her since she told me she's here to lose weight. Apparently she's starting an exercise regimen."

"Good for her," Kurt said, nodding his approval. "So what happened over there earlier? Did she start the machine up too fast and couldn't keep up with it?"

Adam shook his head. "No. She was doing a live update on some vlog she runs. When she ended the video, she apparently hit a button on the machine, and it sped up suddenly."

Kurt paused before pulling out his phone and then began typing.

Adam regarded him a moment before asking, "What are you doing?"

"Looking up her vlog," Kurt replied, tapping on his phone. "I've got to see that video." He scrolled with his finger and tapped again. After a few more seconds, he said, "Ah, I think this is it."

"How did you find that so fast?"

"Her membership form said she worked at the antique shop here in town, so I figured her vlog would be connected to the website. I was right."

"Oh."

As Kurt started the video, curiosity got the better of Adam, and he moved closer. The moment Preslee appeared on the screen and her soft voice reached his ears, warmth filled him, and he found himself smiling back at her. Well, at the phone screen anyway. The endearingly sweet woman was talking about some new antiques coming into her store soon, and her excitement was infectious. Clearly, she was passionate about her work.

Adam could relate.

As she wrapped up, Preslee said a quick farewell to her viewers and then reached for her phone. Adam expected that was where the video update ended and her misadventure with the stair-climber began, but that wasn't quite what happened. Well, it was. Just not particularly in that order.

Instead, he watched her fumble for her phone, heard a beep on the machine, and then she began cursing like mad as the machine sped up to a level that even he wouldn't dare attempt. She ran hard, breath panting out of her, as her hands held a death grip on the side bars.

Although Adam knew she was no longer in danger of injuring herself, he couldn't help but hold his breath as the seconds ticked by. Seeing the panicked expression on her face a second time and the terror shining in her eyes up close and personal did something to him that he couldn't explain. Like he wanted to jump through the screen and save her all over again.

No sooner had the thought occurred than the machine slowed to a stop and Adam appeared on the screen. Huh? Oh. It was when he hit the emergency stop button. Guess she hadn't turned off the live feed when she thought she had. Which was fine. Or it would have been if Adam hadn't known what was coming up next. Damn it. He cringed in horror as he realized that they were about to watch the one part that he didn't want Kurt to see...again.

Kurt sat quietly with a huge grin on his face, clearly knowing what he was about to witness for the second time. Then his buddy laughed. "Ha! I knew it. You did sniff her hair. Like some kind of weirdo pervert."

"Shut up," Adam grumbled, shaking his head. It wasn't like he'd leaned into the woman or buried his face into her hair. All he'd done was turn his nose toward the delicious scent wafting from her locks and inhale a little. That was it. Nothing nearly as sinister as Kurt was making it out to be.

Moments later, the video ended abruptly, as if Preslee had somehow accidentally turned it off. Adam immediately turned sideways and busied himself with some paperwork to keep from having to endure any more from Kurt. But it didn't work.

Kurt continued scrolling with his finger, his eyes still focused on the screen. "Uh, I hate to tell you this, but I think your hair-sniffing debut is going viral."

Adam's head snapped up. "What?"

"Her followers are steadily increasing, and the video is being shared like crazy. Not only that, but there are tons of comments already on here. Everyone is asking which gym she's working out in."

"Great," Adam said, scrubbing a hand over his face. That was just what they needed right now. Bad publicity.

After another minute, Kurt chuckled. "Man, you really need to read these comments. They're hilarious."

Oh, he could only imagine.

You should've walked down the stairs rather than up them.

This is how the war of the machines starts.

Why is that pervert sniffing your hair?

Adam shook his head. "No thanks. I don't need that kind of negativity right now."

"Negativity? No, you got it wrong. The comments are actually positive. Most of them are by people who laughed at the mishap and then apologized for laughing and said they were glad that she was okay. Then quite a few wanted to know which gym she was at, and to quote some of these women, they want to know who the 'hottie' is in the video with her."

"You're kidding?"

"Nope," Kurt said, his face serious. "This could be a good thing for us, you know."

"Maybe."

Kurt sat quietly in his thoughts for a moment before speaking again. "You said she was here to lose weight, right? Maybe you could help her."

"Yeah, I already told her that if she had any questions, you or I could answer them for her."

"No, that's not what I meant. I mean you could be her trainer."

Confusion swept through Adam. "She didn't ask me to train her."

"So?" Kurt shrugged. "Doesn't mean you can't offer your services. Besides, she seems a bit clumsy, and the last thing you need right now is someone getting hurt in your gym."

"Preslee said she signed the waiver."

Kurt's eyebrow rose, probably from Adam using her first name in a familiar way, but he didn't comment on it. "She did. But while the waiver is ironclad and she won't be able to sue you, it still wouldn't look good to potential clients if someone got hurt here. You know how fast word travels in small towns. And we want to promote a safe workout environment, right?"

"Of course," Adam agreed, glancing across the room at Preslee again. "But she's not the type of client I normally work with. All of the people I train are bodybuilders or fitness models who are trying to build muscle. All of them are here to gain weight."

"Exactly. You're known locally as the personal trainer with the most intense workouts and rigorous bodybuilding sessions around. That's why we get only those types coming into the gym." Excitement lit Kurt's eyes. "But what if you were also known for something else? Something that could possibly draw in a lot of new gym members?"

"What do you mean?" Adam asked, not quite understanding where his friend was going.

Kurt gestured to Preslee. "The stair-climber incident speaks volumes. Lord knows she's going to need someone to guide her. At least until she gets the hang of things. Losing weight is hard enough, but it's even harder when you don't have a good support system in place and someone to help keep you accountable and working toward a goal. *You* could do that for her. And with her vlogging about it... Well, like I said earlier, word travels fast."

The idea struck a chord with Adam, and he realized exactly what had been missing from his gym all along. People like *her*. Non-bodybuilder types who needed a safe, unbiased place to meet their own personal fitness goals. Hell, Kurt was right. Preslee was just what he needed to draw a different crowd into the gym and make it the success he always knew it could be.

But there was one big problem. The woman was pretty as all

get-out. Adam didn't hesitate with his answer. "No. It's a good idea, but that plan won't work. Not with her. We'll have to figure something else out. I can't train her."

Kurt tilted his head. "Why? Because you're planning to give her some personal training of your own...in the bedroom?"

Adam crossed his arms and glared at his friend. "Of course not. Why would you even ask me something like that?"

"Two reasons. One, because you've barely taken your eyes off her ever since you came back over here. And two, because you don't date clients. If you're training her, it would be hands-off all the way. We both know that."

Yeah, no kidding. When Adam had first opened his gym and began working as a trainer, he'd decided right then that he would never mix business with pleasure. Not only because there was a chance it could end in a major disaster, but because there was an imbalance of power about it that he didn't like.

Yet Adam shook his head, dismissing his friend's remarks. Sure, Preslee was beautiful and intriguing. But he was only curious about her, that was all. Probably because she was new to his gym, and he was worried that she might hurt herself. It had nothing to do with bedding the woman. "You're wrong. Neither has anything to do with why I don't want to train her."

"All right. Then that leaves only one other explanation," Kurt said, leaning back against the counter with a grin. "You don't think you can help her get fit."

Adam released a disgruntled sound from the back of his throat. "Don't be ridiculous. Of course I can."

Kurt's brow rose. "You think so?"

"I know so."

"How about we make a friendly bet on it?"

Adam knew what his friend was doing. Besides himself, Kurt was one of the most competitive people on the planet, and in all the years they'd known each other, neither of them had ever turned down a bet with the other. But this was different. "We're not making a friendly bet."

"Okay, so a real bet then."

What? No, that wasn't what he meant.

But Kurt continued before Adam could say so. "Twenty bucks to the winner."

Adam snorted. "Okay. Now I know you're joking. No one in their right mind would accept a twenty-dollar bet in exchange for that many hours of training."

Kurt grinned. "All right. Then here's the deal. If you can convince Preslee to let you train her and meet her fitness goals, then I'll stop bugging you about letting me buy into the gym as half owner."

Adam blinked. What the hell? He hadn't been trying to up the stakes.

While he couldn't think of a better partner for his business than Kurt, he really wanted to prove that he could make his gym successful on his own before bringing anyone else on board. Besides, the last thing he would let his buddy do was buy into a failing business. What kind of friend would he be if he did that?

But as competitive as Adam was, he also couldn't stand the thought of passing up an opportunity to win another bet. Especially one of this magnitude. And the gym really did need the free advertisement that Preslee's fitness goals could possibly bring them. If he used this opportunity to his advantage, it could be the one thing that saved his business. And possibly salvaged any relationship he had left with his family.

"And if I fail?" Wait. Was he actually entertaining this stupid idea?

Kurt didn't hesitate. "If you fail, then you have to let me buy into the gym as full partner for half the cost."

Adam considered it for a moment and then shook his head. "This is dumb. We're not making a bet."

"Afraid you'll lose?"

"Hardly," Adam said, scoffing at the idea. "But there are some things you apparently haven't considered. Such as, who's to say that Preslee wants me to be her personal trainer? Or that she'll stick to the training even if she does agree?"

Especially since the woman didn't seem to want his help. When she'd first run into him and he'd offered her assistance, she'd turned him down flat. More than once. She had come across as nervous and uneasy around him. After all, he was a stranger. A big one, at that. At six feet, two inches, he towered over her. Not to mention that he was built like a tank.

His friend shrugged. "True. From the moment she first walked in, she looked like she was ready to bolt for the nearest exit. Hell, she still does," he said as they both glanced her way again.

"She's wary when it comes to the gym. Like she's not comfortable in her own skin."

Kurt nodded in agreement. "Yeah, but that isn't my problem, Adam. It's yours. Do you want to make the bet or not? Going once, going twice..."

Adam ran a hand through his hair. "You're such an ass."

Kurt smirked. "Maybe. But it's still your move. What are you going to do?"

Adam wasn't really sure. He'd never turned down a bet before and didn't want to start now. But the thought of working with Preslee concerned him. All it would take would be one sprained ankle or some other minor injury, and any progress they made together would be completely derailed. And that was if he could even get her to agree to any of this to begin with.

After he'd saved her from the runaway stair-climber, she'd seemed more comfortable around him. Even went as far as to joke with him and tell him that he was a nice guy. But was that enough to convince Preslee to let him train her? He could definitely help her get fit if she would.

"How do we measure her success for the bet?"

"We'll let Preslee determine that herself. But you can't influence her decision. She sets her own fitness goals. As long as they're safe, of course."

Good. That was a given as far as Adam was concerned anyway. "All right," he agreed. "But that doesn't answer my first question. What if she doesn't want to work out with me?"

Kurt shifted his weight and leaned a hip against the counter. "Like I said, not my problem. That's on you. If you can't get her to train with you or if you two don't meet her goals, you lose the bet. Deal?"

Adam rubbed his hand over the back of his neck. "Hold on a minute. You mentioned the vlog earlier. What does that have to do with this?"

"While you're training her, get her to post some workout videos. It'll be good advertising for us."

Adam's eyes widened. "Come on, man. She isn't going to do

that. I mean, it's an antiquing vlog. You saw it. Besides, with as leery as she seems about exercising, I doubt she is going to want to go public with it."

"She already did," Kurt said, tapping his phone.

"By accident. She didn't intentionally post anything that had to do with her working out or losing weight. We both know that."

"Not really. She posted on her own accord from the gym. Maybe she planned to do that during all of her workouts. You never know. But either way, that's not what we're betting on. The extra publicity would be helpful, but this video going viral might be all the publicity we may get anyway." He paused thoughtfully. "Still, as she gets fitter, I'm betting others notice and ask her about it. So we may actually see more publicity from it after all."

"Okay, but just so we're on the same page, the vlog isn't included in the bet."

"Nope." Kurt peered at something over Adam's shoulder and then frowned before focusing back on him. "But if I were you, I would encourage her to use it. She could post a couple of video updates on her workouts. It would benefit her just as much as it would benefit us."

Adam gave him a *yeah, right* look. "How do you figure?"

"You know why. It's called accountability, Adam. If viewers are following her fitness journey, she won't be tempted to quit so easily. Trust me when I say that she's going to need that motivation."

Adam didn't agree. After all, Preslee was already in the gym on her own, wasn't she? And even after her ordeal with the stair-climber and the two guys laughing at her, she still hadn't given up and gone home out of sheer embarrassment. She'd stayed and stuck it out. He liked that about her. It said a lot about her level of determination and willingness to see her fitness journey through to the end.

Hell, this will be a piece of cake.

Adam smiled and offered his hand to his friend. "All right. It's a bet."

Kurt shook his hand and then fist-bumped him. "Okay, but get ready to lose, sucker."

Adam laughed. "I'm not going to lose. In fact, I'm going to go talk to Preslee about training her right now." He cast a glance around the room, searching for her. "Uh, where did she go?"

Kurt smirked with a glint of humor twinkling in his eyes.

"What?"

He shrugged. "While you were taking your sweet time in deciding whether or not you were going to take me up on the bet, she walked out the front door. And I should probably mention that I saw her throw her membership card in the trash on the way out. Good luck with that."

CHAPTER THREE

Preslee arrived home from the gym and tossed her keys onto the kitchen counter with a huff. Then her mind drifted back to her fast exit from the gym, and out of annoyance, she smacked herself in the forehead. Not only had she quit the gym, but on a frustrated whim, she'd thrown her membership card in the trash on the way out the door.

She hated admitting, even to herself, that she *may* have acted a little hastily. Okay, fine. A lot hastily. But she had gotten into her own head and had allowed doubt to creep in. Instead of thinking clearly and logically, she'd let raw emotions dictate her mindset and then acted accordingly . . . and impulsively. In her defense though, when she'd walked out those gym doors, she'd thought for sure that it would be for the last time.

But how was she supposed to lose weight if she didn't exercise?

Preslee sighed. She didn't know the answer to that question. Nor did she care to figure it out. After a long, exhausting day at work and then the added pressure of trying and failing to start a workout regimen, she was physically and mentally wiped. All she wanted to do now was soak in a hot bath and then head to bed. But first she needed to check her messages to make sure her father hadn't called.

He'd taken a bad spill off the top of a storeroom ladder a few weeks ago and had broken his wrist so badly that he'd needed surgery to repair the damage. That left him with pins in his wrist to fuse the bone back together, plus a splint that he was required to wear for up to ten weeks, and he was now unable to lift anything that required the use of two hands. Therefore, he sometimes needed assistance with basic, mundane tasks that most able-bodied people took for granted.

Because of that, Preslee usually brought her dad dinner and checked on him several times throughout the day to make sure he was okay. But she'd silenced her phone while at the gym and had forgotten to turn it back on. So she pulled her phone from her pocket and turned the ringer back on before clicking on the screen to check for any new messages.

While she didn't have any missed calls from her dad, she couldn't help but notice the impressive number of emails she had received over the past few hours. The spammers must be working overtime tonight. But when she clicked on her inbox and saw the emails were actually comments on her vlog update, she blinked rapidly.

Whoa. That was way more than she'd ever gotten on a single video before.

And that was saying a lot. Not because her vlog was all that popular or she had that many followers, but because she had done a few videos that had actually gained some popularity amongst a small niche group of local antique enthusiasts.

Her most popular video was one she'd done last year on a

vintage Rolex that her dad had helped one of their most prominent customers sell at auction. It was a fine watch in pristine condition and had some unique, custom-made features that were desirable to collectors. The extra-wide bevel had been discontinued, and the blue dial and diamond indexes were exclusive to that particular watch. At the time, it had been the only one of its kind known in existence. For that reason, the watch had sold for a staggering amount at auction, and her father had made an incredible commission from the sale. Even to this day, she still received occasional comments on that post.

Still, the older vlog post had nothing on the numbers of her most current update, and she knew immediately something was wrong. Very wrong. Why had so many people suddenly taken an interest in her vlog?

Not wasting any time, she logged on to see what was going on, and her gaze immediately locked on to the number of her followers. An amazing number of new visitors had followed her within the last few hours. What the heck was going on?

Her mind began racing, imagining every horrible scenario she could think of. Had something been stuck in her teeth during the video? Had one of those two jerks mooned the camera from somewhere behind her? Had an errant nipple snuck out of her top without her permission?

But nothing her feeble brain conjured up prepared her for what she found when she tapped the play button. She wasn't the least bit surprised to see the intended update. But then she watched in horror as her mirror image reached for the camera to end the live feed . . . and the video didn't stop.

Oh no. Please. Anything but this. Where's that damn nipple when I need it?

As the video continued playing, Preslee cringed and sucked in a deep breath in an effort to calm herself, but the air refused to inflate her lungs. Her heart hammered relentlessly inside her chest, beating so fast that she thought it might actually explode.

Dear God. The whole awkward thing had been caught on video. It was all there for anyone to see. Her workout disaster with the possessed stair-climber. Adam coming to her rescue. Her lame attempts at flirting with him. And, the most discomforting part, him ignoring them.

Preslee wheezed out an uneasy breath. How was she ever going to show her face around town again? Judging from the number of comments, a whole slew of people had already seen the stupid video. And from what she could gather, according to the number of shares, a whole bunch more were about to.

Jeez. No wonder people referred to this as "going viral." She felt sick to her stomach, like she was coming down with something. Sure, she could delete the post. But would it even matter at this point? The video had already been up for hours. Besides, someone out there had probably already copied it, and chances were good that they would somehow link it back to her. Then that would only make others think she was trying to hide it.

And they would be absolutely correct. Who in their right mind would want that kind of embarrassing stuff out there? She sure didn't.

When the screen went black, Preslee hit play a second time, hoping to induce the heart attack that would surely come from seeing the horrendous debacle all over again. She couldn't die from humiliation later if she was already dead, right?

But before her impending death took place, something had

her pausing the video and staring in disbelief. Wait a minute. Was she imagining things or had Adam just...sniffed her? She backed the video up a little and played that part over again. He had! He had actually turned his head and smelled her hair. Either that or he had been checking her for dandruff. Which would be difficult since he'd closed his eyes.

But why would he sniff her? Had her hair smelled bad? Granted, she had worked up a pretty good sweat right before he'd stood behind her on the machine and showed her how to properly use it, but she had worn deodorant. And it wasn't like Adam had crinkled his nose in disgust as if he had smelled a stench in the air.

Feeling self-conscious, Preslee grasped the end of her ponytail and pulled it around to her nose, giving it a good whiff. The scent of pineapples and coconut filled her nostrils. Okay, so the smell wasn't the problem. Unless, of course, he just didn't like pineapples or coconut. Maybe that was it. Then again, he did smile afterward. So obviously he—okay, stop already!

It didn't matter. So what if Adam smelled her hair? Even if he did like the scent, he didn't bother to say so. If that didn't say loud and clear, *I'm not into you*, then she wasn't sure what did. So why she was sitting there trying to figure it out was beyond her. What a waste of time.

So instead, she began reading through the comments, hoping that she wouldn't come across someone calling her a bumbling idiot. Thankfully she didn't. But she was surprised by what she did find in the comments. A lot of really funny, well-meaning people who posted kind, positive messages to her.

Almost everyone told her that they were glad she was okay. Some who'd laughed at the video apologized for laughing but thanked her for making their day. Some commented that it was something they would've done by accident too. A few asked where she was working out and encouraged her to keep up the good work. And then there were a ton of messages from women who wanted to know more about her rescuer and referred to Adam as a *cutie*, a *hottie*, *sexy guy*, *hot stuff*, *handsome*, and *muscles*.

Preslee couldn't help but laugh at the saucy messages. Mostly because she had all the same thoughts about Adam herself. Was he single? they asked. What did he look like without a shirt on? Did he like to be on top or bottom? Oh wait, that one was from another guy. Well, okay then.

Then she saw one question that made her sigh heavily. *Are the two of you dating?* That was one she could answer herself. Nope. Definitely not. She clearly wasn't the type of woman Adam went for. Otherwise, he would've answered her when she asked him if he had a wife or girlfriend. Or at the very least told her that her hair smelled nice.

But he hadn't. He probably just—

Ugh. There she went again.

Enough.

She needed to stop mind reading and obsessing over him. And the video too. Obviously, a bunch of strangers had gotten their jollies off an embarrassing, unfortunate event in her life. One that was now over. Probably by tomorrow, the comments would stop and everything in her life would go back to normal.

So she needed to do herself a favor and put down her phone, dunk herself into a steaming tub full of bubbles, climb into her comfortable bed to get a good night's sleep, and forget all about the stupid video.

And the hottie who had come to her rescue.

Three days later, Preslee sat behind the large mahogany desk at her father's antique shop, wondering how much it would hurt if she banged her forehead against the hard wood. She had thought the whole viral video thing would blow over the day after, but she had been sorely mistaken.

Not only had the comments and the shares kept coming from strangers online, but it seemed like everyone in town had seen the video as well. The store had been busier than ever, and while that wasn't necessarily a bad thing, she was certain her cheeks were now permanently stained with a red hue from all the blushing she'd done. Everyone kept asking her about the video. They wanted to know more about her workout, if she was trying to lose weight, and how she was doing it. Then they brought up the one subject she really didn't want to think about. Adam Caldwell.

Jeez. Why her?

Preslee bumped her forehead against the smooth flat surface of the desk. Ouch. Okay, yeah. That hurt. But she probably deserved it after all the lies she'd told whenever someone asked her which gym she belonged to. But what else could she say? That she quit the gym on the first night? While it might be true, that didn't mean she wanted to admit it out loud to everyone.

Besides, it wasn't actually a lie. She *had* paid for her first month already and was technically still a member of the Body Shop, even if she had thrown her membership card away. She just sort of left that last part out.

"Uh, Preslee," a male voice sounded, puzzlement filling his tone.

Her head snapped up from the desk to find the shop's new delivery driver staring curiously at her. Crap. "Oh, uh...hello."

"Can I interrupt you for a second?"

She swallowed the knot forming in her throat. "Of course. I was just...um, taking a break. Did you need something?"

"Not really. I was just letting you know that Greg and I are going out on a delivery. We're taking that dining room table set over to Sycamore Avenue. It shouldn't take long."

She nodded. "Okay."

"Greg said we'd probably take our lunch break when we get back since we don't have any more deliveries until this afternoon."

"Sounds good." She twisted her fingers together in her lap. "I'm, uh, going to eat lunch too," she said, her voice warbling a little.

Josh grinned. "Well, yeah. Most people do."

Preslee cringed internally. Why did she always have to spout out stupid things whenever a cute guy was around? What the heck was wrong with her? She reached for her water bottle to ease her dry throat and knocked a stapler off the desk. Josh went for it at the same time as she did, and their heads collided. "Ow."

"Sorry," he said, wincing as he placed the stapler on the desk.

She rubbed at the sore spot on her forehead. The second one. "That's okay. It was my fault. I should've watched where I put my head." Oh, for goodness' sake.

An awkward silence sat between them.

He shuffled his feet. "Well, I guess I better go get that delivery done."

She nodded. "Okay."

Josh offered her one last friendly smile before strolling toward the door, and Preslee admired his rear end as he went. *Not bad. Not bad at all.*

She should probably thank her father for the nice view since he'd been the one to hire Josh a few weeks before. Not that he'd had much of a choice. With her father unable to work after his accident, they'd needed the help. Even though the antique shop still had one delivery guy—a married, middle-aged man named Greg—moving heavy antique furniture was a two-person job. They'd needed someone to help with the physically demanding aspects of the business.

Hopefully, for the long term. Because, while she hated that her dad had gotten injured, there was a plus side to it. It had forced him to slow down. He was getting up there in age, and she worried constantly about his safety and well-being. With Josh now working in his place, she no longer had to. Well, at least until the bones in her dad's wrist fused back together. Then he would probably be right back on top of that ladder pulling another one of his daredevil balancing acts.

Ugh. Preslee rubbed her temples.

She hoped that by the time her dad's injury healed, she'd finally be able to convince him to retire and allow her to take over the family business. After all, it wasn't like she didn't know what she was doing. As the unofficial manager of the antique shop, she'd been taking care of the paperwork, accepting orders, scheduling deliveries, and handling the everyday business side of things for years. She could do it blindfolded with both hands tied behind her back... if only her dad would let her.

And if he ever actually handed over the reins, she already knew what her first order of business would be. Without a doubt, that

would be making Josh a permanent, full-time employee. He'd
been doing a great job since he'd started. The guy had a serious
interest in antiques and knew a lot about them. That kind
of vast knowledge would come in handy whenever she needed
to attend estate sales and auction houses in her father's place.
Which only made Josh an asset to the business...and, to her
delight, a perfect match for her.

Had her father done that on purpose? It wasn't normally like
her dad to play matchmaker. Especially with his own daughter.
If anything, he'd always done the exact opposite. Like when she
had begun dating in her teen years. Her dad had thought it
funny to greet each of her dates at the door, give a few intimidating glares, and wave the two of them off as they'd left.

That part hadn't been so bad. But as he'd stood there waving
goodbye to them, he would always say, "Have a nice time, kids.
Keep your clothes on."

Out loud. In front of her date.

No doubt it had been a deliberate warning for her date to keep
his hands to himself and a not-so-subtle reminder for Preslee to
behave like a lady. And, as if that hadn't been bad enough, her
dad would wait for her to get home by standing guard at the
front door and then flicker the porch light the moment her date
tried to kiss her good night. How was a girl supposed to get any
action like that?

Okay, so maybe that had been the point. But it hadn't made
it any less embarrassing.

Thankfully, his tactics hadn't worked forever. Because eventually, she'd managed to lose her virginity, something she assumed
her father had probably figured out by now. After all, she was
twenty-eight. And over the past few years, she'd even been

in a few relationships that had lasted a considerable amount of time.

But even then, her father had always steered her in the opposite direction of those boyfriends and suggested she find someone who was meant specifically for her. Someone who held the same interests. Someone who she could build a good life with. Someone who loved her as much as he did. Which was sweet and all.

But that only brought her back to her original question. Could that be why he'd hired Josh in the first place? For her? In hopes that they would hit it off and become a couple? Sure, her dad had needed to hire someone to fill the position, and Josh *did* know his stuff when it came to antiques. But her dad couldn't have picked a more perfect guy for her if she'd chosen him herself.

On paper, Josh was exactly what she wanted. He was cute in that boy-next-door kind of way, but not so good-looking that he would be vain about it. He stood almost six inches taller than her and had a decent build on his medium frame. Then there was the fact that he'd been nothing but polite and respectful toward any females who had come into the shop, which led Preslee to believe that he would probably be the same way with any woman he dated. And the guy planned to, one day, go into the antique business himself.

See? Perfect.

Only Josh didn't know Preslee had secretly dubbed him her future husband. Yet, more than once, she'd imagined them running the antique shop together as a married couple until the day came that they would retire from the business and pass it down to their own children.

Preslee leaned back in her chair and rolled her eyes so hard that they hurt. *Oh God. Just stop already. That's nothing more than a fairy tale you keep telling yourself. It's never going to happen.*

She sighed in frustration. While Josh might be the man of her dreams, she apparently wasn't the woman of his.

Over the past few weeks, either her feeble attempts at casual flirting had gone unnoticed or Josh had purposely ignored the subtle overtures altogether. Actually, he hadn't paid any more attention to her than a customer would a dusty lampshade tucked away in a dimly lit corner on the gallery floor.

Darn it. This was exactly why she liked for a guy to make the first move. She'd never been good at reading men, much less figuring out what their intentions were. Sadly, in Josh's case, he didn't seem to have any whatsoever. At least not in regard to her.

It wasn't because he was dating someone. Greg had already informed her that Josh was as single as a one-dollar bill...and that he wasn't gay. Although why the two of them had even had *that* conversation was still one of the great mysteries of the world that would probably never be solved.

Whatever. It didn't matter. The end result was the same, and although it stung a little, one thing was perfectly clear. Josh wasn't interested.

And she knew why.

Preslee glanced down at her figure and pursed her lips. Although she had a pretty face and great hair—at least that was what others had told her—she was the heaviest she'd ever been and didn't feel attractive. So she couldn't really blame the guy if he wasn't feeling it either.

Maybe Josh just wasn't into curvy women. Big deal. Not all

guys were. Or maybe it was her own discomfort with her recent weight gain that he found unattractive. After all, confidence was sexy. Unfortunately, it just wasn't something she'd ever had much of when it came to her body.

So while the two of them might be perfect on paper, that probably meant little when compared to sexual chemistry. That was important. Because everyone needs to feel wanted, including her. Especially her. She longed to feel a man's desire and to know that he craved every inch of her body. No matter what size she was. Because if she didn't have that, then what was the point in being with someone at all?

She wasn't one of those women who believed they had to be skinny to snare a man. After all, she'd had boyfriends before. But what she did believe was that attraction sometimes grew between two people unexpectedly.

So yeah. Maybe Josh wasn't into her right now. But that didn't mean that wouldn't change in the future. His attraction to her could grow over time. And if she shed some pounds, so would her level of confidence.

She wasn't losing weight *for* Josh though. She was doing this for herself. Regardless of where he stood, she needed to make this change for health reasons. That was first and foremost on her mind. Yet that didn't mean she couldn't benefit from her weight loss in other ways.

Preslee wanted to buy cute clothes that fit well. She wanted to feel confident and sexy. If Josh happened to notice the change in her and asked her out, well then, it would just be an added bonus. Sort of be like her playing the part of her own fairy godmother while turning herself into a healthier after-version of Cinderella.

Besides, she deserved her happily ever after. All women did.

That wasn't confidence oozing from her. It was determination. And maybe a bit of motivation. Now she just needed to figure out how she was going to get fit.

Her doctor had recommended making specific lifestyle changes, which included reducing her caloric intake and increasing her activity level.

Yet there was the issue. The problem had never been that she didn't know *how* to lose weight. She did. She'd read enough magazine articles about health and fitness. But unfortunately, it was a lot like churning homemade butter. She knew what needed to be done and could easily instruct others on how to do it. But the long process of actually churning the butter was the hardest, most daunting part. That was probably why people like her took the easy way out and bought their butter from the grocery store. Little to no effort required.

Great. Now I'm craving buttered toast.

She was tempted to go to the break room and make herself a slice, but that wouldn't be the best thing for her diet. Besides, her legs were still a little sore from the evil stair-climber she'd encountered at the gym the other night. Sadly, they felt much better now compared to the past few days.

When she'd gotten out of bed the morning after, her legs had ached so badly that she'd hoped they would just fall off. Every step she'd taken toward the bathroom had been filled with pain, misery, and lots of grumbling.

On the second day, when she'd had to stand in front of the sink for an extended period of time to do her hair and makeup before work, her poor leg muscles had quivered relentlessly until they'd nearly given out.

This morning there still had been some lingering stiffness in her calves that had made itself known every time she walked downstairs to the storeroom or back up again. But thankfully, the pain had mostly faded away. Well, the physical pain anyway. The mental anguish of the past three days was still very real and present.

Her head flopped forward and banged onto the desk again. Ouch. Yep, it didn't hurt any less the second time. But she planned to stay like this for the next fifteen minutes. By then, Josh and Greg should be back from their delivery and heading into the break room for lunch, and she planned to join them in hopes of starting another casual—and probably awkward—conversation with Josh.

The bells on the entrance door chimed, and Preslee groaned. There was no way Josh had gotten back that fast. Which meant it was probably another townsperson who had seen the video and decided to stop in and pepper her with questions. Ones that she didn't feel like answering.

Yet when her head lifted, her gaze fell directly on Adam Caldwell sauntering toward her with a confident swagger. Her stomach twisted, and she blinked rapidly, as if she expected him to vanish suddenly like some sort of mirage. But no. He was really there, moving toward her with a devastating smile that made her pulse quicken.

What the heck was he doing here?

Adam stopped in front of her desk. "Hey, Preslee. How are you?"

Still reeling in shock, she could barely get words out. "Uh, fine. H-how are you?"

"Great. Thanks for asking." He leaned one hand against her

desk as he glanced around the gallery. "Great little shop you have here. You have some pretty cool vintage stuff."

She stared at him warily, still not understanding why he was standing in her dad's store. "Um, yeah, everything here is vintage." She shrugged lightly. "That's kind of the point of it being an *antique* shop," she said, offering him a teasing grin.

"Right. I knew that." He gave her another heart-stopping smile. "So where have you been the past few days? I haven't seen you in the gym since the other night."

Oh my God. That's what he came here for? Jeez. Pushy much?

She crossed her arms defensively and scowled at him. "Do you stalk all of your members like this ... or only the heavy ones?"

The smile melted from his face. "What are you talking about?"

"I'm talking about you showing up at my place of business to find out why I haven't been back to your gym. Frankly, I find it rude and obnoxious."

His brows collapsed over his eyes. "You're right. That would be very rude and obnoxious of me ... if it were true. I, ah, didn't know you worked here. I just came in to buy my mom a gift for her birthday. When I saw you sitting behind the desk, I thought I'd come over and say hello." He lifted one wary brow. "But now I'm starting to regret that decision."

Oh man. Of course he didn't know where she worked. How would he? She hadn't mentioned it at all during their conversation the other night. Why didn't she take that into consideration before she opened her big mouth and jumped all over him, accusing him of something as stupid as stalking her?

Like a guy who looked like him would need to stalk anyone.

Preslee cringed. "I'm sorry. I feel like such a presumptuous idiot right now. I assumed that you ... well, you know."

He shrugged. "It's okay. I probably would've thought the same thing had I been in your shoes. It's no big deal."

"Stop that," she ordered, her eyes narrowing. "Don't you dare let me off the hook that easy. I shouldn't have jumped to conclusions, and I'm trying to offer you a sincere apology."

"It's okay. You already did."

"Yeah, but you negated it when you started making excuses for me. You can't do that."

Adam smirked. "Fine. Then I accept your apology." He cocked his head. "Is that better?"

She blew out a frustrated breath. "Not really. Now I feel like you're placating me to make me feel better."

He chuckled. "Okay, let's make a deal. You tell me why you got so defensive when I asked about why you haven't been back to the gym, and we'll call it even."

She scrunched her nose. "Um, I'd rather just apologize again."

A slight smile stretched his lips. "Why? What's the big deal?" When she hesitated, he added, "You can tell me, Preslee. I'm not going to judge you, I promise." He touched her arm.

The gesture was probably meant to comfort her, but instead it had her heart stuttering inside her chest and words rushing past her lips. "I wasn't planning on coming back, okay?"

God. Why'd she tell him that? Couldn't she have made up something lame . . . like she'd broken her leg or something?

He leaned forward, concern etched in his features. "Why? Did something happen?"

Man, he was the last person she wanted to talk to about this, but he was staring, waiting for an answer. "Something did happen. But it didn't factor into my decision. I just . . . ah, don't think your gym is going to help me any."

His brow rose again, higher this time. "Really? How come?"

Frustration rushed through her. Did he have to keep asking questions? He was as bad as the townspeople. "Look, it's overwhelming and intimidating. I'm not comfortable working out in an environment where a bunch of strangers—most of whom are male—stare at me constantly. It's nerve-racking. And to be completely honest, no one else in your gym looks like me." *There, damn it. She said it.*

He shrugged one muscled shoulder. "Well, of course they'd stare at you. You're pretty."

Though her heart fluttered inside her chest, she frowned. "Is that supposed to be funny? Because, if so, I'm not amused."

He blinked. "No, why?"

"Oh, come on, Adam. That isn't what I meant, and you know it. They aren't staring at me because they think I'm pretty."

"Says who?"

Her eyes narrowed onto him. "Says *me.*"

"Okay, so not only do you work in an antique shop, but you're a mind reader too?"

"Very funny," Preslee huffed out. "But I can tell the difference in the way someone looks at me."

"Oh yeah? Then tell me how I'm looking at you right now."

She expected him to give her a silly gaze, something playful and light. But no. Instead, he glowered at her, his fierce gaze piercing hers as something hot flashed in his dark eyes. Anger? No. It was...blatant disapproval. But what could she possibly have done to cause that?

Oh, wait. Quitting the gym. Yeah, he would definitely disapprove because he owned the place and his entire life was wrapped up in everything fitness. But surely he'd had members quit before. So why did he seem so affronted when she'd done it?

As she searched his face for an answer, his hardened expression suddenly melted and morphed into something else. His direct, unwavering gaze regarded her curiously, as if he were trying to figure her out as much as she was trying to decipher his thoughts. The steady eye contact was nearly too much for her to bear, but she managed to maintain the connection. That was, until his gaze lowered and raked unabashedly over her figure.

With a sharp intake of breath, she quickly averted her eyes, hoping he would do the same. The last thing she needed was a fit, good-looking man like him eyeballing her figure in a way that made her heart pound faster.

She lowered her head. "Those two guys in the gym who were laughing at me..." She glanced back up in time to see him nod. "Are you going to try to convince me that they weren't being jerks?"

Adam released a sound of disgust from his throat. "No, they absolutely were. That's why I canceled both of their memberships and threw them out. You missed the action though, since you'd already left."

"Oh no." She bit her lip. "I feel bad that you lost two members because of me."

He shook his head. "Don't worry about it."

Her heart squeezed. "Well, I'm sorry. You didn't have to do that, but I appreciate you standing up for me."

"You have nothing to apologize for." He smiled at her. "And I didn't lose any business because of you. Instead, I actually gained some. I've had new members signing up every day since you posted that video."

She cringed. "Oh God. You know about the video?"

"Yep."

"I'm sorry."

His head tilted to the side. "For what? People loved it. It was funny, endearing, and...well, sweet. Thank you for promoting the Body Shop through your vlog. I appreciate it."

Her cheeks heated. "It was no big deal. Some people had asked what gym I was in, so I replied and shared the link to your website. I hardly did anything at all."

Adam shook his head. "Not true. It was good promotion for my business, and it was nice of you. So thank you."

She smiled. "You're welcome. I'm glad you got some new members from it."

"Me too. Now I'm hoping I can return the favor."

Intrigue swept through her, and she tapped her pen on the desk. "What do you mean?"

He smiled. "The other night you mentioned wanting to get more fit. I'm assuming you still feel that way, right?" She nodded slowly, and he continued. "Well, as I said before, I'm a personal trainer. I want to help you."

She jerked so hard that the pen in her hand sailed across the room. "You, uh...what?"

His gaze followed the pen and then returned to hers. "You heard me. I want to—"

"No, I heard what you said." She giggled as though he'd told her a funny joke. God, he was too cute for his own good. And sweet too. "I hate to tell you this, Adam, but with as much as I have to learn, it would cost me a small fortune to hire you."

His brows furrowed. "I wasn't planning on charging you. I'm happy to offer my services for free."

Confusion coursed through her, and she squinted at him. "Why?"

"Because, like I said, I want to help. It's what I do. I assist others in reaching their health and fitness goals. I'd like to help you reach yours."

"That's the only reason?" She eyed him, trying to figure out what he'd gain. In her experience, people didn't usually do something for someone without wanting something in return.

"Nope," he said, shifting his weight. "I actually have a selfish reason for wanting to help."

Yeah, she figured as much. "Tell me."

Adam released a hard breath. "Look, I don't like that you felt uncomfortable in my gym. I would love the chance to prove to you that you *do* belong there. Anyone who walks through that door does. But the only way I can do that is by getting you to come back."

Oh. Okay, that made sense. Sort of. And he did seem sincere. But she still didn't understand why he would be willing to give away his valuable training time to help her. Then again, the guy *was* all about fitness. One look at his hard, muscular body would convince anyone of that.

Maybe it bothered him to see someone like her, who was completely out of shape, not doing anything to improve their health. Was that why he offered to train her for free? Because he wanted to entice her into accepting his offer because he felt sorry for her and was looking at her like some kind of charity case. Oh God! That was it, wasn't it?

She glanced back at him, and his deep-set eyes softened.

Of course it was. It was just like him to do so. He'd already proven what a nice guy he was. Like the other night when he'd tried to take the blame for her bumping into him. And he'd been the only one to come to her rescue when the machine had gone crazy. Now he was going out of his way and offering to help her again. The guy was clearly suffering from a severe case of white knight syndrome.

Which was kind of sweet, if you asked her.

Not that it mattered though. The last thing she wanted was a smokin' hot personal trainer who looked like a Greek god standing over her while she sweated like a pig and panted like a braying donkey. "Thanks for the offer, Adam. It's nice of you. But no thanks."

He blinked, as if he hadn't expected her to refuse him. "Why?"

"Because it's for the best. I'm not comfortable at the gym, and I don't think that's going to change."

"You won't know unless you try. Give it a shot."

She shook her head. "I don't think so."

"Okay," he said, although the look on his face said otherwise. "You sure there's nothing I can do to change your mind?"

Strange. She hadn't expected him to look so disappointed. "No, sorry. But I really do appreciate it. It means a lot."

Before Adam could respond, the bells on the entrance door chimed once more, and Josh strolled inside, looking just as good coming as he did going earlier. While he was definitely no Adam Caldwell, Josh was likely more in her wheelhouse and closer to the type of guys she'd dated in the past. Not that any of those relationships had worked out in her favor. Oh well.

Still, she at least had a slight chance with Josh, which was much more than she could say about Adam. Yeah, he was devastatingly handsome and took her breath away whenever he moved closer or turned that dark, piercing gaze on her. But she wasn't silly enough to believe that a guy like Adam would ever date a woman like her. Even if she did have a pretty face, great hair, and a fun personality.

No, Adam was in a completely different realm than Josh, and those two worlds should never collide. Ever.

She glanced up as Josh approached the desk with an outstretched hand. "Hey, Adam. How's it going? I didn't expect to run into you here."

Preslee's stomach twisted. *Adam and Josh know each other?*

Oh no.

CHAPTER FOUR

Adam shook Josh's hand. "It's going well, man. Good to see you," he said, settling back into a more comfortable stance. "What are you doing here—looking to buy something?"

Josh shook his head. "Nah, I work here."

"Oh yeah. That's right," Adam said, recalling a conversation he'd had with Josh the week before when he'd run into him at the gym. "You said you had a new job delivering furniture. Guess this is it."

"Yeah, it's temporary though. Preslee's dad hired me to help out while he's recuperating from surgery."

Adam's gaze swung to her, unease spiraling through him. "I'm sorry to hear that. Is your dad okay?"

He didn't know why, but she hesitated and glanced back and forth between them before answering. "Um, yeah. My dad, uh...broke his wrist when he fell off a ladder...ah, in the storeroom." Her uneven voice shook, and her eyes darted to Josh once more and then back to Adam as she fidgeted in her seat. "But he's...fine now. Just not happy, um, that he can't use his wrist or go back to work." She cleared her throat.

Adam sensed something was off, though he wasn't sure what. "You all right?" he asked, worry cascading through him.

"Of course," she replied, nervously tapping her fingers on the desk. Her voice pitched higher. "Why wouldn't I be?"

His brow rose. He might not know Preslee well, but the woman apparently couldn't lie worth a damn. She'd been fine a minute ago. Up until something had thrown her. What the hell had changed?

Josh must not have noticed her weird behavior because he started droning on about how many sets of something or another he had done during his last workout. Adam didn't know because he wasn't really listening. His mind was too focused on what had caused the sudden change in Preslee's demeanor.

Was she feeling sick? Maybe he should check her for a fever. Her cheeks did look a little flushed. But as Adam studied her curiously, she leaned toward Josh, listening intently as he spoke. Almost as if she were hanging on his every word. Her shiny eyes flickered over the guy with something that looked a lot like interest, and when Josh directed attention her way, the soft pink hue in her cheeks brightened.

Oh. Okay. So that was it. She had a thing for . . . Josh? *Really?*

Not that there was anything wrong with the guy. At least he didn't think so. They'd only really spoken a handful of times, but he seemed like a decent enough person. For the most part. Still, something didn't feel right about Preslee and Josh as a couple. Well, as far as Adam was concerned. He didn't really know either of them well, but he couldn't help the way he felt.

Maybe his unease was just because Josh didn't seem to return Preslee's interest.

Adam glanced over at Josh and eyed him. In fact, he didn't seem to be paying her much attention at all. Hell, he'd barely looked at her the entire time he spoke.

Weird.

Because Preslee was a knockout. Even if she didn't seem to realize it. But he kind of liked and appreciated that about her. Still, Adam couldn't imagine any single guy not recognizing it. Well, unless he was batting for the other team. That was the only thing that made any sense to him.

Adam's gaze shifted back to Preslee, and his eyes roamed over her. When he'd first met her, she'd worn a ponytail and little to no makeup. But now her auburn hair hung loose around her shoulders, framing her heart-shaped face. Long, dark eyelashes lined her gorgeous blue eyes. And a pretty pink gloss shone on her full, perfect lips, matching the color of the nail polish on her toes that were peeking out from beneath the desk in a pair of stylish sandals.

Two very different looks, yet he couldn't decide which one he liked best. Natural and alluring. Or elegant and appealing. Both were sexy as hell. The thought barely filtered through his mind when the tip of her wet tongue darted out and slid slowly across her bottom lip. Something clenched hard in his stomach.

Fuck. Pink gloss for the win.

But as Adam lifted his gaze to meet hers, he realized that she still wasn't looking at him. Her eyes lingered on the rambling dude next to him, the one she apparently had the hots for. Irritation swirled in Adam's gut. He'd have to figure out later why that bothered him. Surely it had to do with how Josh treated her as if she weren't even there. The blind bastard.

"Adam?"

His head shot up. "Huh?"

Josh grinned. "You're spacing out on me, man. I asked you what you were doing here."

"Oh, sorry. I'm just, uh…shopping." Damn. He almost forgot what his lame excuse had been for stopping by. "My mom's birthday is coming up," he said, a surge of guilt rushing through him.

Adam regretted lying to Preslee about knowing where she worked. It definitely wasn't the best way to start off a working relationship between a trainer and his newest client. Then again, she still hadn't agreed to work with him. Yet. But, either way, it wasn't like he could tell her that he got her personal information from the new member form she'd filled out at the gym. There was probably something illegal, or at the very least unethical, about doing so.

He didn't want to come across as desperate, but damn it, he had been. She'd left that night before he could talk to her, and he'd needed to find her. Pronto. Not only because he loved his job and didn't want to lose his business, but because the last thing he wanted was to admit to his family that he couldn't hack it as a trainer, much less a business owner.

At the moment, it didn't look like he had much of a choice since Preslee wasn't interested. At least not in anything *he* had to offer. Adam lifted his head and followed her relentless gaze back to Josh. *Bet she wouldn't have told him no.*

Wait a minute. That errant thought gave him an idea. Not necessarily a good one, but he *was* desperate. Maybe what

Preslee needed to accept his offer was the proper motivation. It was kind of an underhanded move on his part, but it wasn't like he was forcing her to say yes. She would do that on her own. Well, probably.

Time to find out.

Adam cleared his throat. "So, Josh, did you know Preslee joined the gym a few days ago?"

Her eyes widened, and her head snapped to Adam so fast and with such force that he was surprised it hadn't kept going around in a circle on her shoulders.

Josh smiled. "No," he said, turning his focus onto her. "That's terrific. The Body Shop is the best gym around. Maybe we should all meet up and work out together."

Panic flashed in her blue eyes, and she squirmed. "Oh, I, um…"

Adam folded his arms across his chest. "Ah, well, that won't really be possible. You see, Preslee has decided to—"

"Hire Adam as my personal trainer," she blurted out, cutting off his words. Her eyes probed his helplessly as a weak smile stretched her lips. "Right, Adam?"

He grinned. Yeah, he'd thought Josh might change her mind. "Uh, yep. That's right," Adam said, playing along. "Preslee hired me today. I'm excited to start working with her." Well, at least that much was true. "Unfortunately, though, since we'll be doing one-on-one sessions, she won't be available to meet up with you for a workout." Preslee scowled at him so he sighed and quickly added, "Not yet anyway."

Josh shrugged. "That's cool. I'm sure we'll still run into each other. When do you guys start working out?"

Adam gazed at her. "Great question." One he desperately

needed Preslee to answer. Because the last thing he wanted was her to back out on him the moment Mr. Motivation walked away. "How about tomorrow?"

She shook her head. "I can't. I work until five. That's when the shop closes."

"No problem. I'll meet you here at five. I'm happy to work around your schedule. Besides, we have some preliminary stuff to get out of the way before we begin the actual workouts."

Her eyes narrowed again, but she didn't say anything. She couldn't. Not unless she wanted Josh to know that she'd quit the gym and wasn't planning to work out with Adam at all. Judging by the way she kept silent, she clearly didn't want that to happen.

Josh glanced at his watch. "Well, I guess I better leave you two and go eat lunch. My break is almost over, and I've got some deliveries to make this afternoon before I clock out."

"See you around," Adam told him, although Preslee only smiled her goodbye. Then he turned his head and watched as Josh headed toward a back room. When Adam turned back to face Preslee, the smile had slid off her face. Anger lit her vibrant blue eyes, and one brow rose in question as she crossed her arms. Unease twisted in his gut, but he shrugged innocently. "What?"

Gritting her teeth, she leaned over and pinched him. Hard.

"Ow," he said, peering at the small red mark forming on his arm. "What the hell was that for?"

She straightened in her chair and tucked a loose strand of hair behind her ear. "For telling Josh that I quit the gym."

"But I didn't—"

"Only because I stopped you," she said angrily. "You were going to say it. Out loud. Right in front of him."

Damn straight he was. Because he was counting on her stopping him and used her attraction to Josh to his advantage. But he couldn't tell her that. "What's the big deal? You *did* quit the gym, remember?"

She sighed. "Yeah, but I didn't want Josh to know. Now he thinks you're training me."

Adam settled his stance. "That's because I *am* training you." The moment she began to protest, he raised a hand to stop her. "Nope. Save your breath. It's too late to back out. You've already agreed. Besides, if you don't go through with it, Josh will know you lied." He grinned. "So, like I said before, we start tomorrow. See you then." He turned to leave, not wanting to give her another opportunity to back out.

"Adam."

He kept walking.

"Hey! You forgot something."

Damn it. He spun back and glanced at the desk. He hadn't brought anything in with him, and he didn't see anything that belonged to him. "What did I forget?"

She smirked. "You said you needed to get your mother a present."

Oh. Right. He did say that, didn't he?

Adam glanced around the gallery and frowned. He hated shopping, and there was way too much stuff crammed into this tiny shop. "Hmm, I don't really know anything about antiques. Tell you what. You pick something out, and I'll pay for it. Deal?"

Her brows drew together. "How would I pick something out for your mother? I don't even know her."

Oh. Right. "Well, she likes unique stuff and collects colored glass. Does that help?"

"Hmm. Actually it does. I may have the perfect thing for her," Preslee said, rising from her chair and circling around the desk, heading to a glass case. She unlocked it and pulled out a small glass bowl with a matching lid and brought it over for him to get a closer look. "It's a carnival glass candy dish. My dad found it at an estate sale before his accident. It's a rare ice-blue color too, which isn't easy to find. Pretty, right? Do you think your mom would like this?"

Adam nodded. "Yeah, actually she'd love it." He pulled out his wallet. "How much?"

"Three hundred."

His eyes widened, and he had the sudden urge to dig a finger in his ear to clean it out. Because surely she hadn't said what he thought she had. "Three hundred? As in American dollars? For a tiny candy dish? You're kidding me, right?"

She giggled. "It's a combination of vintage and rare. Neither of which is cheap. Our prices range between affordable and high-end though. If you'd like to find something cheaper, we can look around and see what else we can find."

God no. Every minute he spent in the shop gave Preslee another opportunity to back out on him. If given half the chance, he had no doubt, that was exactly what she would do. So he'd buy the ridiculously expensive candy dish, eat the three hundred dollars, and call it a day. It'd be worth it in the long run. Besides, his mom's birthday was coming up in a few weeks, and she really would love the little dish.

"No, I'll take it," he told her, handing her a credit card.

After ringing him up and handing his card back, Preslee carefully wrapped the delicate dish in tissue paper and placed it inside a white gift box that she then tied with a pink ribbon.

"I took the price tag off and gift wrapped it." She slid the box across the desk. "I hope your mom likes it."

"She'll love it. Thanks."

Preslee offered him a genuine smile. "You're welcome."

Wordlessly, he stared at her, noting that her pretty blue eyes were a color similar to the candy dish. Probably just as rare too. He'd never seen any woman with eyes like hers, and every time he looked into them, he breathed a little harder.

Then a rampant thought cruised through his head. Had Josh ever noticed Preslee's eyes? Probably not, if earlier was any indication. Which was weird. Because Adam was finding it hard to look away.

He almost regretted taking her on as his client because of that strict rule about not dating clients. Not that it mattered anyway. The lovely woman in front of him with all those magnificent curves apparently only had eyes for Josh.

Lucky man.

✑

The next day, Adam stood inside the small bathroom of Preslee's one-bedroom apartment. The ultra-feminine room smelled like her hair—a heavenly concoction of coconut and pineapple—but had been decorated with so much pink that it looked like a carnation had exploded in there. But that, by far, wasn't the worst of his problems.

He threw his head back in frustration, eyes staring at the white textured ceiling above, as he slapped the clipboard in his hand against his thigh. He'd only been there ten minutes, yet he was already at the limit of his patience for the day. He lowered his head, gazed over at Preslee, and sighed. "Just do it already."

She shook her head. "No."

"Look, we agreed on this. You said you didn't want to weigh in at the gym because you didn't feel comfortable. So we said we'd do it here. Now get on the scale."

She crossed her arms. "Not going to happen."

He lowered his chin, glaring at the infuriating woman standing near the bathtub. "Why the hell not?"

"Because it's evening time."

"And?"

"And I've eaten today." She placed one hand on her belly. "Several times, in fact."

Adam shook his head. "So?"

"I'm supposed to weigh myself in the morning. Everyone knows a person weighs less before they've eaten. God, Adam. You're not a very good personal trainer if you don't even know that much."

He closed his eyes and counted silently to ten. Then he opened them and tried again. "For the record, I *do* know that. But it doesn't matter. You're the one who wanted to use the scale to measure your fitness goals, and we're just trying to establish a baseline. Even if it's a little higher, an extra pound or two isn't going to make a difference." Though it technically might be an extra pound or two that she wouldn't have to lose later. Kurt wasn't the only one who could cheat.

"Sorry, but no."

He firmed his tone. "You have to."

She shook her head again. "No, I don't."

"Yes, you do. You need to have a starting point."

"I will. In the morning."

He sighed again. "Fine. How about a compromise? Step on the scale, and I'll deduct two pounds from whatever number appears."

She blinked at him through horror-filled eyes. "You're kidding, right? I'm not showing you how much I weigh! That wasn't part of the deal."

Adam rubbed his temples. Damn it, this woman was more trouble than a box of puppies. "Preslee, this is ridiculous. I'm not here to judge or make fun of you. I don't care what you weigh."

"Then I don't need to get on the scale."

He groaned and rubbed the back of his neck, irritation riding him hard. "Come on. I'm trying to do my job, and you're making it difficult. How would you like it if someone came into the shop to buy something but refused to give you any information about what they needed?"

She rolled her eyes. "You mean someone like *you*?"

Okay, so maybe that wasn't the best example. Because he had done that. And Preslee had been a good sport about it...even if she wasn't doing so now. "All right, enough. Just get on the scale already."

"No."

He seriously considered pulling his hair out, but instead, he tried to appeal to her rational side. "Listen, I don't care about your numbers. What I care about is you being able to see your progress. Not only will it motivate you, but those weeks where you don't think you've lost, you'll see for yourself that you did. Those moments make a difference."

She was quiet for a moment. "Fine," she agreed, finally moving toward the bathroom scale. "Let's get this over with then."

Adam breathed out a sigh of relief. *Thank God.*

Preslee stepped on the digital scale timidly, biting her bottom lip as a bright pink hue flooded her cheeks. The moment her weight popped up on the screen, she released a distressed squeak and jumped off the scale as if it were a land mine. If he hadn't been paying close attention, he wouldn't have even had time to read the number before she leaped off.

Not wanting her to be embarrassed, he lifted his clipboard and nonchalantly wrote down her weight. "Okay, let's move on."

At first, she looked confused, her forehead crinkling, as if she expected him to comment on her weight. But she must've realized that he wasn't going to, and her body relaxed, a slight smile stretching her lips. "All right."

He clicked his pen. "How much weight would you like to lose?"

Her eyes widened. "I have to tell you that too?"

Oh dear God. This woman. His fingers tightened on the clipboard. "Of course. Somehow you're missing the part where I signed on to be your trainer. How am I going to help you reach your goals if I don't know what they are?"

She considered it for a moment and then blew out a breath. "All right. I, uh, was thinking I'd like to start off with losing, um...forty pounds or so." She winced, as if saying the words out loud had been painful.

Start off with? Adam's discerning gaze swept over her voluptuous figure, scrutinizing every inch of her body. While it would be possible for her to drop that much weight, the thought of her losing some of those magnificent curves bothered him. More than it probably should.

Then his eyes fell on a small wicker basket sitting on the floor next to the tub. Inside was a pink loofah, an inflatable pillow, and several white votive candles. The thought of Preslee's curvy body nestled in a warm, candlelit bubble bath, water lapping at her full breasts as she rubbed the rough loofah between her soft, womanly thighs, had him stifling a thick groan.

Whoa. Wait a minute. Where the hell did that come from?

He mentally smacked himself. Damn it. She was his client. He shouldn't be picturing her naked...even if it was one hell of a visual.

Adam ran his hand through his hair as he shifted his weight subtly to adjust himself. He glanced back at Preslee, focusing hard to keep his thoughts from going to the wayside again. "Okay, forty pounds is your goal. But as we progress, if I think for one second that you're losing too much, I'm going to speak up." Even if that meant forfeiting the bet.

Preslee nodded. "All right."

That was settled. Good. Especially since Adam couldn't influence her goals. But all bets aside, he would never let her do anything as dangerous as losing too much weight. Her health and safety were way more important than winning some stupid bet. Besides, it wasn't like he hadn't lost to Kurt before. He'd live.

And he didn't really give a shit about her number on the scale either. There were other ways to monitor a person's weight loss without focusing on numbers. Her clothes would fit differently. The exercises would become easier. Her body would grow stronger. All good indications of progress. If it weren't for the bet, he wouldn't have even agreed to weigh her. But he had no choice.

Still, no matter how much weight she lost, the important

thing was for her to feel good about herself and be proud of her beautiful body. That was what he wanted most for her. Everyone deserved that.

"Now," Adam said, glancing up from his clipboard, "how long would you like to give yourself to reach your goal weight?"

She squinted at him. "I'm really starting to doubt your abilities as a trainer, Adam. Aren't you the one who's supposed to figure this stuff out?"

He grinned. Yeah, usually. But the stupid bet was changing the rules on him. "Well, these are *your* goals. I want to hear your thoughts and know what your expectations are. If I think you're being unrealistic or feel like it's not a healthy timeline, I will steer you in the right direction." Whether Kurt liked it or not.

"Okay, how about three months? Is that enough time to lose forty pounds?"

"Normally, I would recommend someone shooting for no more than two or three pounds a week, but some people tend to lose double that in the first week anyway. So I think that losing forty pounds in three months is a reasonable enough goal. If you work hard, it's definitely doable." God. Couldn't she have made it easy on him and said four months?

Preslee nodded. "Good. Because, if I'm going to do this, then I really want to take it seriously and push myself hard."

Adam smiled. Hell, he might just win the bet after all. "That's what I like to hear. It's a great attitude to have. Being positive will only help you stay motivated and reach your goals."

Her smile beamed. "Now that this is done, what's next on the agenda? Is it time to start working out?" Preslee raised both arms over her head and arched her back in a stretch. The move shoved her breasts out, and her nipples jutted through the thin fabric of her green T-shirt.

Heat swirled in his gut, and he licked his lips, his mouth watering at the sight. Then he paused. *Dear God. What the hell is wrong with me?*

"Adam?"

Shit. She'd asked him a question, hadn't she? "I'm, ah... getting into your drawers next," he blurted out. When her eyes widened, he realized what he'd said. Damn it. "No, I...mean I'm looking at your drawers." Oh man. That didn't sound any better. "Ah, your cabinets. I'm going to rummage through your cabinets and drawers so we can go over your diet." He exhaled a hard breath and resisted the urge to punch himself in the face.

"Oh. Okay, then," she said, heading out of the bathroom and toward the tiny kitchen.

Shaking his head in complete and utter disgust, Adam followed behind her until they stood in the kitchen together. She pulled open her cabinet doors and drawers, showing him where she stored her dry food and canned goods, and he immediately pulled everything out and set it on the countertop. He'd never seen so much unhealthy food in a kitchen before.

That was about to change.

He sorted through her cabinets, her refrigerator, and then her freezer, removing all the junk food he could find. He could tell whenever it was something Preslee liked because she flinched as if he'd reared back to slap her. But the only assault he committed was on her kitchen, and she stood on the sidelines watching as he continued to violate the place thoroughly.

Anything unhealthy that was open was tossed into the trash,

while everything that was brand new and sealed in its original container, he placed into plastic grocery bags in order to donate it to a food pantry. There was no sense in wasting perfectly good food. Healthy or unhealthy. Not when people in need could use it and would appreciate it.

Once the food was finally sorted, Adam put the healthier items back into her cabinets and closed the doors. Only about a third of her groceries remained, and since he'd figured that would happen, he had planned ahead.

Adam strolled over to the plastic grocery bag that he'd left on her small dining room table when he'd arrived. "I didn't want you to hate me for throwing out all the good stuff, so I brought you something that you might like."

Interest gleamed in her eyes. "What is it?"

Adam pulled out a large white container. "Do you like protein shakes?"

Preslee shrugged. "Yeah. I mean, they're okay. I've had worse things in my mouth."

He blinked. Had the woman really just said that? Surely she wasn't referring to...

Within seconds, the realization of what she'd said dawned on her, manifesting in blushing cheeks and a fit of giggles. She cringed, slapping one hand over her mouth. "Oops. That wasn't what I meant."

A laugh rumbled from his throat. Man, she was adorable. "It's okay. I knew that." Sort of.

"Ignore my dirty mouth," she said, still laughing.

He smirked. There were lots of things he wouldn't mind doing to her mouth and none of them included ignoring it. "I'll do my best."

"So what now? Do you have some kind of eating plan I have to follow?"

"Yep," he said, dragging her back into the kitchen and stopping in front of the trash can and the donation bags on the counter. He pointed to both. "See all that stuff I bagged up or threw away?" He waited for her to nod. "It's crap. Don't buy it anymore."

She squinted at him. "That's your big diet plan? Jeez. You really are bad at this whole personal trainer thing."

Amusement bubbled up inside him. "Ya know, you might consider being nicer to me since you start training in the morning and I'm the guy who's going to be making you sweat." Man. Why was everything suddenly sounding so...sexual?

"True," she replied, the corners of her mouth tipping into a grin. "But if I don't figure out what I'm allowed to eat, then I'll probably die halfway through the workout anyway. Then it won't matter whether or not I was nice."

Adam chuckled. "Well, we can't have that now, can we?" He handed her a list of healthy foods that he wanted her to eat and a list of the ones she was allowed to have in moderation. "This is your new meal plan. Be sure to have a protein shake and eat a good breakfast. I'll need you in peak form and ready to go. Meet me at Windsor Park at eight o'clock tomorrow morning."

"Eight o'clock? But it's Saturday, and it's my day off. I planned on sleeping in."

He shook his head. "Not anymore."

She crossed her arms. "What happened to you working around my schedule?"

"I lied," he said with a grin. "The only exception is your job. Of course I'll work around that. Otherwise, sweetheart, you belong to *me*." The moment the words left his mouth, his heart thumped hard in his chest, and her eyes widened. Okay, he probably shouldn't have worded it quite like that, but...ah, well. "You know what I mean."

The look of confusion on her face told him that she wanted to argue though she wasn't quite sure what they'd be arguing about. So he made a hasty retreat for the front door while he was still able to. "Cut out any fast food, soda, and candy. Focus on protein and fiber. Drink lots of water. Also limit your carbohydrates to good carbs only and watch your portions. Any questions?"

"Yeah. Do you have a nutritional plan that doesn't suck?"

He shrugged. "Not really. But I can teach you how to satisfy your cravings."

"Thank God for that."

His gaze trailed down to meet the nipples still poking through her T-shirt, and he suppressed a strangled groan. Yeah, he could teach her how to satisfy her cravings, all right.

Though there wasn't a damn thing he could do about his own.

CHAPTER FIVE

Preslee stopped near the wooden bench in Windsor Park, wheezing as if she'd just run up ten flights of stairs. Tree branches swayed above her, offering shade, as the mid-morning breeze whipped across her face, cooling her skin. She needed a minute to catch her breath.

Adam must've realized that she was no longer jogging beside him because he circled back and sprinted over, coming to a dead stop next to her. A shrill sound pierced the air.

She held her ears and winced. "Damn it, Adam. If you blow that stupid whistle one more time, I'm going to shove it up your—"

"Ah, ah, ah," he said, shaking his finger. "That's not a very nice thing to say to your trainer. Just for that, why don't you give me ten jumping jacks, ten squat jumps, ten burpees, and five push-ups. Now."

She blinked at him, her breath panting out of her. "You're a...sadist."

A grin broke out on his face. "No, I'm not."

She nodded furiously. "Are too. And probably the love child

of Jillian Michaels and the Punisher, although I doubt either of them would claim a jerk like you."

He chuckled. "Got anything else you want to call me?"

Preslee smirked. "Don't tempt me."

"All right, enough chatting. Start moving, or I'll blow the whistle again."

Jeez. He was treating her like she was at a military boot camp. She could refuse to cooperate, but the last thing she wanted to hear again was the sound of the little silver torture device hanging around his neck. Her ears couldn't take much more. Neither could her nerves.

Aggravated, she began jumping up and down while flapping her arms and legs through the air in an uncoordinated rhythm. Sweat slid down her back, adding more moisture to the wet patterns on her gray T-shirt. At least she'd worn a good sports bra. It didn't wick away boob sweat, but it was doing a great job at keeping her girls nicely in place.

That was something at least.

"Keep going," Adam said, reaching over his shoulder to his back and yanking his white tank top over his head in that sexy way a man does. Then he wadded it up and tossed it onto the ground before dropping into a push-up with ease.

Holy shit. Preslee scanned his shirtless physique, and her mouth went dry.

She knew the guy was ripped, but she hadn't seen him without a shirt up until now. The magnificent view was better than she'd imagined and totally worth the wait. He was in peak physical condition, and his body was as hard as reinforced steel. She wouldn't be the least bit surprised if those chiseled abs set off metal detectors nationwide. From here.

Bulging muscles in his tanned back flexed as he pushed himself up, holding his body in perfect alignment with the ground. Then he slowly lowered himself using strong, tension-filled arms. Watching him work out was quickly becoming her favorite pastime, especially now that he was wearing less clothing. Why hadn't he taken off his shirt sooner? It would've distracted her from being so tired.

All morning long, every time he'd given her exercises to do, he'd also worked out alongside of her. She wasn't sure if that was meant to motivate her or just provide himself with an additional workout, but it didn't matter since it accomplished both tasks anyway. Besides, there was an added bonus to him staying busy. If Adam was working out, then he wasn't blowing that damn whistle.

She grinned about that.

Unfortunately, he noticed. "What's so funny?"

The smile slid from her mouth as she quickly dropped to the ground to do the push-ups he'd requested. "Nothing," she said, grumbling under her breath.

His eyebrow rose. "Do I need to give you another set of reps?"

See? Sadist. She shook her head and did another push-up that didn't look nearly as polished and smooth as his. "No, thanks," she said sweetly.

His low chuckle wafted to her ears as she pushed up once again. "What? No snappy comebacks?" he asked.

She grunted as she did her last wobbly push-up and then collapsed back to the ground, her arms trembling. "Nope. I guess I'm losing my will to live." She rolled over onto her back with a groan. "But now us mere mortals need a break." She hated to wave the white towel of defeat, but she needed to rest before she passed the hell out.

"Do a five-minute cooldown first."

She waved him off. "That's okay. I'm good."

Adam pushed up from the ground, landing on his feet. "No, you should never skip a cooldown. If you stop working out too suddenly after a cardio session, you'll risk getting light-headed."

She had news for him. She was already light-headed. "I'm fine, Adam. I just need to lie here for a moment and catch my breath."

He smirked. "Thought you said yesterday that you wanted to push yourself? What happened to that, huh?"

Her head lolled back onto the ground. "Oh, trust me, I do want to push myself. Right off a damn cliff."

A warm chuckle rumbled from his chest. "Come on. Get up and do your cooldown."

"No thanks."

"Now, Preslee." His command held bite.

Stupid drill sergeant wannabe. Why wasn't he off running a boot camp for troubled teens or something? Maybe then he'd leave her alone and let her die in peace.

She groaned and shoved to her feet, every cell inside her body screaming at her to ignore him and stay down. But if she did, he'd blow that dumb whistle again. Her poor ears begged for her to follow his instructions. "Fine, I'm up. What do you want me to do?"

His mouth curved. "Lean over the back of the bench and kick your legs out behind you to do leg lifts. It'll enhance your flexibility and range of motion in your joints while also safely decreasing the intensity of your workout by gradually lowering your heart rate and blood pressure. I don't want either of them to drop too rapidly or you could faint."

Huh. Well, if he was that worried about her fainting, then maybe he shouldn't take off his shirt during their workout. Besides, fainting didn't sound all that bad. If she passed out, at least she'd be back on the ground again. "How many?"

"Three sets of twelve on each leg. Keep your back straight and your legs fully extended as you lift them behind you. Nice and slow. Don't bend the knee."

Preslee took position and began. The faster she got them done, the quicker she could fall back to the ground and resume her slow death.

It was strange though. She'd expected exercising and sweating in front of Adam to be an awkward and unpleasant endeavor. But after he'd stretched with her during warm-up, jogged beside her in the park, did the exercises—or some variation of them— beside her, and then annoyed her with the whistle, she hadn't thought twice about being embarrassed.

Something about him obviously put her at ease. She dared to say that she was even somewhat comfortable around him. More so than she thought possible. Well, at least until he began removing clothing. But that would've thrown any woman off.

Adam maneuvered around to the front of the bench and sat on the edge, facing away from her. Bracing his shirtless body with both hands on the seat, he slid his butt off the edge and let all of his weight reside in the strength of his arms. Then he proceeded to do deep bench dips that would've broken both of her arms off had she attempted them.

The guy was seriously strong. Even the tight control he had on his breathing while working out was admirable. Especially since her labored breaths sounded like a dehydrated wildebeest slogging through thick mud.

After only a few leg lifts, her thighs burned and trembled with each motion, and she silently considered pleading for mercy. As if he read her mind, he said, "Keep going."

She pushed through the burning sensation until the last set was finally complete. "Am I done?" she asked, still breathing heavily, although her heart rate had actually slowed since their jog.

"Yes, you can recover now."

Oh, thank heavens.

She trudged over to a thick patch of green grass beneath a nearby shade tree and collapsed, rolling once again onto her back. The blue sky peeked through the branches above her as the balmy breeze dried the perspiration dotting her hairline. Moisture clung to her neck. She sucked in a deep breath and then released it slowly as her body relaxed, melting into the soft grass. "I'm going to be sore tomorrow."

"Yep," Adam said, joining her on the ground beneath the tree. No sympathy in his voice. Just stating a mere fact. "You'll feel like quitting too. Don't. Work through the soreness. This is a process, and fitness doesn't happen overnight. So show up, keep working, and you'll see results, I promise."

She smiled. "Speaking of showing up, why did you ask me to come to the park? I thought you'd want to meet at the gym. Isn't that normally where you train your clients?"

He lifted one shoulder. "You didn't feel comfortable there, so I felt like you were ill equipped to handle it on your first day. I didn't want to overwhelm you."

Her stomach fluttered at his sweetness. "Thank you for considering my comfort level. I appreciate that."

"Don't thank me yet," he said with a sly smile. "We'll get back into the gym soon enough. I just figured it wouldn't hurt to give you a day or two to get used to the way I train before I unleash the fires of hell on you."

"Big of you," she said, rolling her eyes.

Fires of hell?

What the heck had she gotten herself into?

C~

Adam had meant to take it easy on Preslee during their first workout, but things hadn't gone according to plan. Not only because she was much stronger and more capable than he'd thought after witnessing her stair-climbing incident, but because it had been fun as hell annoying her with his whistle.

Besides, he couldn't make the workout too easy. What kind of trainer would he be if he didn't push his clients to their limits and show them their true potential? Not a good one, for sure. But he didn't want to push her too much. *Yet.*

He hadn't brought up the viral video again or encouraged her to vlog her first day because he wanted them to get a feel for each other first. She needed to be comfortable with him, and he wanted to see what she could handle. And vlogging would've only gotten in the way of that.

It was best to ease Preslee into the workouts—and the vlogging—rather than go for the gold on the first day. Otherwise, she might injure herself, which would be a needless setback. She had motivation at this point, and he wanted to use that to keep the forward momentum. But once he got her into the gym, he was going to have to bring it up and encourage her to make those videos. The gym needed the promotion.

Adam rose to his feet. "You did great today. Ready to hit the showers?"

"Definitely. I can't wait to get out of these sweaty clothes."

At the mention of her taking off her clothes, a mental image flashed through his mind of her in the shower with soapy hands trailing all over her voluptuous body. Only it wasn't *her* hands roaming over that shapely figure. They were his. His eyes closed to preserve the erotic vision flashing so vividly in his mind, and he nearly groaned out loud.

Wait. What the...?

Adam's eyes flew open, and his gaze landed on a fully clothed Preslee lifting herself from the ground. Why did this keep happening to him? It was as if his subconscious wanted her naked...and apparently soaking wet.

His dick twitched at the thought, and he glanced down with a frown. *Nope. Not happening, buddy. She's a client, and you know we never...* Oh dear God. Now he was trying to reason with his penis. Had he lost his mind?

She *was* his client, damn it. That meant hands off. Period. He wasn't allowed to make flirty passes or ask her out, no matter how pretty and funny and likable she was. And she *was* all of those things. But maybe his attraction to her was just a side effect of not having been laid in a while. It'd been too long, and any guy would be attracted to a desirable woman like Preslee.

"I didn't see a vehicle in the parking lot when I pulled up earlier," she told him. "How did you get here?"

He picked up his shirt from the ground. "I was at the gym early this morning so I jogged over."

Her eyes widened. "B-but the gym's two miles away."

He shrugged. "So?"

"My apartment is closer, and I didn't even consider doing anything other than driving. Guess that shows the difference in our mentalities when it comes to exercise. You seek it out, whereas I avoid it at all costs."

He pulled his shirt over his head and shoved his arms through. "Not true. You just spent your Saturday morning working out with a trainer. You're no longer in that category of people who avoid exercise." He waggled his eyebrows playfully. "You're in my world now, baby."

She laughed. "Well, I wouldn't go that far after only one day. Maybe give me a few weeks to see if I stick to it first."

Adam's insides twisted. He didn't like that she thought she didn't belong in his world. Nor did he like the idea of any of his clients quitting on him. But for some reason, it bothered him more to picture her doing so. Why? He wasn't sure. Maybe it was because of the bet he had with Kurt. After all, Adam hated to lose. But he wasn't about to let her quit. He'd just have to keep her motivated and working toward her goal.

He glanced at his watch and cringed. "I didn't mean to be here this long. I'm going to have to run, literally, or I'm going to be late. I have to meet another client in fifteen minutes."

"Want a ride? I'm heading into town. I'm going to the post office to check the store's mailbox."

"That'd be great."

"I'm parked over there," she said, gesturing across the open field to the green Honda Accord in the parking lot.

Adam nodded. "All right. Wanna race?"

Preslee didn't hesitate. Hell, she didn't even wait around long enough to answer him. She just lit out for her car. The unexpected move caught him by surprise, and he stood there blinking at her backside for several seconds before a smile cracked his face in two and laughter rumbled from his chest. He'd only said it in a joking manner. He hadn't expected her to take him up on it.

But since she did...

Adam gave chase by launching into a full-tilt run. He had to. He'd accidentally given her one hell of a head start, and it was the only way he was going to catch up, much less beat her. For someone who claimed not to be in good shape, Preslee was much quicker on her feet than she gave herself credit for. He was in great physical condition, and it still took him a good distance to catch up and pass her. Even then, he only made it to the car a few seconds before she did.

"You won," she said, panting heavily as she headed for the driver's-side door.

He scowled at her over the hood, breathing only a little harder than normal. "And you cheated."

She laughed as she opened the door. "No, I didn't. You didn't say when to go."

"Exactly. You're supposed to wait for that part."

One shoulder raised nonchalantly. "Well, you should've been clear about the rules." She blew out another hard breath as she slid behind the wheel. "When you ask someone to race, you should be ready. It isn't my fault you weren't prepared."

Adam slid into the passenger seat and grinned. The woman was so full of it. "Just to be clear, I'm never playing poker with you. You'd probably have aces up both sleeves."

She started the car as she turned to face him, blinking in mock surprise. She placed a hand to her chest and batted her lashes. "I can't believe you'd accuse me of that."

His eyes narrowed playfully. "Yeah, right. You probably don't play fair on board games either. You can't be trusted. In fact, I was going to ask you how you've done on your new diet, but you probably cheated on that too."

She laughed as she pulled out of the parking lot. "Actually, I didn't. I considered it though. Multiple times. My healthy dinner had the texture of wicker furniture and the taste of cardboard. I now know why people lose weight by eating 'healthy' food. It's not because it's better for you. It's because they starve to death."

Adam chuckled. "It's about finding the right foods that work for you. Anytime you make a big change to your diet, it's going to take some getting used to."

She nodded. "I know. I'm giving it time. I'm not planning on cheating on my diet any time soon."

He glanced down and caught sight of something nestled between two receipts in the center console. His brow rose. "You sure about that?"

"Yep."

He cocked his head toward her. "Really?"

She nodded solemnly. "Of course."

He gave her a *yeah, right* look. "You're sure?"

Her brows drew together. "Yes. Why do you keep asking that?"

He reached for the golden snack cake and held it up. "Because of this."

She smiled meekly. "Oh. Um, I can explain."

He grinned and shook his head. "It's okay. No need."

"I bought that the other day *before* I joined the gym. I'd tossed it into my console, and I forgot it was there."

He held up a hand. "Preslee, you don't have to explain. I was kidding."

"I know, but you probably think I planned to eat it. I wasn't going to, I swear."

He tore open the clear plastic wrapper. "Too bad. I was going to share. Guess I'll have to eat it myself."

Her head jerked toward him with disbelieving eyes. "You're eating my Twinkie?" A quick but heated look exchanged between them before she blushed beet red and turned her gaze back to the road. "My snack cake, I mean."

He shrugged. "Why not? You said you didn't want it." He broke off a piece of the sponge cake with some of the cream filling and popped it into his mouth, humming in appreciation.

She blinked in shock, as if he'd eaten a dog turd. "But... you...y-you can't eat that."

Adam swallowed and tossed another piece of the soft golden cake into his mouth, mumbling around it, "Why? Because it's yours?"

"No, because you're a trainer," she stated, completely dumbfounded. "You're supposed to be all about fitness and health food. You can't just eat...snack cakes."

"Really? Hmm. Guess I missed that memo," he said, licking vanilla cream filling from his lips. "You should try it. It's really good." He held a piece up to her lips.

"No, I—"

When she opened her mouth to protest, Adam tucked the small piece of sponge cake between her parted lips. For a moment, she seemed to panic. Her eyes bulged, and her mouth opened wider. As if she didn't know what to do with the bite of cake and considered spitting it out. But the sugary filling must've melted on her tongue because she finally closed her lips around it, and her eyes drifted shut on a small, satisfying moan. One that sent electricity shooting straight down his spine and directly into his groin.

But he didn't have time to contemplate his visceral reaction to her because there was a more pressing issue. "Preslee, open your eyes before you drive us into the ditch."

Her eyes shot open, and her hands tightened on the wheel, keeping the car in its lane. "Oh. Sorry."

Well, he wasn't. He liked watching her lose herself completely when it came to something pleasurable. The thought alone had him shifting in his seat, wondering when his shorts had become so tight. He subtly reached down and adjusted himself, hoping she wouldn't notice.

Preslee glared him. "You shouldn't have done that."

Uh-oh, had she caught him rearranging his—

No, wait. She was referring to the cake. "Why? What's wrong?"

That only seemed to make her madder. "I'm on a diet, Adam. Or did you forget that?"

"Doesn't matter."

Her eyes narrowed. "Of course it does. How am I going to lose weight if you're feeding me cake? God. You're the worst personal trainer I've ever had."

He chuckled. "I'm the *only* trainer you've ever had, aren't I?"

"Yes, but don't let that comfort you," she said, pulling into the gym's parking lot. "I have zero experience whatsoever with other trainers, and I still think you're the worst. That should tell you something." She parked the car and turned to him. "If I were paying you, I'd ask for a refund."

He grinned. "Good thing you aren't paying me then."

She squinted at him. "And why is that again? I still can't figure out why you would offer your services to me for free."

"I told you. I want to help."

She snorted. "Oh, right. By feeding me cream-filled cake. Trust me, I don't need you for that."

He sighed. "Look, you seem hung up on that so let me explain. When it comes to your diet, you don't want to deprive yourself. It's okay to splurge occasionally as long as you do so in moderation. You can have anything you want, healthy or not, as long as you do it the smart way. Allow yourself to have a little and don't overindulge. That's the key."

"So you aren't going to be upset with me if I veer off my diet a little from time to time?"

"No. You're an adult, Preslee. I'm not going to tell you that you can't have something you want. Everyone gets cravings. Even if it's for chocolate, then eat it. I would probably just advise you to go for dark chocolate for the added benefits of the antioxidants. But even if you ignored my suggestion, it's not like I'm going to bend you over my knee and spank you."

A mental image of her bending over that bench earlier materialized out of nowhere like a submarine surfacing in the middle of a lake. His palm itched relentlessly as he thought of how he'd like to smack it lightly across her bare butt.

Preslee. Nudity. And water.

Damn it. Not again.

CHAPTER SIX

Preslee strolled through the doors of the Body Shop and glanced around warily.

Here she was. Again.

What was she thinking? Even though she'd spent the entire weekend working out with Adam in the park and had even started to gain a little confidence in her abilities, she still felt like a loser walking back into the gym after quitting the first day. Who does that?

Well, besides *her*.

At least Adam would be there to guide her this time and she wouldn't be working out alone. That made her feel infinitely better about showing up and giving it another go. Then again, that also meant she would be followed around from one machine to the next by a hot guy who resembled a rock-hard bodybuilder.

She sighed. This was such a bad idea.

But unfortunately, it was too late to back out. Adam stood at the check-in counter with Kurt, and they had both glanced up as she'd entered the building. Ah, well, at least she could take comfort in the fact that Adam was the only one, besides her, who knew she'd quit that night.

She moved toward them.

"Right on time," Adam said, glancing at his watch. "I'm just finishing up with something. Why don't you get scanned in while you're waiting?"

Oh crap. She'd forgotten all about the membership card that she'd thrown into the trash on the way out the door last week. "I, um, seem to have lost my card. Is it possible to get a new one?"

A slow grin lifted the corners of Adam's mouth. "Sure," he said, turning to Kurt. "Could you set Preslee up with another card? Hers is apparently"—he used two fingers on each hand to gesture air quotes—"missing.""

"No problem," Kurt replied, chuckling under his breath.

They gazed at her with the same amused grins.

She fisted her hands on her hips. "All right, which one of you saw me toss it?"

They both laughed.

"Kurt did," Adam admitted, his smile widening. "I didn't find out until later."

Later? How much later?

If she weren't already embarrassed and eager to avoid the conversation, she would've asked him right then. Because she still found it odd that Adam had shown up at the antique shop a few days after she'd quit and volunteered to be her trainer. For some reason, she couldn't let it go. Call her overly suspicious, but something about it seemed way too coincidental.

But why would he lie? What would *he* have to gain by

helping her work out? She'd pondered that question all weekend long and hadn't been able to come up with a single answer that made sense. If anything, Adam was losing valuable time and money by spending his training time with her.

But guilt twisted in her stomach. The guy was going out of his way to help her, and instead of just accepting it with gratitude, she was trying to figure out an ulterior motive. Jeez. How ungrateful could she be?

Kurt grinned as he slid a card across the counter. "I pulled it out of the trash for you in case you came back. For the record, I'm glad you did," he said, sincerity filling his tone. "Most people who quit don't."

Heat crept up her neck. "Thanks for saving it for me. It was a rash decision in the moment. I was frustrated."

"Yeah, I figured," Kurt answered. "No worries. I quit my job and throw my card away at least once a week. It keeps Adam on his toes." He winked.

She smiled. It was kind of Kurt to make her feel better. Obviously, he was as bad as Adam at letting someone off the hook. No wonder they were best friends. "Well, I won't do it again. I'll hang on to it this time."

"You'd better," Adam replied. "We have work to do."

Kurt nodded toward Adam. "I heard you were working out with this clown," he said, keeping his gaze on Preslee. "Don't let him ride roughshod over you. Trust me, he's known to do it."

Adam snorted. "Only when I trained you, maybe. But that's because you don't know how to follow instructions."

"That's because you suck at giving them," Kurt jabbed back. "My three-year-old nephew could've trained me better...and in less time than it took you to do so."

She grinned at their exchange. They sounded more like brothers rather than best friends. "Don't worry. I can handle Adam. He acts like a drill sergeant, but he doesn't scare me." Much.

Adam lifted one eyebrow, as if he were about to rise to a challenge, and Kurt chuckled. "I love your bravery, Preslee. But you probably shouldn't say stuff like that in front of Adam. It turns him on...and not in a good way."

Preslee smiled wider and gave a nonchalant shrug.

Adam grabbed a clipboard and rounded the counter, stopping in front of her. "You can handle me, huh?" He smirked. "You know I can make you eat your words, right?" He cocked his head, as if he was waiting to see if she would take the bait.

Preslee stiffened, and heat flashed in her cheeks. God, did he have to say things like that to her? Or challenge her so? Not that she was stupid. Deep down, she rolled her eyes at Adam's empty threat, but she wasn't about to poke the sleeping beast within him to see if she could rouse him. She believed in a little thing called self-preservation.

Her eyes raked over his broad shoulders, toned biceps, and muscular chest. Through his thin cotton T-shirt, she could make out all the firm bulges and hard planes of his strong body. Her mouth watered.

Yeah, she was hot for him. But she would never admit it, to him or anyone else. That would be disastrous and serve no other purpose than to make things weird between them. So instead she shrugged and gave him an innocent smile. "Of course."

Kurt laughed. "Man, she's got your number."

Adam grinned. "We'll see about that."

Her pulse sped up. Okay, so maybe she wasn't as totally at ease with him as she thought. But *he* didn't need to know that.

Adam had gone out of his way to make her feel as comfortable with him as possible. She appreciated the effort, even if it hadn't quite worked out the way he'd meant for it to.

Didn't matter.

He didn't need to know that her heart raced whenever he took off his shirt. Or that when he touched her body in different places to show her the proper form, he set off an array of fireworks inside of her. It was *her* problem, not his.

"Yes, we will," Preslee said in a coy voice.

No. She wasn't the least bit worried. Adam had been nothing but kind, patient, and encouraging during their other workouts, even if she did tease him about being the spawn of Satan. In truth, the workouts weren't as bad as she'd thought. Sure, they kicked her butt and left her on the ground in a sweaty heap, but they never involved anything that wasn't within her capabilities. Somehow, he had geared the exercises specifically to her and made sure they would challenge her.

She liked that. It motivated her and made her feel stronger.

He was a great trainer for someone like her who needed the extra incentive to keep going. His positivity and enthusiasm were contagious, and she could tell he had genuine concern for her health and well-being... which only made her feel worse for doubting his intentions.

Her earlier suspicions about an ulterior motive in helping her were clearly just her being paranoid. If she'd learned anything from her past, it was that she couldn't always trust her judgment when it came to other people. Especially men. She obviously needed to get over that. So far, he seemed like a "what you see is what you get" type of guy. She could trust him, couldn't she?

Of course she could. They were becoming fast friends. Well,

as far as he was concerned anyway. It wasn't like she didn't want to be Adam's friend. It was just hard for her to think of him that way since she kept having these vivid fantasies of him being in her bed. Or her in his. Honestly, she didn't care which. She wasn't that picky. But that was all they were. Silly fantasies.

Adam clapped his hands together. "You ready, Preslee?"

Dazed and distracted, her wide eyes lifted to his. "For what?"

His brow lifted curiously. "To work out."

"Oh. That," she said, heat flooding her cheeks. She hoped he wouldn't be able to guess what she'd been thinking. "Yep, let's do it."

"Come on," he said, pivoting on his heel and marching across the room.

She followed, uncertain as to what they were doing. And that made her nervous since a handful of men were working out at different stations. But as they passed by two of them, one spotting the other on the bench press, Preslee stopped in her tracks.

She recognized them both. "Max? Brett? I didn't expect to run into you two here." At least not together. The last she'd heard, they hated each other. But she didn't want to say that aloud.

Both men grinned as Max sat up on the bench. "We get that a lot. But since Brett decided to quit being such a punk, we're cool now and have been working out together."

Brett snorted from behind the bar where he'd been spotting Max. "What Max means is that he finally stopped being a cry-baby so now we get along great."

"I see that," Preslee said, a giggle slipping past her lips. "Well, I'm glad you two were able to put aside your differences."

Max shrugged. "Didn't have a choice. I needed my truck fixed, and this guy is apparently the best mechanic in town."

"About time you admitted that," Brett said.

"Well, it's very...mature of you." Preslee smiled at them before her eyes fell solely on Brett. "I'm looking forward to your wedding. I received my invitation last week."

"Good. Sidney will be glad to hear you're coming." Brett glanced over her shoulder at Adam, who was standing behind her. "Speaking of which, I had her send you and Kurt invitations. I know the gym stays open late on Saturdays though, so I'll understand if y'all can't attend."

Adam shrugged. "No problem. We're just going to close up early that night. Neither one of us wants to miss you getting hitched."

"Sweet," Brett said, his tone sarcastic. "Didn't know you two cared so much."

"We don't," Adam replied with a smirk. "We just figured that Sidney's the only woman willing to put up with your sorry ass and thought we better be there to make sure you don't screw it up."

Max laughed.

"Whatever." Brett rolled his eyes with a good-natured grin. "You guys don't need to worry about me messing things up with Sidney. I'd do anything to keep her happy. She's the best thing that's ever happened to me."

Max smacked him on the back. "She's the best thing that's ever happened to *all* of us. She's made you more tolerable to be around. Now we can work out together without me wanting to kill you. At least for an hour or two anyway."

Wiping the sweat off his neck with a towel, Brett shook his head at Max and then glanced at Preslee and Adam. "That's another thing. We realized we had something in common. Max and I both like lifting weights. Who knew?"

"I did," Adam told them.

Preslee giggled. Both men were gym rats, and it made sense that they would have that in common. "It's amazing how things work out."

"It sure is." Brett cocked his head at her. "So what are you doing here?"

Adam stepped closer to her. "She's training with me."

Confusion filled Max's eyes. "Really? I didn't even know you were a member here, much less working with Adam. When did this happen?"

She fidgeted in place. "I, uh, started a few days ago."

Max rubbed his chin in deep thought. "Jessa mentioned that she might start working out. I'll have to let her know that you're a member. Maybe she'll sign up, and you two can work out together."

"Uh, sure," Preslee replied. "How has she been? I haven't seen her lately. Did she like the vintage dessert cart you bought for her grand opening at the restaurant?"

A smile stretched across his face. "She loved it. Thanks again for the suggestion, as well as going out of your way to locate one for me. I never would've found it on my own. It was the perfect gift."

Preslee's chest swelled with pride. "You're welcome."

Adam spoke up. "Sorry to break this up, but we should really get to work."

"Right. Sorry." She waved at the other men. "Be sure to tell the girls hello for me."

They nodded in unison and went back to lifting weights.

Adam led the way through the gym with Preslee following behind him once again until he stopped in front of a large treadmill at the far end of a row. "We're going to start with cardio, so I thought we'd begin on this treadmill first. Sound good?"

"All right," she agreed, although she wasn't sure what was wrong with all the other treadmills they'd passed. This one didn't look any different. What was so special about it?

But as she stepped onto it and glanced back to see if anyone besides Adam was watching her, she realized exactly why he'd chosen it. It was the only treadmill in the entire gym that was partially hidden from view by a huge support column. Which meant she couldn't be easily seen—or watched—by others.

Suspecting that Adam had done that on purpose, her heart swelled inside her chest. She'd never met a man who was as kind, considerate, and thoughtful as Adam had proven to be. Actually, he was perfect. Then an errant thought ran through her head so fast that it made her dizzy.

He was perfect all right. *For her.*

Too bad he'd never know it.

The moment Adam caught Preslee glancing around the gym to see if anyone was watching her, he pulled out a set of black wireless earbuds and held them out to her. Time for a distraction. "Here. Put these on."

She gazed warily at his outstretched hand, as if he were asking her to pick up a hairy tarantula. "Uh, why?"

"Just do it," he said, pulling his cellphone from his pocket and thumbing through the screen until he found the playlist he wanted. "If this is too loud, the volume control is on the right side." He pushed the play button and waited for her response, but she didn't give him quite the one he'd expected.

Surprise registered in her eyes as her gaze flickered to him and then a wry grin tugged at her mouth. "Did you make this playlist for me?"

He paused the music and shook his head. "No, it's the same one I always listen to when I work out. Why do you ask?"

Amusement spread across her face, reaching her eyes. "You listen to Britney Spears?"

He raised one brow. "Something wrong with that?"

"Not at all," she said, grinning. "I guess I just didn't expect it. You seem more like...the heavy metal type."

"Well, I've got some Metallica and Megadeth on there, as well as some jazz, oldies, and even some of the King's greatest hits."

"Elvis?"

He nodded. "The one and only."

"My dad would love you. He's a huge Elvis fan."

"I'm assuming that's how you got your name?"

"Yep. He loved the King of Rock and Roll so much that he named his only daughter after him."

"Your mom didn't have anything to say about that?"

"Uh, no," she said quietly, her voice barely above a whisper. "She...loved Elvis too." Sadness filled her eyes.

Adam wasn't sure why she suddenly seemed so forlorn, but he didn't want to pry. It wasn't any of his business, and if she wanted to share something with him, she would. He wasn't pressuring her to do so. Instead, he chose to get her mind in a better place.

He leaned one hand against the arm of the treadmill. "Well, it was a good choice. I love your name."

Her cheeks flushed. "Thanks," she said, lowering her head. "I, uh...like it too."

Ah, man. He hadn't meant to make her blush. Was she not used to receiving compliments? Because if so, then he needed to correct that immediately.

But Adam changed the subject in order to keep them on track and force her to focus on something beyond whatever had put that heartrending look on her face. "You're doing a brisk ten-minute warm-up to get those muscles primed, and then we'll pick up speed. You ready?"

"Sure," she said, nodding as she began walking on the treadmill at a moderate pace.

Adam hit the play button on the music and then set a ten-minute timer on his phone before moving off to the side several feet away. Knowing how self-conscious she was about others watching her, he didn't want her to feel as though he was looming over her. Even if he couldn't take his eyes off her.

Soon, the timer on his phone beeped, and he turned it off as he stepped toward the treadmill. "Good job. Now let's kick up the pace and get you sweating."

"I'm already sweating," she said with a laugh.

He grinned. "Yeah, but not enough for my liking." When she stopped the machine and blinked at him, he realized how that may have sounded. "Uh, sorry. I didn't mean that the way it came out."

She smiled politely. "That's okay. I didn't read anything into it."

"Good," he said, nodding. "Don't sweat it." Then he paused and held one finger in the air. "Actually, sweat as much as you want. Just not about *that*. It didn't mean anything."

An unreadable expression flitted over her face before quickly disappearing. "Yeah. I know," she said, her tone much lower than before. "It's fine."

With the way she clipped her words and turned away from him, he would most definitely say it wasn't fine. He hoped he hadn't offended her. Or was it possible that she'd caught on to his attraction for her, and he'd put her in an uncomfortable position?

Because that was the last thing he wanted to do.

Adam was just about to ask her when he spotted her staring at something across the room. His gaze followed hers and landed on Josh at the check-in counter. Oh. So it wasn't anything Adam had done. She must've seen Josh walk through the front door and gotten flustered. That would explain the sudden change in her demeanor. "So, uh...Josh, huh?"

Preslee turned wide eyes onto Adam. "Um, what?"

He smiled at the surprise evident in her tone. "Have you asked him out?"

"Who?" She seemed genuinely confused, as if she hadn't heard a word he said.

"Josh. You like him, right?"

Her cheeks flushed as she stared back at him. In shock? Or was that horror? "Of course. He's nice and...well, he works for my dad. He's a great employee."

Adam stared at her. "That's not what I meant. I'm asking if you *like* him."

"Oh." She hesitated so long that he began to wonder whether she would answer at all. "I suppose," she said, lowering her chin. "But the whole thing is pointless, so it doesn't matter."

"Why do you say that?"

She sat there in silence, as if she wasn't willing to elaborate. But her bright pink cheeks spoke volumes. He folded his arms. "Wait a minute. Is that why you want to work out? For him?"

She shook her head. "No, of course not. I'm trying to get fit for health reasons."

Thank God. That's a much better reason.

She cleared her throat and then added, "But it wouldn't hurt if getting into shape came with an added bonus. Like catching Josh's attention."

Adam's jaw tightened.

He didn't like the idea of her trying to make herself more attractive for a man. Any man. She was beautiful just the way she was. Didn't she know that? Because if she didn't, Adam would have been happy to explain it to her.

But the one thing he couldn't do was discourage her from going after something she wanted. Even if it was some dude who didn't seem to give her the time of day. "Well, you never know if you don't give it a shot, right? Go for it."

Her shoulders slumped. "I don't know. It's probably a lost cause. Josh, uh, doesn't seem interested."

Because he's an idiot. "So what are you going to do about that?" Adam asked, hoping his words would fire her up to go after what she wanted.

"Give up," she said quietly. "It's what I always do when something isn't working for me. I quit."

Adam frowned. Her admission reminded him of the night when she'd thrown away her card and left. She'd given up too easily. He'd thought it was out of frustration, not that it was a pattern.

While he was confident that he could help her attain her goals, that was going to be hard to do if she decided to quit every time she got discouraged. If they were going to work together, he needed to find something to encourage progress and keep her coming back to the gym. Even if that meant...

Damn. Adam sighed. He knew firsthand how competitive men could be. Especially when it came to women. If he had to use Josh to keep her motivated, then so be it. That was exactly what he would do. Even if he didn't know what she saw in the guy. "I can, uh...help you with the Josh situation."

She squinted. "The Josh situation?"

"Yeah. You want him to notice you, right?" He waited until she nodded hesitantly before continuing. "I can help with that."

Confusion swamped her face. "How?"

"By flirting with you in front of him."

Her eyes widened. "Uh, I don't think that would—"

"It'll work," he said. "Trust me. The moment he sees another man taking an interest in you, it'll pique his own. I guarantee it."

She didn't even hesitate. "I can't ask you to do that."

"You didn't. I offered."

She paused. "But why? What do you get out of this?"

He frowned. "Do you always expect someone to have ulterior motives? Can't someone just do something nice for you?"

She crossed her arms. "Answer the question, Adam."

"All right," he said, grinning. "You and Josh can name your first kid after me."

Preslee huffed out a breath. "I'm serious, Adam. Why would you want to...flirt with me? Wouldn't that be awkward for you?"

Oh yeah. Flirting with a beautiful woman was a real hardship. As if. But it wasn't like he could tell her that. Nor could he tell her that he wanted to use Josh to motivate her. "I technically wouldn't be flirting with you. I'd be pretending."

Yeah, right. Liar.

"But that doesn't explain what you'd get out of it."

Shit. She wasn't going to leave it alone. "Look, how about we make this into an arrangement of sorts? I'll help you with Josh if you do me a favor. You could, ah..." Well, he had to bring it up sooner or later. "Help promote my gym."

Confusion filled her eyes. "How?"

Not sure how well it was going to go over, he thought it best to ease her into it. "For starters, you could recommend it to your friends. I could always use some new members."

Her cheeks reddened. "I, um, don't really have any friends."

Adam blinked. "What do you mean? You just stopped and spoke to Max and Brett. And Max said you knew his wife and that Jessa might be willing to join."

She waved a hand through the air dismissively. "Yeah, I know her. But Granite is a small town. That doesn't mean she's a friend. I don't...uh, never mind."

"No, say it."

She sighed. "I don't...get close to people."

"How come?"

Her head lowered, and she fidgeted with her hands. "If given the chance, people let you down. I don't open myself up for that kind of heartache anymore. I've done it too many times in the past."

He paused. "But what about Josh? If you start dating him, wouldn't you be doing just that?"

"Yes. And it scares me. But I don't want to be alone forever." She blinked, surprise flitting through her eyes, as if she hadn't meant to admit that out loud. Then she shook her head. "Look, I don't want to talk about this. All I can say is that I don't mind promoting your gym. You can leave flyers or business cards on the desk at the shop, and I'm happy to recommend the Body Shop to anyone who comes in. Other than that, I don't know how else I can help."

Her comment bothered him. Why did she feel so alone? People obviously liked her. Hell, he liked her. A lot. And his nerves were firing like rockets through his veins with the need to say just that. But he didn't want to push her. Otherwise, she might shut down completely. That was the last thing he wanted.

So instead, he forced himself to appear casual and, not knowing how she'd react, make the suggestion he had led up to. "How about doing another video on your vlog?"

Preslee threw back her head and laughed. A lot. "Yeah, because that went so well last time."

He shrugged. "I don't think it went that bad. Even now, you're still getting followers and comments on the post." Yeah, he'd been watching it. "People seem very interested in hearing more about your fitness journey."

Her head snapped up, and her pupils dilated. "Wait, you aren't kidding?"

"No," he said, smiling. "I think it would be in your best interest to do more video updates and talk about your workouts. It will help you with accountability, but it could also inspire others."

She shook her head. "B-but it's an antiquing vlog. It doesn't have anything to do with fitness."

He leaned forward. "That doesn't seem to matter to the viewers who are following you. Besides, you said business had picked up at your shop since you posted that first video. We had new members sign up because of it too. It might be worthwhile to do a few more. It could be good for both of us."

She considered his idea long and hard before speaking. "Well, I have been wanting my dad to retire so I can take over the business. Maybe if I show him that I can bring in more customers and handle things on my own, he would be willing to do so."

Adam hadn't known about that, but he nodded anyway. "Couldn't hurt."

"But what if it doesn't work?"

"Then nothing changes. You're still in the position of trying to convince your dad to let you take over the shop."

"And trying to get Josh to notice me?"

He shook his head. "No. I'll still help with that."

Another moment of silence passed. "So, basically, you scratch my back and I scratch yours?" Her nose squished up as if she wasn't convinced.

"Yep," Adam told her, though he wasn't really feeling it either. Because the fact was, although he couldn't ask her out, the last thing he wanted to do was help her date some other guy.

Who was he kidding? This stupid plan would never work. Good thing she didn't seem any keener on the idea than he was. "It's okay if you aren't interested. We'll just forget I said—"

Preslee thrust out her hand. "It's a deal."

CHAPTER SEVEN

P reslee pulled out her phone and got ready to go live.

She couldn't believe she'd agreed to this. It was one thing for her to do a video about antiques, because she knew what she was talking about. But it was a whole different thing to do one about working out. What the heck did she know about it?

Sighing, she tried her best to straighten her hair and tame any loose strands. Thank goodness she had worn her cutest workout attire and her favorite waterproof mascara. That made her feel infinitely better about being in front of the camera. But she still wasn't confident that this was going to go well.

Fake it until you make it, girlfriend.

Confusion twisted Adam's features. "You're going to do one right now?"

She nodded. "Yep. I would rather do it before I become more sweaty than I already am. Besides, I don't want to be winded and unable to speak clearly." Actually, she'd rather not do it at all. Therefore, it was now or never.

Adam moved out of the line of the camera.

Preslee shook her head and motioned him closer. "Nope. If I'm going to do this, then you're going to be on video too. Get over here."

He stepped back over and leaned on the treadmill's side railing. "Why me? You're the vlogger."

"Yeah, but you're the one the women want to see."

Adam frowned. "What are you talking about?"

"Oh, please. Don't tell me you didn't see the comments about you."

He shrugged. "It was just a few silly comments by some flirty women. Oh, and at least one dude," he said with a grin. "I didn't take it seriously."

Well, she sure as heck did. How else was she going to keep people coming back to her vlog? "I don't suppose you'd be willing to take your shirt off for them on camera?"

He glared at her.

"Okay, fine. Didn't hurt to ask." *Jeez.*

"What would that accomplish?"

"It might help keep people's attention." Lord knows it had worked on her.

He laughed. "Preslee, I have news for you. You don't need me. I didn't take my shirt off in the first video, and you did just fine."

"Well, yeah. But I don't plan on practically falling on my face this time around. So I need something to entertain the viewers."

"You have it. They wanted to know more about you and your workout. Just be yourself. That's all you have to do."

There he went being nice again. But it was hard for her

to believe that anyone would prefer a curvy woman talking about working out over a hot guy like Adam showing off chiseled abs.

Still, if she didn't do this now, she was going to back out on the whole thing. She could already feel herself trying to come up with excuses as to why this was such a bad idea. And it probably was. But she propped her phone on the dashboard of the treadmill and pushed the button anyway.

Preslee offered a friendly smile to the camera. "Hi, everyone. Welcome to my vlog. Normally this is where I talk about antiques, but since I had such an overwhelming response to my last post, I thought I'd take the time to do a short follow-up and answer some of your questions." She paused, not knowing what to say next. "I, ah..."

Adam placed his hand on her back and smiled, encouraging her to continue. The unexpected warmth his hand provided sent electricity shooting through her nerves, giving her the jolt she needed. Like a cattle prod guiding her into a narrow shoot.

She cleared her throat. "I've just started my fitness journey, so there isn't much to tell. But I've got someone with me who is better equipped for answering your questions." She gazed at Adam and smiled. "Would you like to introduce yourself?"

He returned her grin with a glint in his eye, as if he knew she'd purposely cast the focus onto him. But he didn't call her out. Instead, he was a good sport and turned those warm, deep-set brown eyes onto the camera. "Hi, I'm Adam Caldwell, owner of the Body Shop in Granite, Texas. I'm also a certified trainer, and I'll be working with Preslee for the next several months as she goes on this journey."

When he glanced back at her, Preslee took the look as her cue to speak. "Um, some of you asked about what kind of foods I'm eating and what my workout schedule looks like. Well, Adam has given me a low-carb, high-protein diet plan to follow, and we're going to be working out together five days a week with two rest days in between. Right, Adam?"

"Yep, that's the plan."

She nodded and gazed back at the camera, addressing her viewers once again. "Some of you have also asked how much weight I've lost, but unfortunately, that isn't a question I can answer since I've just started and my weigh-in day isn't until Monday."

Adam cut in. "That sounds like a perfect day to make a weekly vlog post to give your viewers an update, don't you think?"

Preslee blinked in shock and then gritted her teeth. "Um, yeah. I guess I can do that."

His grin faded slightly, as if he realized that she wasn't happy with that request. "I'm sure everyone will love hearing about your progress as we go."

Irritation sprang up inside of her, but she managed to shove it back down. Before she unleashed it, she needed to finish the video and turn the camera off. She didn't need to make an unintentional blooper reel of her murdering her trainer. "Okay, guys. I know we didn't answer all of your questions, but we'll try to get to those during another update. If you have more questions, leave them in the comments below. Until next time."

"Take care," Adam said, raising a hand as a goodbye gesture.

She ended the video, making sure the camera was off, and then glared at him. "Why did you do that?"

He gave her a sheepish look. "What?"

"On a live video feed, you volunteered me to give weekly updates on my weight loss. That was the equivalent of you throwing me under a bus and then running me over with it. Twice. What the hell?"

"I'm sorry. That wasn't my intention. I was just trying to help you stay accountable. It was just a suggestion. If you didn't want to do it, you could've said no."

"And then I would've felt like a jerk. Probably looked like one too."

He smiled. "You wouldn't have looked like a jerk."

"Well, I will if I don't lose any weight on Monday."

"If you're following the diet plan and working out with me, you'll lose weight. I promise. But either way, you need to quit worrying about what other people think." Adam covered her hand with his. "This is about you. Not them."

The heat of his hand surrounding hers melted away any annoyance she felt, and she sighed. "I know. But it's hard for me not to care what others think. It shouldn't matter, but it does."

Adam frowned. "Sweetheart, we live in a world where people judge harshly. If you let their opinions matter, you'll always have someone spewing negativity your way. The only opinion that matters is your own. You get what I'm saying? No one else matters. Not society. Not your viewers. Not even me."

Preslee's gaze met his. "No, Adam. You definitely matter."

His eyes darkened, and his lips formed a thin, tight line. His hand wrapped around hers more firmly as his thumb moved in slow, sensual circles on her palm. "Preslee."

Her heart thumped faster at the husky way he murmured her name. His intense gaze bored holes into her, and she got the sense that something was about to happen. What, she wasn't sure. But something was definitely coming. And, holy hell, it would most likely be her if he didn't stop looking at her like that.

Adam opened his mouth to speak, and Preslee held her breath, waiting to hear whatever he would say. But before he spoke a single word, Josh appeared next to them. "Hi, how's the workout going?"

Preslee stared between the two men. Oh. Adam must've known Josh was on his way over. That was obviously why he'd looked at her that way. He'd promised to flirt with her to draw Josh's attention. But while Adam had only been pretending for Josh's benefit, unfortunately, it wasn't only him who Adam had fooled.

She sighed. "Just great."

$\backsim$

Adam took a step back and blew out a breath. "Hey, Josh."

He wasn't certain where the guy had come from, but he was thankful Josh interrupted when he had. Adam had been so keenly focused on Preslee that there was no telling what had been about to come out of his mouth. And with the way she continued to stare at him with those mesmerizing blue eyes, she must've wondered the same.

But nothing good could come from saying it out loud.

Still, he couldn't deny that he'd felt something in the moment. Something he had no business feeling. Not after knowing her only a week. And especially not after volunteering to help her attract another man.

Yeah, the reminder sucked. Preslee wasn't into him. She wanted Josh. And Adam sure the hell didn't want to be a stand-in for him. Even if she changed her mind and wanted to date Adam, it wouldn't matter. She was still his client. Therefore, off-limits. There was no getting around that.

Why did he ever agree to help her with Josh in the first place?

Agree? It was your idea, idiot.

And too late to back out.

Adam ran a shaky hand through his hair. She had done her part by doing the video update. The least he could do was hold up his end of the bargain.

Josh smiled. "You two are getting along well, I see."

Adam stepped closer and draped an arm over her shoulders. "Preslee's great to work with. She's so likable that it's hard not to love everything about her."

She turned her face up to his, and a deep shade of pink colored her cheeks. "Um, thanks."

He winked flirtatiously. "You're welcome."

Josh cleared his throat. "Yeah, I know. I mean, I've technically worked with her longer than you."

Although Adam didn't think the comment was meant as a challenge, his chest automatically rose. As if he were a puffed-up rooster that had just realized there was another cock in the henhouse. "So I've heard."

Preslee stiffened beneath his arm. "Uh, how was your day off, Josh?"

He smiled. "Just another day. Most of the time, I'd rather be hanging out at the shop. You know how much I like being around antiques."

She returned his smile. "About as much as I do."

Adam gritted his teeth and forced himself to say, "Looks like you two have one thing in common."

Josh nodded. "Two, actually. We both work out."

"So do I," Adam said in a heated rush, head lowering.

Silence came over all of them.

Preslee blinked but didn't speak. Was she picking up on the weird tension radiating off him? Because he was pretty sure Josh had, judging by the blank stare.

Adam dropped his arm from around her and winced internally. What was he doing? He was acting all territorial, and he really needed to cool it. And remember that Preslee wasn't his.

"So," Josh said, breaking the uncomfortable silence, "has Adam been kicking your butt into shape?"

Irritation sizzled in Adam's veins. Was this guy blind? She already had a great shape. And a great butt. Comments like that were what made it hard for women to love their bodies just the way they were. Insensitive moron.

But before he could say anything, Preslee spoke up. "Adam isn't putting me through the wringer, if that's what you mean. He's been a pleasure to work with. I'm getting a good workout."

"Good," Josh said, smiling at her. "Nothing like working out with someone to get your heart pumping and break into a nice sweat."

Adam eyed Josh, noting the slight change in his voice. Had he meant that in a sexual way? Because if so, he was going to . . .

Shit. *Do nothing.*

Adam fisted his hands at his sides. He was going to do absolutely nothing because that was what he signed up for. To help Preslee get Josh. Which meant Adam would have to sit idly by while another man flirted with her. In front of him. Wonderful. Maybe they would let him watch them make out later too.

God. He hoped not. The last thing he wanted to see was Josh touching her.

Yeah, Adam was jealous. And that fact only annoyed him more.

CHAPTER EIGHT

After spending the entire week in the gym, Preslee had a new-found appreciation for people who worked out without anyone to guide or motivate them. What on earth made them not want to quit? Pure strength and willpower? A need to burn energy? A death wish? Because if so, she didn't have any of those.

What she did have, though, was Adam.

If it hadn't been for him, Preslee would've already given up. She hated to admit it, but he'd been the only thing that had gotten her through the past week. Between working at the shop during the day and spending her evenings in the gym, she'd completely exhausted herself.

Every night, she'd arrive home with tired limbs and sore muscles. She would force herself into the shower, quickly blow-dry her hair, and then fall into bed without even watching TV, an activity she used to do before bed to wind down. Now sleep came easily.

Thank goodness it was Friday though. She looked forward to having the weekend off so she could get in some extra rest and relaxation. It would be a well-deserved break after her first week of working out.

So far, Adam had done a great job at varying up their sessions to keep her from becoming bored. And as surprising as it was, she had actually begun to enjoy the treadmill. Who knew the repetitive motion of walking would have a meditative quality to it?

If anyone had told her before that she would enjoy exercising, she would've laughed. Funny how things changed.

Yet one thing hadn't changed. She'd run into Josh almost daily in the gym. Since they both worked at the shop during the day, it made sense that he would also work out in the evenings. But did it have to be at the same time she came in?

After agreeing to Adam's stupid plan concerning Josh, she'd immediately regretted that decision. Adam—a guy she was hot for—had flirted with her just so another man she thought might make a good husband would notice. Needless to say, that had only made things awkward amongst all of them.

And the rest of the week had been more of the same.

This isn't going to work.

Preslee worried that the only thing they were going to succeed in was making things weird between her and Adam. Well, weirder. But at this point, all she could do was keep running on the treadmill and hope that Josh didn't walk through those gym doors today. Or any other day.

She glanced at Adam, who stood nearby watching closely as she sprinted on the machine. She was jogging at a much faster clip than she would've liked, and a sharp pain in her side made breathing difficult as her lungs strained for oxygen. Her tired legs hurt with each stride, and sweat ran in rivulets down her back beneath her shirt. Adam shouted encouragement from the sidelines, but she was panting too hard to understand the words coming out of his mouth.

Wait. Had he just said this was fun?

For who? Because it sure as heck wasn't for her. She took back all of her nice thoughts about treadmills being therapeutic. They weren't. They were evil.

Preslee glared at him with a look that she hoped resembled a death threat, and he finally motioned for her to stop. Thank heavens. She hit the button and breathed a huge sigh of relief as the machine slowed.

Once it stilled, she reached for the small towel that she'd left hanging over the rail. She blotted moisture from her forehead and then swiped the towel over the back of her sweaty neck to keep her hair from sticking to her skin. She sighed. *Too late.*

"Great job," Adam said, giving her a high five. "I'm impressed. I didn't expect you to run the entire time. That was awesome."

She blew out another breath as she reached for the water bottle she'd left in the cup holder. "Yeah, well, if you keep working me out this hard, I'm going to have to fake my own death soon."

He laughed. "What? No way. This wasn't even the toughest part of today's workout. We were only getting your heart rate up. Now the real workout begins."

She gaped at him. "You're kidding?"

"Nope. It's Friday, and you're going to have two days of rest over the weekend. So we're going to work on arms and shoulders today. Trust me, you'll thank me later."

Preslee wandered over to the nearby cleaning station to grab some paper towels and the sanitizing spray the gym provided.

She returned and began to wipe down her machine. "Didn't we work on those earlier this week?"

"Yep. But you do know that you have to do these exercises more than once to get results, right?" His mouth quirked up.

She rolled her eyes as she tossed the paper towels in a nearby trash can. "Funny."

"Come on," he said, motioning for her to follow him. "I had you lifting weights before, but today we're using the cable pulley machine."

"The cable pulley machine?" she asked, trudging along behind him. "Why does that sound so... *Fifty Shades*?"

Adam chuckled. "Well, I should probably give you a safe word. Because you will definitely be in pain and begging me to stop by the time I'm through with you." He turned to wink salaciously at her.

Her heart lurched wildly in her chest, but she ignored it and released an uneasy giggle. "And I bet you're going to take a lot of pleasure in that, right?"

He stopped in front of the cable pulley machine and turned back to face her with an amused grin. "No doubt."

Preslee put her hands on her hips. "I knew you were a sadist."

❧

By the time Monday evening rolled around, Adam was a simmering pot of mixed emotions. Irritation. Aggravation. Annoyance. Okay, so maybe they were all pretty much the same emotion. Whatever.

There was only one reason for his foul mood. He'd gone the entire weekend without seeing Preslee once. He'd been waiting—rather impatiently—for her to stop by the gym to say hello. But she hadn't come in.

Where is she? What has kept her so busy?

Sadly, he had only known Preslee for two weeks, yet he couldn't make it through two days without thinking about her. And it was driving him nuts. Mostly because it was none of his business where she was or what she was doing.

That was the real kick in the pants.

He enjoyed spending time with her. Way more than he should. Her fun personality and witty sense of humor made their workouts fun. Somehow, she could always get him to laugh at the most mundane things. Even when she was only complaining about the workout itself, grumbling that she was sweating like a sinner in church or accusing him of being the devil reincarnated.

He glanced up to see Preslee swinging through the gym's entrance door, and just like that, his irritation melted away. She wore a white tank top covered by a lightweight workout jacket, dark leggings, and a pair of navy-blue sneakers. The fitted outfit clung to her curves and accentuated her shapely figure in a way that had his gut clenching.

She stopped in front of him, smiling brightly. "Hi, Adam."

"Hey, stranger. Long time, no see." He hadn't meant to say that, but he couldn't seem to stop it from tumbling out of his mouth. It *had* felt like forever. He wondered if she felt that way.

She giggled. "It hasn't been that long. I just saw you on Friday."

Okay, so that was a hard no. Not seeing him for two days apparently hadn't affected her the same. Wonderful. How much more proof did he need that Preslee only had eyes for Josh?

He tapped the clipboard in his hands. "You know what today is, right?"

The horror in her expression made him smile. "Oh God. Do I have to?"

"Yep," he said, toting her over to the large scale near the bathrooms. "Hop on."

Reluctantly, she did as he asked, but her tightly closed eyes spoke volumes. Preslee hated getting weighed in.

But after adjusting the sliding bars and giving his paper a cursory glance, he beamed a smile at her. One she couldn't see because her eyes were still closed. "It's been only a little over a week, and you're already down eight pounds."

Her eyes flew open. Unblinking, she stared at her current weight. Almost numbly, she asked, "W-what? How is that possible?"

He chuckled. "You put in the work. That's how it's possible." He gave her a high five. "I'm proud of you. I knew you could do it."

Excitement lit her face. "Not without you, I couldn't have."

While his ego appreciated the compliment, he wasn't about to let her believe that. "No, this was all you. You didn't need me to get the results you wanted. I'm just a tool that can help, but I can't make anyone stick to their fitness or diet plan. You have to want it enough to follow through. You did that."

Pink bloomed on her cheeks as she stepped off the scale. "Thanks. That's nice of you to say."

"I'm not being nice. I'm being honest. You worked hard, and you earned it. By yourself. You deserve to celebrate your accomplishment." Then he gave her a teasing grin. "Just not right now because it's time for your next workout."

She laughed. "Figures."

"You ready?"

"Sure, I just need to get scanned in," she said, heading for the front desk. Adam watched as she waited for Kurt to scan her card. Then she headed back to him.

"Okay, now I'm ready. Bring the heat," she said, challenge rising in her voice. "Losing eight pounds has me pumped and ready to lose more. Do your worst."

"Be careful what you wish for," he warned, his tone lowering.

She faltered momentarily, but then fire flashed in her eyes and that stubborn chin lifted. "I can handle anything you dish out," she said, daring him to retaliate.

He smirked. "Oh, you're asking for it, baby." Shit. Had he just called her baby?

Thankfully, she didn't seem to notice and only shrugged.

Brave woman.

Adam grinned. "I'm not going to push you too hard. Not yet, anyway."

"But—"

"No buts. You've only been working out for a little over a week. Your body has to get used to the new limits that we're pushing it to. So while it's adjusting, we need to be careful. I don't want to do anything that sets you back. You need to stay on track with your workouts for both our sakes."

Her brows furrowed. "What do you mean? How does it affect you if I don't stay on track?"

Adam winced internally and scrambled to cover his tracks. "Uh, I'm your trainer. What affects you affects me. Besides, if you have a major setback because of an injury, I'll have to work up a whole new fitness plan for you, and that's time-consuming. It's also harder to get in a good workout if you're injured."

"Oh. I guess that makes sense."

Guilt crashed through him. Man, he hated this. He didn't like lying to her...even if it was mostly by omission. A lie was still a lie. But the last thing he wanted was for her to find out that he and Kurt had made a bet concerning her. Somehow he didn't think that would go over well.

He probably should've thought about that at the time. But when he'd accepted that bet, he hadn't known Preslee. She'd just been a random woman who'd wandered into his gym and declared that she wanted to get fit. Something he could help her with, and in return, she would help his business. He hadn't really considered her feelings at all. That made him sound like a jerk, but regardless, it was the truth.

Not that he could tell her that. The bet situation had gotten out of hand, and he already felt like an ass. He didn't really want to look like one to her as well. Especially since she'd only enriched his life since the first day he'd stumbled onto her. Actually, she'd stumbled *into* him. Didn't matter. Either way, the more time he spent with her, the more he liked her. Her spunky personality, her kindness, her sweetness. Even her clumsiness was endearing.

Which was a problem.

Training Preslee was doubly challenging because of his attraction to her. He never thought he'd be in a position where he would develop feelings for one of his clients. He'd always been so careful about drawing boundaries and—

Wait. Did I just admit that I have feelings for her?

Adam sighed. This was so not good.

He firmly believed a trainer dating his client was unacceptable and irresponsible. So he wouldn't go there. But eventually, he would no longer be working with her on a professional level. Only then would he feel comfortable asking her out. Until then, he had no choice but to wait it out. And hope that Josh hadn't knocked him out of the race. Which was exactly what it felt like at the moment.

Preslee had already made it clear that she wanted Josh. Maybe she wasn't even attracted to Adam. During their workouts, there had been times when he thought she might be flirting, but the woman loved to joke around. Was it possible that those times he thought she was flirting, she was just kidding around instead?

Adam had never in his life been so upside-down over a woman before, much less doubted himself to this degree. He'd always been confident and secure in his ability to attract a woman. Yet Preslee didn't really seem all that interested. At least not in him. She was too busy trying to get Josh to notice her.

A voice broke through the invisible fog surrounding him. "Adam."

His head snapped up. "Huh?"

Preslee giggled. "Did you not get enough sleep last night? You seem to be spacing out."

"Oh, sorry. I . . . uh, haven't been sleeping well lately." Because he couldn't stop thinking about her.

"Is something bothering you?"

Definitely. The thought of him not being able to ask the beautiful, voluptuous woman in front of him out, all because she was his client and hung up on a guy who was blind as a mole. "No, I'm fine."

"Good," she said, casually twining her arm into his. "So what are we working on today, friend?"

Friend? Well, that was just great. He'd accidentally called her *baby*, yet all he got in return was being friend zoned. Perfect. He might as well go ahead and buy her and Josh a wedding gift now.

He sighed. "I'll show you when we get there," he said, gazing around the room to pick out the least busy area of the gym. He wanted her to be comfortable. The treadmills were empty, so he decided to start there first. A little cardio to begin their workout was a great way to get her heart rate up.

Adam had barely settled on the idea when a man's voice rang out from behind them. "Adam?"

Recognizing the voice immediately, his feet stalled beneath him. He didn't need to turn around to know who was standing behind him. Michael had always had impeccable timing.

While Adam used to be close to his older brother, their relationship had been strained ever since Adam began medical school. Probably because Michael had followed in their parents' footsteps and pressured Adam to do the same. That had only led to some resentment on Adam's part.

He'd hoped Michael would take his side and defend his right to make his own career choices. After all, he was Adam's older brother, and that would've presented a united front. But that wasn't what had happened.

Instead, Michael had left his rebellious little brother hanging precariously by his fingertips out on a shaky, unstable limb of their family tree. A limb that his parents had threatened to take a chain saw to when he'd told them that he'd dropped out of medical school. They hadn't actually disowned Adam, as they'd threatened, but their harsh words had hurt. Much like his older brother's lack of support.

Michael had always been competitive. Hell, that was where Adam had gotten his own competitive streak from. He'd learned it from the person he looked up to the most. But the one time Adam had needed his older brother, Michael hadn't been there for him.

That day, his brother had made his choice. And it had been the wrong one, as far as Adam was concerned.

He dropped his arm to let go of Preslee and pivoted to face his brother. "What the hell are you doing here?"

Beside him, Preslee stiffened at his curt tone, probably because she'd never heard it before. At least not this particular one.

Michael smiled at him though. "It's been a while since I've heard from you. I thought I'd drop in for a visit and see what my little brother has been up to."

"Why?"

"Maybe you missed the part where I said you were my brother."

Adam chuckled sardonically. "Nope. Didn't miss it. But since when did you give a shit about that? You sure didn't back when I needed—"

Michael raised his hand. "This isn't the time or place for that talk."

Adam's jaw clenched. "Then why are you here?"

"It's simple," Michael said, shrugging. "I missed my little brother."

Damn it. Adam gritted his teeth. He really wanted to throw Michael out on his ass, yet he'd said the one thing that guaranteed Adam wouldn't. Unless...

He leveled a gaze at his brother. "Tell me the truth. Did they send you?"

"Why would they do that?"

"I don't know. Maybe they think you'll talk some sense into me. Who knows why they do anything? Just answer the question or this conversation is done."

Michael sighed wearily. "No, Adam. Our parents didn't send me. They don't even know I'm here. I swear."

Adam paused a moment as he decided whether or not to believe his brother. Michael could be a jerk at times, but he wasn't usually a liar. Adam's posture relaxed. "All right. Fine. I believe you."

"Big of you," his brother said, smirking, his own rigid frame releasing some tension as well.

"Well, I can see you haven't changed much," Adam told him, leaning against a rail. "Still the same smart-ass as always."

Michael grinned. "Look who's talking, punk."

Though he was still pissed at his brother, Adam couldn't help but grin at the old nickname his brother used to call him. He hadn't heard it in a while. He'd missed that. "Where are you staying?"

Michael rocked back on his heels. "With you, if you'll let me. You still have a guest room, don't you?"

Adam was tempted as hell to say no, but unlike Michael, he wasn't about to leave his own brother out in the cold. Not that it was cold in Texas during the summer, but still... "Yeah, I have a spare bedroom. It's yours if you want it."

"Good. Thanks," Michael replied with a nod. Then he glanced at Preslee, his gaze traveling down her body and back up again. His eyes darkened, and he grinned, as if he liked what he saw. "Are you going to introduce me to your pretty friend?"

No. Adam didn't want to introduce them and allow the two of them to become acquainted. What he wanted to do was punch his brother in the mouth for the way he'd just checked out his wom—

Ah, shit.

Preslee. Her name was Preslee. She was his client. Maybe even his friend. But she definitely wasn't . . . *his*. He'd do well to remember that before the crazy ideas and erotic images of her floating around in his head complicated matters even more.

"Adam," Preslee said, gaining his attention.

"Oh. Right." It wasn't like he had a choice. "Preslee, this is my brother, Michael Caldwell."

"I didn't know you had a sibling, Adam."

He glanced at Michael and grinned. *Ouch. That must've hurt.*

Sure enough, Michael winced at her comment. Adam didn't think she'd said it to get a dig in at his brother, but it served his traitorous brother right.

Michael quickly regained his composure though. "Well, that's fair enough. Because I haven't heard anything about you either. You must be Adam's, uh . . . girlfriend?"

She didn't even hesitate. "No, we're just friends."

Man, that stung. Apparently the woman was on a roll tonight.

"She's a client," Adam stated, hoping his brother would get the message that she was off-limits . . . to the both of them.

Preslee gazed at him with an unreadable expression before turning to his brother and offering a handshake. "I'm Preslee. It's nice to meet you, Michael."

"The pleasure is mine, I assure you." Adam's brother grasped her hand and brought it up to his lips, gently kissing the back of it. Well, so much for him getting the message.

Adam groaned under his breath and rolled his eyes. Michael had always been more sophisticated than him, but that fake, debonair crap wasn't going to work on an intelligent, modern woman like Preslee. She would see right through his brother's chivalrous act and realize what a piece of work he was.

Her blue eyes widened. "Wow! Such a gentleman. I've never had a guy kiss my hand before. I thought it was something they only did in old movies."

Michael winked at her. "Then you've clearly been hanging out with the wrong guys."

She smiled adoringly at him.

Oh, come on! Really? Why did women fall for that kind of stupid crap?

Just because Michael pressed his lips to her hand didn't make him any more of a gentleman than Adam. In fact, Michael had just kissed her hand *without* permission.

Adam cut in, his tone gruff. "How long are you staying?"

His brother shrugged. "Depends. I heard there's a 5K charity mud run coming up on Saturday. I know how much you like stuff like that, and it's not far away. Thought maybe we could participate in it."

Adam blinked. "Together?"

Michael chuckled. "Well, that is usually what *we* means."

Though he had always run on treadmills to keep in shape, Michael had never before participated in any races that Adam knew about, much less a more-challenging mud run obstacle course. Why was he so interested in doing so now? "What's your motive?"

"Don't have one. We haven't spent much time hanging out the last few years. This is more your thing than mine, but I thought it would be something fun for us to do together. If you're interested, I mean."

Adam gazed at his brother, who was apparently trying to fix things between them. He wasn't sure if that was possible, but if Michael was willing to give it a shot, Adam would too. "All right. I'm in."

"Good," Michael said, a smile tipping the corners of his mouth. Then he glanced over at Preslee. "Would you like to join us? I wouldn't mind having something pretty to run after." Then he winked at her again.

Adam's hand fisted. One more wink from Michael in Preslee's direction, and Adam was going to punch his brother in his eye and close it for good. Or at least until the swelling went down.

CHAPTER NINE

Preslee couldn't believe Adam hadn't mentioned having a brother.

Well, actually she could. It wasn't like Adam had been very forthcoming with personal information. In fact, he knew way more about her than she did about him. He knew where she lived, where she worked, what she liked to eat, what exercises she hated, what kind of car she drove, and the most personal information of all—how much she weighed. No one, not even her father, knew the answer to that question.

Adam had come to her work, stood in her bathroom, raided her kitchen, and even ridden in her car. Yet she hardly knew anything about him. He owned a gym and worked as a personal trainer. Oh, and apparently he had a brother.

That was it?

Man, she really didn't know jack about him. Probably because he was the trainer and she was the trainee. It was his job to know things about her. Yet she had somehow fooled herself into thinking that they were becoming friends. But how could they be friends when she knew nothing about him?

Apparently, she was just a job to him. Nothing more. And she would do good to remember that. If for no other reason than to not get hurt when they eventually parted ways. After that, she'd probably never see him again. The thought had her stomach clenching. Damn it. This was why she always kept people at a distance.

Adam gazed over at her. "You ready to work out?"

"Sure," she said with a nod before glancing at Michael. "But what about your brother? Don't you...ah, want to spend some time getting caught up? We can always meet up tomorrow evening."

Adam frowned. "No, you've already taken the weekend off. You're not missing out on another workout. I don't want you to lose the ground you've gained over the past two weeks."

"But, Adam, your brother is in town—"

"It's fine. I can give him a key to my house, and he can let himself in. That way he doesn't have to wait around for me to finish up."

Michael spoke up. "Actually, if you don't mind, I was thinking I'd hang out here for a while. If we're going to do that mud run next weekend, then it probably wouldn't hurt to get in a little pre-event training." His eyes cut to Preslee, and he gave her a flirty smile. "You're going to join us for the mud run, right? It'll be fun."

She wasn't planning on it. But before she could tell him as much, Adam stepped sideways in front of her, blocking her body as if he were protecting her from his brother. "She's busy," he said, his low, menacing voice sounding like a warning.

Preslee blinked. What? No, she wasn't. But even if she were, it wasn't Adam's place to speak for her. Her temper stirred, heat spiraling through her. Where the hell did he get off? She was a grown woman, and she could damn well answer for herself.

She maneuvered around Adam to see Michael's smiling face. "Actually, I'm *not* busy, and I'd be happy to come along. It sounds like fun."

Whoa! Why the hell are you agreeing to this? It doesn't sound fun. It sounds like . . . torture.

"Good," Michael said, nodding with approval. "It'll be . . . uh, interesting, I'm sure."

Adam glared at his brother through narrowed eyes as he ground out, "Preslee, we really need to get started on your workout."

"Okay," she agreed warily, still not quite sure what was going on.

Thick tension hovered in the air around them. It was almost palpable. Clearly, there was some weird dynamic going on between the two men that didn't have anything to do with her. At least not as far as she could tell.

Michael cleared his throat. "If you don't mind, Preslee, I'd like to tag along and work out alongside of you. I've never seen Adam in action. I'd love to get a feel for what my brother does with his clients."

A muscle ticked in Adam's jaw. "Why? So you can report back to Mom and Dad and tell them all about—"

"Knock it off," Michael demanded, anger present in his tone. "I already told you they don't know I'm here. I'm a grown man, and I'm here of my own volition. Our parents don't have a say in what I do."

Adam scoffed. "Well, that's a fucking first."

Preslee glanced around, noting that other gym patrons were

beginning to stare. While it might be none of her business, she didn't want Adam to look bad in his place of business. She placed a hand on his arm. "Adam, stop. Please. You're causing a scene. This isn't the place."

He gazed around at all the prying eyes and nodded. "You're right. It's not." He glanced back at his brother and groaned. "It's fine. In fact, we'll all work out together. I could use a good sweat right about now."

Preslee released a breath. Thank goodness things hadn't escalated. There was obviously no love lost between the brothers, and whatever the issue was between them probably wasn't going to be resolved tonight. Sad, since Preslee would have given her right arm to have had a sibling to grow up with and share things with.

Like DNA.

Preslee let out a disheartened sigh. She'd spent her entire childhood alone. Sure, she'd had both of her adoptive parents. At least until her mom died when she was six and left her to be raised by her father. Since he'd never remarried, it had always been just the two of them. But that wasn't the same as having a sibling to confide in or even fight with.

The closest thing she'd had to that kind of relationship was the best friend she'd had when she was nine. But Jenny's family had moved away the following year and they'd lost touch. After that, the only close relationship she'd had was with a small brown mutt that she'd found wandering near a dumpster behind the grocery store. But even he hadn't stuck around.

Story of my life.

With Michael on their heels, she followed Adam to a section of the gym that wasn't occupied. They stopped in front of several vacant treadmills, and Adam pointed at them. "We'll start here to get the heart rate up before moving on to strength training."

"All right," Preslee said, doing some arm stretches.

Adam had taught her that stretching her muscles would help reduce the buildup of lactic acid and therefore help her to feel less sore and stiff after her workout.

"How are those shoulders doing?"

"A little stiff and sore," Preslee admitted as she continued to stretch. "Especially in my shoulder blade area. But it's not too bad."

Concerned filled Michael's eyes. "Should I take a look?"

Preslee squinted at him. "Why would you want to do that?"

Adam smiled. "He's a doctor."

"Oh." Well, that made sense then.

But Adam shook his head at Michael. "No need to check her over. She just has some tight postural muscles." His voice lowered, and his tone grew bitter. "And I didn't even need a degree to determine that."

Wow. Adam was right. He *could* probably stand to work off some of the frustration or resentment he'd apparently been holding on to when it came to his brother. Because she'd never seen this side of him before.

Michael nodded at Adam but gazed curiously at her. "Are there isolated areas of contraction that refer pain to elsewhere in your body?"

Uh, what? How was she supposed to answer a question like that when she didn't even know what he was talking about? "I, um . . ."

Thankfully, Adam intervened. "She's fine. We did some shoulder work on Friday. That's why she's sore."

"Oh? What part of the shoulder did you work on?" Michael asked, his interest piqued. "The superior angle of the scapula?"

"Yep. And the upper trapezius, which extends in an infero-lateral direction."

Preslee blinked rapidly, her brain fuzzing as she tried to absorb this information. But trying to follow their rapid-fire conversation was pointless and absolutely maddening. What were they talking about? Were they even speaking English any-more? Because it sure as hell didn't sound like it.

Michael continued using medical jargon she didn't under-stand. "She pointed to her shoulder blade. If that's where it's sore, then that could be the pain pattern of the C5–6 level in cervical discography or from the zygapophyseal joint. Did you consider that?"

Adam shook his head. "What do I look like—an idiot? Of course I did. But if she continues to be sore, I will show her how to lie down and massage her infraspinatus with a tennis ball. It'll make her feel better."

Whoa! Wait a minute. Preslee didn't know what they were saying, but she held up a hand to stop them from going any further. "Time out. You want me to massage my what with a tennis ball?" she asked incredulously.

Both men chuckled, but she didn't care. At least they weren't arguing anymore.

Adam smiled as he offered up an explanation. "Your infra-spinatus muscle is one of four muscles that form your rotator cuff." Then he laughed again. "What did you think I was talking about?"

She giggled. "I didn't have a clue. Actually, I wasn't sure you did either."

He shrugged. "I'm a personal trainer, Preslee. It's my job to know about muscles and how they work. Not to mention, I have more training than most in my field."

Michael snorted. "Careful, brother. Those medical school roots are showing."

Preslee blinked at Adam. "You went to medical school?"

Adam cut his brother a displeased look before gazing at her. "Yeah."

"B-but you aren't a doctor?"

"No."

Michael laughed. "His handwriting is way too legible for that."

Adam cleared his throat. "I attended medical school for a short time. But I...dropped out."

Michael chimed in. "Yeah, Mom and Dad weren't happy with you when—"

"Shut up," Adam said, glaring at his older brother. "The last thing I want to discuss is our parents and how I'm a disappointment to them."

Preslee's eyes widened. Well, so much for them not arguing anymore. They'd almost gotten along for a whole thirty seconds.

Michael sighed. "Adam, I wasn't—"

"I don't want to talk about it. Just leave it alone."

Preslee blinked at him. Adam was normally so easygoing and friendly. He'd never been this uptight about anything before. At least not in her presence.

But Michael nodded. "All right. I will...for now. But we're going to have to talk about it at some point."

Adam made a rude noise in the back of his throat at the underlying threat in his brother's words.

Preslee didn't know what to say. Apparently there were a lot of things she didn't know about Adam and his family. And now wasn't the time to ask about them. But she did want to know more and hoped he would open up to her later. "If you two are done poking at each other, we should probably get to the workout."

She went for the treadmill in the center, hoping to keep the brothers from being near each other, but Adam steered her toward one on the end and kept the middle treadmill for himself. As if he was purposely keeping her away from his brother. Weird. Was Michael that big of a jerk? Maybe that was why Adam hadn't wanted her to go on the mud run. Because it *was* clear that he hadn't. She just wasn't sure why. It was exercise, for goodness' sake. Wasn't that what he wanted her to do?

Oh. Wait. Was he afraid she wouldn't be able to keep up and would embarrass him during the event? If so, he'd probably be correct. Undoubtedly, she would lag behind them the entire time. Maybe she should back out and not go.

But then she remembered how Adam had treated her like a child and spoken for her as if she didn't have a mind of her own. So rude. And she decided right then that she wasn't backing out of anything. The mud run's obstacle course would probably kill her, but she'd at least die a slow death as an independent woman who had made her damn point.

The three of them walked at a brisk pace for a few minutes until Adam said, "Time to up our speed to a jog."

She groaned under her breath even though she did as he said. Each of them increased their speed until they were jogging next to one another. While she was already perspiring like crazy, Adam and Michael weren't even sweating. They weren't even breathing hard. Sure, they were both in good shape, but couldn't they even act like this was as hard for them as it was for her? Jeez.

As she watched them eyeing each other like two bulls trying to size each other up, Michael suddenly increased the speed of his treadmill, making him jog a little faster. He grinned mischievously at Adam. A determined look came over Adam's face, and he increased his speed as well until he was sprinting slightly faster than his brother was moving. Challenged by the move, one of Michael's eyebrows rose, and he upped his speed again. Apparently not wanting to be outdone, Adam cranked his treadmill up until he was flat-out running, as if he were in a race for his life.

Watching him run like that, Preslee shook her head. Clearly someone had been holding back on their buddy runs in the park. Adam had kindly kept pace with her the entire time. Yet now he was running at a speed she would never be able to maintain. Not without falling on her face within the first three seconds.

While she knew Adam had a competitive streak, she hadn't expected his older brother to bring it out of him to this degree. The brothers looked like two warriors going head-to-head, although she wasn't quite sure what the battle between them was about. She'd heard enough to know that it had something to do with their parents and Adam quitting medical school but not enough to put the pieces of the puzzle completely together.

But enough was enough.

She needed to put a stop to this absurd contest between them before one or both of them fell over dead from exhaustion. She stopped her treadmill and motioned for Kurt to bring over some water. Then she walked behind Adam and Michael, located the plugs for each of their machines, and yanked them out simultaneously. Both treadmills immediately slowed to a stop.

Huffing out a deep breath, Adam glared at her. "What the heck...did you...do that for?" he asked, panting between words.

Michael leaned over, his hands on his knees, as he wheezed in and out. "Yeah...I was...winning."

Adam turned steel eyes onto him. "Wrong." He sucked in another deep breath. "I was running...way faster."

She narrowed her eyes. "I don't care who was winning. I just wanted you two to stop competing before you killed each other."

Adam snorted, his breath starting to regulate a little. "He's my older brother. We'll never stop competing."

"It's our way," Michael said, straightening as he released a steady breath.

Kurt appeared with three bottles of water and paused when he started to hand one to Adam's brother. "Michael? Man, I haven't seen you in a while. You look good. What are you doing in town?"

"Surprising my brother," he said, accepting the water from him and wiping sweat from his forehead. "How have you been, Kurt? You still using the web to self-diagnose your ailments instead of visiting an actual doctor?"

Adam chuckled under his breath.

Kurt grinned. "I'll never live that down, will I?"

Returning a smile, Michael shook his head. "Nope. Not when your so-called smallpox outbreak turned out to be nothing more than a hangover and a mosquito bite."

Preslee bit her lip to keep from giggling.

Kurt shifted his weight. "Hey, some of the symptoms were the same. I had a headache, nausea, vomiting, and a bump suddenly appeared on my forehead..."

"Most of those are symptoms of everything," Adam said, smirking. "I'm just glad the bump wasn't bigger and didn't appear on your stomach. You might've thought you were pregnant."

Everyone laughed. Even Kurt, who wore a good-natured smile and took their ribbing in stride. "Don't forget I have things on both of you guys. Like that time Adam asked out that pretty model, and she—"

"Okay, okay," Adam said quickly. "We don't need to go there."

Preslee winced internally, although she wasn't really all that surprised that Adam dated models. A guy who looked like him could probably have any woman he wanted. Models included.

Michael coughed. "Or what about that time Adam was sixteen and got caught looking at dirty magazines? I thought Mom was going to strangle him."

Preslee sighed. It wasn't all that shocking to find out Adam—along with a lot of the male population—had looked at naked pictures of pretty women when he was a teenager. Especially if the guy was into models. He'd apparently been judging women by their looks for years.

"Enough," Adam said, aggravation embedded in his tone. He glanced over at Kurt. "Don't you have work to do?" He didn't wait for a response before turning his hard gaze onto his brother. "And you. You're about one sentence away from sleeping in your car tonight."

Michael grinned. "I think that's my cue to get going."

"Good plan," Adam agreed. "Kurt, my keys are on my desk

in the office. Can you please give them to Michael? He's going to need them to get into my apartment."

"Don't suppose you still have any of those dirty magazines under your bed, do you?" Michael asked, waggling his brows.

Adam blew out a hard breath. "Would you leave already?"

"Hmm. Well, that wasn't a *no*." Wearing an amused grin, his brother turned toward Preslee. "It was nice to meet you."

"Same to you," she replied. "I hope to see you again."

"You will...at the mud run next weekend," he said with a quick wink.

She smiled politely. "I guess so."

Michael smirked and then followed Kurt toward the office just as Adam called out, "No snooping through my stuff before I get home."

His brother waved a hand in the air dismissively.

As they watched him leave, Preslee said, "So that's your brother, huh?"

"Yeah."

"Any other siblings?"

"Nope. Just Michael. Trust me, he's enough." Adam's eyes met hers. "Do you have any siblings?"

"No, it's just me," she said, feeling the internal cringe that always happened whenever someone asked her that question. "I, uh, was adopted by a couple who couldn't conceive. They'd planned to adopt again, but after getting me, things sort of changed."

Adam grinned. "You must've been quite a handful."

She smiled, realizing what he thought. "No, it wasn't me that changed their minds."

"Yeah, sure. That's what they all say."

"Actually, I'm telling the truth," she stated, feeling a sudden weight on her chest. "My mom, uh...passed away when I was only six."

He blinked, surprise registering in his eyes. "Oh. I'm sorry. I shouldn't have said—"

"It's okay," she said with a shrug. "You didn't know."

Adam lowered his voice. "How did she..."

"Lung cancer. Stage four." Preslee rubbed at her chest absently, remembering how she would lay her tiny hands on her mom's chest while she slept, wishing a magical fairy would take away her pain so she could breathe easier. "She only lived eight months after her initial diagnosis."

"I'm sorry."

Tears pricked her eyes. "Don't be. My mom was in a lot of pain toward the end. While it was devastating to lose her, it's comforting to know that she isn't hurting anymore. And I still have my dad. Although he had to raise me by himself, he's always treated me as if I was truly his. I couldn't have asked for more."

Adam's eyes softened. "Preslee, I don't know your dad, but I'm sure he would agree when I say that you *are* his. Not being biologically related doesn't make you any less significant. In fact, I think it's the other way around. Your parents weren't stuck with you. They chose you."

Her heart squeezed inside her chest. The guy was just too sweet at times. "Thanks for saying that, Adam. I appreciate it."

"You don't have to thank me. I'm just being honest. You're great. Who wouldn't want you?"

Well, she could think of a few people. But there was one who stuck out in her mind the most. Him. Preslee began to fidget uncomfortably. "We should, uh, probably get on with the rest of our workout."

"All right," Adam said, smiling. "Let's head over to the weights."

"Okay."

Once the strength-training session was over, Preslee went home soaked in sweat and probably smelling like it. After a quick shower, she pulled out her laptop and looked up some mud run competitions online. Mostly because she wanted to know what she had gotten herself into.

Unfortunately, it had been a horrible mistake.

In the forums she read, the past participants referred to the races as marathon hell, while others compared them to running the gauntlet. She cringed at that, remembering a story her dad had once told her.

He'd said that back in the day when he was a young marine, they had an old form of punishment in the military called "running the gauntlet." Whenever someone got into trouble, that person was forced to run between two lines of marines who were armed with weapons, and they'd beat him as he passed by them. Brutal, if you asked her.

But while that was a horrifying thought, it wasn't like she expected anyone to hit her with anything if she passed them. Not that she *would* pass anyone. It was highly unlikely that she'd be able to outrun their worst competitor. And really, what would they hit her with—a water bottle? Maybe a sweaty headband slingshotted at her?

Either way, she was certain there was a good reason people online—who competed in these events regularly—called these races such terrifying names. Undoubtedly, this would be a tough, challenging course. Not to mention intimidating. But by the time she read the forums, it was already too late to back out.

Not only because she'd already agreed, but because the competition was a fundraiser with all the proceeds benefiting a charity for a nearby children's hospital. She would've felt like an insensitive jerk if she pulled out after learning that bit of information.

No. Like it or not, she was stuck participating in the event. Even if her body didn't have the kind of conditioning needed to complete such an arduous race: three treacherous miles over grueling obstacles, each sure to wear her out.

From everything she read online, a mud run required strength, stamina, and endurance. Adam and Michael had all three, since they were both in excellent physical shape. But she was nowhere close to being on their level.

No wonder Adam hadn't wanted her to participate.

Preslee sighed and closed out the forums before logging on to her vlog to respond to any comments that had come in on her latest video. She read through the first few with a smile on her face. Adam had been right to encourage her to post more videos. She liked hearing from others who were struggling with their own workouts. It made her feel . . . less alone.

But then she saw some comments that had her blinking in shock.

Why did you let yourself get so fat?

You shouldn't have gained the weight to begin with.

What the hell? Preslee couldn't believe anyone would write such hurtful things to someone they didn't even know. Yet there seemed to be two offenders: *trucks304* and *fitsmartguy*. She quickly deleted their comments and then scanned the others for any other vile remarks. When she didn't find any, she checked her previous video. Sure enough, there were more responses from both men.

Your face isn't bad. But that body? *shudder*

I bet you're single. No one wants to be with anyone that heavy.

Dear God. The comments were only getting worse.

Preslee deleted the vitriol and, not wanting to see any more, shoved her laptop away. What was wrong with people like that? Did they get off on putting others down? Did they think it was funny? Because it wasn't. If anything, it only made them look like jerks. And made her feel like crap, which she was sure had been their intention.

But they were right about one thing. She *was* single. And it did probably have a lot to do with her size. Lord knows that Josh hadn't paid her any mind. And Adam had made it clear that his only interest in her stemmed from helping her train.

In fact, the only person who flirted with her was Adam's brother, and she was almost certain that Michael had only done so because he'd thought she was Adam's girlfriend. Preslee doubted she would've ever seen Michael again if it weren't for him inviting her to tag along next weekend. But after reading the daunting forums and the nasty comments on her vlog, she really wished she hadn't agreed to go.

But it wasn't like she could back out. What would she say? That she was too out of shape to do the race? Man, that would be mortifying to admit out loud. Especially to two fit guys like Adam and Michael.

No, she had to participate. But how?

Desperate to keep from embarrassing herself, Preslee pulled

the laptop back to her and spent the rest of the evening searching for ways to prepare for the competition. Unfortunately, she couldn't find anything that would give her performance a boost. Not when the mud run was only a week away.

She was just about to give up when she clicked on something that piqued her interest. Maybe it was a little drastic. But after reading the harsh comments on her vlog, she was ashamed of herself for letting her weight get so out of control and was determined to keep from embarrassing herself, as well as Adam.

At this point, she was willing to try almost anything.

Pride be damned.

CHAPTER TEN

Adam leaned over to Preslee as they stood side by side in the registration line. "Do you know what you'd be without me?"

"Late?" she asked sarcastically, remembering how he'd hustled her out the door this morning before dawn and practically shoved her into his truck, where Michael had been waiting impatiently in the back seat. Apparently, the two brothers had gotten up early and were amped up and ready to compete. Figured.

"No," Adam said, grinning as he handed her an orange bottle of sunscreen lotion with a high SPF rating. "Unprepared."

She accepted it with a smile. "Good thing I have you then," she replied, not realizing how it sounded until the words had already popped out of her mouth. Crap. So she quickly followed it up with, "Good friends are hard to come by, you know?" Then she turned away from him, wincing at how stupid she sounded.

She silently berated herself as she flipped open the top on the sunscreen and squirted some onto her palm. Her comment must've been as weird for him as it was for her, because he didn't speak as she smeared the sunscreen over her bare arms, rubbing it in until her skin absorbed all of the lotion. Then she reached down and did the same on her lower legs where the spandex Capri leggings she wore didn't cover her shins or calves.

"Next," the woman at the registration desk called out.

Preslee nudged Adam. "You go."

"That's okay. You can go before me."

She shook her head. "I'm still applying sunscreen. Go ahead."

He nodded and stepped up to the registration desk.

Preslee applied sunscreen to her face and rubbed it in until the lotion had soaked completely into her skin. The last thing she wanted was for Adam to see her with white streaks of sunscreen making her look like a clown. As clumsy as she was, she usually didn't need help in that area. In fact, she'd be lucky if she didn't trip over her own feet today while running.

She glanced over at Michael, who was smiling at her as if he were a mind reader. Then Michael pulled out a pair of dark sunglasses and slid them onto his face, covering his eyes. The same warm brown eyes he shared with his little brother.

But that wasn't what had caught her attention.

Instead, Preslee had noticed an emblem on the side of Michael's sunglasses that had her doing a double take. After being in the antique business so long, she had developed a great eye for recognizing brands. Not only old ones, but newer ones as well. It came in handy when trying to determine the age and worth of an item found at an estate sale.

She cleared her throat. "Oakleys, huh? Those are some

expensive sunglasses you're wearing. Aren't you worried that you'll break them or lose them during the run?"

He shrugged. "If I do, I'll just buy another pair."

Oh. Well, all right then.

But when Michael squatted down to tighten his shoelaces, Preslee gawked at him. She hadn't noticed before—probably because he'd been sitting in the back seat—but Michael sported a white pair of Bally Aston sneakers on his feet. If she was correct, those shoes were genuine calf leather and cost somewhere around six hundred dollars. "Um, you're going to run through mud in those?"

He gazed up at her. "Sure, why not? They're just shoes. I can always get a new pair."

Jeez. She knew he was a doctor, but how much money did this guy make that he could just throw away six-hundred-dollar shoes on a whim? She thought it might be rude of her to ask, so she didn't.

As she waited for her turn at the registration desk, she glanced around. A fine mist rose from the ground, cooling the slight breeze wafting over her skin. It was still early, but the blue morning light was already fading and the dew-covered grass sparkled with the first bright rays of sunlight peeking over the horizon. It wouldn't be long before the blinding sun would be blazing down on them with the sizzling summer heat that South Texas had always been known for.

Michael glanced over at Adam, who was almost finished registering, and lowered his voice. "So, you and Adam are an item, huh?"

Preslee nearly choked on her own saliva. So much for not asking a question because it might be considered rude. "Um, no. Of course not," she said, quieting her voice as well. "Your brother is my trainer. We're just friends."

"But you like him, right?"

"Sure," she said with a nod before glancing back down. "Apparently more than you like those expensive shoes you're about to ruin."

He chuckled but didn't say anything else, since Adam had finished at the registration table and rejoined them. Thank goodness. It was her turn, so she hurried over to the table and got started. Once she was officially registered, she returned to them and they headed toward the starting line in silence. When they got there, Adam led them in some stretches as a warm-up while they waited for the race to begin.

Preslee did a quick internal check of her energy level and found that she felt strong and capable. Empowered even. Almost like someone who believed in her abilities. She could totally do this. Of course, that was probably just the exhilaration of the race humming in the air around her. But she hadn't really experienced the discomfort and anxiety that she'd expected to feel this morning.

It hadn't hurt that Adam had increased the intensity and pace of her workouts this week, in order to prepare her for the event. That probably had somehow added to this newfound sense of confidence. But more than likely, it was the extra thirty-minute sweat sessions she'd added on herself this week that had left her feeling undaunted by the upcoming race.

She hadn't told Adam that she'd upped her daily training schedule by incorporating two extra workouts per day. Mostly because she was too embarrassed to admit that she was afraid of not being able to keep up during the race. Or even worse, that he would purposely lag behind everyone else in order to stay with her. Both scenarios would only make her feel like a loser.

Preslee thought losing a few more pounds over the week might be enough to give her a boost in her running ability and help her out during the race. And it had worked! When she'd weighed in the day before, she had been pleased to see that she'd lost almost fifteen more pounds. Adam had been a bit perplexed and concerned that she'd lost that much during her second week. But clearly her plan had worked, and she couldn't think of her weight loss as anything other than a win.

As the race was about to start, one of the coordinators grabbed a microphone and reminded everyone that the run would be a 5K race with a layout that wound around forty acres of natural terrain. He told everyone that they would encounter various natural and man-made obstacles in their path, but that the mud run volunteers had gone through and removed sticks and such to make sure the obstacles were safe. And that this year, they weren't doing a beginners' course and an advanced one, which would've allowed each participant to choose their own difficulty level. Instead, they were having the first timers compete side by side with the seasoned athletes.

Of course. Just my luck.

As the coordinator wished everyone a good race, people began to crowd in around the three of them, trying to get closer to the starting line. Adam and Michael flanked her though, which gave her plenty of room and kept her from getting squished by the other competitors. Both brawny brothers commanded their space, and no one seemed interested in crossing into it. Well, except for a few of the female competitors who Preslee had seen eyeing the men at her side. Not that she could blame them.

When the air horn sounded, signaling the start of the race, all of the participants took off at once. Adam had told her earlier in the week that she needed to pace herself so she wouldn't burn out, so she found her rhythm almost immediately and stuck with it. Adam ran alongside her, praising her efforts, putting a smile on her face, and inspiring her to keep going. She felt good. After all, she was running next to two seasoned pros, and if you asked her, she was doing a damn good job of keeping up.

Five minutes into the run, the wide dirt path narrowed considerably as it rounded a corner, and some of the outside runners around them had to fall back in order to stay on the trail rather than end up in the weeds. When the three of them reached the first obstacle, Preslee slowed her pace. A huge patch of ankle-deep mud sprawled out before her, and she waded through it carefully to keep from slipping and sliding around in it like some of the runners ahead of them had done.

As usual, Adam was in beast mode and powered straight through it. His lean, muscular physique was like a well-oiled machine with an unstoppable momentum. Michael displayed the same athleticism with his perfectly toned shoulders and muscled thighs. He didn't slow down either as his trim, powerful body blew through the obstacle with little resistance.

Although she was sure it was killing them to wait, both men stopped on the opposite side of the mud patch and encouraged her to move faster. Not wanting to disappoint or hold either of them back, Preslee moved through the mud as quickly as possible. Which wasn't easy. She sank deep, which only suctioned her shoes to the ground. But she treaded through it and got to the other side. Then they all ran full-bore to make up for the lost time, kicking up bits of mud in their wake.

The sun had risen higher, and the air heated up. As she ran, Preslee wiped her brow and then fanned her hot face. She was perspiring so much that the sunscreen she'd applied before the race had started mixing with the sweat and dripping into her eyes, making them sting.

So much for avoiding sun damage.

There was no way she would quit. She was devoted to finishing this race, even if it killed her. And, at this rate, it was looking like it just might. They'd only made it through one obstacle, and she already felt like she needed a break. Or possibly a nap. Maybe even a vacation.

Sweat continued to pour off her in rivulets as she made it to the next obstacle, which was a natural barrier rather than a man-made one. A mostly dried-up creek with a large puddle in the middle and steep banks sat before them, blocking their way to the next path. Without hesitation, Adam and Michael ran forward and leaped across to the other side before turning to urge her on. It didn't look like much of a jump, so Preslee went for it.

She probably would've made it, too, had her foot not caught on a large cypress knot by the edge of the bank. She stumbled forward and landed directly in the middle of the large puddle. Thankfully, the water was deep enough to cushion her fall and keep her from getting injured. But when she pulled her wet hands up to shove her hair away from her face, a rotten odor infiltrated her nostrils.

Oh yuck. The water must've been stagnant. Either that or there was something dead in the small, algae-infested pool. Just the thought alone had her scrambling out of the water and up the side of the bank as quickly as possible.

"Good girl," Adam said, cheering her on. "Way to hustle." Clearly he didn't have a clue what had lit a fire under her. But it only took seconds for him to catch the horrific smell coming off her. His nose wrinkled with disgust. "Oh God."

Michael took a step back, his upper lip curling. "Man. What the hell was in that water?"

"Besides me?" she asked, her tone filled with repulsion. "I'm not sure, but I'm certain I don't want to know."

"Uh, you're up to date on all your immunizations, right?" Michael asked, his voice serious.

Preslee blinked in horror.

Adam punched his brother in the arm and gave him a dirty look. "Don't scare her like that, you idiot."

Michael offered a wry grin. "Sorry. I can't help myself. I'm a doctor, you know. It's my job to worry about people catching infectious diseases." Panic shot through her, and a gasp escaped her lips. Michael caught what he said and cringed. "Oh. I'm sure it's fine though."

Adam's jaw clenched as he gave his brother another hard gaze. "What he meant to say, Preslee, was that it's probably just the smell of the black mud. Or maybe algae. It's not a big deal."

Another small group of runners jumped the creek. As they started past Preslee, she saw the looks on all their faces before they took off running. It was the same look a person got when they were stuck on an elevator with someone who had just passed gas.

Preslee wanted to cry, but weeping wasn't going to help any. There was nothing she could do about the horrible smell. So instead, she crossed her fingers that she didn't end up contracting some kind of deadly flesh-eating bacteria from whatever was rotting in the creek. "Can we just go already?"

Without waiting for them to answer, she took off at a dead run, keeping a good pace. Not fast enough that they wouldn't be able to catch up, though neither of them did. They both lagged behind her at least five or six feet. She couldn't really blame them.

By the time they reached the next obstacle, the unpleasant smell must've dissipated some because both men were running beside her once again. Or maybe they'd just gotten used to the stench like she had. Didn't matter. She was determined to put it out of her mind and not think about it anymore. Because every time she did, she longed to soak her body in a warm, bleach-filled bathtub while sipping on a cocktail made up of several strong antibiotics.

Adam pointed to a huge dumpster trailer in front of them that made up the next obstacle. "Oh man. I hate this one. Who wants to go first?"

Jeez. If even Adam didn't want to do it, then it had to be really bad. What did they have to do—crawl through rotting trash to get to the other side?

Michael shook his head. "I'm not diving into that water first. You go."

Preslee's head snapped up. "Did you say water?"

Adam nodded. "Yeah, they line the dumpster with some kind of plastic or vinyl to keep it from leaking and then fill it with water."

Although he continued to speak, Preslee stopped listening. Her focus instead was on another contestant, who climbed the ladder on the side and jumped into the oversize dumpster. A splash followed, and it was music to her ears.

She didn't bother to respond to Adam or wait for either of them. Just the thought of submerging her body in clean water and rinsing the smell of death off her was enough to persuade her to climb the ladder and throw herself over the edge as if she were bungee jumping from a bridge. But the moment she hit the water, she shrieked as her entire body froze.

Not figuratively either.

Preslee had just unknowingly tossed herself into a large vat of ice water, and the shock to her system had not only taken her breath but practically caused her to drown. Thankfully she'd managed to get her legs under her and stand up in the chest-deep water before that happened.

She wrapped her arms around herself and shivered violently, her chin and lips quivering. Goose bumps rose on her prickling skin. The water was so cold that the ice cubes floating on the surface felt sharp against her sunburned flesh. At least for the first few seconds. After that, her entire body went completely numb, and she couldn't feel a thing. Including her hands and feet.

Somehow, she managed to ease her way over to the other side. But once she got there, she was unable to pull herself out. Her limbs were so cold that she couldn't get them to work properly, and her freezing hands were shaking too much to be able to grasp anything. It wasn't until Adam and Michael had both reached her and given her a boost that she was finally able to climb over the ledge of the dumpster and out of the icy water.

Adam and Michael exchanged a look of concern before they lifted themselves out of the freezing water. They did it with such ease that Preslee almost wanted to laugh at how pathetic she must've seemed. They grasped her arms, which were still as cold as her legs, and guided her down the stairs until they were on solid ground.

The hot Texas breeze engulfed her, and she sighed in relief. Adam briskly rubbed her two hands between his and blew his warm breath across her cold fingers. "You all right, Preslee? You were in that ice water longer than most people."

"I-I'm f-f-fine," she managed to get out, her teeth chattering.

Michael rubbed the outsides of her bare arms, lending her his body heat as well. "Don't worry. A few minutes under the hot sun will warm you."

Probably. But she didn't want to wait for the sun to warm her. Moving her body should be enough to get her blood pumping. And it would be faster too. She climbed shakily to her feet. "No. L-let's g-g-go."

Adam shook his head. "No. Just rest here for a minute. Let your body warm up first."

Her lips trembled. "It'll be f-f-faster if we r-run. We're g-getting b-behind."

Adam's lips tipped downward. "I don't care about that. I just want to make sure you're okay."

"I am. Just d-don't want to l-lose."

Actually, she didn't give a damn if she came in last place or not. She wasn't all that competitive when it came to stuff like this. But she knew Adam was. The last thing she wanted was to be the reason *he* came in last place.

Adam glanced at his brother. "Is it safe? Or should we wait for her body temperature to rise?"

Michael gazed at her before answering. She wasn't sure if it was her pleading eyes or if he really thought it was okay to continue, but he nodded. "It's fine. If she's up to it, then we can keep going. As hot as it is, it shouldn't take long to regulate her body temperature."

They started out again, though she moved much slower than before. Adam must've still been wary about them carrying on before she had thawed out because he stayed close, watching her as if she would face plant at any moment.

But Michael had been correct. Her body warmed fairly quickly under the hot sun, and she was able to move her limbs enough to power walk and then finally jog. Although there was now a new level of weariness that had settled into her bones that hadn't been there before.

Since they were moving at a snail's pace compared to before, it took a while before they reached the next obstacle. It was a huge wall with a curve at the bottom. Participants had to run up the wall as far as they could and then jump up while others at the top grasped their hands and pulled them up and over onto the other side.

Michael went first and scaled the wall with ease as a stranger grasped his hand at the top and pulled him over the ledge. Adam went next and ran up the wall, latching on to Michael's outstretched hand, and climbed onto the wall as well. When it came to her turn, she hesitated. But after a few shouted encouragements, she got into position and darted for the wall, running up the curved part as fast as she could, and jumped for all she was worth.

She missed Michael's hand but managed to grasp on to Adam's, who dangled her in mid-air until he pulled her dead-weight over the ledge and onto a platform. Unlike either of them, she hadn't bothered to even try climbing up. She was too tired for that and knew she would only hinder Adam.

Earlier that morning, she'd been riding high on a buzz that had now completely faded. But her shoulders went back and her chin lifted as she put on her game face and summoned the energy to keep going. The platform dropped off into muddy brown water, which they waded through to get to the other side. Then they continued on the dirt path toward the following obstacle.

Thankfully, the next couple were fairly easy. She only had to balance herself as she walked across narrow beams over another mud pit and then crawl across a large section of rope netting. Both were a piece of cake. Especially compared to the one that followed. This one was tough. She moved hand-over-hand across a set of rings that were hanging in a straight line over a small pool of ice water. But some of the rings were greased so, of course, she ended up back in the cold water. Though she had expected it this time and rushed out of the pit before the freezing liquid numbed her limbs and paralyzed her.

"You're doing awesome," Adam told her as they continued on their way. "Only one more obstacle to go."

Thank heavens.

The last obstacle was a huge pit. They'd have to army crawl in the mud beneath barbed wire, through a dark tunnel, and then dodge a bunch of hanging wires. This was their big grand finale? Weird. It seemed too easy. She had expected the last obstacle to be the hardest, but apparently she'd been wrong.

But as they lay in the mud and began crawling, Preslee changed her mind. The mud pit wasn't easy to navigate. She made it under the barbed wire with no problem, though her muscles ached from fighting her way through the thick, sticky mud. But though she wasn't usually claustrophobic, the tiny, dark tunnel that was half filled with mud had a suffocating effect that left her gasping for breath before she made it out the other side. The guys looked unfazed though, as if they did this kind of stuff daily. In fact, both were even smiling, enjoying themselves to the fullest.

Adam nodded toward the hanging wires. "Last section of this obstacle."

Preslee rose unsteadily to her feet. "What are the wires for?"

"They have electricity running through them. Ten thousand volts."

She gaped at him. "They're going to shock me?"

Michael chuckled. "Not if you don't touch them."

Preslee glanced again at the wires. There were so many of them that there was no way to make it through without touching at least some. "That's impossible," she argued. "No one can make it through there without touching them."

Adam grinned. "That's kind of the point. But it doesn't hurt that bad. It's tolerable pain. Just crawl through as fast as you can. It'll be fun."

Fun? This is supposed to be fun? Haven't these people heard of Scrabble?

Preslee followed Adam and Michael as they crawled through the mud and made it to the wires. She followed Adam's advice to scurry through as quickly as she could, but screeched loudly when the first jolt of electricity ran through her.

Ow, that hurt! Who comes up with this sadistic shit?

She slogged through the mud on her belly to the other side while painful zaps occasionally coursed through her whenever she accidentally touched another wire. By the time she finally scaled the small wall out of the pit behind Adam, she had never in her life been so glad to be done with something. Thank goodness they only had to make it to the finish line now. That shouldn't be so bad.

She followed the guys down the trail, and they picked up their pace until they were running again, mud flinging from their shoes. The event volunteers had done a good job of cleaning the paths of fallen tree limbs and other debris. With nothing to trip over, it would be smooth sailing the rest of the way.

Well, mostly.

While both Adam and Michael contained a seemingly endless supply of energy, it wasn't a sustainable speed. At least not for her. Her strength had slowly dissipated throughout each obstacle, and the hectic pace Adam set was too intense while she was this depleted. So she slowed down to give herself a breather.

The moment Adam realized he was pulling away, he shortened his stride to match hers. "You okay?"

"Yeah," she panted out. She was just more distracted than usual. Mostly by the incredible burning in her calves. "I'm just not as fit as you two."

His forehead wrinkled in disapproval. "You're doing great. Ditch the negativity."

Easy for him to say. He wasn't the one struggling. Maybe he didn't like her to say that kind of negative stuff out loud, but it was true and he undoubtedly knew it. That was probably why he didn't bother to argue the point rather than just get mad at her for commenting on it.

"If you need a break, we can walk."

Hell no. Besides, if he told her to engage her core one more time, she would probably punch him in the face. "That's okay," she said between heavy breaths. "Keep going. Don't slow down."

The faster they got to the end, the quicker she could go home, take a hot shower, eat something, and fall into bed. She was looking forward to that. "We need to keep moving. Why don't you guys go on ahead of me?"

Adam shook his head. "We aren't leaving you behind."

"Why not? You said it yourself. That was the last obstacle. I know how competitive you two are. Go race to the finish line." She grinned at him. "You can let me know who wins when I get there."

His brow furrowed. "I don't want to leave you."

She motioned to a passing runner and blew out a hard breath. "I'm hardly alone, Adam. There are dozens of other contestants in the vicinity. Besides, I'm a big girl. I'll be fine. I'll see you at the finish line."

"You sure?" Michael asked warily, jogging on her other side.

Preslee glanced at him. "Absolutely. Go already."

Michael shrugged. "If you say so," he replied with a grin, taking off at a dead run in the direction of the finish line.

Hesitating, Adam glanced at her one last time. Only after she smiled and nodded did he finally take off after his brother. Adam shot off like a rocket, and within moments, she couldn't even see them anymore.

Oh well. They were better off. And so was she. At least now she wouldn't have to kill herself to keep up with them.

Not that she wouldn't continue to push herself. She absolutely would. But it would be done at a pace that was far more suitable for an out-of-shape person rather than two buff dudes. She wasn't worried about catching up. Like she told Adam, she would meet them at the finish line. No big deal.

Preslee slowed down and fell to the back of a large group

of contestants who passed by. She thought she could stay with them, but even their leisurely pace was too intense. Within minutes, they disappeared around a bend in the path ahead of her. That was probably the last time she would see them.

Didn't matter. It wasn't like she was worried about getting lost. Signs positioned on the trail pointed out the way at every turn, and it didn't require a significant amount of navigational skill to follow them. Besides, without any obstacles to cross, it wasn't like she needed anyone's help to finish the run on her own.

Well, probably.

It was an uphill battle, and the steep gradients required larger and longer ascents and descents than when the path had been flat. Her thighs burned on the inclines, and her shins and ankles hurt on the declines. But she willed the pain away and kept going.

Misery swamped her entire muscular system, and she had no doubt that she'd be next-level sore the following morning. For now though, her body absorbed the pain and converted it into motivation.

Her damp clothes had kept her cool—even if they did reek of death—but it hadn't taken them long to dry out under the hot sun. The black mud caking her clothes and body had dried to white and cracked with each movement. Clumps of mud stiffened her hair, making her feel like Medusa on a bad hair day.

She licked her dehydrated lips, wishing she had a bottle of water. Her parched throat burned with every breath panting out of her. When her sides began to ache, she breathed out evenly through her nose. It didn't help. Her lungs no longer expanded to maximum capacity, and she felt like she wasn't getting enough oxygen, making her light-headed.

She went through the motions of running, her legs pumping hard while her arms swung in tandem, but her mind was no longer fully present or aware of the movement. Between the heat, the humidity, and the intensity of the run, she began to wilt under pressure.

She couldn't let that happen.

Preslee swallowed the large knot in her throat. She was pretty sure it was her pride. She hated admitting that she was completely wiped out. Maybe she'd pushed herself too hard, but she had been spurred on by the need to prove she could do this. Whether to Adam or to herself, she wasn't sure.

But her resolve waned. Her nostrils flared as she dug deep to find the strength to carry on. And she did. But every step was a small battle that she had to overcome in hopes of crossing the finish line and winning the war she had waged on herself to keep moving. Because one thing was certain. If she stopped now, it would be over. She wouldn't be able to start again. So stopping wasn't an option. Not until she reached the finish line.

By the time she made it to the paved section of the path, her head was spinning. It felt like there was no end to the race and someone had tied sandbags to both of her legs. Was she so out of shape that she couldn't finish three miles?

Stop it. Focus on the end goal.

She tried, but there was no gas left in her tank. Her body hurt in a way she'd never experienced before, and she wanted to weep in agony. She had major cramping in her legs and sides. Each step was staggeringly painful, but she powered through it.

Finally, she rounded another bend and caught sight of the finish line ahead. Well, barely. Thick plumes of gray smoke lined both sides of the track leading to the finish line and minimized her visibility. Not that it mattered. The sweat dripping into her eyes blurred her vision, making it hard to see anything anyway.

She blinked it away and gazed at the finish line again. This close, it still seemed like an impossible distance. But she wasn't giving up. She pulled from the last of her reserves and ran through the haze of polluted air.

God, her poor lungs.

A wave of heat and nausea washed over her. Erratic thoughts swept through her, and her mind drifted. Was she having a hot flash? Going through menopause? Okay, she was only twenty-eight, so menopause probably wasn't the culprit...yet stranger things had happened, right?

Jeez. Why couldn't she think straight?

Come on, Preslee. Focus.

It was bad enough that she was panting like a teenage boy who'd just gotten to third base for the first time, but now she was also straining to catch her breath while gasping for clean air. She groped desperately for the last threads of her strength and stumbled, her feet dragging on the ground.

She was critically close to face planting into the pavement when she spotted Adam standing off to one side up ahead. He smiled as he congratulated other participants crossing the threshold. But when his gaze found her, his smile quickly faded and he wore a look of concern. Probably because her sporadic, uncoordinated movements looked more like she was playing around rather than participating in a serious event.

She didn't care though. Completely exhausted, she had nothing left to spare. She could barely hold herself upright, and the loss of balance only compounded matters. Yet she was driven to reach the end and only her incredible will kept her moving those last few steps.

When her shoes finally met the white finish line, she nearly cried. It had been a seemingly impossible task for someone as unfit as her, but she had completed a three-mile mud run. She did it!

Or maybe she *overdid* it. Because, after that small, fleeting moment of success, everything happened in slow motion. Preslee swayed in place, and her vision blurred. Her stomach cramped. The air thinned, and she couldn't catch her breath. A throbbing sensation in her head had spots floating in front of her eyes. Then she spun into darkness and collapsed.

She didn't remember hitting the hard ground, though pain reverberated through her body. A crowd immediately huddled around her in shock, forming a half circle. Some people asked if she was okay while others called out for help.

Next thing she knew, Adam was there, running his hands over her body as if he was searching for an injury that he wouldn't find. His voice rang in her ears. She heard him calling her name and asking questions, but she was unable to respond. Then his voice became muffled, as if he were underwater. Or maybe she was. Either way, she could no longer make out what he said.

But that wasn't even the most pressing issue. It was getting harder to breathe, much less hear or see anything. Her vision had blurred again, but this time, it wasn't due to sweat in her eyes. She wasn't sweating any longer. Instead, a cold chill traveled the length of her spine.

She tried to get her legs under her so she could rise under her own power, but it was no use. She couldn't move, and her heart raced. What the hell was wrong with her? Was she having a heart attack? Or possibly a stroke?

Adam slid one arm under her legs and another around her back before carefully lifting her from the ground. He cradled her to his warm chest as he carried her through the crowd. To where, she didn't know. All she knew for certain was that she needed someone in that moment, and Adam was the only one there for her.

CHAPTER ELEVEN

Adam hurried toward the emergency medical unit that had been on standby as a precaution since the start of the event.

Two medical personnel saw him coming toward them with a barely conscious woman in his arms, and they opened the back of the ambulance. One of them instructed him to lay her on the gurney inside and started asking him questions—most of which he couldn't answer—and then ushered him back outside.

He didn't want to leave her again, but they insisted that he would only be in the way. So he did as they asked, frowning when they closed the doors behind him. He hoped it was to keep the cool air in rather than to keep from having an audience if she flatlined on them.

Oh God. Terrifying images of her fighting for her life flooded his brain. Was she that bad off? No. She couldn't be. The thought of never seeing her smiling face again scared the hell out of him. He'd never forgive himself if something happened to her. She had to be okay. Just had to.

As he waited for news about her condition, Adam stayed just outside the ambulance, wearing an oval track in the dirt beneath his feet. He was still pacing when his brother found him.

"Adam?" Michael emerged through the crowd, heading in his direction with a bottle of water in hand. "Hey, is Preslee all right?"

"She collapsed," Adam said, his tone uneven and tinged with panic.

"I know. I heard a commotion while I was waiting in line for the water. I came right back, but you had disappeared. What happened?"

"I don't know. I've been waiting for an update." He gazed at the back of the ambulance and then back to his brother. "Do you think you can pull the whole doctor act so we can get them to give us any information?"

Michael squinted at him. "It's not an act, moron. I *am* a doctor."

Adam sighed. "You know what I mean."

Before Michael could respond, the doors of the ambulance opened, and one of the medics helped Preslee out. Adam rushed forward, grabbing her hand to help her down the last step. She still looked dreadful, with mud-caked hair, sunburned skin, and a bandage on her arm, but at least some of the color had returned to her face.

"Preslee?" Adam asked, concern evident in his tone. "How are you, sweetheart? You okay?"

She blushed furiously. "Yes. I'm sorry if I worried you. I was just a little dehydrated. I feel better now that they've pumped some IV fluids into me."

"Good. I'm glad to hear it," Michael told her.

But Adam was confused. People didn't usually pass out

just because they were a *little* dehydrated. She'd probably been slightly dehydrated dozens of times while they'd worked out together, yet she'd never passed out on him before. Something was off about that explanation, but he didn't know what. "Are you sure you're okay?"

"I'm fine." She wrung her hands together. "I, uh, didn't remember how I got here until they said a man carried me. I'm assuming that was you."

"Yeah, it was me," Adam replied, running an unsteady hand through his hair. "When you collapsed, it scared the hell out of me. I got you here as fast as I could."

Her pink cheeks deepened in color. "I'm sorry."

"You don't need to keep apologizing. I just want to make sure you're all right. That's the important thing." His eyes flitted over her, looking for any sign that she wasn't as okay as she claimed to be. "You are, right?"

"No permanent damage," she said with a half smile. "They wanted to transport me to the emergency room to get checked out, but I refused. There's no point. I feel fine. Once they gave me some fluids to counteract the dehydration, my vitals all returned to normal."

Michael cut in, his low voice filled with concern. "Maybe you should go to the hospital and get checked out anyway. Just in case."

She shook her head. "No, that's okay. I'm seriously fine. Honest."

Michael sighed. "Would you allow me to take a look at you then? I'd feel much better if you were checked over more thoroughly and given a proper assessment. Free of charge, of course." He winked at her.

Adam wasn't sure if his brother was flirting with her or if he was actually concerned something might be wrong. It better have been the latter. But either way, Adam liked the idea of her getting looked at by a doctor. Even if it was his brother. "Good idea," he agreed.

Preslee exchanged glances with both of them. "Well, since you two are ganging up on me, I guess I don't have much of a choice, do I?" Then she grinned. "All right. Fine. But can we go back to my place to do this? I'd rather not draw any more attention here than I already have."

"No," Adam said, not wanting to leave her alone for the night. "We'll go back to my apartment. It's closer."

"Okay," she said. "But I'm telling you, I'm all right. This is a waste of time."

Michael shrugged. "That's for me to determine."

As they walked to the truck, Adam stayed right beside Preslee in case she had another episode. Michael must've been thinking the same, because he flanked her other side. But they made it to the truck without incident and headed for Adam's apartment.

Once there, Adam directed her to the bathroom to take a shower. He loaned her a T-shirt and a pair of sweatpants and threw her muddy, smelly clothes into the washing machine. She emerged from the bathroom smelling much better than when she'd gone in. She looked better too.

Michael jumped into the shower next while Adam showed Preslee to his bedroom, where they argued over whether or not she would be spending the night. Adam won easily enough, since she was at his mercy. She'd ridden with him in his truck and didn't have her car with her. He hadn't meant to hold her hostage, but he wasn't going to let her go home to an empty house after collapsing either. There would be no one there to watch over her.

When Michael came into the room, fresh from the shower, Adam stepped out to give them some privacy. He wasn't keen on leaving his brother alone with her—especially in a bedroom—but he was fairly certain Michael would behave professionally and keep his hands to himself. At least he'd better, if he knew what was good for him.

While waiting, Adam took a shower and then added his and Michael's dirty clothes to the washing machine before measuring out some detergent and turning it on. Then he sat in the living room, drumming his fingers on his knee as he waited patiently for his bedroom door to open. They were taking much longer than he'd expected.

It wasn't until the washing machine had run through an entire cycle that Adam began to worry. He busied himself by swapping their clothes from the washer into the dryer, but he couldn't help but let his imagination run wild as he planted himself back onto the couch. Had Michael found something wrong? Or, even worse, was he in there making a move on her?

The irritating thought sent lava flowing through his veins. Brother or not, he'd kill him. But when the bedroom door finally opened, all of his jealousy-induced urges to murder his sibling went dormant.

Adam shot to his feet as Michael stepped into the living room. "Is she okay?"

"Shhh. She was so exhausted that she wasn't able to keep her eyes open. I examined her, and she fell asleep while we were talking."

"But she's all right?"

"Yes. Technically." Michael stood there with a contemplative look on his face, as if he was mulling something over.

Adam frowned. "What do you mean 'technically'? What's wrong with her?" Damn it. He knew something was going on.

His brother hesitated. "I think it would be better coming from her."

Adam squinted at him. "What would be better coming from her? Did she ask you not to tell me some—"

"No. Actually, she said I could tell you. But I think it's something she needs to tell you herself. And she agreed. But then she fell asleep, and I didn't have the heart to wake her. She was so tired. But it's definitely something you need to know."

Adam had no idea what the *something* was, but he felt like his head was about to explode. "Well, apparently she can't tell me because she's asleep. And I'm not going to wake her either. So spill." His brother stood there, not saying a word. "Michael, damn it. Tell me."

"Fine. But you're going to stay calm."

Adam clenched his fists at his sides, making a conscious effort not to punch his brother in the face. "Would you just tell me already?"

"Okay. While we were talking, Preslee admitted that, for the past week, she's been on a new crash diet. One that promised she would lose twenty pounds in a week if she followed a strict diet regimen that included appetite suppressants and intermittent fasting."

Adam blinked. "What?"

"Hold on. That's not all. She's also been squeezing in extra workouts without telling you to lose weight faster. And she's been suffering from bouts of insomnia—probably due to whatever appetite suppressants she's taking since some of those have stimulants in them. She hasn't slept more than three or four hours per night for the past week. Which is what most likely added to her severe exhaustion."

The words were like a verbal slug to the gut. "You're kidding."

"No. I wouldn't joke about something so serious."

Adam blurted out a mindless oath and paced the room furiously. God, he wanted to throttle her. "Why would she do that?" he asked, burning with frustration. "And why the hell would she tell you that but not me? I'm her trainer, damn it."

"Maybe she felt more comfortable with me because I'm practically a stranger. Or maybe she was afraid you'd blow your top...sort of like you're doing right now."

True. Adam was wound up tighter than a rubber band, ready to snap. "Do you blame me? I didn't okay her adding more workouts. And nowhere in the diet I gave her did it say for her to fast or to take diet pills that could possibly harm her. If she isn't going to follow my instructions, then I'm as useless to her as air-conditioning on a fucking bicycle."

"Calm down. From what she said, I'm pretty sure it was a onetime thing. The episode she had earlier scared her, and I explained the consequences of crash dieting. I advised her not to do it again, and I'm certain she isn't going to."

"She shouldn't have done it the first time. It's dangerous." Adam rubbed at the back of his neck. "If I had any idea she was doing something so stupid, I would've said something. But there were just no signs that anything was wrong."

Michael shook his head. "Bullshit. There were signs. You just didn't see them."

Adam gaped at his brother. "Gee, thanks for making me feel better."

"I'm not trying to comfort you," his brother stated. "I'm trying to point out what you missed."

Adam scowled. Had he missed something over the past week? After all, it was *his* job to be in tune with what his client's body needed. Thinking back, he'd noticed that she had been dragging a little during their workouts. She had also looked tired. Maybe even a little on edge. At the time, he'd thought it was because they were pushing her beyond her regular limitations. So he hadn't spoken up.

Now he knew better.

He'd apparently created a monster. One who'd done something harmful to her health in order to fast-track her weight loss. And while he knew he was not to blame for her actions, there was still guilt on his part. Because it ripped his heart in two to know that she hadn't trusted him enough to come to him about it. If a trainer didn't have his client's trust, then he didn't have anything.

Adam swallowed his anger. "I guess there were things I noticed. I didn't say anything because I'd intensified her workouts and thought I was just pushing her harder. I was trying to prepare her for the mud run so she wouldn't struggle during it." He sighed, although annoyance still hummed in his veins. "I'll talk to her about this when she wakes up."

Michael nodded. "Okay. But I don't think you getting mad at her is the best way to approach this."

He shook his head. "I'm not mad at her. I'm mad at myself. You're right. When I noticed something was off with her, I should've spoken up. I regret not doing so."

"Don't beat yourself up, Adam."

"How can I not?" Adam asked, rubbing a shaky hand over his face. "You don't get it. When Preslee collapsed, I didn't know what was wrong. I couldn't...do anything."

"You felt helpless."

"Well, yeah. She could've died," he said, the words rushing out. "I kept thinking that if I were a doctor, I could've done something to help her." He huffed out a weary breath. "Maybe Mom and Dad were right. If I had stayed in medical school, then I—"

Michael raised his hand to stop him. "Quit being so dramatic. Preslee didn't die. Nor would you have been able to help her. Because we both know that if you had stayed in medical school, you would've never met her."

Okay, so his brother had a point. "Maybe. But I still can't help but feel I let her down. Especially since I missed the signs that she was in trouble."

"I get that, but you also have to remember that she was the one who kept this from you."

"I know, but still..."

Michael blew out a hard breath. "Look, if you kept a secret from her, would you want her taking the blame for not realizing it?"

Guilt slapped Adam across the face, and he winced. He was keeping a secret from her, and of course he wouldn't blame her for not realizing it. Why would she ever suspect that he and Kurt had made a bet about her fitness goals? Damn it. He wished he had never accepted that stupid bet.

He shook his head. "No, I wouldn't. But it's my job to coach my clients into a healthier lifestyle. I should've realized—"

"Like I said, you can't blame yourself. It happens."

Adam scoffed. "Right. That comes from a hotshot doctor."

Michael lifted one brow. "You think I've never missed signs before?"

"Have you?"

"Yes, unfortunately." Michael paused thoughtfully. "I basically did the same thing with a patient of mine. I noticed something was off and didn't mention it. I thought if something was wrong or he wanted me to know about it, he would tell me. I was wrong."

Adam hesitated momentarily. "What happened?"

His brother swallowed hard. "An hour after my patient's appointment, he was found dead inside his car. It was still parked outside the hospital's professional building I used to work in. He'd had a massive heart attack right after walking out of my office. I knew something wasn't right that day. This guy was normally the loud, animated type, but during his office visit, he was quiet and practically motionless. He looked weary and uncomfortable, as if something was causing him pain. Unfortunately, I didn't realize what until it was too late."

"Damn, I'm sorry. That had to be rough."

Michael shrugged. "It was. I blamed myself. Although it wasn't my fault, it was tough knowing that had I just said something, the outcome might've been different. But I learned an important lesson that day. Now if I see it, I say something. It could save someone's life."

"I'll do the same from now on. I don't want this to happen to any of my other clients."

Michael nodded. "It's a smart move."

"Wait a minute. Did I hear you right? You said the building you *used* to work in. Aren't you still working there?"

"I quit."

Adam blinked. "What do you mean you quit?"

"I don't work there anymore."

Adam grinned. "I know what quitting means, dumbass. But why? You were the only internal medicine doctor in that entire building, you were making a ton of money, and . . . well, you had a nice office. Why leave?"

Michael's tongue poked against the inside of his cheek. "I found another job elsewhere."

"Ah, I see," Adam said with a nod. "You got some fancy job at a more prominent hospital."

"No."

"Better pay, then?"

His brother shook his head. "Nope."

"Good benefits?"

Michael shrugged. "Not really."

"Then why leave? Where the hell are you working now?"

His brother grinned. "You're talking to the new internal medicine doctor in Granite, Texas."

Adam stood a little straighter. "You're joking."

"Nope. I crossed paths with Dr. Fowler at a Houston medical conference last year, and he mentioned that he was retiring this year. I thought it was a good opportunity to get out of the big city and move to a place where I could slow down and open my own practice. It's what I've always wanted."

"I didn't know that."

"Neither did our parents." A broad grin spread across Michael's face. "Mom and Dad are pissed at me."

Adam couldn't help but laugh. "Welcome to the club."

"Look, I'm sorry for not standing up for you when you dropped out of school. I was wrong, That's been a thorn in our relationship for a while, and I'm ashamed to admit that I didn't consider your feelings at all. I don't blame you for being upset with me. I should've been on your side. Hell, I was on your side. I just didn't say anything.

"But that's partly why I'm here. I'm done being silent. I know showing up and admitting I was wrong probably doesn't mean much, but I'm hoping it'll be a start. You may not believe this, but I miss my little brother."

Happiness mingled with relief inside of Adam. "Good. I've missed you too," he said, giving his older brother a manly side hug and a slap on the back. "And just for the record, you showing up and admitting you're wrong means a lot."

"I knew you'd say that, you punk."

Adam laughed. "So what changed?"

Michael crossed his arms. "Our parents have always thrust their ambitions and overachieving ways onto us. Don't get me wrong. I like being a doctor. But at the time, I didn't have the courage to go after what I wanted like you did. I really admired you for that. Still do, in fact. After you stood up to them and held your ground, I realized I didn't have to live up to their ridiculous standards either. I only had to live up to my own."

"Exactly. I wish our parents would see it that way."

"Good luck with that," Michael said, smirking. "They aren't talking to me right now. You're on your own."

Adam shrugged. "Well, I'm glad to hear that you're doing what you want and not what our parents expect. They really need to learn that success isn't nearly as important as a person's values."

"I agree. Maybe one day they'll wake up and realize that they can't choose our dreams for us. But they're both stubborn and steadfast in their overinflated opinions. So it'll probably take years. Until then, it's just us." Michael clapped Adam on the shoulder. "Hope you're okay with that."

"Sounds good to me," Adam said, glad to have his older brother back in his life.

Michael glanced at the clock on the wall. "I wasn't planning on leaving until tomorrow, but I think I'll go ahead and get on the road today. It's still early enough."

Adam never thought he'd have to say this to his brother, but... "What's the hurry? You don't have to leave."

"Actually, I do." Michael nodded toward the closed door down the hallway. "You need the guest room since someone is occupying your bed." Then he grinned. "Unless, of course, you planned on slipping into bed with her."

Adam shook his head adamantly. "Of course not. I was going to sleep on the couch. Preslee and I are just friends."

"Yeah, right. I see how you two are with each other. There's more going on there than just friendship. Whether either of you admit it or not."

"Wrong. She's into another guy."

"Yet she's in *your* bed."

Adam chuckled. "Yeah, but you know why. She's exhausted... and it's not because of anything I did to her. Unfortunately."

His brother grinned. "Listen, all I'm saying is that I approve. Not that you need my blessing. But I like her a lot. She'd make a great sister-in-law."

Adam scrubbed a hand over his face. Had he just heard his brother right? "We aren't even dating, and you already have us married?"

Michael nodded. "Like I said before…if I see it, I say something. And I definitely see it. You two are perfect for each other. I hope it works out for you, little brother. Now if you'll excuse me, I'm going to go pack. If I hurry, I can get back to Houston before dark." He turned toward the guest bedroom.

"Michael?"

"Yeah," his brother said, turning back.

Adam extended his hand. "Thanks. For everything."

Michael shook his hand. "What are big brothers for?"

"Well, that thank-you includes you helping Preslee. I appreciate you checking her over and making sure she's okay."

A grin tugged at Michael's lips. "What are future brothers-in-law for?"

CHAPTER TWELVE

Preslee awoke to the sound of voices coming from somewhere on the other side of the door. Adam's bedroom door, to be exact. She figured it was just the two brothers talking, but she couldn't make out the hushed words and was too exhausted to walk to the door to find out for sure.

Waking up in an unfamiliar place normally would've unnerved her, but not this time. She smashed her face into a soft pillow that smelled like Adam, and the comforting, masculine scent wrapped around her like a warm blanket. So she lay there motionless, allowing herself to drift in and out of sleep for a while longer.

When her eyes fluttered open again, she gazed around the room, which had grown considerably darker. To her relief, she stretched her limbs and didn't feel pain. Only achiness. The hot shower and nap she'd taken had really helped. Although she suspected that she would probably be stiff for a few days.

Other than that, she felt... good.

Tired of lying in bed, Preslee climbed to her feet. Still weak and creaky, she opened the door and padded barefoot down the hall. Something delicious scented the air, instantly spiking her hunger to atomic proportions, and her stomach growled. It'd been a while since she'd last had anything; she hadn't eaten at all today. Skipping breakfast hadn't been the smartest move. Stupid crash diet.

Preslee rounded the corner into the living room and spotted Adam in the kitchen. He had his back to her while stirring something on the stove and whistling an upbeat tune. He didn't hear her approach.

She'd never seen him in jeans and a T-shirt before. The ripped, faded denim fit him snugly, showing off muscular thighs and a nice rear end, while the worn shirt stretched tightly across his magnificent back and broad shoulders. Bare toes stuck out from beneath the frayed, distressed hem of his jeans. That alone lent an intimacy to the atmosphere. Maybe because she was barefoot too.

Adam usually wore workout clothes when they were together, such as athletic shorts and a tank top that showed off his toned, sculpted biceps. While she always appreciated good arm porn, the jeans and T-shirt look was somehow better.

He seemed...relaxed. And comfortable.

It was strange though. Before today, she'd never even been inside his home. Now, she was not only in it, but she'd showered in his bathroom and slept in his bed. Not that she was complaining. His small two-bedroom apartment had a quaint, homey feel.

On his bar sat a soy wax candle, flickering gently as it gave off a faint cinnamon aroma. At the other end, there was a miniature herb garden in a small wooden box that held three terra-cotta pots labeled BASIL, ROSEMARY, and THYME.

On the opposite counter, two salad plates overflowed with mixed greens next to a glass bottle that held some kind of homemade balsamic vinaigrette dressing that had slightly separated. A wooden cutting board sitting nearby on the counter was covered with a chopped tomato, leftover juice, a sharp-looking knife, and a bunch of scars in the wood.

Apparently Adam cooked. Who knew?

She cleared her throat, and his head whirled in her direction. Their gazes met, and his dark stare made her wish she hadn't alerted him to her presence. Thick tension congested the air around them. She wanted to look away but couldn't bring herself to do so. She needed to face him. More for herself than for him. But still...

After the sun they'd received today, the hard planes of his tanned face looked more rugged and manly than before. Veins bulged from his arms, and a muscle twitched in his corded neck. His face was stoic, and she couldn't read him.

Had Michael told him about the crash diet? If so, what was Adam thinking? Should she say something? Should she wait for him to speak first? She didn't know what she was supposed to do here.

Finally, he put her out of her misery with a smile. Yet unease still flared to life inside her. What if he was mad and didn't want to say so?

Adam broke the silence first. "How are you feeling?"

Her shoulders relaxed as she attempted to joke with him. "About fifteen pounds lighter than I was a week ago."

"I'm not interested in your weight," he said with a lackluster tone. "I want to know how *you* feel." He pivoted toward the stove.

Okay. So maybe he wasn't mad. But he definitely wasn't happy either. "I, uh, feel better. The nap helped a lot."

"Good." His tone was distant and remote.

She hesitated. "Adam?"

"Yeah."

"Look at me."

His back muscles tightened. "Why?"

"Because I don't want there to be any awkwardness between us. So if you're going to be upset, then just give me a verbal lashing now and get it over with."

He didn't turn around, but his head lowered. "I'm not mad."

"Bullshit."

Adam turned off the burner and spun to face her. "I'm not mad, Preslee. *Disappointed* is probably a better word."

Ouch. That was worse. "I'd rather you be mad."

A grin tugged at the corner of his mouth. "That's not how it works. You don't get to pick my emotion."

"Come on, Adam. I was prepared for pissed off. I can't handle you being disappointed. That's something else entirely."

He crossed his arms. "Sorry. It's the feeling I choose. Deal with it."

Defeated, she sighed. "No, I'm sorry. What I did was stupid. And as idiotic as this sounds, I knew it was stupid while I was doing it. Which only makes it worse. But I was...I don't know. Desperate. I wanted some small edge over my weight loss."

Adam shook his head. "There are no shortcuts. You want results, then you put in the work. It's simple math. There's no magic pill that is going to get you to the end goal faster. Even if you did lose weight, chances are good that you will put it back on."

"I know. It's just that—"

"Don't make excuses," he said calmly. "And no more cheating the system. What you did was harmful, dangerous, and extremely unhealthy. It was a formula for disaster, and if you do something like that again, I'm done training you."

Preslee blinked at him. "Wow, that's harsh."

"No, it's not. But it is the truth. I won't work with someone who refuses to trust me to help them. It would be pointless. I would only be wasting my time."

"Okay."

Although he'd kept his cool thus far, his tone suddenly hardened. "And just for the record, no damn guy is worth you harming yourself for him. You need to realize that your heart matters more than your weight does. Screw what Josh thinks."

"I...I wasn't doing it for Josh. I did it for *you*."

Shock morphed his features. "For me?"

"I didn't want to embarrass you by not completing the run. I was worried that I would hold you back and wanted to give a top-notch performance."

He stared at her in disbelief. "Who the hell asked you to do that?"

"No one. I just...wanted to impress you."

Adam raised his brow. "Do I look very impressed with you right now?" he asked. "I would rather you come in last or not finish at all than to do something so ridiculous as to endanger yourself. It's not worth it."

She bit her lip. "I know that now."

"Look, you're focusing on the wrong thing. Instead of worrying about what you can't do, you should be worrying about what you *can* do. The only person you're ever competing with is yourself. No one else matters but you," he said, reinforcing his previous statement. "Trust yourself to get there. If nothing else, trust *me* to get you there."

The wounded look on his face made her feel guiltier than she already had. "I really am sorry, Adam. I should've come to you about this. Next time I will."

"I'm hoping there isn't going to be a next time," he told her. "That's why I'm rethinking our whole strategy. I'd like to adjust your workouts to include more stretching and strengthening. So I'm going to bring in a yoga instructor several days a week too."

She cocked her head. "Just for me?"

"Not exactly. More women have been joining the gym lately, thanks to your vlog, and I want to be sure I'm meeting their needs. And I figured that some of my other clients might benefit from yoga as well. So I'm going to make it a regular thing and take part in it too. Not only because I want to show my male customers that men can do yoga, but also because if any of these new female members can't make it to one of the yoga classes, I can work with them privately."

Preslee frowned, not liking the sound of that. "Oh."

"Hey, don't look at me like that. Yoga has mostly to do with matching your breath to your movements and thinking about each muscle as you squeeze or stretch it. It also has to do with tuning in to your body and letting it guide you. Basically, it incorporates a mind-body connection. My personal belief is that anytime you can get to a healthier place in your mind, your body will follow. So I think this would be a good fit for you. I'd like you to try it."

That was what he thought she'd frowned about? Not even close.

She nodded. "Okay. I'm willing."

"One thing though. Please don't call the new yoga instructor a sadist...at least not to her face."

Preslee smirked. "I won't. I reserve that special nickname only for you."

"Lucky me," he said, grinning. He turned back to the stove and gave his dish another stir.

The scent had her mouth watering. "So, what about my diet? Is that changing too?"

"Yep. I'm going to bring in a dietitian one day a week and set up appointments for each of my clients. I don't want any of you starving yourselves. That isn't going to make your body stronger or help you during workouts. Your body needs fuel. It's about choosing the right foods in order to get the correct levels of nourishment so that we can boost your metabolism and provide you with a good energy source."

Preslee smiled. "I'll commit to that. I think seeing a nutritionist would be a good idea for me. I recognize that it's something I need. Besides, I'm on board with any diet that allows me to eat more."

"It's not a diet. It's a lifestyle change. As long as what's on your plate is healthy, I want you to fill up. Speaking of which, dinner is ready. Are you hungry?"

"I assumed the other plate was for your brother." She glanced into the living room. "Where's Michael? Apparently I was so tired that I fell asleep while he was talking. I'd like to thank him."

"You missed him. He headed out after you dozed off. But I'm sure you'll get your chance to properly thank him. He's moving to Granite next week. He's going to work with Dr. Fowler for a few months to get acclimated, and then he's going to take over the practice so the old doc can retire."

"Really? I knew Dr. Fowler wanted to retire, but I never thought the grumpy man actually would. He's been my doctor so long that I assumed he would die with a stethoscope in his hand."

"Well, apparently he has other plans."

"Good for him. I'm glad to hear that. He's a bit of a crab sometimes, but he deserves to live out the rest of his years in peace." She smiled up at Adam. "And, of course, that's great news for your brother. Is it possible that you two will get over your issues?"

"Already have. We worked them out before he left."

"That's great, Adam. I'm happy to hear it. And I'll be sure to congratulate Michael on his new job the next time I see him. I'm sure everyone here will love the new doctor in town. Especially the single women," she added with a saucy wink.

Adam chuckled. "He does have a way with the ladies. Although I'm not sure he's ever been in a relationship that has lasted longer than a few hours."

Preslee gave a nonjudgmental shrug. "Well, I'm sure there are some women in this town who aren't looking for anything permanent. They'd probably be happy to welcome a hot new doctor to town with open arms."

His brows furrowed. "You think my brother's hot?"

"Oh. I...ah," she stuttered as heat crept into her cheeks. "I mean, he's good-looking." Not as handsome as Adam, of course, but it wasn't like she could say that out loud. "Definitely not my type though."

"Oh, I see," Adam said, his tone lowering. "Because Michael's no Josh, right?"

Preslee bit her lip. *No. He's no you.* "Exactly." Adam's brow lifted, as if he hadn't expected her to agree with him. Oh man. Had she just offended him by talking about his brother like that? Of course she had. After all, that was his family she was referring to. "Sorry. I didn't mean to insinuate that—"

"Don't apologize," he said, though he seemed to be gritting his teeth. "You want what you want. And if Josh is the one you want, then there's nothing wrong with that. Besides, the last thing my brother needs is another woman fawning all over him." He lifted a skillet from the burner and turned toward the plates. "If this gets any colder, it's not going to be any good. Why don't you have a seat at the table while I plate our meal?"

"I could help with—"

"I've got it," he said hastily. "Just sit."

Preslee stared at him momentarily, but his eyes wouldn't meet hers. If that wasn't a dismissal, then she wasn't sure what was. So she maneuvered around the bar and sat down at the small dining room table that separated the kitchen from the living room. While waiting, she gazed around the room, admiring the open floor plan of the unit, which always made small spaces look much larger.

Moments later, Adam appeared at the table juggling two bottles of water and two plates of salad. Before she could jump to help him, he'd placed one of each squarely in front of her and deposited his across from her. Then he returned to the kitchen to grab their plates of food, which he promptly delivered before taking his seat.

Everything looked and smelled amazing. The scent of Dijon

mustard and rosemary wafted up from the grilled chicken breast that had been paired with a side of couscous as well as some sugar snap peas and baby carrots that were vibrant in color. She could tell the crisp mixed greens on her salad plate were fresh and had been drizzled with a small amount of the dressing she'd seen on the counter.

"This looks great," she told Adam. Then she took her first bite and hummed in appreciation at the perfectly seasoned chicken. "Mmm. It's so good. Where did you learn to cook like this?"

Adam smiled, apparently having left his weird mood in the kitchen. "Kurt and I were roommates for a while. He can't boil water, so it was up to me to learn to cook to keep us from starving to death. A person can only live off of microwavable noodles for so long."

"Kurt sounds like my dad. He can't cook either. The only dish he makes is soup from a can," she said with a laugh. "That's why I prepare a couple of meals for him each week and always make enough for him to freeze the extras. Especially since his fall. All he has to do is thaw them out and warm them up. My dad is—" She hesitated and then rose from her seat. "Crap. I didn't call to check on him today. I bet he's worried sick."

Adam held up a hand. "Actually, he called your phone while you were sleeping. I let him know you were okay."

Preslee blinked rapidly. "You talked to my father?"

He shrugged. "Well, I wouldn't normally have answered your phone like that, but I figured you would've wanted him to know where you were. I hope that was all right."

"Yes, it's fine." She sat back down. "What did you tell him exactly?"

"That you were spending the night with me."

She gawked at him. "You said what?"

A grin spread across his mouth. "Yeah, that was pretty much his reaction too."

Preslee shook her head. "Tell me you did *not* really say that to my dad."

"Okay. I didn't really say that to your dad."

She studied his face and noticed a muscle ticking strongly in his jaw, as if he were clenching his teeth together to keep from grinning. Oh dear Lord. "You did! You actually said that to him." She slapped a hand over her face and dragged it downward over her mouth in disbelief. "Why would you say that to a girl's father? Do you have a death wish or something?"

Adam laughed. "Maybe because this *girl* that you speak of is a grown woman and doesn't need her daddy's permission to spend the night at a man's home. Besides, I told him that I was only your trainer and that there was no funny business going on. That we were just friends."

Friends. God, she was starting to hate that word. "Yeah, but it's my dad we're talking about. He's not going to believe that."

Confusion filled Adam's eyes. "Why would I lie?"

"The same reason all of my old boyfriends lied when they said they would keep their hands to themselves. Because that's what guys say to overprotective dads who are safeguarding their daughter's virtue."

"But I wasn't lying about keeping my hands to myself."

Of course he wasn't. Figures. "Yeah, *I* know that. But my dad doesn't. He probably just added you to his top-ten most wanted list for guys who've tried to get frisky with his daughter. Actually, knowing what you said, I bet you made it into the top three. Might even be number one at the moment."

Unconcerned, Adam took a bite of his dinner. "I'm not the least bit worried about your dad, Preslee. We're both adults here." Then he shrugged one shoulder. "Besides, he doesn't even know where I live."

"It's a small town, Adam. It wouldn't be hard to figure out," she said, rolling her eyes. "Just consider yourself warned. If you ever happen to meet my dad and he asks if you want to run the gauntlet, be sure to tell him no."

He looked at her as if she'd lost her mind but didn't bother to ask what it all meant. It wasn't like he was ever going to meet her dad anyway. "All right," Adam agreed.

After finishing dinner, they cleaned up together and then lounged in the living room on the oversize chaise sectional while watching the latest Marvel movie. Adam sat on one end with his feet propped up on the huge matching ottoman while Preslee lay on the longer end with her legs stretched out in front of her.

But halfway through the movie, a rhythmic thumping began against the living room wall. It started low and then got louder as time went on. She tried to ignore it, but when it got so loud that she couldn't even hear the movie anymore, she gazed over at Adam.

He apparently was just as annoyed by the sound because he rubbed his temples and glared at the offending wall with a clenched jaw. "Damn it. Not this again."

"What is it?" she asked, confusion tainting her voice.

Adam sighed. "Sorry. It's my neighbor. I've asked him to quiet down whenever he has a guest over at least half a dozen times, but he never does."

The banging coming from the other side of the wall grew louder, and it started to alarm her. "What's he doing—

renovating? It sounds like he's hammering on something pretty hard."

"You could say that," Adam said with a wry grin. "The guy is apparently a ladies' man, and these walls are way too thin."

"Oh God," Preslee stated, cringing at the thought.

"Yep. That's what the women call him. Well, that and Jesus. Basically, he holds a very loud and inappropriate religious revival almost every Friday or Saturday night."

Preslee laughed. "That's terrible."

"Tell me about it." A raucous moan penetrated the wall, and Adam shook his head. "I get tired of hearing it. Happens all the time."

They tried to return to the movie, but no matter how much they increased the volume, it was no match for the vocal sexual encounter going on in the next apartment. But then the moaning suddenly changed, eerily mimicking the sound of a cat after someone's stepped on its tail and the poor thing has to fight for its release.

Preslee winced. "That's a horrific noise. Are you sure he's not killing someone over there? You're assuming he's having sex, but he could be a murderer."

"He's not," Adam said with a chuckle. "Man, your imagination is really out there at times."

The entire wall shook as a man's guttural voice pierced the air. "Oh yeah, baby. I'm gonna make you scream until you're begging me to put you out of your misery."

Preslee's brow rose. "See? Murderer. Told you so."

Adam shook his head. "You're ridiculous."

They went back to watching the movie, although they had to turn the captions on so they could read the rest of it. Hearing it was no longer an option. After another twenty minutes of earsplitting shrieking and explicit pounding, the lurid sexual activity finally ceased to exist.

"I think he ran out of fuel," Adam told her.

"Well, it's about time. If that went on any longer, that poor woman wouldn't have been able to walk normally tomorrow."

Adam chuckled. "I think that was what he was aiming for."

Lucky girl.

Oh man. Had she really just thought that? Heat crawled up her neck, landing in her cheeks. She was blushing like a teenage girl who had just watched her first porn video. She needed to change the subject. Fast.

She inhaled a deep breath. "At least you'll be saved from this torture next weekend."

"How's that?"

"Brett and Sidney's wedding. With the reception taking place at Bottoms Up Saturday night, I'm sure there will be plenty of drinking and dancing to keep you busy into the wee hours. You and Kurt are still going, right?"

"Yeah, we'll both be there. Wouldn't miss it for the world."

She beamed at him. "Good. It'll be fun."

Adam smirked. "Will your dad be there? I'm just wondering if I should wear Kevlar to the afterparty."

She giggled. "No, he won't be there. You're safe...for now."

"Good to know."

She cocked her head. "What about your parents?"

"They won't be there either," Adam told her with a grin.

Indignation crossed her features. "I know that, funny guy. But that isn't what I meant, and you know it. I was asking where they live."

"Houston. It's not far, but it's enough distance to keep them off my back. Well, most of the time."

Her expression dulled. "You mean because they don't approve of you dropping out of med school?"

"Not just that. They don't approve of my career choice either. They've been upset with me about both for a long time."

"Why?" Preslee asked, genuinely confused. "Anyone can see how great you are at what you do and how happy it makes you. Why wouldn't they want you to follow your dreams?"

He shrugged. "My parents look at me like a rudderless ship. I was going full steam ahead in medical school when I suddenly lost course. Now they think I'm drifting along with no sense of direction."

"But that isn't true. You have great things going for you."

"Yeah, but they don't want to hear that. Both of my parents are surgeons at the top of their fields, and they want their sons to follow in their footsteps. To be doing anything other than what they expect is unfathomable. And now that Michael has disappointed them by choosing to become a small-town doctor rather than work in the city at one of the higher-paying hospitals, they're really going to be on the rampage."

"You don't think they'll come around?"

"Maybe. But it's going to take time. When I told them I dropped out of medical school, they threatened to disown me. They never did though. So I think they'll eventually get over it."

"Sorry. I bet that hurt."

"It did, but I think I always suspected they wouldn't do it. They were just upset. Still, I'd like to prove them wrong. If I can show them that I can run a successful gym, then that would go a long way in helping them to let go of their ridiculous expectations. But first I need to make the gym more profitable. Otherwise, I won't be able to keep it open, and that would only prove my parents right."

"Oh. I didn't realize the gym was having financial difficulties."

"It's not that bad. I just need to pull in some more gym members and maybe book some more clients. Things will be fine."

She wasn't sure if she believed him and had a feeling he was minimizing the problem for her benefit. After all, he was training her for free. No wonder he wanted her to bring some of her friends into the gym. He needed the extra money. "I can start paying for my training sessions."

He didn't even hesitate. "No."

She frowned. "Why not?"

His jaw tightened. "Because I said so."

"That's not a good reason."

"Sure it is."

Preslee sighed. "Adam, I don't mind paying for your services. I've never understood why you offered to train me for free anyway. We were strangers. Technically, it still doesn't make sense."

He hesitated, as if he were searching for an explanation himself, and then he scowled. "Can't someone do something nice for you without having a reason behind it?"

She winced. Okay, yeah. It was probably rude of her to question him when he'd done nothing but help her. And really, what would he gain from it anyway? She was using up his valuable time and energy, and if she was being honest, she'd only given him grief about the eating plan and exercises. Even if it was in good fun, it was a wonder the man was still helping her at all.

"Sorry. I guess I'm just not used to others going out of their way for me. So I tend to question it when they do."

"Why do you think that is?"

She gave a halfhearted shrug. "I don't know."

He raised a brow. "I'm betting you do."

Well, she had a few ideas. But it wasn't anything she wanted to discuss with him of all people. Especially after he'd already threatened to stop working with her earlier. It was embarrassing to admit that she had trouble forming attachments to others, and she didn't want anyone having that kind of power over her. Including Adam.

She sighed. "I guess I just like to make sure a person's heart is in the right place before I open myself up to something that might turn out bad."

"That seems awfully cynical."

"Maybe. But I'm speaking from experience."

He stared at her for a moment. "Who hurt you?"

She blinked at him. "Uh, no one."

"Someone obviously has."

Preslee shook her head adamantly. "No, I just meant in general. People can be cruel."

"Has someone been cruel to you, Preslee?" He sat straighter, his intense eyes focusing directly on her. "And tell me the truth this time because you can't lie worth a damn."

He was right. She'd never been able to lie well. "It's nothing, Adam. Just drop it, okay?"

"Tell me. Was it your dad?"

"What? No, of course not."

His brows furrowed. "Then it had to have been Michael or Kurt. What did they say?"

"No. Neither of them said anything."

He paused thoughtfully. "Was it me? Did I say something that—"

"No, it wasn't you." Jeez. He was like a dog with a bone. "It was two strangers on my vlog, okay? They said some things that ... well, not very nice. It's part of the reason I went on the crash diet. I was already panicking about embarrassing myself at the mud run, and their comments only made me feel worse about myself. So I let two nameless, faceless jerks who wrote crappy comments on my vlog have power over me."

A muscle ticked in his jaw. "What did they say?"

"Does it matter?"

"Yes. Because it matters to *you*."

She inhaled a deep breath and told him all about the two men and their negative comments. She blushed and stammered through the whole thing, embarrassment heating her face the entire time.

Clearly pissed, his mouth formed a tight thin line. "Damn it. Those are the same two assholes who I banned from the gym."

She blinked. "What? How do you know that?"

"Their usernames are similar to their email addresses we have on file. I know because I added them to our banned list myself."

"B-but how did they know about my vlog? How would they even find it?"

He shook his head. "I don't know. They saw you making a video. Maybe they overheard you talking. Or maybe they just heard about it in town. Lots of people have been commenting on it."

"But why go to the trouble of going on my vlog and writing hateful comments? What purpose did it serve?"

He cringed. "I guess that's my fault. I told them that night that I was banning them for harassing you. So apparently they are blaming you for them getting kicked out. They are taking their anger out on the wrong person. I'm sorry."

"You shouldn't have to apologize for those jerks."

"No, but they aren't going to do it so someone should. But I promise you that I will make sure they leave you alone from now on. I have their addresses still on file. I'll pay them a visit tomorrow and have a word with them about what they're doing."

She waved her hand through the air dismissively. "Don't bother. I've already blocked both of those idiots and deleted their comments. I doubt they are going to go through the trouble of making new accounts just to spew more vitriol my way."

"They might."

She shrugged. "Then I'll block those accounts too. It takes a lot longer for them to make new accounts than it will take for me to block and delete. I'm not worried about them or anything they have to say. I made the mistake of letting them bother me once. Trust me, it won't happen again."

"Good. But if they keep harassing you . . ."

"They won't. When a bully doesn't get a response out of the person they are bullying, the fun is taken out of it. And I didn't respond. They will move on, if they haven't already."

"Okay, but if they don't leave you alone, I expect you to let me know. You don't deserve their abuse. And I can take care of it, if you want."

"It's okay. I appreciate it, but it's not necessary."

He nodded. "I'm only trying to help. I like you, Preslee."

She smiled. "I like you too."

An awkward silence stretched between them.

She didn't want him to continue talking about this anymore, so she glanced up at the clock on the wall and yawned. "It's getting late. I should probably get some more rest."

"Good idea. You need all the sleep you can get right now so that your body can recuperate from the exhaustion."

She nodded. "Thanks again for everything you did for me earlier today. I appreciate it."

"You're welcome. And just so you know, you did great on the mud run. I really was impressed."

Her chest filled with pride. "Thanks."

"Sleep well."

"You too," she said, rising from the sofa and heading for the hallway.

"Um, Preslee?"

She stopped in the doorway and turned back. "Yes?"

"About earlier today."

"You mean the passing out thing?"

He nodded solemnly. "Promise me that you won't ever do that to me again. I don't know what I would do if something happened to you."

Her heart swelled inside her chest. "I promise."

CHAPTER THIRTEEN

Adam released a pent-up sigh.

He couldn't believe how crazy the past few days had been. Or how quickly everything had come together.

Besides his regular training schedule, he'd interviewed and hired a part-time yoga coach and a certified dietitian, both of whom would be meeting with his clients to help them with their fitness goals. Not only that, but he'd also spent the past few nights helping with renovations going on inside the gym. Ones that were now finally done.

When he'd first mentioned the idea about renovating to Kurt, his gym manager had balked, stating that they didn't have the funds needed to do any remodeling. Which was true. But business had been increasing each week, thanks to Preslee and her vlog. She'd only done two more posts since the first one went viral, but it really seemed to be helping. More so than anything else Adam and Kurt had tried.

Just last month, before meeting Preslee, they'd done all the free advertising they could think of—posting flyers, sharing business cards, social media giveaways, and even updating the Body Shop's website. None of which had worked. Someone might have wandered through their doors on occasion, but the underwhelming response hadn't come close to the number of new members they were now signing up daily. And every one of them mentioned Preslee's vlog.

But even though business had been good, Adam hadn't wanted to use the gym's cash flow to do the renovations. Instead, he'd used money he had saved. It wasn't a lot. Just a few thousand dollars. But he figured it was enough to do something with. And thankfully he'd been right.

Lucky for him, Adam had three buddies that had helped him out. Max Hager, Brett Carmichael, and Nathan Price. All three were members of the gym, as well as mutual friends with Sam Cooper, the owner of a local construction company.

Brett had attested to Sam's fair prices since he had apparently done some work in Brett's new auto shop. Max was Sam's best friend, as well as the electrician that the man used on all of his jobs. And Nathan, otherwise known as Nate, actually worked for Sam full-time as his job foreman.

Nate had really been the most help. He had introduced Adam to his boss. And then, as the two of them discussed the cost to erect a few walls inside the gym, Nate had spoken up and reminded Sam of how they still had some unused building materials left over from a previous job that he'd wanted to part with. After that, a little unexpected horse trading had taken place.

Sam hadn't hesitated to offer the building materials to Adam at a deep discount, while Adam had offered up yearlong gym memberships to Sam and any of his employees who showed up after hours to help with the work. Even though they wouldn't be getting paid in cash, four of Sam's guys had voluntarily shown up, including Nate. And with his expertise, they had formed a skeleton crew and knocked the entire job out in only two nights.

One newly constructed wall separated the weight room from the rest of the gym, while the other new walls sectioned off an entire area specifically for yoga classes. And since the dietitian had agreed to use Adam's office, he hoped that all of the changes they'd made would help his members—new and old alike—feel more comfortable and less intimidated in the gym. Especially when it came to Preslee.

He'd barely finished the thought when someone came swinging through the gym doors, catching his attention. *Speak of the devil.*

But when he glanced in the direction of the doors, he saw it wasn't Preslee at all. It was Max and Nate. "Hey, what are you two doing back here? You didn't get enough of me for the past two nights?"

Max grinned. "It must be that pretty face of yours."

Nate chuckled. "Or maybe it's that hard body."

Adam shook his head. Smart-asses. "Yeah, yeah. Seriously though. Did you guys need something?"

Nate nodded. "Yep, my tools. I left a few of them here last night. Kurt said he would keep them in your office until I got off work."

"But how did you get anything done today if you didn't have your tools?" Adam asked, confused.

"He borrowed mine," Max explained. "Which is why I'm here to make sure he gets his back. Borrowing another man's power

tools is like asking to borrow his woman. You just don't do it."
Then Max glared at Nate.

Nate chuckled and raised his hands innocently in the air, as if
surrendering. "Whoa, I didn't ask to borrow Jessa."

"No, not exactly," Max agreed. "But you did say that you
thought about asking my wife out."

Adam's eyes widened.

Nate laughed and then shrugged halfheartedly. "Yeah, but I
didn't do it."

"Close enough," Max muttered.

Grinning, Nate shook his head and then glanced at Adam.
"You mind if I grab those tools real quick? Maybe you can talk
some sense into this guy while I'm gone."

"Um, yeah." He pointed toward the office across the room.
"Through that door."

Nate strolled toward the office, whistling a happy tune.

Adam returned his attention onto Max. "What was that
about?" Knowing Nate's reputation, Adam couldn't help but
add, "Did he really say that to you? That he thought about asking
out your wife?"

"Yeah. On the way over here, he told me that he'd thought
about asking Jessa out back when she was single."

Adam grinned. "Oh. That wasn't at all where I thought that
was going."

"I know, right? Can you believe the nerve of that guy?"

Confusion swept through Adam. "No, I mean that I don't think
what he said was as bad as what I had originally thought."

"Not as bad? The little punk said he would've asked my wife
out."

"Yeah, but he was talking about when she was single."

"So?"

Adam smiled. Apparently Max wasn't going to see reason where Jessa was concerned. Then again, she was his wife. Adam would probably feel a little possessive too if Preslee were his wife and some guy talked about dating her back when she was single. "Okay, so maybe you've got a point."

"I thought you'd see it my way. Let me guess. You were thinking about how you'd feel if someone said the same about Preslee."

Adam nearly choked on his own saliva. "Uh, no. We're just—"

"Friends?" Max laughed. "Right. I'll believe that the day you start sniffing my hair and staring at my ass while I run on a treadmill."

Adam cringed. "I take it you saw the video?"

"Hasn't everyone?"

"Probably." He ran a hand through his hair. "It's that obvious, huh?"

Max shrugged. "Maybe not to everyone. Preslee doesn't seem to have a clue about your intentions." He paused. "They are intentions, right?"

"I can't. I mean, she's my client."

"So?"

"As a rule, I don't date clients. I never have."

"Your loss. Preslee's great. She really came through for me with that vintage dessert cart. And Jessa has gotten other antiques from her since then. My wife adores her. She's always singing her praises."

"So they're friends then?"

Max nodded. "Yeah, why?"

Adam frowned. Then why had Preslee told him that she

didn't have any close friends? "I was just curious. I've never seen her hang out with anyone."

"That's because she doesn't. Jessa and Sidney have both invited Preslee to join them on multiple occasions, but she never does. I was surprised that day when she said she was actually going to the wedding. But then Brett told me later that Sidney had called Preslee the day before and wouldn't take no for an answer. He said she told Preslee that all of her girlfriends needed to be there on her big day because she could use the emotional support. Probably true, since she's marrying Brett." Max grinned.

Adam thought about that for a moment. Did it have something to do with what Preslee had said the other night? That other people would only let her down, if given the chance. Was he one of those people?

"You're thinking awfully hard. Is there a problem?"

"No. Not really."

"Then why are you scowling like that? Did something happen with Preslee? Is she in trouble?"

"No," Adam said, shaking his head. "Not anymore. I took care of it. Or at least I think I did."

"That doesn't sound convincing. Is there anything I can do to help? Especially if it involves Preslee. I still owe her one."

"Maybe. She always seems to go out of her way for others, yet she doesn't like to ask for help in return. I know she could use some extra support with this whole fitness thing. I don't really want to go into specifics, but she, uh, did something recently that could've been harmful to her health. I just want to make sure it doesn't happen again."

"Was it diet pills or some extreme fad diet?"

Adam blinked. "Both. How did you know?"

Max held up both palms. "I've struggled with a food addiction my entire life. Been there, done that."

Adam had forgotten about that. He'd been surprised when he had heard about Max's food addiction last year because the guy was always in the gym and had a strong physique. Something he had obviously earned through a lot of hard work. But that only went to show why no one should be judged by appearance alone. You never know what someone is struggling with on the inside. "Sorry."

"Don't be. I've learned to control it." Max gazed at Adam sincerely. "So what can I do to help? Do you want me to talk to her?"

"Actually, I was thinking more along the lines of you talking to your wife."

Max cocked his head in confusion. "My wife?"

Adam nodded. "Yeah, I was thinking maybe you could ask her if she's willing to join the gym. You had mentioned it before, and I think it would be a good idea. Preslee having a workout buddy would be a great way to stay on track."

"Already on it. I talked to Jessa about it last week, and she was excited to learn that Preslee was a member. The only reason you haven't seen her in here yet was because she had several catering events already scheduled for this past week. She'll probably be in sometime over the next few days. I'll put a rush on it."

"Good. I'm glad to hear it. I'm happy to comp her membership too."

Max shook his head. "No need. She was going to join anyway. And I wouldn't be surprised if she brings in others. All the girls know Preslee and love her. So the moment I mention to Jessa that she may need some extra support, I don't doubt they'll all rally together."

"That would be great. At least tell them to ask Kurt for a group discount. I'm happy to provide it. I'd do anything for Preslee."

Max grinned. "I see that. Does she?"

Adam hesitated. "I...don't know. Probably not."

"Well then, maybe you should rectify that."

"Rectify what?" Nate asked, returning with his tools in hand.

"Adam is having a problem with a woman," Max stated simply.

Nate grinned. "You mean Preslee?"

Adam's head snapped to him. "How the hell did you..."

His smile widened. "Dude, you sniffed her hair like a drug dog needing a cocaine fix."

Dear God. Had everyone seen that damn video? He rubbed a hand over his face and sighed. "Just great."

Nate chuckled. "Don't worry too much about it, Adam. When it comes to women, we've all done stupid stuff before. Trust me when I say I've done worse."

Adam wasn't sure what he was talking about. "But you aren't even dating anyone." In fact, for a guy with such a bad reputation for being a ladies' man, Adam had never actually seen Nate with a woman.

"Yeah, and why do you think that is? Maybe it's because the woman I fell for left town years ago. She couldn't get away from me fast enough and has never been back. *That's* how badly I screwed up."

"Yikes!" Adam said, wincing. "I would definitely take some ribbing over a hair-sniffing video rather than not seeing Preslee again." Oh. Wait. Was that him admitting that he was falling for her?

Max and Nate both grinned.

Shit.

On Friday, Preslee strolled through the gym doors earlier than usual with an entire entourage of women. She led them to the front desk and had Kurt scan her in before gazing around the room in search of Adam.

She spotted him organizing equipment across the room so she turned to her group and said, "You girls go ahead and get signed in. I'll be right back." Then she moved in his direction.

Adam's head lifted and then he glanced at his watch. "Hey, you're here early today. We weren't supposed to meet until six o'clock."

"I know," she said with a sigh. "But... well, something sort of came up. Sorry for the last-minute notice, Adam, but I won't be able to train with you later."

"Okay. Is something wrong?"

"No, it's just that we're apparently holding an impromptu bachelorette party for Sidney today," she said, motioning to the gaggle of women standing at the front desk. "I didn't know about it until just a little while ago. It all happened really fast."

He nodded. "Ah, I see. But I thought Brett and Sidney decided that they weren't doing those. Did that change?"

"Yeah. From what Valerie told me, her brother didn't want to have a bachelor party because he was afraid that some of his single friends would take things too far."

Adam grinned. "You mean like with strippers and drinking?"

Preslee raised both palms. "I guess so. She said he was trying to avoid any issues. Probably smart on his part. Things can quickly get out of hand whenever alcohol is involved."

"No kidding. And Brett should know. He liked to party

pretty hard back in the day. Hell, some of his single friends still do. But Brett isn't like that anymore. He's changed."

"I know. But Sidney didn't want her husband to have to give up having a bachelor party all because a few of his friends don't know how to control themselves. So the married couples got together and planned out both parties. That way neither of them miss out. You only get married once, right?"

Adam's gaze met hers. "If you're lucky."

"Yeah," she said, her heart thumping. Then she sighed, banishing the crazy thoughts swirling in her head. It wasn't like she would marry Adam. But some lucky girl would one day. Damn it.

"So what are the men doing today?"

She paused. "Didn't someone call you? Jessa said they were going to invite you and Kurt."

Adam pulled his cellphone out of his pocket and checked it. "Damn it. Yeah, Max called me a couple of times and left a message. I forgot I turned my ringer off earlier while working with a client. I'll call Max back in a minute."

"Well, if you can't get ahold of him, let me know. Leah can tell you how to get to her house. The guys apparently all gathered at Sam's to play poker. I'm sure they would love for you to join them."

Adam shook his head. "Unfortunately, I can't. I still have a client I have to meet with at five. But there's no reason why Kurt shouldn't go and have a good time. I can keep an eye on things during my next training session."

"That's nice of you."

"It's no big deal. I'll get to hang out with them all tomorrow anyway." He rubbed his chin. "The reception is still at Bottoms Up, right?"

"Yes. The wedding ceremony will take place at the church at six o'clock tomorrow evening and then the reception will follow immediately after at the bar."

"Good. That gives Kurt plenty of time to close up the gym in the afternoon and then get dressed and to the church on time."

"Perfect."

"Yeah." His gaze swept over her and confusion settled onto his features. "Wait a minute. Why are you in your workout clothes? I thought you said you were attending a bachelorette party?"

Preslee grinned. "We are. The women are all working out together and then heading over to that new spa that opened recently to get manicures, pedicures, and massages. Who knows? Maybe even a few brave souls will get something waxed."

"Sounds like fun," Adam said, chuckling.

"I'm sure it will be. They're a fun group to hang out with. And the best part about it?" She pointed to the eight women chatting with Kurt. "I held up my end of the bargain."

Confusion flashed in his eyes. "What do you mean?"

"I brought in some new members. That was part of our agreement, remember? You help me with Josh, and I help promote your gym."

"Oh. Right. I remember."

"Good. Because I heard he's supposed to be at the reception tomorrow. I thought maybe we could, you know . . . try out more of what you suggested." Heat bloomed in her cheeks. "The flirting, I mean."

Adam's brow rose. "You want me to flirt with you at the reception?"

She bit into her bottom lip. "Um, yeah. I think your plan

is working. I've noticed that Josh has become more attentive toward me. So I thought we'd up the stakes a little since we'd be in a social setting. Like maybe you could dance with me or something. Just to see if Josh responds to it."

His mouth set in a firm line as his jaw tightened. "Okay. If that's what you want."

She hesitated. "Um, it is."

"Great," Adam said, although his gravelly tone and the look in his intense eyes said something else entirely. "Well, that's perfect. Thanks for bringing in some new members. I better go help get them all registered so that you can get in a workout and then get on with your bachelorette party." He didn't wait for a response. He just walked away.

Preslee watched in confusion as Adam marched stiffly across the room toward the front desk. What the hell was that? She wasn't sure, but whatever it was had stunned her senseless. Why had he been so curt with her? Had she upset him?

And, if so, what the heck did she do?

Adam had been the one who'd suggested making the deal to begin with. If he found the whole idea of flirting with her that damn repulsive, then maybe he should've thought about that before opening his big mouth.

It wasn't like she was looking forward to him pretending to like her any more than he was. Okay, maybe that was a lie. She liked the idea of him flirting with her. She just wanted it to be real. Because the whole idea of him fake flirting with her only made her feel more pathetic than she already did.

It was embarrassing enough that Adam felt the need to flirt with her just so she could get another man's attention. Scratch that. *Force* himself to flirt with her. Because judging by

Adam's response as he stomped away, that was exactly what he'd be doing.

She hadn't at all been prepared for the weird vibe he'd given off, and it had completely caught her off guard. Now she regretted even bringing it up. Well, she learned her lesson there and definitely wouldn't do it again.

Preslee caught movement out of the corner of her eye and glanced over to see Leah, Valerie, Jessa, and Sidney heading in her direction. The other four women were still registering at the main desk, but judging by the way they smiled adoringly at the two handsome men helping them, none seemed to mind being left behind.

Leah glanced back and grinned. "I think they're going to be a while. They found some pretty men to look at."

Preslee giggled. "Well, I guess that's one way to get your blood pumping." She swallowed hard, remembering all the times her heart had pounded faster whenever Adam had gotten close to her. The man seemed to have that effect on females. In fact, Kurt did too. "Why don't we go ahead and start working out? The others can join in when they get through."

"Sounds good to me," Sidney said. "Lead the way."

Choosing to stay together, all of them climbed on machines in the same area so they could each see and hear the others. Three ladies jumped on treadmills while Preslee and Valerie opted for the rowing machines that sat across from them.

"So this is where you've been hanging out, huh?" Sidney asked.

Preslee nodded. "Only in the evenings and during the days on the weekends."

"Well, it's definitely paid off," Leah told her. "You look great. You have such a healthy glow."

Jessa smirked. "I have a feeling that glow isn't all because of her workouts. Did you guys see her trainer?" She turned her attention to Preslee. "Max said you've been working out with Adam."

She nodded. "Yep, for the past month."

"Which one is Adam?" Leah asked.

"The dark-haired one," Valerie explained.

Leah was still staring in Adam's direction. "I see what you mean about the glow, Jess. He's good-looking. I'd be glowing too if I was a single girl who spent all my extra time with him." She winked at Preslee.

"See? Told you so," Jessa said, giggling.

Valerie snorted out a laugh. "The blond isn't bad either."

Preslee couldn't help but smile. "Have y'all met them? They're both great guys."

"Sort of," Jessa replied. "They come into the restaurant sometimes. Always polite. Good tippers too. Max introduced me. He knows them from the gym, of course."

"Same," Sidney replied. "Brett introduced me too. He said Adam and Kurt had a huge hand in getting him to start working out with Max. They probably deserve a medal for that."

Jessa nodded. "No kidding. I never thought our guys were going to get along. I'm glad to see that things have changed. We can actually have dinner together now without the two of them trying to kill each other."

"True," Sidney agreed. Then she turned to Preslee. "So how are things going with Adam? Brett says he's a good trainer who likes to get hands-on with his clients."

Although Preslee knew she hadn't meant anything sexual, she couldn't help but squirm a little. Probably because she wished

Adam *would* get hands-on with her. Not because she couldn't go without sex. She could. And had. But if anyone asked her how long it had been since she'd last had sex with something other than her vibrator, she would be too mortified to answer.

Sex was like oxygen. It wasn't a big deal unless a person was deprived of it for too long. Then they either ended up in a vegetative state with irreversible brain damage or...well, dead.

She seriously needed to get laid before that happened to her.

A sigh fell from her lips.

"Preslee?"

Her head snapped up to see four pairs of eyes staring curiously at her, and she realized that she hadn't answered Sidney's question. Heat blasted through her cheeks. "Sorry. He's...um, great. I highly recommend him."

Valerie's head perked up. "Hmm. Do I sense something there?"

"What do you mean?"

She grinned. "You know, something more. Like maybe there's something between you and Adam."

Preslee scoffed. "Ah, no."

The corner of Sidney's eyes crinkled slightly. "Why not? He's hot."

With a shake of her head, Preslee laughed. "I don't think the bride-to-be is supposed to be checking out another guy the day before her wedding."

"It's perfectly okay if I'm looking for *your* benefit," she argued playfully.

Valerie coughed out a laugh. "Dear Lord. I think you've forgotten who you're marrying tomorrow. Brett would probably kill Adam if he knew you thought he was hot."

Sidney shrugged. "Actually, he does know. The first time

I met Adam, I told Brett that I thought his friend was very handsome and that we needed to set him up with one of my girlfriends."

"Really?" Valerie asked, blinking. "And Brett didn't have a coronary?"

Sidney laughed. "No, he actually was the one who suggested that maybe Preslee would be a good fit for Adam. And I agree. They would make a perfect couple. She's smart and kind and—"

"And sitting right here," Preslee said, chiming in.

"Oh. Right. Sorry about that. I was on a roll."

Preslee smiled at her. "Well, I hardly think I'm perfect for him. Nice of you to say though."

Sidney tilted her head. "Why do you say that?"

"Oh, come on. As if I could get a guy like him. Men who look like that don't look twice at someone like me."

A frown marred Leah's pretty face. "Don't say that. You should be kinder to yourself. I should know. I spent my entire life listening to my mother spew negative comments." Leah shook her head and gestured to the other women. "Besides, what you're saying... it's just not true. Look around you. You're surrounded by four other plus-size women who all have really hot men."

Three heads bobbed in unison as the other women agreed with her.

Preslee sighed. "Yeah, but it's different with Adam. He's a personal trainer. He literally spends his days getting others into shape."

"So?"

"So why would he want me?"

Valerie blinked at her. "Why would he want you? Because you're gorgeous. And you're one of the nicest people I've ever met. You deserve to be with a great guy. One who makes you happy."

"Thanks. But I don't think he's interested."

Sidney sighed. "Have you asked him?"

Preslee shook her head. "God no. I don't handle rejection well. The last thing I want to do is put myself out there and get turned down flat. I don't want to embarrass myself."

Jessa pursed her lips. "I understand that. I really do. But, honey, how will you know if he's interested if you don't give it a shot?"

"We're just friends. He doesn't want anything more."

Valerie leaned toward her. "You don't know that for sure. How could you?"

Preslee rubbed a hand over her face. "Look, it's not hard to figure out. He's shown no interest in me whatsoever. I don't blame him though. He's in shape, and I'm not even his type. I mean, look at me. I'm f—"

"Fucking beautiful?" A husky male voice slashed through the air unexpectedly.

Everyone jerked their heads in the direction of the sound until all female eyes were on Adam. He stood there with his arms crossed, a muscle ticking in his strong jaw, with his dark eyes trained on Preslee. He looked pissed, and every bit of that anger seemed to be aimed in her direction.

Her heart rate sped up, and her palms dampened with sweat. Crap. How much of their conversation had he overheard?

"Fucking beautiful?" he repeated, still staring at her. "Was that what you were going to say?"

No one answered him. All of the women had been stunned into silence by his sudden arrival, including Preslee.

"Or how about smart? Sexy? Out of his league? Because if you say anything other than those words about yourself, then you're not nearly as self-aware as you should be."

Preslee blinked in shock as the other women exchanged glances with one another and bit into their bottom lips to keep from smiling. "Uh, Adam. We were, um, just talking about—"

"I know what you were going to say," he said, interrupting her. "But I don't like it when women talk about themselves that way. No dropping F-bombs in my gym."

"But you just did," she accused playfully.

"Yeah, but mine wasn't the same one that you were going to use."

Her nose crinkled. "*Fat* is a word that most people use, ya know?"

"Not in my gym, they don't." He came closer and shrugged. "I mean, what exactly is fat, anyway? Is it a size six? A size twelve? Eighteen? Twenty-eight? Who gets to decide that? Society? Well, that's bullshit. I've seen women in every one of those sizes looking gorgeous as hell. Sexy isn't a size."

Preslee shook her head. "Not all men agree with that statement."

He nodded. "You're right. But there are plenty of men out there who love curvy women. And yeah, there are some who don't. But you don't have to check any boxes for that guy. He doesn't matter. *You* do. Don't ever think you need to shrink yourself just to squeeze into some narrow-minded view of an unrealistic beauty standard." He smiled at her. "You're beautiful just the way you are."

Preslee's heart lurched wildly inside her chest, and her muscles tensed. She hadn't expected Adam to have this kind of powerful effect on her. But he'd blasted through all of her defenses, and she could no longer ignore the way he made her feel. The man paid attention to her, even when no one else did. As if she was special and he valued her as a person. But the complimentary words? As a woman, those made her feel feminine and desirable. Something she hadn't felt in a long time.

She'd definitely needed that.

Preslee didn't want to admit that she was falling for her trainer, but dear God...she was. He challenged her to be a better person and constantly showed her what true kindness was about. He was consistent, reliable, and honorable. A true man. One she could depend on and trust implicitly.

And knowing all of that left her utterly speechless.

He gazed over their group and smiled. "I have to meet my other client soon, but you ladies have fun. And thanks for coming in. I hope to see you all on a regular basis."

As Adam walked away, silence reigned amongst them. For several moments, they all stared at her slack-jawed, eyes blinking. Finally, Valerie cleared her throat and smirked. "Just friends, huh?"

CHAPTER FOURTEEN

The next evening, Adam leaned against the bar with one elbow, dangling a longneck bottle between two fingers. He lifted it to his mouth and tipped it back, taking a long pull of his beer before setting it on the bar. Then he glanced around the crowded room.

When he'd first heard Logan and Valerie were hosting Brett and Sydney's reception at Bottoms Up, he didn't think it was a good idea. The reception was an invite-only event that was to be closed to the public, but Saturdays were always the busiest night of the week for the popular bar. He thought for sure they would lose money.

But when he'd arrived, Adam couldn't help but grin. The bar was brimming with the same locals who usually frequented the bar. Go figure. Guess that was the thing about small towns. All of your neighbors *are* your friends.

In fact, the only person Adam hadn't spotted in the bar yet was Preslee. Then again, he'd overheard someone say that some of the ladies had gone home to change before heading to the reception. Maybe she was one of them.

Kurt stood next to him, eyeing a pretty brunette as she passed by. "Damn. There's some hot women in here tonight."

Adam nodded. "Sounds like you're hoping to take one home with you."

"Well, yeah. Aren't you?"

Adam shook his head. "Hell no. That's your thing, not mine."

"What's my thing? Sex?" Kurt asked, his brows drawing together. "Since when do you not like sex?"

"No, I'm talking about one-night stands. Next to my brother, you're the king of them. However, I'm not interested."

Kurt's eyes narrowed. "Oh, give me a break. Like you've never had one."

"I didn't say that. But doing something once or twice isn't the same as doing it all the time." God. Counting his neighbor, his brother, and his best friend, he was surrounded by man whores.

His friend shrugged. "Don't knock it until you try it."

"I'm not knocking it . . . or you. If that's what you want to do, then more power to you. As long as you're treating the women with respect, not leading them on, and being safe about it, then I don't care how many one-night stands you have."

"Well, thanks . . . Dad." Kurt grinned.

Adam chuckled. "No problem, son."

"So just for clarification purposes, you're saying that you aren't interested in taking anyone home with you?"

"Exactly. The last thing I need right now is a distraction. Business is good. Memberships are up by forty percent, and I've taken on four new clients this week alone who want to start training with me. Sex is the last thing on my mind."

Kurt lifted one brow. "You sure about that?"

Confusion spiraled through Adam. "Why do you keep asking me that?"

"Because Preslee just walked in," Kurt said, grinning as he nodded toward the door.

"What does that have to do with any—" The words dried on his tongue as he turned and spotted her near the entrance.

Across the room, Preslee stood chatting in a small circle with two other women, her shoulders back and her head held high. He'd never known her to show off her body, but his eyes drifted almost immediately to the ample amount of cleavage swelling out of her sexy, low-cut top. Her glistening chest sparkled under the colorful strobe lights flashing throughout the room, and Adam couldn't help but wonder if she'd dusted herself with some kind of glitter.

Glitter was nontoxic, wasn't it? He mentally shrugged, not able to summon the urge to care. Who gave a damn? One taste would undoubtedly be worth dying from glitter poisoning.

His dick stretched awake.

Whoa! Down, boy. She wants someone else...someone who isn't us.

But his persistent erection refused to take a hike. It wasn't going anywhere as long as Preslee's full pink lips moved silently in time to the lyrics of the slow song playing in the background. Or while her magnificent body swayed sensually to the somber beat of the music.

So much for eliminating distractions.

The stunning woman filled out every inch of the tight jeans she wore, and watching her lush body move like that only made him want to run one large hand over the sexy curve of her waist as his other hand gripped those shapely hips and pulled her against his hardness.

Preslee's bright blue eyes scanned the crowd, looking for someone. Probably Josh. Why was she so damn infatuated with him? What the hell did that guy have that Adam didn't?

Her attention. The unspoken words hung in the air around him like a noose cinching his neck.

Frustrated, Adam lifted the beer he'd abandoned on the bar and downed the rest of the contents in one large gulp. If he was going to have to sit here all evening, watching her moon over Josh, then he was going to have to do it with a buzz. That was the only way he was going to get through this night with his ego unscathed.

Kurt clapped him on the back. "You okay?"

"Yeah. Why do you ask?"

"Oh, I don't know. Maybe because you went from smiling to scowling in a matter of seconds." He nodded toward Preslee. "I'm guessing you have a thing for her."

"No, I don't."

Kurt grinned. "That's cute."

"What is?"

His grin broadened. "You denying it."

"She's my client," Adam reminded Kurt, as well as himself. "So no. While I think she's beautiful, I'm not interested in Preslee."

"Liar. That gal is on your hit list, and you know it."

Adam blinked. "My what list?"

Kurt chuckled. "A hit list refers to a list of women you'd like to hit the sheets with."

Adam shook his head and laughed. What kind of stupid, sexist bullshit was that? "What are you—a teenager? I haven't talked like that about a woman in years. Shouldn't have even done it back then, but I was young and stupid at the time. Thank God I grew out of that."

"Says who?"

Adam ignored his friend's playful jab. "Ya know, I never took you for the sexist type. At least you've never been in the past. But I'm guessing you have one of these so-called hit lists?"

"Hell, no," Kurt said, shaking his head adamantly. "I overheard my teenage nephew talking on the phone to one of his buddies about how he had a 'hit it and quit it' list under his mattress with all the names of the girls in his class that he'd like to sleep with. I just didn't mention the 'quit it' part because it's such a dick thing to say. Honestly, the whole list thing is the stupidest shit I've ever heard."

Adam agreed. "Did you tell him that?"

"No, I let his momma tell him that. The moment I told my sister what the list was for and where it was located, she marched up to his room to give him a firm lesson about respecting women."

Adam chuckled. "Like I said, young and dumb."

Kurt shrugged. "Yeah. But be honest, Adam. Say you did have a list of women you'd like to sleep with..." He lifted his beer bottle to his lips, tipped it back, and then swallowed. "Would Preslee be at the top of that list?"

"No," Adam said, his tone serious. He gazed across the room at Preslee and decided it was time to quit lying to Kurt, as well as himself. "She'd be the *only* damn woman on it."

Kurt laughed. "Thought you said you weren't interested?"

"Shut up."

His buddy chuckled again. "Damn, man. I reckoned you had a thing for her, but I didn't realize you had it that bad. What are you going to do?"

"Nothing. Like I said, she's my client. I don't date any-one who I have a business relationship with. Besides, Preslee's interest lies with Josh, not me. I walked up on a conversation between her and her friends yesterday where they were talking about Josh and how he's not showing interest in her. Personally, I think the guy is a moron for that, but he's what she wants. She's already made it perfectly clear that we're just friends."

"That sucks."

Adam ran a hand through his hair, tousling the strands. "Yeah, but it doesn't matter. Even if there was something between us, there are other things to consider. Like the bet we made."

Kurt shrugged. "It was just a harmless bet between friends. It's nothing."

Adam lifted one shoulder. "Maybe. But I don't think Preslee would feel the same. After all, it was her workouts that we were betting on. The more I think about it, the more I feel like we crossed a line. Not intentionally, I guess, but that doesn't change the fact that we did."

"Well, you only have eight weeks to go before the final weigh-in. After that, the bet will be over, and she won't be your client anymore. Since Josh isn't showing any interest, maybe then you could slide in there and—"

"No," Adam said, shaking his head. The last thing he needed was to get his hopes up. Especially after he'd heard her talking about Josh yesterday. "I don't think so."

They sat in silence while Adam continued to stare across the room at Preslee. Then Kurt finally said, "Well, you can't just sit here watching her from afar all night like a damn hawk on a telephone pole who just spotted a field mouse."

"What else am I supposed to do?"

"Go over and talk to her."

Adam's brows drew together. "Why? So I can watch her flirt with Josh some more? No thanks. I'd rather find a dark corner to loiter in, console myself with beer, and drink myself into oblivion."

"Well, that's a healthy attitude," Kurt said with a groan.

"You've got a better idea? If so, I'd love to hear it."

"Yeah, how about going after what you want? Who cares if she's your client? If you want her, then make a move. Hell, if nothing else, just ask her to dance. Anything is better than you sitting here looking so pathetic."

Adam grinned. "Was that your version of a pep talk? Because, if so, you really suck at it."

"At least I'm not too chickenshit to go after a woman, all because there might be a little competition."

Fire lit in Adam's stomach. "You think Josh is what's holding me back?" He scoffed. "You know better than that. It has nothing to do with him. Not going after Preslee has more to do with her not looking at me as anything other than her trainer...and her pal."

"So that's it. You two are just friends?"

Shrugging, Adam glanced over at her again. "Probably."

"You don't even know for sure?"

"No. I mean, she says we're just friends, but then I sometimes get the feeling that there's...I don't know, something more."

Kurt threw back his head and groaned. "You're killing me here, man. I've never known you to be such a quitter. Or to run away from a challenge. Especially of the female variety." He motioned to Preslee, who was ordering a drink at the main bar. "If you don't get over there and ask that pretty young woman to dance, I'm going to pull a junior high move by going over there and telling her that you like her and ask her if she likes you too. I'll even draw a little diagram on a bar napkin with checkboxes that say yes and no."

Adam laughed. "You wouldn't dare."

Kurt lifted one brow, and Adam's chuckle dissipated.

Shit. Okay, maybe he would. "Fine, I'm going. Just keep your mouth shut. If you say anything to her about this, I'm going to fire you. For real this time."

Kurt grinned. "All right, but you might want to hurry. Josh just showed up, and his eyeballs are dangling in your woman's cleavage."

Adam spun around to see Josh's mouth hovering close to Preslee's ear, as if he was trying to talk to her over the loud music, and his laser gaze was pinpointed directly between her breasts. Damn it.

A low growl rumbled from Adam's throat. Before he even realized what he was doing, his feet propelled him forward through the crowd. But as he advanced on Josh and Preslee, an errant thought ran through his head. Preslee was his client. His friend. But not . . . well, *his*.

As much as he hated it, he needed to remember that.

❧

Preslee leaned toward Josh, straining to hear what he said over the blaring music coming from the speaker over their heads. She probably couldn't have picked a worse place to stand inside the bar if she'd tried.

Ah, well. At least it gave her a good reason to get closer to him. Well, that was until she spotted him blatantly staring at her chest. She'd worn her auburn hair down and loose, but now she fought the sudden urge to pull her hair forward over her shoulders to hide the deep cleavage she had on display.

Why though? Wasn't that what she had wanted—to grab his attention? Because, boy, had she gotten it. But for some strange reason, his leering made her feel cheap. Almost like she had to bribe him with some boob to get him to notice her. Which wasn't exactly an endearing quality.

She angled her body away from him as she reached for the margarita the bartender handed to her. She brought it to her mouth and licked the salt-dipped rim before taking a drink of the tangy, potent concoction. "Wow, he made this really strong," she said to Josh.

Overhearing the comment, Valerie leaned over the bar and grinned. "That's because you're more likely to tip well if you're served a generously poured cocktail. Bartenders are banking on that." Then she lowered her voice so that only Preslee could hear. "Then again, it probably doesn't hurt that your low-cut blouse highlights your boobs." Valerie gave her a salacious wink and then went back to work.

"What'd she say?" Josh asked.

Heat crept into Preslee's cheeks. "Uh, nothing," she said, taking another sip of her margarita. She held her drink in front of her, blocking his view of her chest, as she gazed out over to the dance floor. "So, uh, do you wanna..."

"What? Dance?" Josh shook his head. "Nah. I'm not the kind of guy who gets out on the dance floor and shakes my ass in public."

Before she could respond, a male voice rose behind her. "Good thing I am."

Preslee's head snapped in the direction of the familiar voice, and her tongue practically rolled out of her mouth and onto the ground. Adam stood there in dark jeans and a cream-colored Henley that hugged his prominent pectoral muscles and strong, broad shoulders. He sported his usual tousled bed-head look, but his deep-set brown eyes were focused on her with an intensity that had her breath backing up in her lungs.

Damn, he looked good.

She had always thought Adam was handsome, but right now, he was downright devastating. Her throat tightened, and she barely managed to squeak out a nasal-sounding, high-pitched "hi."

"Hey, Preslee." Without precedent, Adam wrapped his arm around her waist and pulled her into his warm chest for a hug.

The spit instantly dried in her mouth.

He held her close in an intimate embrace, and she could smell the subtle hint of sandalwood cologne lingering on his shirt. But it was the familiar scent beneath the fabric that had her turning her face into his neck and taking a deeper breath—all heated skin and testosterone-filled musk. She'd never before understood what other women meant when they said a guy smelled like "a man." Until she met Adam. Now she totally got it.

Mouth watering, she took another deep breath before he released her and then smiled up at him. "Having a good time?"

"Yep. And I hear you need a dance partner." He lifted one brow.

She stilled. "Oh, I . . . well, I was . . ."

"Good, let's dance." He snagged the margarita from her hand and passed it to Josh. "Keep an eye on her drink, would ya?"

Josh nodded but looked almost as confused as she felt. What was Adam doing? Was he drunk or something? Josh was finally showing some interest in her—well, in her breasts anyway—and Adam was messing it up. What the hell?

"Come on," Adam said, dragging her toward the dance floor.

He kept a gentle hold as he pulled her through the crowd. A fast song was already playing as they reached the middle. He spun her to face in the direction they had just come from, and she spotted Josh watching from afar.

Adam moved in behind her, the hard planes of his body surrounding hers, as he molded himself to her backside. One strong arm slid around her waist, palming her stomach. She tensed and sucked in an unsteady breath.

He bent his head until his firm lips brushed against the lobe of her ear and his hot breath fluttered over her neck. "Relax, darlin'. Josh is watching. I promise this isn't going to hurt one bit."

Josh? Who the hell cared about him?

Something hot had slid through her veins at the sound of the sexy, demanding tone whispered into her ear. Why was he talking like that? God, how much had he had to drink tonight? Couldn't have been much. It was early, and he didn't even smell like booze.

Intrigue spiraled through her, and she released a deep breath, letting her body go lax against his. The large hand resting on her stomach settled in just below her navel, his fingers lightly caressing, as he placed his free hand on her hip and tightened her body against his.

Desire winged through her, but she bit her lip and ignored the sensations. The last thing she wanted was for him to think that he was turning her on. Even if it was true. They hadn't even started dancing yet, and her blood pressure had already spiked sky-high.

When Adam finally began to move, her stomach twisted in automatic response. He ground himself against her, and blood thrummed in her veins in time with the pounding in her ears.

God. She was so going to regret this.

The darkened dance floor was lit only by strobe lights, and the music hammered so loud in her ears that it vibrated into her chest. Something hot and all-encompassing simmered in the air around them, as if the atmosphere was sensually charged.

She reveled in the pleasure of him against her, which in turn had her batting away thoughts of the two of them turning into anything more. He was just helping her with Josh, damn it. It was all for his benefit. She needed to remember that.

But the flood of thoughts wouldn't stop coming. Images bounced in her head of her and Adam as a couple, taunting and teasing her mercilessly. It was a cruel thing to do to herself. Mostly because that dream would never come true.

By the time he'd led her off the dance floor and returned her to the bar area where Josh waited with her drink, her knees were as weak as limp noodles. But it wasn't because of the dancing.

Adam offered her a smile, the one she'd always found so sexy, and said, "Thanks for the dance, sweetheart. I enjoyed it."

Her cheeks warmed at the way he was looking at her, even if she did know it was him just putting on a show for Josh. Still, she somehow managed a smile. "Same here."

"Good. We'll have to dance again when another fast song comes on." Adam winked at her before meandering away.

She put her hand to her chest and gasped a little as her shoulders slumped forward. It was as if her body was so weak that she couldn't even hold herself upright.

Josh gazed at her. "Are you okay?"

"Yes," she lied.

But she wasn't okay. She couldn't seem to catch her breath, although that had nothing to do with dancing either. It was Adam. Well, that and the fact that she'd just realized that she'd fallen head over heels in love with the wrong guy.

CHAPTER FIFTEEN

Adam leaned back in his chair and huffed out a breath.

"You all right, buddy?" Kurt asked, a note of concern in his voice.

"Yeah, why?"

Kurt grinned. "Oh, I don't know. Maybe because you've been shooting daggers at Josh with your eyes for the past ten minutes. Every time he so much as touches Preslee or gets too close to her, you growl under your breath like a territorial male dog."

Yeah, well, maybe he was feeling territorial. But it wasn't all his fault. The way Preslee had shimmied against him while they were dancing had caused the circulation in his brain to go haywire. His entire body ached relentlessly.

Still on edge, Adam slumped in his chair in misery. He needed to get a handle on all of the raw urges and sensations spiraling through him. So he would maintain his distance while silently observing her from afar.

What was wrong with him? He wasn't supposed to be looking at her this way. Clearly, he was losing his ever-loving mind. Because that one sexy dance had put an enormous crack in his control.

He wanted her. All of her. And he didn't want to share her with Josh, who was so blatantly wrong for a woman like Preslee that it wasn't even funny. She was charming, playful, and so damn sweet. While Josh couldn't seem to spot a good woman standing directly in front of him.

Adam glanced across the room and caught sight of them again. Only this time, Josh was talking to another woman while Preslee stood there waiting patiently. Her eyes met Adam's, and she gave him a weak smile. A fake one at that.

Was Josh flirting with the other woman? Because from where Adam stood, it sure looked like it. Man, if so, Preslee had to be so disappointed.

But when Adam watched Josh leave Preslee by herself to head to a table with the other woman, anger seared his insides. That was it. He'd had enough of Preslee being ignored by that idiot. Maybe it wasn't a good idea for him to react when he was so heated, but he didn't care.

Tuning out the cacophony of the crowded bar, Adam marched across the room toward Preslee, weaving through bodies as fast as he could. She saw him approaching, and there must've been something predatory in the way he moved because she looked nervous.

Good. She should be. Because he wasn't playing around anymore. Josh was going to notice this beautiful, sexy woman even if he had to pick Preslee up and beat the moron over the head with her.

Adam stopped in front of Preslee, and the aroma of raw coconuts and sweet, fresh pineapple sent his blood humming through his veins. "Do you want Josh?" he asked her hastily.

She paused, as if stunned by his candor. "Um..."

Adam didn't even wait for her to finish her answer. He had asked on a whim, but he had no doubt she would say yes, and damn it, he didn't want to listen to that. Not from her. He didn't want to hear that she wanted another man.

He stepped into her space, and her eyes widened. His hand slid around the back of her neck as he lowered his lips to her ear. "Just how far are you willing to go to get him?" he asked.

She hesitated to answer again, and her awkwardness only made her even more endearing. "Um, how far?" she asked, her voice shaky.

"Yeah," he said, snaking an arm around her waist to pull her closer.

Her body tensed. "W-what are you doing, Adam?"

"I'm going to kiss you," he told her. "Just once."

She blinked in shock, as if he'd told her that he was going to make her eat a live cricket. Her breathing quickened. "W-what do you mean?"

"If you want to make Josh jealous, then you're going to have to step up your game."

Worry creased her forehead. "By kissing you?"

"Yes," he stated, knowing that he was trying to win her over. But she wanted Josh, and Adam was going to show her why that wasn't her correct match. If this didn't work, then at least he'd have this one kiss to remember her by. "I'm going to kiss you now."

She drew back slightly, her eyes wide in disbelief. "Okay," she agreed, although there was still hesitation in her tone.

His gaze fell to her lips, and he hoped like hell she understood what he was about to do and didn't full-out deck him in front of everyone. Even though he probably deserved it between the bet and getting himself involved in her relationship with Josh. He really needed to learn to stop while he was behind.

Tomorrow, he thought. He'd learn that lesson tomorrow. Because right now, he had something more pressing to do. Something he'd been wanting to do for the past month.

Adam moved his face slowly toward hers as she watched him from beneath her long, dark lashes. Just thinking about kissing her sent a flash of heat swirling in his gut.

But before he could kiss her, she leaned forward and kissed his cheek with a quick peck. It wasn't at all a sexual kiss. More like a thank-you kiss you would give your grandma for the ugly Christmas sweater she'd knitted you. Which wasn't at all what he'd planned.

He scowled. "What the hell was that?"

"Um, a friendly kiss?"

Yeah, fuck that. Because it wasn't nearly enough. Which was strange. In his experience, putting off cravings usually lessened or weakened the strength of desire behind them. But that rule of thumb apparently didn't apply to this woman. Because he was going to kiss her *his* way...and there would be nothing friendly about it.

Adam grasped the back of her head and angled it to the side. His eyes dusted over her pale pink lips, watching her lick them nervously. Then he lowered his head and covered her mouth with his. It was like touching a live wire. Of all the women he'd kissed in the past, never before had this much electricity shot through his system.

Maybe it was because he'd spent so much time jonesing for her. Or maybe there was just something special about her.

Probably both. All he knew was that he'd barely brushed his lips over hers and something unexpected had ignited inside of him, engulfing him in flames. Not like a small fire that had grown out of control in a matter of seconds. More like the equivalent of someone accidentally launching an entire space shuttle into orbit all because they'd carelessly thrown a lit cigarette on the ground beneath the platform.

Unable to stop himself, he parted her lips with his tongue and deepened the kiss. Sweeping inside, he tasted the tangy margarita she'd been drinking, along with something else. Something sweet and undeniably Preslee. He explored the curve of her full, pouty lips and then traced her perfect mouth with his tongue before stopping to suck on the tip of hers.

She responded with an unintelligible moan, and he froze. Was she playing along? Because if so, she was clearly a darn good actress. Emmy-worthy, if you asked him. Because the sound that had just hummed from the depths of her throat sounded real. Like she had really been turned on.

Although Adam had frozen in place, Preslee hadn't. She continued to kiss him, her body molding to his like it had been made to fit there. But he was surprised when her breasts flattened against his chest and two tightly pebbled buds poked through her shirt. He'd worried that she hadn't been attracted to him at all. But apparently, she wasn't as unaffected by him as he'd thought. Good to know.

His lips moved once more, manipulating hers, as his hands traveled down her curvy waist and landed on the swell of her hips. He bit back a groan. This woman would be the death of him. Just thinking about getting her clothes off was enough to keep him hard as a rock for a solid week.

It took every bit of strength he had to pry his mouth from hers. But he finally managed to pull away, nipping her bottom lip one last time and scraping it lightly with his teeth as he did.

That was the kind of kiss he wanted from her. Not some generic version.

Maybe this was a mistake of epic proportions. He should probably move on and let her and Josh work things out on their own. But Adam couldn't do it. Because the only male attention he wanted focused on that curvy body of hers was *his*.

Preslee blinked in complete confusion. Had that really just happened?

She licked her lips and released a contented sigh. She could still taste Adam there. He had kissed her. Like really kissed her.

Out of the blue.

In the most phenomenal way imaginable.

She couldn't remember a time when she'd ever been kissed so thoroughly. At least not with any clothes on. It had felt... She wasn't sure. All she knew was that she hadn't wanted it to end.

The scandalous, R-rated meeting of tongues that had taken place was nowhere near the sweet kiss she'd expected. Maybe it was the spontaneity of the steamy kiss, but it hadn't felt like a pretend one, and the way he'd touched her hadn't felt very friend-like.

Instead, she felt like he'd stripped her bare with only his mouth. As if she should be restoring her clothing to order even now, although it wasn't even necessary. When their lips had touched, everything in the room had disappeared. The room itself had disappeared. Nothing had existed beyond her and Adam.

If they hadn't been in a public—

Oh.

Blinking away the lust-filled haze, Preslee gazed around the room to see a bar full of people staring at her. Lovely.

Even her female friends were all looking in her direction with raised brows. Yeah, they would definitely have some questions later. Especially after she'd sworn that she and Adam were nothing more than friends.

And they were.

He'd only been pretending, and the kiss hadn't meant anything. But damn him for being a star performer. Someone should give him an Oscar. Because even *she* was having a hard time convincing herself that the kiss hadn't been real.

It had felt real. Like something special. Meaningful.

Yet she knew better. Adam was helping her with Josh, that was all. Her eyes darted around the room again to find the rest of the bar still staring at them. Including Josh. He was sitting with that other woman, but he was glaring awfully hard in Preslee's direction. And he didn't look happy.

His mouth formed a tight line, and his narrowed eyes shot daggers from across the room. He looked . . . jealous? Strange, since *he* was the one who had been flirting with another woman right in front of her and then abandoned her to go hang out at the woman's table. What did he have to be jealous about?

In the past, Preslee had all but begged for his attention, and he hadn't given it. Not once. Not until tonight. When it had been convenient. But now that he wanted to give her attention, she was annoyed by it.

She glanced over at Adam, who was wearing a devilish grin.

"I, ah . . ." She didn't know what to say. "Seems we had an audience for that spectacular performance."

He licked his lips and grinned. "Can you blame them? That kiss was pretty hot."

She blinked. He thought their kiss had been hot too? Then she shook her head, realizing that he'd meant for it to come across that way to others. "No, I meant Josh in particular. Apparently he saw the kiss. And judging from the irritated look on his face, I'm certain he didn't like it."

A small crease formed between Adam's eyes. "Well, that was the idea behind the kiss, right?"

"Yeah, but I don't want . . ."

Whoa! What was she doing? She couldn't tell Adam what she was thinking. No way was she going to admit that Josh wasn't who or what she wanted, all because she'd stupidly allowed herself to fall for Adam. Just because she'd developed feelings for him didn't mean that he returned them. What if he outright rejected her? Oh man, that would suck.

She shook her head. Okay, so maybe Adam was nice enough that he wouldn't purposely try to hurt or embarrass her. Especially in front of others. But that didn't mean she wouldn't be regardless. She would. No matter how nicely he turned her down.

Adam frowned as he gazed across the distance at Josh. Then he turned his attention back to her. "Can we go somewhere to talk?"

"Okay, do you want to grab a corner table or step outside?"

"Neither. I would rather go back to my place so that we can be alone without any interruptions. Is that okay?"

She nodded hesitantly but had a strong feeling that she wasn't going to like where this was heading. "Sure."

"You want me to drive?"

"No, I'll take my car and follow you." If this was going the way she thought it was, then she wanted to be able to leave on her own.

His forehead creased. "But you've been drinking."

"Not really. I only had a few sips of that margarita. Before that, I drank club soda. You probably had more than I did."

"I only had one beer. And I was nursing it."

"Good, then we can both drive."

He stared at her for a moment, but she couldn't read his strange expression. "Actually, I'd rather you ride with me. Even if you didn't have much, it was a hard liquor."

"Okay, fine," she said, just wanting to get this over with. "Then let's go."

His apartment complex was only a couple of miles away, and they walked to his front door in silence. He hadn't said a word on the drive over, and even when they went inside, he still didn't speak. Just closed the door behind them, as if something weighed heavily on his mind. So she sat on the edge of the sofa and waited for the bad news that she expected to come.

She hated this. Why couldn't he have just done this at the bar?

Adam stood in front of her. "Do you know why I wanted to talk in private?"

Yeah, he was going to dump her as a client. She figured it was bound to happen sooner or later. But did it have to be right after he kissed her? That was why he was doing it, but still…she didn't want to lose him. "I do. But it's not necessary. The kiss didn't mean anything."

He paused. "I disagree. In fact, in the last hour, everything changed for me. For the better, I might add. But I had to make some hard decisions first."

Wow. That was remarkably insulting. Her being out of his life was for the better? Really? Preslee shot to her feet and scowled at him. "Well, I'm sorry I ever took up any of your time, Adam. Trust me, it won't happen again," she said, heading toward the door.

He marched after her and grasped her arm gently before she could make it to the door. "Hey, why are you acting like this?"

"Me? Are you kidding? You're refusing to train me anymore, all because you kissed me and didn't like it."

His eyes widened. "What are you talking about?"

"I'm talking about you and the enormous jerk you're being right now," she blurted out, blinking back the tears stinging the back of her eyes. "I didn't ask you to kiss me, you know."

"You didn't have to. I wanted to kiss you. Still do, in fact."

"Yeah, well you shouldn't have done it if you—" Preslee froze in place and blinked at him. "Wait. What did you say?"

He smiled. "I want to kiss you again."

She shook her head, still not quite understanding what he meant. "Uh, I don't get it. Why would you want to kiss me again?"

"Because I liked kissing you the first time."

Her mind scrambled to catch up. "Then why are you not wanting to train me anymore?"

He chuckled. "I don't know where you got that idea. I never said anything like that. I think you somehow concocted that in your head."

Thinking back, Preslee realized he was right. He hadn't actually said those words. She'd just assumed that was what he was going to say. "Sorry. I jumped to conclusions when you said you wanted to talk to me in private. In my head, I went straight to the worst-case scenario."

"I see." Adam moved closer. "But that isn't what I want."

The way he was looking at her was somehow different than before, and the intensity behind it was making her nervous. "Um, then what do you want?"

"This," he said, leaning toward her slowly as if he was giving her time to move away from him. When she didn't, his lips lightly brushed against hers. "And this," he added, running his tongue along the seam of her lips before pulling back once more. "And a lot more of this," he whispered, wrapping his hand around the nape of her neck and pulling her mouth back to his in a devastating kiss.

One she felt all the way to her toes.

The man kissed with so much unrelenting passion that it stemmed the flow of blood from her heart to her limbs. Her knees buckled, and she drooped in his arms, marveling at his strength as he held her upright. Fire licked beneath her skin, and her body softened against his like warm butter.

But she managed to place one shaky hand on his chest and give him a little push. "Adam," she whispered, the warning unmistakable in her tone. "I don't think we should do this." Huh? What the hell was she doing?

He rested his forehead against hers and sighed. "Maybe not. But it feels so damn..."

"Yeah," she agreed, licking her lips and blowing out a hard breath. "I know."

"Then why stop?"

He was adorable and tempting as hell, and she couldn't help

but be susceptible to his charm. "Because I don't think it's smart to continue." *Who cares? Do it anyway.*

"Why? Didn't you like it?"

She wasn't going to lie to him. Or herself any longer. "Yes. I did. More than you know. But you're my trainer, Adam. You know it's not a good idea. It's safer to stop now before one of us regrets anything tomorrow." Wouldn't be her, though, that was for sure.

He frowned but nodded. "Okay, if that's what you want."

Preslee sighed. Well, that had gone over well. On his part anyway. For her, it wouldn't have taken much for him to convince her to kiss him again. But she was right about what she said, even if she didn't want to be. Man, being an adult really sucked at times. But now that she had Adam in her life, she would do anything to keep him there. Including avoiding anything romantic with him.

Adam took a step back, giving her some space. "Tell me something. Why did you assume that I was going to stop training you?"

"I don't know. Like I said, I just thought you were bailing on me."

"Yeah, but why?" he asked, his eyes wary. "It seems odd that you would think that about me. Is that what you're used to—men dropping you for no good reason?"

She shrugged. "It wouldn't be the first time someone left me."

"Ex-boyfriends?"

"Every one of them," she agreed. "It's the story of my life. When I was younger, I even lost my childhood best friend. She moved across the country. Although it was her parents' decision and not her fault, it still hurt a lot."

He gazed at her for a moment and then said, "But that's not all, right? There's someone else who left."

"Well, yeah. But I already told you about my mom dying when I was six." Just mentioning it had sadness spiraling through her.

He nodded. "I know, but that's different. It's not the same as someone leaving. She didn't have a choice, and you can't really blame her for that either."

"I know."

He gave her a *yeah, right* look.

"Okay, fine. Deep down I know that. Or rather the adult in me knows. But to the six-year-old inside of me, it still feels a little like she left. Not on purpose, but that doesn't make her any less gone."

His eyes softened. "I'm sorry."

"It's okay. I know my mom would've stayed with me if she'd had a choice, unlike..." Her words trailed off.

Adam raised a brow. "Unlike who?"

Of course he latched on to that. Figured. "No one."

"Who else left you? You're leaving someone out."

She hesitated. "Well, my dog ran away from home when I was younger," she said, laughing uneasily.

A muscle ticked in his jaw. "Come on, Preslee. I'm being serious."

"Me too. My dog really ran away from home."

"But that's not what you were talking about. Someone didn't want to stick around. Who was the person who had a choice and left anyway?" He gazed at her intently. "Who hurt you so badly?"

Horror spiked through her, and she bit into her lip to keep it from trembling. "No one."

"Was it a man?"

She shook her head and lowered it as anger and sadness mingled inside her. "I told you. It's no one."

"Then why won't you look me in the eyes?"

Preslee lifted her gaze to meet his and blinked back a tear. "There. Are you happy now? Let it go, Adam."

He sighed. "Why won't you tell me? Maybe I can help."

"I don't want to talk about it. I just want to forget the whole thing." She motioned toward the door. "Why don't we just go back to the bar?" She turned away from him to face the front door as she contemplated bolting through it. "I told you I don't want to talk about this. Just leave it alone already. Please."

"Sweetheart, this is something that clearly still bothers you. Let me help. Tell me who hurt you."

Rage coursed through her, and she whirled on him with her hands clenched into tight fists. "My biological mother, okay?" she said, straining to speak the truth as tears filled her eyes and blurred her vision. "Are you happy now? Is that what you wanted to hear?"

Adam stood there motionless, not saying a word, as he stared at her with big, sorrow-filled eyes.

Irritation welled up inside of her. "Don't you dare stop now. Ask me why. You want to know, right?" Her heart thundered in her chest, and she took a deep, shuddering breath. "You want to hear all about how I went looking for my biological mother, expecting one of those emotional reunions that you see on TV, yet that isn't at all what I got. Instead, I found the exact opposite."

"I'm sorry, honey." He tried to grasp her hand, but she moved out of his reach.

She wouldn't be able to hold herself together if he touched

her right now. "I'd always pictured my biological mom as someone who put me up for adoption because she wanted a better life for me, one she wouldn't have been able to provide. As if maybe it was a teenage pregnancy situation or something like that. I could've forgiven her for that. But what I found instead was a drugged-out woman who had..." She choked back a sob welling in her throat.

After a moment, Adam's low voice sounded. "Go on."

She took a deep breath and let out the truth. "Twenty years before, this woman had traded her own newborn baby girl to a drug dealer just to get her next fix."

The shocking words took him by surprise, and his eyes widened. "God," Adam said, rubbing the back of his neck. "I'm sorry."

"Don't be. I was one of the lucky ones. If the person she had traded me to hadn't been an undercover investigator running a drug sting operation, who knows what would've happened to me. Not that she would've cared. They put me in foster care, and my biological mother signed away her rights to me while still in jail. Because, in her own words, she had never wanted me, and I had been nothing more than a burden to her." Her voice cracked.

Fire shot through Adam's eyes. "That's unforgivable."

She nodded. "After telling me all of that, this woman then had the nerve to look me in the eye and ask if there was anything else she could help me with. As if she had done me a favor." She breathed out a heavy sigh. "The only thing I could say was no...because she hadn't really helped me to begin with. Then she dared to ask me if I had any money on me, as if I needed to pay her for her time."

"You didn't deserve that, sweetheart."

"I know I didn't. But on the drive home, I realized something. She *had* actually helped me, after all. Twice in my life, to be exact. When I was a baby, she had given me up by signing away her rights, which allowed me to be adopted by the best parents anyone could ever ask for. And twenty years later, this same woman told me the truth about how I ended up in foster care when she didn't have to." Her voice softened. "For those two things, I'll always be grateful."

He stared at her slack-jawed. "You're a much kinder person than I am, Preslee. The way you look at things amazes me at times. I don't know that I could be that forgiving."

"It's not easy. I wanted to hate her."

"With good reason," he said, nodding. "But I bet your dad was proud of how you handled that situation."

More tears filled her eyes, and regret coursed through her. Damn it. She didn't want Adam to see her looking so weak and defeated. In the past, he'd always brought out her strong side. She didn't like feeling vulnerable in front of him. "I . . . didn't tell my dad. He doesn't even know that I found my bio mom."

Confusion lit his eyes. "How come?"

She shrugged. "I was afraid that he would think that he wasn't enough of a parent for me and that it was the reason I went looking for my biological mother in the first place. None of which is true. So I kept quiet."

A frown crossed Adam's face. "That's not healthy, honey."

"Yeah, tell me about it."

"Why did you go looking for your biological mother?"

Preslee hesitated. "Because I wanted to know that she cared. That I mattered to her. To someone. But it was a lost cause. She never cared about me. Not when she left me in the arms of a supposed drug dealer who happened to be an undercover cop, not when she left me in foster care, and not when I was sitting in a diner eight years ago watching her walk away from me for the last time. The woman just didn't give a damn."

"Now something inside of you thinks everyone is going to leave. Like she did. And you blame yourself for that. Because why would anyone want you when your own biological mother didn't even want you. Am I right?"

Her head snapped to him, her voice trembling. "What? No."

"Yes," he said, nodding slowly as if he was waiting for it to sink in. "That's what you think. But it's not true, Preslee. It's not your fault that she left."

"I never said it was."

"You didn't have to. But that is what you believe."

Preslee held up a hand. "Okay, slow your roll, Dr. Phil. Stop trying to psychoanalyze me."

"Why are you denying it?"

"Because it's not true."

His eyes gleamed. "Bullshit. That's why you stopped kissing me too. You're afraid."

"Of what. A kiss?" Preslee rolled her eyes. "Get real."

Adam lifted one brow. "No. But you're afraid of something. What is it?"

She hesitated and licked her lips nervously as she glanced away. "Nothing. I just...don't know."

"Yeah, you do. Tell me what's scaring you." He surveyed her, confusion flashing in his eyes. But he must've seen the fear in her shaking body because he grasped her chin gently and turned her face fully up to his in order to look into her eyes. "Are you afraid that I'll leave, Preslee? Tell me the truth."

Overwhelmed, she didn't speak. She couldn't. Because he had hit the nail on the head, and the truth was cutting through her like a sharp blade. Her heart seized up inside her chest as tears began to leak onto her cheeks, but she didn't speak.

"I'm right, aren't I? You think that if we get involved, I'll eventually leave. Like your mother did."

She sniffed, swiping a tear from her cheek. "Like everyone does."

His eyes filled with sympathy, which was exactly why she didn't want to admit it to begin with. But then he smiled warmly, his eyes intense on hers. "I need you to understand something, Preslee. I'm not like everyone else."

"Don't say it. Don't say something you don't mean."

He smiled. "I'm not going anywhere. Ever."

CHAPTER SIXTEEN

Adam wasn't going to let this go. It was too important. Preslee needed to believe that not everyone would leave her, and he was happy to be the one to deliver the message. Loud and clear. "Do you understand me, Preslee? I want you."

She blinked her glassy blue eyes. "What do you mean?" she asked hesitantly, her voice low.

"You heard me. I. Want. You."

She shook her head in disbelief or possibly denial. "You mean as friends."

"No, I'm talking about these feelings I have for you." He breathed out a heavy sigh. "Look, I've tried to ignore them because you're my client. But it's impossible to do anymore. Damn it, I'm too far gone."

He kissed her temple, breathing in the sweet scent of her hair, before nibbling on her earlobe. One hand tangled into her soft hair and tugged gently, guiding her to tilt her head back as he slowly licked his way down her jawline, seeking her lush mouth. When he found it, her full lips were already parted, and he made a shallow sweep inside with his tongue. She immediately returned the gesture, and her fingernails scraped the back of his neck.

He was tempted to linger at her mouth but forced himself to pull back and look at her. Tension charged the atmosphere. The sweet innocence of her pretty face veiled her thoughts, but those glassy blue eyes gleamed with something wild as her pupils dilated. He ran the tip of his thumb over her bottom lip and swallowed hard. Man, he needed to know what she was thinking right now. Needed to know if she wanted him as much as he wanted her.

Adam opened his mouth to ask just that, but nothing came out. Silence sat between them like a disgruntled chaperone. What the hell? It was like his head was suddenly underwater, and he couldn't breathe. He tried again. "Preslee, I..."

But the barest hint of a smile flirted with her mouth, and the words died on his lips. He couldn't really ask her to sleep with him, could he? He didn't think he'd ever wanted a woman this much in his life. And probably never would again.

Just ask her already.

All right. He could do this. Adam ran a shaky hand through his hair and then blew out a long, slow breath.

Here goes nothing. "Preslee, I... would like to, um... do you."

Her eyes widened.

Oh dear God. Realizing what he said, Adam shook his head furiously. "No, that's not what I meant. What I'm trying to say is that I want you to do me."

Her mouth hinged open, and she blinked at him rapidly.

Nope. Not better.

So he spit out, "I mean, we'll do each other."

Holy shit. Stop fucking talking already.

Had he really just said that to her? How the hell did he mess that up? Out of all the things he could've chosen to say . . .

I want you in my bed.

Will you spend the night with me?

Please stay.

I want to make love to you.

Cringing, he glanced at her face to see her staring at him fixedly as one would a tragic car accident. One part morbid curiosity and one part sympathy for all parties involved.

He rubbed a large hand over his face and swore. "I'm sorry. That came out all wrong. Forget everything I just said. I didn't mean any of it."

An amused grin spread across her face until it reached her eyes. "So you don't want to *do me*? Or me to do you? Or us to do each other?"

His eyes riveted to hers as her smile morphed into a smirk. "Are you enjoying making fun of me?"

"Yes, I am," she said playfully, her tongue darting out to wet her lips. "But I was having a lot more fun before you so graciously offered to *do me*."

He winced. "Sorry. Like I said, that came out horribly wrong."

"Does the offer still stand?"

He chuckled. "Which one? I gave you three."

"Any of them. Maybe all of them. I do like to keep my options open," she said with a giggle. "In fact, I think maybe I'd like to try the 'me doing you' one first, if you don't mind."

He blinked. Did she mean . . .

He barely had time to brace himself for impact before Preslee threw herself at him. Literally and figuratively speaking. She pulled him close, and her mouth crashed against his. She kissed him with so much passion and fire and demand that he could barely catch his breath. When warm, feminine hands found their way under his Henley and onto his bare abs, his whole body went rigid.

She lifted his shirt over his head as he ducked to help her slide it off. The cool air from the air-conditioning chilled his torso, but it didn't matter. At the moment, he was hotter than he'd ever been. But was she as affected as he was right now?

A random thought crossed his mind, and he shook his head adamantly. *No. Don't do it. Don't you dare ask...* "Are you wet for me?" he asked, his throaty voice sounding as if he'd chewed glass and then swallowed it.

Her long, dark eyelashes fluttered around those beautiful baby blues of hers, and her tongue darted out to lick her bottom lip. "Why don't you find out for yourself?"

Oh, praise the Lord.

He yanked her into his bare chest. His erection pressed errantly into her stomach as his mouth took hers, his lips moving over hers at a frenzied pace. He shuffled her backward down the hallway toward his bedroom and didn't stop moving until the back of her knees bumped into his bed. Then his hands reached for the hem of her shirt.

Preslee stiffened and placed her hands over his. "Uh, maybe we should...slow down a little."

Huh. Okay. He hadn't seen that coming. "All right," he agreed easily, taking a step back. His hands itched to touch her again, but he kept them firmly planted at his sides. "Is something wrong?"

"No."

He focused intently on her, staring deep into her eyes. "Preslee, if I did anything to make you feel uncomfortable..."

"No, it's not that," she said, shaking her head furiously. "You didn't do anything wrong, I swear. It's just...me."

The expression on her face was unreadable, and he couldn't gauge her current state of mind. But something had caused her to suddenly put a halt to things, and he wasn't entirely sure what it was. That only worried him more. "It's okay if you changed your mind. If you don't want to—"

"No, that's not it. I *do* want to, but I...well, I'm just worried that I..." She winced at the words that wouldn't come as red heat slashed across her cheeks. "I'm not a thin woman, okay?"

His brow lifted. "You're kidding, right?"

She glared at him and pursed her lips.

"Wait. I think you misunderstood what I'm trying to say."

"Really? Because I think it came across perfectly clear." She lowered her head, her gaze shifting to the floor.

He stepped toward her and slid one finger under her chin, lifting her face back to his. He smiled gently. "Do you really think I care about your weight?"

"Yes."

"Then you're wrong."

"Am I?" Preslee asked, clearly not convinced. "I mean, look at you." Her eyes raked over his bare chest and then flickered back to his face. "You probably don't have a clue what it feels like to be uncomfortable in your own skin."

"How do you figure?"

"You own a gym, Adam. Not only do you like to stay in shape, but you train others to do the same."

"Do you want to know why I started working out? Because I was one of those scrawny kids who got picked on growing up."

Her eyes widened, and her mouth hinged open slightly. "You were?"

"Every day. At school, after school, at the park. Basically everywhere I went. I was a magnet for bullies who wanted someone much smaller to push around."

She shook her head. "I...I'm sorry. I wish things like that didn't happen in this world. It's unfortunate that they do." She bit her lip. "So that's how you got into weight lifting?"

"Pretty much. I met Kurt not long after that. He wasn't into the lifting as much as I was, but he liked to work out to stay in shape. Over time, we became best friends." Adam smiled. "It took a while, but through training, I was able to go from being the littlest guy in the room to being the biggest."

"Really?"

He shrugged. "I haven't had a single bully try anything with me since. Now I stay fit just because I like the way it feels. But that doesn't have anything to do with us. I only mentioned it because you said I don't know what it feels like to be uncomfortable in my own skin. Trust me, I do."

She sighed. "Come on, Adam. You know what I'm saying. Why would you want to be with someone who looks like me when there are plenty of thinner women who would jump at the chance to be with someone who looks like you?"

Anger swept through him. "Okay, now you're pissing me off. Since when did you become such a hypocrite?"

Her eyes widened. "What? I'm not a hypocrite."

"Oh yeah? You're sitting here worried that I'm judging you for the way you look, yet you're doing that exact thing to me.

It's a double standard, Preslee. Yeah, I own a gym and enjoy working out. But that has no bearing on who I'm with or what they look like. I'm not even sure why you think it should."

She shook her head. "It's not that I think it should. I'm just saying that it does happen. A lot."

"Maybe so. But a woman shouldn't want to be with me just for the way I look any more than I should want to be with her for the way she looks."

She nodded. "I'm sorry. You're right about it being a double standard. And I get what you're saying about being with someone just for the way they look. But isn't that how physical attraction works? You can't tell me that you would want to be with someone who you're not remotely attracted to. Because if so, I call bullshit on that."

He nodded. "Of course there should be physical attraction. But what I'm saying is that no one is going to tell me what I should want in a woman or dictate who I'm allowed to be attracted to. Not society. Not my family or friends. And not you either."

She shook her head. "I'm not telling you who you're allowed to be attracted to."

"Oh yeah? Then why is it so hard for you to believe that I'm attracted to you?"

Preslee hesitated. "You can be mildly attracted to someone and want to sleep with them for one night. Especially when it's convenient. That's not unheard of, you know?"

"Yeah, well, neither is a guy who appreciates curves on a woman. You may not believe this, but some men actually prefer women with some meat on their bones. They get turned on by soft curves, love handles, or even a well-rounded booty. Maybe not all guys have that mentality, but I do. No one has to fit into a certain mold for me. I don't want a woman with a perfect body. I just want a woman who is perfect for *me*."

She rolled her eyes. "Says the guy who dates models."

Adam grinned. "It was only one model, thank you very much. But I didn't go out with her because of that. I dated her because we both shared an interest in old movies, Preslee."

She stared at him without blinking for a full thirty seconds. Apparently, he'd shocked her into silence. Good. Served her right.

While he still had the floor, he added, "And just for the record, not all women like muscled-up guys either. There are plenty of women who have refused to date me for that alone. So it's not always as one-sided as you might think."

That comment must've snapped her out of her trance. "Maybe so. But I have a feeling you probably don't run into that wall as much as I do when it comes to men who don't want to date a woman who weighs more than them."

He shrugged. "Possibly. But I bet I run into more plus-size women who aren't willing to even give me the time of day or take me seriously because they assume that I won't find them attractive. All because of the way they look. So I somehow get lumped in with the assholes who judge people just because of the way *I* look."

She stared at him for another good ten seconds before speaking. "You know, I didn't even consider that, Adam. It's actually a really good point."

"Well, do you want to know the most frustrating thing about it all? I've probably missed out on some pretty great women, all because of the hang-ups society has pushed onto them. And they might've missed out on a pretty decent guy who would've been happy to show them that they were worth way more than their number on a scale. Not that I'm trying to toot my own horn or anything." He shrugged. "If owning a gym has taught me anything, it's that people come in all shapes and sizes, none of which determine their worth as a human being."

She grinned. "I think it's fair to say that you just earned the right to toot your own horn. I like how self-aware you are. I wish more guys were like you." She hesitated and gazed up at him. "I'm sorry for what I said earlier. You were right. It was hypocritical of me, and it wasn't fair of me to make assumptions about you."

"It's all right," he said with a nod. "Let's just forget about the stupid assumptions that society has taught us all to make and move on. Besides, I have something else I'd like to clear up between us right now."

"Oh. Okay," she said, concern tightening her voice.

"I want you to answer one question." He grasped her hand and placed it directly on his rock-hard cock. "Does this at all feel like I'm only mildly attracted to you?"

She blushed and chewed on her bottom lip. "Um, no. Not really," she said, her mouth quirking. "But just for argument's sake, I might need to check it more closely. Ya know, in case there are any changes that I need to monitor."

Adam laughed. "Baby, you can check it all you want, but I guarantee you that thing isn't going down for quite a while."

"Such a pity." Her eyes glittered.

"Yeah, it would be a shame to have to go to the emergency room to have them do something about it so I don't hurt myself. You don't know how dangerous this can be. Something like this can get slammed in doors, caught on furniture, and even strangled with clothing."

She licked her lips. "Well, then you should probably do something about it. Maybe I can help you with that." She gave him a good, hard squeeze.

Lord have mercy.

Adam groaned under his breath. "I was hoping you'd say that." He leaned forward and pressed a gentle kiss to her neck. "Now where were we?"

"I think we were right about *here*," she said, yanking her top over her head and tossing it on his bedroom floor. A pink hue swept into her cheeks.

His heated gaze dropped to the swell of her nicely rounded breasts spilling over the cups of her black bra, and he ran one finger gently across one as his other hand moved to her waist, pulling her closer.

He knew what it had cost her to pull her shirt off in front of him. Even through the tight smile on her face, he could still see the fear in her eyes that she might possibly be rejected for the way she looked. Which was silly since there wasn't a damn thing wrong with the way the woman looked. She was beautiful, and he couldn't get enough of her gorgeous body.

To punctuate that, he told her, "You're fucking perfect the way you are. Don't ever let anyone tell you otherwise."

She smiled and pulled his face down to hers to kiss him. Her lips brushed over his timidly, but he pulled her closer and deepened the kiss. He didn't want her timid. He wanted her filled with confidence. No more with the narrow, specific idea of beauty she had. He wanted to show her how beautiful and desirable she really was. He wanted to celebrate her body and show her that it was something to be proud of...even if it wasn't perfect in her eyes.

It didn't matter. She was perfect...for him.

He reached behind her and, with a flick of his fingers, undid the clasp on her bra. The straps loosened marginally but the bra stayed mostly in place. His fingers slid slowly under the straps by her collarbone, and her body tensed.

He paused. "Is this okay?" he asked, wanting her to grant him permission to move forward. Just because she'd granted it once didn't mean a woman couldn't change her mind after the fact. He wasn't a guy who would take advantage of a situation. He needed to know she stood by her decision. Otherwise, it wasn't going to happen, and he'd return to his respective corner.

She bit her lip and gave him a barely perceptible nod.

He shook his head. "No, Preslee. I want you to be very clear about what you want. Say the words or this stops right here. I don't want there to be any regrets later. Nor do I ever want you to be uncomfortable with me. You don't have to do anything that makes you feel awkward. It's okay to say no. We don't have to do this. Not yet. We can take things slower. It's up to you."

"I want this. But just in case that isn't enough for you..." Preslee slid the bra off her arms and let it fall to the floor. "How about now? Is this clear enough for you, Adam?"

Holy hell. His heart thumped in his chest. Hard.

"Um, yeah. Loud and clear," he said, swallowing hard. He tried to be gentlemanly enough not to stare directly at her full, nicely rounded breasts tipped with tight pink nipples. Ones he badly wanted to pinch just so he could hear her gasp. "So beautiful," he told her, his breath coming faster.

"I want this," she said, her voice not wavering in the slightest. "I want to spend tonight with you."

"Thank God," he ground out. "That would've been the longest, coldest shower of my life."

She smiled up at him. "Same here."

"Well, before this goes any further, there's one more thing I need to clear up between us."

Her brow rose. "Anyone ever tell you that you talk too much?"

He grinned. "Last thing, I promise."

"Okay."

Adam stepped into her and ratcheted her up into his arms. Her soft bare breasts flattened against his hard chest, and his mouth hovered a breath away from hers. "I never said anything about this being only for one night."

CHAPTER SEVENTEEN

Preslee swallowed hard, unable to speak.

Not because Adam was touching her in any blatantly sexual way. It was because of what he'd just said. This wasn't a one-night stand for him.

He clasped a lock of her auburn hair between two fingers and smoothed his thumb over it. This close, she could feel the heat of his body and smell the spicy aroma of his cologne and clean scent of his skin. It stole her breath.

Adam gently drew her toward him and covered her mouth with his. Weakened by lust, she just stood there while he kissed her. Her breasts tightened against him, and her stomach pinged with excitement. She had fantasized about Adam's hands and mouth on her many times, but this was way better than she'd imagined.

But when his fingers moved down to unbutton her jeans, Preslee sucked her stomach in, and her body went rigid. Adam hadn't done anything. But that one little move of his had triggered a reaction, an involuntary one that she thought she'd surely gotten past after removing her shirt and her bra.

Apparently she hadn't. Scaredy-cat.

Adam stilled. "Preslee, are you sure you want this? We can wait. There's no rush. I want you to feel comfortable with me."

That was the thing. She *did* feel comfortable with him. But it was hard to let go of these hang-ups she had about her body. After all, she'd had them most of her life. But she wasn't going to wimp out now. She knew this irrational fear was only in her head. He'd done nothing to cause it. "No, it's fine. I don't want to stop."

In a reassuring gesture, he brought her hand up to his mouth and kissed her palm. "Are you really sure? I don't want you to regret this tomorrow."

Preslee nodded. She would be much better off making peace with her body now than fighting insecurities for the rest of her life. The only way to do that was to make a conscientious effort to get past her physical imperfections. Everyone had some, didn't they?

"I won't, Adam. Besides, if I was going to have regrets tomorrow, I'd much rather it be for something I did instead of something I didn't do."

His cheeks creased with a slow grin. He reached once again for the button on her jeans, moving slowly as if he were sneaking up on it. His knuckles brushed against her stomach as he managed to get the button undone and her pants unzipped. Then he kissed her neck as his thumbs slid inside her waistband on both sides and shoved her tight jeans down over her hips. Once they made it to her knees, Preslee used her own legs to work them the rest of the way down. When they fell to her ankles, she stepped out of them and kicked them aside.

Adam wrapped an arm around her and lowered them both to the bed, where he took one distended nipple between his firm lips and sucked hard. Electricity shot through her, and she arched in response, shoving the rigid bud farther into his hot mouth. Then his tongue swiped over to the other one to pay his respects.

His fingertips brushed against the underside of her breasts as he licked his way down her stomach to the waistband of her panties. "Lift," he told her, yanking her panties down as she did and tossing them in the same direction as her jeans had landed. When he tried to spread her legs, she tensed and gave resistance. "Open them," he said. "Please don't hold back."

Mentally chastising herself, Preslee blew out a nervous breath and allowed his large hands to part her legs. The intimacy of the position made her cringe inwardly, but it also sent erotic sensations cascading through her. She glanced down at him, and he gave her a sexy little smile before his tongue darted out to taste her. Her head fell back with a deep moan.

Adam settled in between her legs, taking his time to slowly kiss, lick, and suck on every inch of her flesh before his mouth finally covered her. His tongue concentrated solely on that little bundle of nerves that had her squirming from his ministrations. He hummed against her appreciatively as he relished in torturing her until she was writhing against him.

A buzzing started in her ears and traveled south, causing her blood to fizz in her veins. Her skin ached from the sensitivity as her muscles quivered with anticipation. All until that one exquisite moment when the world as she knew it exploded and ceased to exist any longer.

She cried out, lost in a maelstrom of emotions and sensations.

Her brain scrambled, and something warm unfurled in her stomach, spreading outward to each of her other limbs. Steady waves of pleasure washed over her, each cresting before the next wave hit. It was the longest and slowest and most powerful orgasm she'd ever had, unraveling little by little, all the while drawing heat from her center.

Adam rose and pinned her with a very male gaze as he licked his lips. "So sweet and delicious."

Heat filled her cheeks. How was a woman supposed to respond to a guy saying something like that to her?

Thank you?

Okay?

You're right. I should be on a dessert menu?

Fortunately, she didn't have time to reply to his comment before he started stripping off his pants. They hit the floor, and he rose to his full height. God, the man was built. And she wasn't just referring to the wide span of his broad chest or those spectacular abs of his.

Adam climbed up the bed until he was between her knees and leaning over her with his elbows holding him up. He gave her a wolfish grin. "Did that take the edge off a little?"

A little? That had been enough to keep her satisfied for the rest of her life. "Mmm-hmm," she murmured, not sure if she was even able to speak anymore.

"Good. So now we need to talk about something else. You aren't allergic to latex, are you?"

She froze and blinked at him repeatedly. Why the hell would he be asking her something like that? Oh man. If he pulled out a latex glove because he was into some weird kink or fetish, she was outta there. "Uh, no."

He nodded. "Okay, good. Then a latex condom is all right with you?"

Oh. So not a strange kink then. Whew. Thank goodness. "Yes," she replied, fighting back a giggle. "But just so you know, I'm on the pill."

He groaned and leaned his forehead into hers, hesitating. "It's your call, sweetheart. I get tested every year and haven't been with anyone since my last test. But I don't expect you to take my word for it."

"Why not? You're taking my word for it that I'm on the pill, aren't you?"

"I trust you, Preslee. I don't think you'd lie about something like that."

"Nor do I think you would. You trust me, and I trust you. So we're covered. If you want to forgo the condom, I'm okay with—"

She barely had time to brace herself for the onslaught of Adam's thrust, and the words died on her lips. Her mouth went instantly dry as she sucked in a resounding breath, a gasp that she was pretty sure woke up people sleeping in the next county over.

Adam released a groan so guttural that it vibrated into her chest and sent sparks shooting through every nerve. He was as hard as steel inside her where they were intrinsically linked, and just that one initial thrust promised so much power and stamina that her nipples pebbled at the thought.

He began moving, gaining speed and strength as he went, and her entire world narrowed to only him. Clutching his shoulders, Preslee absorbed his eager thrusts and tried her best to keep her eyes from rolling into the back of her head. But the man was a machine, and the sensations he was inflicting sent chills through her yet made her feel like she was running a high fever. His mouth found hers, and their lips molded together.

Lost in the kiss, Preslee responded to his mouth on hers by rubbing against him more fully. Like she was a cat trying to wind her body around his. And she probably purred as well. Because the things he was doing to her were...

Oh, sweet heaven.

Adam stifled a groan.

The low moans and occasional sighs slipping through her parted lips weren't helping him quell his need to come. But he was determined to give her the best climax of her life before doing so. No matter what.

Yet when a soft smile curved her pretty pink lips, a yearning that he'd never felt before flared to life in his gut. Desire ripped through him, and need coiled tight at the base of his spine.

He took a deep breath. But her sweet scent lingered in the air around him, filling his nostrils. The woman smelled like coconuts, pineapple, and...pure heaven. And she tasted just as delicious.

Adam trailed kisses down her lovely neck and buried his nose into the hollow at the base of her throat. His ears rang from the pressure building inside of him, and his heart pounded furiously.

By the time Preslee cried out, Adam was trembling from head to toe due to the strenuous effort of holding himself back. But when her body tightened around him, he closed his eyes and let go. Pushing inside of her one last time, he allowed his orgasm to chase after hers by mere seconds.

He held himself over her as he stared at the beautiful woman beneath him. Flushed cheeks. Full lips. And a heavy-lidded gaze that met his and unraveled something deep inside of him.

Adam considered himself a strong individual—physically and mentally. But Preslee was his one, true weakness, the only thing he really wanted to overindulge in. Yet she still gazed up at him with an unsure expression that melted his heart.

He didn't need an excuse to kiss her again, but it was a good one, if he did say so himself. Because the woman just didn't get it. She still didn't understand what she meant to him. Although they were different, they fit together perfectly. And he meant how they fit so easily into each other's lives.

Although it hadn't been all that long ago, he couldn't even remember a time when Preslee hadn't been in his. And he didn't want to. She was everything good in this world, and he had fallen hard for the stunning woman. It all happened so fast, but he loved Preslee and would do everything in his power to help her achieve every single one of her goals in life.

Then he remembered about Josh.

Huh. Well, maybe not *all* of them.

CHAPTER EIGHTEEN

Early the next morning, Preslee awoke to a wandering hand traveling slowly up her bare back. She didn't need to open her eyes to know who it belonged to. After last night, she'd recognize Adam's touch anywhere.

Still groggy, she lay on her left side, facing away from him, with a soft sheet tucked under her arm and pulled up over her breasts. A slight chill lingered in the darkened room, but the heat of his large muscular body had kept her warm throughout the night.

She had hoped to get up before him so that she could do the walk of shame before he had awoken. But apparently that wasn't going to happen now. Not that it really mattered. She didn't feel any amount of shame for what happened between them last night.

Oh, she was certain they were about to have a very awkward morning-after conversation. But right now, she was still too relaxed and content to move. So she didn't. Instead, she lay there enjoying the sensations of his light touch as his broad hand traveled over her spine.

Adam shifted closer, his ripped body slanting more firmly into hers as he propped himself up with an elbow and hovered over her right shoulder. His erection pressed strongly into the back of her thigh as the scent of soap and eager male encompassed her. They'd taken a hot shower together the last time he'd awoken her before falling back into bed and dozing.

Long fingers threaded into her hair, gently moving it off her neck and out of his way. Then he pressed a hot, open-mouthed kiss to her shoulder before sucking and nibbling his way up to her throat. The intimate gesture sent an electrical current of desire surging through her, and her body stirred to life, a soft moan sliding past her lips. If he hadn't known she was awake before, he definitely did now.

She arched back against him to provide better access to her throat since he was still behind her. But her neck apparently wasn't what he wanted anymore. A broad hand slid up the front of her body and grasped on to her chin, tilting her face up to his. Then his mouth took hers.

While his hands were gentle, the kiss was anything but. His mouth moved over hers with an urgency that took her breath away. As if he had a dire thirst that needed to be quenched. Or a desperate hunger that needed to be fed.

Her heart fluttered. Never had she been woken up in such a delightfully sexy way before. She looked up at him as he continued to lean over her. "Good morning," she said, beaming a smile at him.

His heated eyes glimmered. "It's damn sure about to be."

Preslee didn't know exactly what that meant, but his low, guttural tone stirred something deep inside. So much so that she didn't even protest when Adam rolled her onto her back and yanked the sheet off her naked body. So much for having an awkward morning-after conversation. Adam apparently wasn't planning on doing much talking.

Fine by her.

Cold air caressed her nipples, hardening them instantly. His gaze lingered on them briefly, as if he contemplated reaching for them. But instead, he positioned himself between her thighs and smiled with wicked intent.

Resisting the urge to cover herself, she swallowed hard and met his gaze with a confidence that she hadn't had before. She'd been growing more and more comfortable with showing him her body. Hell, he'd already seen and touched all of her anyway. Three times during the night, in fact.

Adam lowered himself and let her support some of his weight before levering himself back up and resting his forearms on both sides of her head. Then he sank into her with such slow precision that her eyes nearly crossed. When he filled her completely, she dug her nails into his back and blew out a sharp breath.

Then he began to move.

Exquisite pleasure washed over her as he rocked gently into her, awakening nerve endings that she didn't even know she had. It was as if his magnificent body was attuned to hers in every way imaginable.

Her breath bottomed out. It was too much and not nearly enough, all at the same time. She teetered on the brink of orgasm for way longer than she thought humanly possible before she noticed the determined look in Adam's eyes.

He was purposely delaying his own gratification until she came. He apparently planned to wring every ounce of pleasure out of her that she could, because every time the intense bomb building inside of her got anywhere near detonation, he'd blow out the fuse and start the onslaught again.

"Adam."

"Yeah, baby?"

"Enough playing," she said, unable to keep the exasperation out of her tone. "I want to come."

He grinned. "You will. In due time."

She gasped at a particularly hard thrust that sent delightful butterflies winging through her. "No. Now. As in right now."

"Soon," he said.

A loud banging noise suddenly shook the nearby wall, and Adam's neighbor yelled out, "Hurry up, man. Y'all have kept me up all night. I'm trying to sleep here."

Preslee blushed and covered her mouth. "Oh God," she whispered. "He heard us last night."

Adam chuckled softly and shrugged. "He's probably just pissed because I have more stamina than him."

The rough voice penetrated the wall once more. "I heard that, asshole."

Preslee sighed.

Adam was breathing deeply, having just dropped off into sleep. The poor guy was exhausted from an entire night of hot sex. Like really hot sex. So hot, in fact, that she was surprised the neighbor hadn't called the fire department to come out and put out the flames.

Shamelessly, she smiled. With Adam asleep, she had a clear escape route and could've gotten up and left. But after their little tryst this morning, she didn't want to. Instead, she wanted to lie in his strong arms with his warmth against her naked body. Because she loved the way he held her. Loved the way he touched her. She even loved...

Him? Oh no.

She had known she was falling for him, but she hadn't thought anything would actually come of it. That silly belief had comforted her into accidentally letting down her guard. Why had she done something so stupid?

Well, she guessed it was too late to do anything about it now. Besides, she was no longer falling. She'd already hit rock bottom, and her heart had burst wide open upon landing. This was so not good.

A person wasn't supposed to fall for their personal trainer any more than they were supposed to fall in love with their doctor. Not that Adam had anything to worry about when it came to Dr. Fowler. Or his brother, for that matter. But these things were against the rules. Well, *her* rules anyway.

Mixing business and pleasure wasn't easy to do, and that kind of complicated relationship should always be kept on sacred ground. Otherwise, it could negatively affect a working relationship, as well as a friendship.

She probably should've stuck to her guns last night and never let this happen. But it was too late. She couldn't go back and change anything now. Not that she really wanted to. Maybe Adam didn't know it, but he had stripped her bare last night. Not just in the literal, physical sense. He had touched something deep inside of her, a depth no one had ever reached before.

Although Preslee wasn't sure exactly what that entailed, the two of them making love had signaled a shift between them.

Good or bad, she wasn't sure. There was a huge chance that, along with the light of day, a whole new set of challenges would arise that they would have to face. Starting with where they stood as trainer and client.

All she knew was that she couldn't lose him from her life. Not now. Not ever. She snuggled more fully into his side, her head lying just over his heart, listening to it beat. He stirred, and she felt the warmth of his hand on hers before he dozed off again.

God, this man. She wanted nothing more than to stay in this intimate, magical place the two of them had created for as long as she could.

CHAPTER NINETEEN

Adam pulled up beside Preslee's car, which was still sitting in the empty parking lot outside of Bottoms Up. The sky was a murky gray, and rainwater sluiced off the shiny metal of the car, falling in puddles on the ground. "Need an umbrella?"

She peered at her passenger-side window, which sheeted water from it. "No, that's okay. I'm not scared to get wet."

"Oh, baby, I know that already," he said, grinning. "But you still might not want to get rained on."

A pretty pink blush bloomed on her cheeks. "Stop it."

"Stop what?"

"Stop . . . looking at me like that."

He chuckled. "Like what?"

"Like you're ready to strip me down to nothing and have your way with me again."

He waggled his brows. "I like the way you think."

"Uh-uh." She pointed at him. "If you hadn't looked at me like that earlier, we would've been here before the rain started. But no. You insisted on me staying for breakfast."

He shrugged. "I was hungry."

"Well, you couldn't have been too hungry seeing how we ended up back in the bedroom before we finished cooking and didn't even eat anything."

"*You* didn't," he corrected. "I had my breakfast in bed, and believe me, I ate until I was completely satisfied. In fact, I believe we both were." He winked.

"Oh my God." She snorted. "I'm leaving. You know, before you break your arm trying to pat yourself on the back."

He grinned at her sarcastic remark. God, he loved that about her.

She started to open the door but hesitated. "Um, thanks for earlier though. It was really good."

His smile widened. "My pleasure."

He loved that about her too. Even though she was embarrassed beyond belief, she would still always state the truth no matter what. It was a refreshing quality that was hard to find in most people. Including him.

Guilt coursed through him. He still hadn't told her the truth about his bet with Kurt. While he hadn't exactly lied, he *had* sort of gone around the truth. As far as he was concerned, that was just as bad. He was pretty sure she would agree.

Adam didn't want to spend one more night without telling her the truth. All of it. Though he didn't like the idea of hurting her. But it wasn't like he had much of a choice. Unless...

Maybe if he put an end to the bet first, she wouldn't be as upset. It would be in the past, and he could prove to her that he didn't care about the bet. *She* was the important thing to him. He didn't give a damn that he would lose to Kurt by forfeit. In the end, as long as he had Preslee, he would come out a winner.

She rolled her neck. "My muscles are still a little sore from last night. We could head to the gym and get in a workout before I check on my dad."

"Actually, I have something I need to take care of right now, but we can meet up later. I need to talk to you about something anyway. It's important."

Her head snapped up, and something flashed in her eyes. Was that panic? Fear? "What is it?" she asked, her voice low.

Damn it. He shouldn't have said anything. Now he'd worried her for nothing. "I'd rather not get into it now. This is a conversation for when we have more time and neither of us has to be somewhere. Okay?"

She scowled. "Fine."

God. He was already screwing this up. He should've known she would assume the worst. "Preslee, trust me. I'll explain everything later. Until then, try not to jump to conclusions, okay?"

She paused thoughtfully. "All right. I'll try not to."

He smiled, hoping it would appease her fears. "Thanks for giving me the benefit of the doubt."

She nodded and moved to get out, but he snagged her arm, stopping her. She gazed back to see what he was doing, and he used that moment to pull her to him and plant a searing kiss on her. Her lips parted in surprise, and he slid his tongue between them, deepening the kiss.

But lightning cracked in the distance, bringing him back to his senses. If he didn't stop now, he would be taking her right there in the truck in the middle of a parking lot...and a rainstorm. Wouldn't be a bad way to spend the afternoon, but the last thing he needed was for them to get caught fornicating in public. That news would surely travel fast in a small town.

He slowed the kiss and pulled back to nibble on her bottom lip before setting her away from him. "You should probably go before we, uh..." His gaze shifted downward, and her eyes followed.

She smiled, apparently liking the reaction his body had to hers. "Okay. See you later."

"Definitely," he promised, glad that he'd managed to vanquish any fears she might have had about what he wanted to talk about later.

Preslee threw the door open and hurried to her car. It only took seconds to get her car door unlocked, but in that short amount of time, her hair and shirt became soaked through. Stubborn woman. She should've taken his umbrella. But she made it inside her car, started it, and waved as she pulled away.

Adam headed in the direction of the Body Shop as the rain dissipated. The gym had opened several hours before, and Kurt would already be there going over yesterday's paperwork. Adam had never backed out of a bet before so he wasn't sure how Kurt would react, but in the end, it didn't matter. Because he cared too much about Preslee to lose her over a ridiculous bet.

When he arrived, Kurt was busy spotting a guy on the bench press so Adam waited behind the counter. He looked over the paperwork Kurt had already finished and was pleased to see that their memberships had nearly doubled from what they were the previous month. Man, that was great.

Kurt appeared and gave him a wary look. "Why are you here this early?"

Adam checked his watch. "What do you mean early? It's already after noon."

"Yeah, but ever since you've been training Preslee, you haven't been coming in until later in the day. This is early... for you."

"I need to talk to you about something important."

Kurt leaned his hip against the counter and glared at him. "You're firing me?"

"What?" Adam shook his head. What was up with everyone jumping to conclusions? "No. Where did you get that idea?"

Kurt's arms relaxed. "From you, moron. You said you wanted to talk about something important. When a boss tells you that, it's because you're getting fired."

"Yeah, maybe. But employees don't usually call their bosses morons either. So clearly we're more than that. I told you our friendship would always come before our work relationship. I meant that."

A genuine smile tipped Kurt's lips. "Then what did you want to talk to me about?"

"The bet."

Kurt squinted. "The one about Preslee?"

"Yeah," Adam said, crossing his arms. "I want out."

Kurt didn't hesitate with a reply. "Okay."

Adam gazed at him, unsure as to why he was letting him off the hook so easily. That wasn't like Kurt. Was he pissed about it? "Look, you know I wouldn't normally forfeit a bet, but I just can't—"

Kurt held up his hand to stop him from talking, but his eyes darted away. "We're good. Don't worry."

Man, Kurt must really be upset if he wouldn't even look at him. Maybe he thought this was Adam's way of choosing Preslee over their friendship. It was a crazy notion. Adam wanted both of them in his life, and he needed Kurt to know that. "Just hear me out."

"You've said enough," Kurt said firmly, his eyes firing warning shots. "It's fine."

But Adam wasn't going to let it go. Not when his friendship was on the line. "No, it's *not* fine. Listen." Kurt shook his head, but Adam wasn't taking no for an answer. "Yes, damn it. Hear me out. I know we needed to draw new members into the gym, and we accomplished that, but we shouldn't have ever made that bet about Preslee and how much weight she could lose with me training her. It wasn't—"

A feminine gasp came from behind him, and Adam stopped cold, the sound chilling him to the bone. No. He recognized that voice.

Without another word, Adam spun to see Preslee standing there with wide eyes and an open mouth. She didn't speak. She didn't even blink. The only sound was the ominous thunder still rumbling in the distance.

Acid bubbled up in his throat as guilt and regret spiraled through him. Damn it. She'd heard what he said. He knew it sounded bad and had no doubt that she was going to be mad once the shock wore off. He only hoped he could explain everything before that happened.

Finally, her lips moved. "You...used me?"

He winced at the bitterness in her tone. His heart pounded in his chest, in time with the throbbing in his head. This was not going to end well. He held out a hand, and she shook her head. "I can explain."

She glowered at him but remained motionless. "What is there to explain? I got the full picture. You got me to agree to let you be my trainer, all so you could use me as some kind of...marketing tool for your gym?"

"It's not like that. There's more to it."

"Yeah, I know. I heard. As if using me wasn't bad enough, you and Kurt made a bet about it." She rubbed her face with both hands in disbelief. "Who the hell does stuff like that?"

Shame filled him, and he lowered his head. "I know it sounds bad. But it wasn't like that." He lifted his head. "I only wanted to bring in more customers and keep my business going."

Her eyes heated and shot flames at him. "By using me to do it. That's why you wanted to make those videos. Because the first one had gone viral."

"Yes, but I—"

"You bastard." Moisture filled her eyes. "Do you know how fucking humiliating that is?"

Pain and hurt flashed across her solemn face, and it made his stomach clench with regret. "Sweetheart, I'm sorry. You have nothing to be embarrassed about."

"Maybe not. But you two should be ashamed of yourselves," she said, pointing at both of them. She apparently wasn't letting Kurt off the hook either.

Adam nodded. "I *am* ashamed of myself. But I want you to understand something. We made the bet the night I met you. I didn't know you at the time. Kurt suggested that I train you and—"

She raised her hand. "Don't you dare do the blame game. You're a big boy, Adam. You agreed to the bet. That makes you just as guilty as Kurt."

He sighed. "I know. I wasn't blaming him. This is on me. I was just explaining how it happened."

"I've heard enough. I don't need to know all the dirty little details about your stupid bet. Besides, do you really think that not knowing someone makes it okay for you to bet on their weight loss or use them like you did me? Because it's not. Ever."

Remorse sat in his stomach like a lead weight while guilt trickled down his spine. "You're right. It's not okay. I'm sorry. I don't know what else to say to make this right."

A disgusted sound came from the back of her throat. "Nothing will make this right." Then she turned her look of disappointment onto Kurt and shook her head, showing how upset she was with him too. "And you. I thought we were friends."

Kurt flinched. "We are, Preslee. I'm sorry. I know you might not believe that right now, but I *am* your friend."

Adam stepped toward her. "Baby, listen. Please. We screwed up. I'm sorry I hurt you. It wasn't intentional, I swear."

"Really? Well, then answer this for me," she said, crossing her arms. "That day you came to the antique shop..." She paused for a moment as if rolling something around in her mind. "Did you use Josh as motivation to get me to say yes to training with you?"

Fuck. Adam closed his eyes. He couldn't lie to her. So he lifted his gaze. "Yes."

She clenched her fists. "*That* was intentional."

He cringed. "Yes."

"That's what I thought." Preslee shook her head. "You know what? It doesn't matter anymore."

"Don't say that," Adam replied, moving closer. God, he wanted to take her into his arms and make this all go away. "It matters. *You* matter...to me."

One teardrop fell onto her cheek and slid beneath her jaw. "Yeah, I'm guessing that's what you wanted me to believe last night when we slept together."

Kurt's surprised gaze darted to Adam, but he didn't say anything. He hadn't known they'd ended up in bed together. Well, he did now.

Preslee didn't seem to notice the look Kurt gave Adam. Either that or she didn't care. "I can't believe I fell for that. Sleeping with you was such a big mistake. One I'll never make again."

"Don't say that. You didn't fall for anything. Last night meant something to me."

"No, that was a charade. What was it? Were you afraid that I was going to put an end to our training sessions? After all, that would really put a damper on all this free promotion you've been getting. Is that why you had sex with me?"

"God, Preslee. It wasn't like that. You have to believe me."

She shook her head. "You're wrong. I don't have to believe anything you say. Not ever again. You told me last night that you had feelings for me. But that was a lie. Because if you did, you wouldn't have ever done this."

Fear caught his breath, and Adam cleared his throat. "I was trying to undo it. Do you remember earlier when I told you that I wanted to talk to you about something later? Well, this was it. I was going to confess everything. I didn't want there to be any lies between us."

She rolled her eyes, and sarcasm fell smoothly off her tongue. "Well, kudos to you for finally growing a pair. It only took you a month for your conscience to catch up with you. Impressive." Sniffling, she whirled around, heading for the exit. Before she got there though, she stopped and turned back. "By the way, Adam, in case I haven't made it clear enough for you, I never want to see you again. You're fired." Then she marched out the door.

Adam started after her, but Kurt stepped in front of him, blocking his path. Anger and betrayal rocketed through him at his best friend's interference, and he fisted his hands at his sides. "Move."

"No," Kurt said, standing his ground. "She was right about me. I haven't been a good friend to her. But I'm going to make up for that starting now. Let her go."

Had it been anyone else, Adam would've bulldozed right through them. But he couldn't do that to Kurt. Not when it was his own fault that he'd messed things up with Preslee. So instead, he slammed his hands onto the counter and lowered his head in frustration as a sharp breath ripped from his lungs. "I can't."

"Why? She doesn't want anything to do with you."

He lifted his gaze. "I can't leave it this way. She needs to know that I'm..."

"You're what?" A broad grin spread on Kurt's face. "In love with her?"

Adam closed his eyes. "Yeah."

Kurt chuckled. "I thought so."

Adam turned incredulous eyes on his best friend. "If you knew before I did, you could've clued me in."

"If I had, would you have believed me?"

Adam rubbed at the back of his neck. "No."

"That's why I kept my mouth shut," Kurt said with a shrug. "But it didn't take a genius to figure out that you were getting in pretty deep. You've been practically drowning yourself in her for the past month. Maybe it's time you throw yourself a life preserver and take a breather on dry land."

Heat simmered just below the surface, but Adam managed to keep his demeanor calm. "You seriously think I want to be saved from her? God, no. I can't lose her, Kurt." Adam shook his head. "I *won't* lose her. She's the only thing that matters right now. She's . . . everything to me."

"I get it, buddy. I do. But she's upset. Right now you're up shit creek without a paddle, and there's some pretty rough waters ahead. If I were you, I'd let the tides calm down before you end up diving headfirst into a whirlpool."

Adam glared at him. "If you use another damn water analogy, I'm going to punch you in the face."

Kurt grinned. "Sorry, they fit."

Adam blew out a breath. "Yeah, maybe. But I need to talk to her, to make her understand. She needs to know that I—"

"No. I meant what I said. She's hurting right now. Just let her be until things settle down."

"And let her think I didn't give a crap about her? That the only thing I cared about was my business? No way. I'd rather die than do that."

"Adam, she's not going to listen to you while her emotions are running hot. Just let her breathe." Kurt gazed at the front door. "Actually, how about I run and catch up to her? I don't know if she'll talk to me, but if I can get her to listen, I'd be happy to explain that I was the one who initiated the bet."

"It's okay. She probably won't believe you anyway. It could just make things worse. She'll think you're covering for me."

Kurt sighed. "Things can't get much worse, can they?"

"True," Adam agreed, his mind reeling. "All right. See if she'll listen. But hurry. I want you to make sure she's okay."

Kurt jumped over the counter and jogged out the front entrance. Adam prayed that he would catch her before she made it to her car. But would she even talk to him? Lord knows that Adam hadn't been able to get her to listen. Served him right though. The whole bet thing had been stupid from the start.

As he waited, Adam stared at the counter, seriously contemplating smashing his head into it. It had only been a couple of minutes, but not knowing what was going on outside was driving him insane.

Kurt returned moments later with a weird, almost somber expression. One that made Adam's gut roil with dread. Had she brushed him off too? Of course she had. She had every right to do so after what they'd done. How were they going to get out of this mess they'd created? "Tell me," he said, hanging his head. "How bad is it?"

Kurt cringed. "Bad, man. Real bad."

Great. "Let me guess. She didn't want to talk to you either?"

"No, I didn't actually talk to her."

Confusion swarmed in Adam's head. "Then what happened? She drove off before you caught her?" Kurt shook his head but didn't speak. Instead, he swallowed audibly and hesitated. "Damn it, Kurt. Tell me what happened."

He let out a hard breath. "She, uh, sort of ran into Josh in the parking lot before I got outside. And he...well, he asked her out to dinner."

"What?" Surprised, Adam rubbed a hand over his face. "After all this time," he said, shaking his head in disbelief. "The idiot couldn't see how great she was back when she was single and trying to get his attention. But now that we are together, the guy wants to chase after my woman? I don't think so."

Kurt frowned. "Eh, buddy..."

Adam waved him off. "Yeah, yeah, I know. We aren't together right now, therefore she isn't technically *my* woman. But I'm going to rectify that."

"Um, yeah. Well, good luck with that. Because *your* woman just accepted a date with another man."

CHAPTER TWENTY

Preslee glanced over at the man sitting across from her and downed her third glass of water as if it were a vodka shot that just happened to be in a large glass.

Josh pushed his glass of ice water toward her. "Thirsty?" he said, commenting on her sudden drinking problem.

She nodded but didn't speak. Sadly, that was the way she'd responded to almost everything he'd asked her since he'd picked her up half an hour ago. It was bad enough that they'd driven in silence all the way to the restaurant. But if she hadn't had to order dinner for herself, she probably wouldn't have spoken at all.

It wasn't Josh though. Not really. After finding out about what Adam had done to her, she just wasn't in the mood to talk. To anyone. She wasn't in the mood to eat either, which was why she was picking at the salmon on her plate with her fork.

"Not hungry?" Josh asked.

Preslee shook her head, still not speaking. She never should've agreed to this date. Not only because she was such crappy company for Josh right now, but pain and fury still battled for position inside of her, and she wasn't sure which emotion would pop out of her mouth if she dared to open it.

Damn it, Adam.

Over the past month, she'd asked him more than once why he wanted to help her work out, and he'd actually convinced her that he was only doing so because he was a nice guy. Hmph. Nice guys didn't go around making bets with their friends about women. Nor did they use unsuspecting people as marketing tools. What kind of jerk did that?

Yet she hadn't actually been unsuspecting, had she? She had known all along that something wasn't adding up. After all, that was why she'd questioned his motives to begin with. But she'd convinced herself that she was reading into things. Why? Because she trusted him and thought she could count on him. Now she knew better.

But why hadn't she trusted herself? Why hadn't she listened to that inner voice of hers telling her that something wasn't right? That was the last time she would ever forgo trusting herself. Especially because she was too busy trusting some guy. It was a mistake she wouldn't repeat. With Adam or any other male.

Man, she hated liars.

She wasn't sure what hurt more. Knowing that Adam had pretended to care about helping her get fit when he clearly had other motives, or learning that their entire relationship had been based on a bet and lies.

She sniffed. The back of her eyes stung, and she knew that if she didn't stop thinking about Adam, she was going to end up crying again. So she shoved him completely out of her mind. Too bad it wasn't as easy to do when it came to her heart.

Preslee took a gulp of the ice water Josh had pushed toward

her and tried to make small talk to ease the tension she felt. "Uh, so what did you do today?"

Josh shrugged. "Not much. Since it was my day off, it was a lazy day for me. I slept in until almost noon and then headed to the gym. That's when I ran into you out in the parking lot."

"I see."

He took a bite of his steak, chewed it up, and then swallowed. "Speaking of that," he said, one brow rising in interest. "I couldn't help but notice that you were upset when I ran into you. Everything okay?"

"Yep."

"Did something happen between you and Adam?"

At the mention of Adam's name, hurt and anger flared inside of her, but she managed to bank her emotions. "What do you mean?"

"For a while there, I thought you two were a couple. You seemed like a couple at the reception. So I figured you guys broke up or something today at the gym."

Well, that was not at all what she wanted to talk about right now. Especially with Josh of all people. "No. We were...never dating."

"But you wanted to, right?"

"Um, nope."

He grinned. "You're a bad liar."

"I'm not..." Oh hell. If she lied to Josh now, she would be just as bad as Adam. "Yeah, okay. You're right. I wanted us to be a couple, but unfortunately it just didn't work out."

"May I ask why?"

She shrugged and scraped the fork across the plate. "He lied to me."

"Oh. Well, that's a dick thing to do to someone you care about."

She couldn't help but laugh. "Yes, it is." Then her smile faded. "But I'm not too sure he cared about me. Because if he had..."

"He wouldn't have treated you like that," Josh said, finishing her sentence.

"Yeah," she agreed.

Josh smiled. "I probably shouldn't ask since it's none of my business, but..." Then he winced as if he was waiting for her to get mad.

"You want to know what Adam lied to me about?"

Although his curiosity was clearly piqued, Josh shrugged. "Only if you want someone to talk to. Like I said, it's none of my business. If it's too personal and you'd rather keep it to yourself, that's fine. Either way, I just want you to know that I'm here for you. We're friends, right?"

She smiled. "Yes, Josh. We're friends."

Actually, that was all they were...and all they ever would be. Well, that and coworkers, of course. While Josh was a handsome guy who had a lot to offer a woman, he wasn't *who* she wanted. Actually, now that she thought about it, he never really was *what* she wanted either.

When her dad had taken such a bad tumble, Preslee had realized her father wasn't as invincible as she'd always believed him to be. And that had scared the hell out of her.

Over the years, she'd lost so many people from her life. But her dad had always been her one constant. She couldn't lose him too. Just the thought of being alone in this world terrified her in ways nothing else had.

That was why she'd decided it was time to find someone to settle down with. Because if something ever happened to her father, she would at least have a husband to lean on. Someone to fill the void her father would evidently leave in her life. The only reason Josh had won Preslee's single guy lottery was because the two of them had so much in common when it came to their shared interest in antiques. But marriages weren't built solely on commonalities.

She smiled back at Josh. "I don't mind telling you what happened. In fact, maybe you can help me make sense of it. Because Lord knows I can't understand any of it."

Josh listened intently as she told him the whole story. Well, okay, maybe not the *whole* story. Because she definitely left out the parts about how she'd wanted to get his attention and how Adam had volunteered to help her with that. Funny thing though. Now that she had Josh's undivided attention, all she could think about was Adam.

Go figure.

"So that's basically what happened," Preslee said, sighing. "He swore that he was planning on telling me the truth when we talked later and that he was going to confess everything, but I'm just not sure what to believe. I mean, he lied straight to my face several times."

Josh cocked his head. "I understand why you're upset. But maybe he really was going to tell you the truth. What about giving him the benefit of the doubt?"

"I did that when I asked him what was in it for him. Repeatedly. He chose to lie to me over and over again. And he used me. I don't appreciate that."

Josh leaned back in his chair. "Do you love him?"

The question caught her off guard, and she faltered. "I, uh..." She closed her eyes to center herself as her heart pounded relentlessly against her rib cage. Then she opened them and gazed at Josh. "Yes. Unfortunately, I do. I didn't mean to fall for Adam, but it happened. It doesn't matter now though. I don't even know how he feels about me. Or if he ever felt anything for me."

"That's easy," Josh said, grinning. "Adam is so in love with you that he's oblivious to everyone around him. When you're in the room, the only thing he sees is you."

She squinted at him. "Why do you say that?"

"I saw the way he kissed you last night. Hell, the whole bar saw it. If that wasn't a claiming, then I don't know what the hell is. With that one kiss, he let every guy in the bar know that you were off-limits and that you were with him."

Absently, Preslee's fingers touched her lips. She loved every second of that steamy kiss he had planted on her in the bar. Adam could kiss. Like *really* kiss.

What if Josh was right and Adam really did love her? It was true that no other man had ever made her feel as safe and as protected and as...well, sexy as Adam had. He had somehow instilled a confidence in her that wasn't there before. Probably because he'd always treated her as though she mattered.

Well, except for the one time he didn't.

But everyone made mistakes. Could she forgive Adam for hurting her and making her feel insignificant this once? She wasn't sure. Maybe he hadn't meant to make her feel that way, but that didn't make it hurt any less.

"I can see your wheels turning," Josh said, reaching across the table and placing one hand over hers. "You don't have to decide anything tonight, Preslee. Just take some time to figure out what you want to do. Sometimes problems take a while to work themselves out."

She nodded. It was good advice. She was still reeling from finding out that Adam had lied and used her. But, with the way she felt right now, nothing was going to get resolved tonight or probably even this week. It would take time for her to come to terms with it and figure out what she wanted to do. "Thanks, Josh. I think I will take some time. It's all too fresh for me to make any decisions right now."

"That's smart thinking."

She shrugged. "Besides, I don't even know what Adam wants."

"He wants you," Josh said with a grin. "Anyone with eyes can see that."

"I don't know. I never thought he was the type who would go after someone like me. But then after last night..."

Confusion warped Josh's features. "What happened last night?"

Her cheeks heated. "Uh, well, I guess you can say I got my hopes up."

"Only to be disappointed by him today."

"Yeah."

His eyes filled with sympathy. "Any guy would be lucky to have you."

She wasn't getting the impression that Josh wanted anything more than friendship, which was fine by her. She didn't want him to want her. Not anymore. But why else would he ask her out?

"Thanks," she said sincerely. "Speaking of that. I'm a little confused about something." She paused, considering the best way to ask the unsettling and embarrassing question. But, in the end, she decided to just be straightforward and ask him outright. "Josh, why did you ask me to dinner?"

"Because you were upset, and I thought maybe you needed someone to talk to. That's what friends do."

"Of course. I just wasn't sure if you were looking at this as more of a..."

"Date?"

She bit her lip. "Yeah."

"Nope. I never looked at this evening as anything more than two friends hanging out. While you're beautiful—inside and out—I know I don't have a chance in hell. Adam won that particular race while I was still standing at the starting gate. But..." Josh's face broke with a smirk. "If he doesn't get his crap together soon, you know where to find me." He winked to let her know that he was kidding.

Well, she hoped he was anyway.

℮

Adam had spent the entire night pacing and driving himself up the wall. He hated knowing that Preslee was out with another man. Especially since there wasn't a thing he could do about it.

Damn it. Why hadn't he told her the truth sooner? Preferably before she found out on her own. While he didn't doubt that she would have been upset either way, finding out like she did had only made things worse. And he'd never gotten the chance to tell her how he really felt about her.

He'd tried to call her several times last night and then again this morning, but her cellphone went straight to voicemail each time. She must've turned it off because she hadn't wanted to talk to him. But he wasn't going to let her go that easily. He loved her. Even if she chose to never forgive him, she needed to at least know that.

And she was about to find out.

Adam shoved open the door to the antique shop and stepped inside, heading directly for the desk. No one was there, so he rang the bell sitting on the counter and waited impatiently. When a door to the back room opened, hope bloomed in his chest. But unfortunately it wasn't Preslee who came through the door.

A tall, dark-haired older man entered, wearing a cast on his arm nestled inside a dark blue sling, his expression curious. "Can I help you, son?"

Adam swallowed. Great. This wasn't at all the way he pictured himself meeting her father for the first time. "Is Preslee here?"

Her father gazed at him warily before answering. "She's not available at the moment. Is there something I can do for you?"

"No, I just need to speak to your daughter. It's important."

"Important, huh?" The old man stared at him, his dark eyes hardening to steel. "You must be Adam."

"Yes," he said, offering his hand.

Her dad only glared at Adam's outstretched hand. "Like I said, she's not available."

Adam dropped his hand as frustration coursed through him. Perfect. Preslee had apparently already told her dad what he'd done. Just what he needed right now. To deal with an angry father who was covering for his daughter so she wouldn't have to face him. "Preslee?" Adam called out, turning in circles. "Please come out. We need to talk."

Something that looked an awful lot like amusement flashed in her dad's eyes. "Like I said, she's not available right now."

Fury spiraled through Adam. "I think we both know that isn't true."

Her father shrugged unapologetically. "Maybe."

"And if I come back tomorrow?"

"Chances are good that she won't be available then either," the man said with a soft chuckle, clearly enjoying himself. "It's really up to her."

"Fine," Adam said, rubbing a hand over the back of his neck. "Could you at least give her a message?"

Her dad nodded. "Sure."

Knowing that Preslee was probably listening from wherever she was hiding, Adam spoke loud enough for her to hear every word. "Tell her that I'm sorry. That I never meant to hurt her. That I'm willing to do anything I have to in order to fix things between us because she means the world to me." He hesitated, hoping she would be tempted to come out and talk to him after hearing that. But when she didn't, he breathed out hard and said with a sigh, "Damn it. I'm in love with you."

Her dad grinned with mirth. "You love me?"

Adam realized that he had stopped referring to Preslee as if she wasn't standing right there and had started talking to her directly...whether she could hear him or not. "No, not *you*," Adam said in annoyance. Here he was pouring his heart out to the man's daughter, who was hiding somewhere in the building and refusing to come out, and her old man kept jacking with him. "I'm talking about your daughter, sir. I'm in love with her."

Her dad nodded. "Then that's something you should probably tell her yourself."

"I agree," Adam said, his gut clenching with the knowledge that Preslee hadn't come out to talk to him even when he'd said he loved her. Was it already too late? Had she written him off for good? "But she isn't speaking to me right now and apparently isn't willing to listen to anything I have to say."

Her father grinned. "I see."

Well, he was of zero help. Regret coursing through him, Adam sighed. "Never mind. I'm sorry to have bothered you," he said, turning to leave. Although he had hoped he'd see Preslee face-to-face, her father was apparently going to be her guard dog from now on and keep him as far away from her as possible. Served him right for hurting the man's daughter.

But as he walked away, Adam heard her father ask, "Have you ever run a gauntlet, son?"

Adam pivoted on his heel, squinting at him. Preslee had warned him to say no if her father ever asked him if he wanted to run the gauntlet. He didn't know why or what it even meant, but it was obviously something bad that Adam didn't want any part of. "No, sir. But I'd do so for your daughter."

Surprised by Adam's answer, her father raised a brow. "You think you're worthy?"

Adam shook his head furiously. "No, sir. No one is worthy of your daughter."

The man smiled with approval. "Good answer."

Adam agreed. But he needed to make something clear to this man. "Look, I know you have no reason to like me after I hurt your daughter. I don't even like myself right now. I messed up. I know that. But I'm going to do everything in my power to make things right between us again. I really do love her."

"My daughter won't date a cheater."

"What?" Adam's eyes widened. "She told you I cheated on her? I've never cheated on anyone a day in my life. I wouldn't do something like—"

The old man raised a hand to stop him. "She didn't tell me that you cheated on her. I'm just letting you know that it won't be tolerated." He glared at Adam. "By her or by *me*."

Breathing a sigh of relief, Adam nodded. "I wouldn't expect anything less. But like I said, I wouldn't do something like that to her. I know there's no coming back from that. And she means way too much to me. She's the only woman I want."

Her father's eyes lit up for only a second before hardening a second time. "I'm going to give you a good piece of advice, son. Don't ever hurt her again. Otherwise, you'll be doing much more than running a damn gauntlet."

Adam grinned. Advice, his ass. That sounded much more like a threat. One he obviously deserved. "I'll never hurt her again. You have my word. In fact, I'd consider myself lucky to have her in my life if she ever decides to forgive me for..." His words suddenly trailed off.

Interest clearly piqued, her father narrowed his gaze onto Adam. "Go on."

As realization dawned, Adam shook his head. "Wait a minute. You don't actually know what I did to her, do you?"

Her dad grinned like a cat caught with the canary. "Nope. At first, I thought you had cheated on her. But after the reaction you had when I brought it up, I knew I was wrong. Good thing. The punishment for that indiscretion is the death penalty as far as I'm concerned."

Insulted by the insinuation that he was a cheater, Adam's jaw tightened. "I didn't cheat. I can assure you of that. But I did lie to her. It started out harmless, and I didn't mean for anyone to get hurt. Especially her. I was planning on coming clean about it all, but she found out about it before I could tell her the truth."

Her father listened intently while he spoke and then gazed at Adam a minute more, as if trying to decide whether or not he believed him. Apparently he did. Because the old man smiled and nodded his approval. "Do you want some more advice, Adam?"

"Advice? Or another threat?"

Her dad smiled, humor glinting in his eyes. "I know my daughter, and she's not someone who gets over things easily. Especially after she's been hurt. Give her time."

Adam nodded. "I'm not going anywhere. Preslee's worth waiting for. I love her more than anything, but I'll wait as long as I have to. It's more than I deserve, but I hope she'll give me another chance."

In a friendly gesture, her dad stretched out his hand to Adam. "Me too, son."

CHAPTER TWENTY-ONE

Preslee let herself inside her dad's house using her own key and found him lounging on the sofa watching TV. A soft cast still covered his right wrist although his blue arm sling lay idly on the coffee table. "Hey, Dad."

Her father sat upright, careful of his arm. "Hi, honey. I didn't know you were coming by tonight." He glanced at the clock on the wall. "What are you doing here so late?"

Preslee smiled. Only her father would consider eight o'clock late. "I came by to check on you after your first day back on the job."

Actually, she'd made the mistake of listening to one of the six voicemails Adam had left and had begun to feel her resolve waver, so she'd gone for a walk to clear her head. Next thing she knew, she'd ended up here.

"It was a good day. It's nice to finally get back to work. But it's also strange."

"You didn't climb on any ladders, did you?"

He grinned. "Nope. Not a one. Josh wouldn't let me."

"That's because, when we were having dinner last night, I made him promise me that he would keep an eye on you today."

He looked confused. "You had dinner with Josh?"

"Yeah."

His brow rose. "What about Adam? He's the one I've heard so much about for the past month. You've spent almost every day with him."

She shrugged. "We had a falling-out."

"That's too bad," her dad said. "What did he do? Do I need to pay him a visit?"

"No, Dad," she said with laugh. "Hold your fire." She plopped down next to him on the couch and leaned into his shoulder— the one on his good arm. "He just...well, something happened, that's all."

"Well, no. Obviously that's not all. Otherwise you two...uh, I mean *you* wouldn't look like a kid whose balloon just got popped."

Yep. She'd never been able to hide her emotions very well. She'd always been too transparent for her own good. "I guess you could say that, in a way, Adam *did* pop my balloon. We, uh...broke up." She blew out a breath. "But it's okay."

His eyes hardened. "I will be paying him a house call. Broken wrist or not. No one is going to get away with dumping my little girl. Not while I'm still breathing."

She patted her dad's arm. "That's sweet, Dad. But I'm not a little girl anymore. And that isn't what happened. Adam didn't leave me. I walked away from him."

"Because he lied to you?"

Her eyes widened. "How did you know?"

"I, uh...didn't," he said, wincing. "I guessed."

Good guess, if you asked her. Almost too good. She eyed him warily. "Well, you nailed it perfectly. Yes, he lied to me about something. He swore he was going to come clean, but I found out about the lie before he had a chance to."

"Do you believe him? Do you think he would've come clean?"

She thought about it for a moment before answering. "Yeah, I do. Not only because he seemed sincere, but from what I overheard him say when he didn't know I was standing behind him, it sounded like he was going to tell me the truth."

"That's good."

"Yeah, but the lie isn't even what bothered me most. I'm just...disappointed in him, I guess. That was what I meant about him popping my balloon. I thought Adam was somebody I could count on. Now, I'm not so sure." Her shoulders slumped.

Her dad gave her a little squeeze. "I'm not making excuses for Adam. But from everything you've told me, he seems like a pretty good guy. So is it possible that this is a onetime occurrence?"

"I...don't know. Maybe. Probably. But even if it is, does that excuse it?"

"That's for you to decide. But I will give you something to consider. Have you ever made a mistake and wished you could undo it? Or maybe kept something from someone you loved and needed to tell the truth but were afraid to? That's not always easy to do. So if Adam was planning on coming clean, then maybe you should take that into consideration. It sounds like he has integrity and wanted to do what was right, even if it put him into an uncomfortable position."

Stunned silent, Preslee sat there quietly as guilt swam

through her veins. Wow, she was such a hypocrite. Here she was upset at Adam for keeping something from her, but she had done the same thing to her dad. Maybe it was time for her to come clean too. "Actually..." She swallowed hard. "Dad, um...there's something I need to tell you."

His mouth fell open. "Oh dear Lord. You're pregnant."

"What? No." She shook her head furiously. "I'm not pregnant. Where did you get that from?"

He exhaled in relief. "When a daughter says that she has something to tell her father, we dads are always going to jump to the worst-case scenario."

She giggled. "Me being pregnant is the worst-case scenario? Really? Because I could think of so many things that are much worse."

He chuckled. "Are you trying to scare your old man? Because if so, you're doing a great job."

Preslee smirked. "Sorry."

"It's okay. Now what did you want to tell me?"

Yeah, that. She hung her head, not wanting to look him in the eyes. "I sort of did something...eight years ago...that I never told you about."

He sat there silently for a moment, taking in what she said. "Okay," he said, puzzlement lacing his voice.

Tears stung the backs of her eyes, but she couldn't stop now. "I want you to know that it had nothing to do with you or anything to do with our relationship. I would never want you to think that. You're a wonderful dad. Always have been."

His brows collapsed over his concerned eyes. "Honey, you're starting to worry me. What did you do so long ago that you didn't want to tell me about?"

She lifted her head, needing to see his reaction when she told him the truth. She needed to know if she was hurting him. Man, she hoped not. "Eight years ago, I went looking for my biological mother."

He stilled. "Oh." He didn't say anything at first. Then he finally asked, "Did you...find her?"

She nodded solemnly. "Yes. I met her in person."

His facial expression remained neutral, and she wasn't sure what he was thinking. "Was she off the...uh..." His words faltered.

Oh. He knew? "Off the drugs?" she asked, waiting for him to nod before continuing. "No. She's not. She's still doing drugs like she was back when she traded me for some dope."

Her dad winced. "I'm sorry, honey. I never meant for you to find out like that. Your mom and I always planned to tell you when you were old enough to understand, but then she died and you were so young. After that, I didn't have the heart to tell you."

"It's okay."

He shook his head. "No, it's not. Otherwise, you wouldn't have kept this secret to yourself all these years. Why didn't you tell me that you met your birth mother?"

"The same reason you didn't tell me that she had abandoned her infant daughter for drugs. Because I didn't want to hurt you. Like I said, I was afraid that you would think it had to do with you. Like maybe you weren't enough of a parent for me. But that was never the case. I was just curious, that's all. I think most adoptees would be. But knowing what I know now, I...wish I'd never looked for her. She never wanted me. I was nothing more than a burden to her."

Fire blazed through her father's eyes. "She said that to you?"

Preslee nodded as tears filled her vision. "Yes."

Her dad shook his head in disbelief. "I can't forgive that, Preslee. I refuse to offer my compassion and understanding to a woman who can say something so horrendous to her child, the daughter she was supposed to love and care for. What kind of mother would do something like that?"

"That woman wasn't my mother." She gazed up at her father and gave him a watery smile. "I had a mom. A great one. One who loved me with everything she had for the short time we were together. That's who will be always in my heart as the only mother who ever mattered to me. I want to be the kind of person who can forgive the woman who gave birth to me for the things she's done, but I . . ."

He placed his hand on top of hers. "You don't have to forgive her, baby. She's done enough to you already, but I want to ask one thing of you. I want you to remember that everyone has their demons, including your birth mother."

She nodded. "I know that, Dad. I do. I guess I just wanted to know she cared, but . . . she didn't. At all. As selfish as she is, I'm not even sure why she agreed to meet with me in the first place. Maybe it was morbid curiosity. Who knows? We met in a diner, talked only long enough for her to tell me all about the horrific ordeal *she* went through when I was a baby, and then she walked out. She didn't even bother to look back once. I just didn't matter to her. Then or now." She sighed heavily. "That's why I've decided to talk to a therapist and work out how I feel about it all. I need that closure for myself. I don't want there to be any lingering unresolved feelings on my end toward a woman I don't matter to."

Being careful with his injured wrist, her dad wrapped his arms completely around her and pulled her into his warm chest. "I think that's a smart decision on your part, honey. But I have one last thing for you to consider. Do you know who you matter to, Preslee? *Me.* Always have, always will. Mom too. We loved you the moment we first laid eyes on you. Maybe even before that. We might have only been your adoptive parents, but you were always meant to be ours, and you brought nothing but joy to our lives. Still do."

Drops of moisture trailed down her cheeks, wetting the front of his navy-blue T-shirt. "I love you, Dad."

"I love you too."

She sniffled. "I miss Mom."

He smoothed his hand over her hair. "I miss her too. She would be so proud of the beautiful young woman you've turned into. Just like I am."

Preslee sobbed in his arms for several minutes before finally pulling out of his embrace and wiping away her tears. Her dad reached for the tissue box sitting on the end table and offered her one.

"Thanks," she said, dabbing at the corners of her eyes. "By the way, there's something else I need to tell you."

"I'm warning you, Preslee. If this is the part where you tell me that you're pregnant, I'm going to ground you and send you to your room."

She smiled. "It might be fun for you to ground me at this age."

His face turned serious. "Preslee."

She laughed. "I'm kidding. I'm not pregnant."

He let out a hard breath. "Okay, then what is it?"

She hesitated only for a moment before taking the plunge.

"After I met with my birth mother and found out what she did to me, I had some...issues that I didn't tell you about. It's another reason why I think therapy would be good for me."

Concern filled her father's features. "What kind of issues?"

"I began having bouts of emotional eating. Lots of them, in fact. Every time I thought about what that horrible woman said to me and the way she made me feel, I caught myself turning to food in order to comfort myself. That's why I gained so much weight over the past eight years. Which, in turn, has also affected my current health."

Worried eyes gazed down at her. "What do you mean?" he asked, his voice filling with urgency. "What's wrong with you?"

"I'm fine, Dad. It's just that I'm prediabetic. That's why I've been trying so hard to work out. Dr. Fowler said it was reversible if I got my weight under control and exercised more. So that's what I've been doing."

"I'm proud of you for taking control of your health. I knew you were trying to get fit, and I can tell it worked. You have a healthy glow about you."

She smiled. It was nice when people noticed all the hard work she had put in to make it happen. "Thanks. Adam had a big part in that though."

"The fitness or the healthy glow?"

"Both. But I'm still only halfway to my goal weight. I just hope I don't gain the weight I've lost back now that Adam and I aren't working out together anymore."

One dark eyebrow rose. "So you aren't going to forgive him then?"

She shrugged. "I don't know. I guess I just need some time to figure that out. I hope he'll give me some space until I do. I'm just emotionally and physically drained right now and have too much on my plate. I want to prioritize my mental health and consider my options about my physical state before I resolve anything on the Adam front. But I have a feeling he's going to be relentless when it comes to wanting me to hear him out."

Her dad grinned. "Not if I have anything to say about it."

Oh Lord. "Dad, don't do anything—"

"I won't," he promised. "But I do want to point out something to you. I've seen how happy you are with him. I don't want that to change. If losing you is his consequence for the mistake he's made, then so be it. But you might want to remember your happiness when you're considering your options. Do what's best for you."

"I will," she promised. "Don't worry about me. Besides, all of this is my own fault anyway. I knew better than to let him get too close. If I had kept my distance, I wouldn't be feeling like this."

Her dad looked puzzled. "Whoa. Hold on. What's wrong with letting someone get close?"

One shoulder came up in a slight shrug. "Why bother? They're just going to leave anyway."

"What do you mean?"

"Everyone always leaves."

"Really? I'm right here."

Preslee leveled a gaze at him. "I'm not talking about you. Well, not yet anyway. But, Dad, you aren't going to live forever. There will come a time when you will leave me."

"Well, I think I still got a few good years left in me. Don't start kicking dirt over my grave just yet."

She laughed. "You know what I mean."

He shook his head. "Actually, I don't. Who left? Are you talking about your mom? Because you have to know she'd have sold her soul to the devil to stay with you. With both of us. Dying doesn't count as leaving. That's something that is just a part of life and can't be helped. You can't hold that against her."

She blinked back the tears building once again in her eyes. "I don't. Not really. I know in my heart that she didn't want to leave. But that doesn't make her any less gone. And the older I get, the more trouble I'm having hanging on to those memories of her. Pieces of Mom are starting to fade away. I was so young when she died. I can barely remember the sound of her voice anymore." She sniffled.

"Oh, baby girl." Her dad grasped her hand. "I forget sometimes how young you were when she passed. Tell you what. Why don't we pull out some of the old home videos tonight and watch them? It would be nice to hear your mother's voice and see her smiling again. It might ease both of our hearts a little."

Preslee smiled. "I'd love that. Do you know where the box of them is?"

"They're up in the attic. Let me just go pull the ladder down and grab those." He started to rise.

She beat him to a standing position. "No way. You are not climbing on another ladder. I forbid it. Especially while you're still wearing a cast. You could reinjure yourself. Besides, you'll have trouble carrying the box. I'll go up to the attic and get them myself."

"All right," her dad said, settling his long frame back on the couch. "But before you do, tell me who else?"

"Huh?"

"You said everyone leaves you. Who else were you talking about? Your birth mom?"

Preslee nodded slightly. "She was one of them, although I'm not sure I care all that much about her leaving. Not anymore. I think talking with you about her helped me move past some of it. I'd like to try and put all of that behind me now."

"Good. I'm glad to hear that. But what do you mean by 'one of them'?"

"Well, I was also referring to the guys I dated in the past. They all left me. Not the other way around."

"Yeah, but they were idiots. They did you a favor by leaving."

She smiled. She doubted her dad would ever think any guy was good enough for her. "Well, even if we don't count them, there are still more."

"Who else?"

She licked her dry lips. "Do you remember Jenny? She was my best friend back when I was nine. She lived next door in that—"

"White house with the ugly green shutters? Of course. She was a nice girl, and you two played together all the time. Well, until her family moved away." Realizing what he'd said, a frown emerged. "But honey, she didn't leave you. Not really. Her dad had received that job offer in California. It wasn't like she could stay here with us. She had no choice but to go."

"Try telling that to a nine-year-old girl who just lost her best friend. At the time, it felt like she'd abandoned me. Especially since she never wrote me a letter or tried to stay in contact."

"Well, that happens. People sometimes move on with their lives and never fully realize what an impact they had on a person. Or how much they could be missed by someone. Have you tried looking her up? She was so young. Maybe she feels the same way you do."

As odd as it was, that was something she'd never considered. "No, but now that you've mentioned it, I may do that. I would love to reconnect with her. It would be interesting to see how much she's changed since we were little."

Her dad nodded. "And who knows? Maybe you'll become best friends again."

She smiled. "True."

He scratched his chin. "Well, that had to cover everyone. I can't think of anyone else who would have left you or disappeared from your life."

"Actually," Preslee said, holding up one finger, "there was one more."

"Who?"

She sighed heavily. "This is stupid, but do you remember that little brown dog that I found behind the grocery store? He was hanging out by the dumpster trying to eat whatever scraps he could find."

"How could I forget? I hated that dog. He chewed up my sneakers more than once. I wanted to strangle him. But what about him?"

"He ran away from home, remember? Even though I took good care of him, he still left me."

Her dad stared at her blankly before whispering, "Oh." He cringed visibly, his lips tightening into a thin line. "I forgot." Then he let out a nervous chuckle. "Uh, I probably should've told you this a long time ago, but..." He ran an uneasy hand through his gray hair.

Her eyes narrowed onto him with laser precision. "But what?"

After a short pause, he finally spoke. "That dog," he said, cringing. "It didn't exactly run away from home."

She stared at him in shock before a terrible thought passed through her head. "Don't tell me you took him to the pound. I knew you didn't like him and threatened him with that all the time, but I didn't think you'd actually do it."

He shook his head. "No, of course I didn't. Although I should have, as many times as I caught him trying to jump onto the kitchen table from one of the chairs. Or the many times he peed on my bathroom rug. He was a nuisance."

Confusion swam through her. "I don't understand then."

Her dad hesitated. "He died."

"Oh my God." Her mouth fell open, and she blinked rapidly. "Y-you killed him?"

He shook his head furiously. "No, not me. I didn't kill him."

"You had to. He wasn't sick. The night before he disappeared he was perfectly fine. What did you do to him?"

"Honey, he got run over by a car."

She glared at her dad suspiciously. "*Whose* car?"

His eyes widened. "Not mine," he swore, holding his hand up. "I promise. The morning he disappeared, that dog of yours had apparently dug his way out from under the fence and gotten hit by a car in front of the house."

Preslee blinked. "What?"

He nodded. "Yeah, I found him before you woke up. He was already dead, so I buried him in the backyard and told you that he ran away. Since there was a hole in the fence where he dug out, it was believable. But I guess I forgot to tell you the truth after all these years." Her dad bit his lip as if he was struggling to keep from laughing. He shrugged sheepishly. "Oops."

"Oops?" she repeated, placing her hand on her hips. "So let me get this straight. My dog got hit by a car and died. But instead of telling me that, you let me believe that he ran away from home because he didn't like me?"

That did it. Her dad couldn't seem to contain his laughter anymore, because he cracked up. He slapped a hand over his mouth to stanch the flow, but it did no good. Preslee crossed her arms and glared at him, but even then, his chortling only got louder. After about a minute of hearing how amused her father was by all of this, Preslee accidentally released an inappropriate giggle of her own. She couldn't help it. His laughter was infectious.

When her dad finally collected himself, he sat back on the couch and took a deep breath. "I'm sorry. I didn't know that you thought the stupid mutt ran away because he didn't like you. Had I known that I would've told you the truth. But you had just lost your mom the year before, and I was only trying to keep you from getting hurt. Please don't be mad. I truly am sorry."

She smiled. Her dad had always tried his best to keep her from getting hurt. Whether he was threatening her dates, or putting up with a scruffy dog who chewed all of his shoes because he didn't have the heart to tell her she couldn't keep him. So how could she ever be mad at him for anything?

"I'm not mad. I am sorry that the dog died though. Now I feel bad. Maybe if I hadn't rescued him from behind that grocery store, he would still be alive."

"No, honey. I don't think things work quite like that. I believe that when it's your time to go, then it's your time to go. No matter where you are or who you're with." Then he smiled wide. "But if it makes you feel any better, I buried him with the last sneaker of mine that he chewed up. Figured he might need a little snack on his way to heaven," he said, another chuckle spilling from his lips.

Preslee laughed too, which only set her father off again. She wasn't sure why they were laughing, but they did so until both of them had tears streaming down their faces. Finally, she caught her breath and managed to say, "Why are we laughing? It's not at all funny."

Her dad's laughter slowed to a halt and he took another deep breath. "You're right. It's not. Sorry. But sometimes you just have to laugh. It makes life easier to deal with."

She wiped at her eyes with the tissue she was still holding. "We're horrible people."

Her father shook his head. "Nah. You know how it is. Something might not be funny when it first happens. But eventually, over time, you can find humor in a situation. This is sort of like that."

"Yeah, but there's really nothing funny about my dog dying." She pushed a strand of hair out of her face. "I was more laughing because you got so tickled by it. Though it still isn't funny."

"Honey, I wasn't laughing about the dog dying either. I started laughing because I realized I never told you that the dog died. Then I got amused when you accused me of killing him." He smirked. "I'm glad to know that you think your old man is capable of running over an innocent dog all because I didn't like him."

"Uh, yeah. Sorry."

"You don't have to apologize, honey. But do me a favor, would you? Maybe share that part of the story with your new boyfriend. It might keep him in line in the future."

She crossed her arms. "Maybe you should tell him yourself since you've talked to him more recently than I have." She raised a brow, daring him to deny it.

Her dad winced. "He *may* have stopped by the shop this morning. How did you know?"

"I didn't. I guessed," she said with a wide smile. "It wasn't like it was hard to figure out. Never in your life have you ever defended—even in the slightest way—any guy that had hurt me. You just wanted to maim them."

"I'm not defending Adam," her dad said, holding up his hands. "In fact, I'm happy to go find him and kick the crap out of him for hurting you if that's what you'd like me to do. But I have a feeling that it's not what you want."

"Then what is it that I want?"

He smiled. "That's simple. You want Adam. Because you're in love with him."

"I...I didn't say that."

Her dad shrugged. "Didn't have to. I can see it in your eyes."

"No, that's anger."

"Yes, it is. And pain. But only a man you love could hurt you that much. I should know. I married the only woman who ever held that much power over me. Your mother."

She sighed. "That's different. The two of you were both deeply in love with each other. That isn't the case with us. Yes, I fell in love with Adam, but he...doesn't love me back."

"Yes, he does."

"How do you know? You barely know Adam."

Her dad smiled. "Just trust me, okay? The guy is definitely in love with you."

Preslee did something to her father that she hadn't done since she was a teenager. She rolled her eyes at him. "Well, it doesn't really matter anymore. Even if Adam is in love with me—which I highly doubt—I'm not ready to face him, much less forgive him. I'm still hurt by what he did. Whether he meant to humiliate me or not, he did so in the worst way possible, and I need some time to figure things out in my head. Only then will I deal with him."

Her father grinned. "I knew you'd say that. Even as a child, you were never quick to forgive. That's why I told Adam to give you some time when I saw him this morning."

"You did?"

"Yep. And he said he would...because you are worth waiting for."

Her throat swelled, and she swallowed the knot forming. "He said that? Really?"

Her dad nodded. "I have no doubt he meant every word."

Preslee inhaled a deep breath and then closed her eyes to keep from shedding the tears building behind her eyelids. Just hearing that Adam had said she was worth waiting for had her heart softening a little. Her first instinct was to go to him and try to get back some semblance of what they'd lost when she'd walked out on him.

But she couldn't.

No way was she going to let Adam off the hook that easily. Just because he'd said something nice about her to her father didn't mean that she would just forget about how he'd hurt and embarrassed her.

While her father fully believed Adam had fallen in love with her, she still had serious doubts. Maybe taking a step back from the entire situation was exactly what she needed and would give her some perspective. After all, Adam said she was worth the wait, right?

Good. Then let him prove it.

"Honey," her dad said, snaring her attention. "I think I'll go microwave us some popcorn while you grab those old home videos from the attic. I can't wait to see your mom and reminisce about her for a while. I miss her every day."

She smiled. "Me too, Dad. I'll be right back."

Preslee headed into the hallway, yanked the pull-down ladder out of the ceiling, and stepped onto it. The wooden ladder creaked a little under her weight but seemed steady enough as she climbed up into the musty-smelling attic.

Once she made it inside, she pulled the string on a light above her head and began searching for the box of old videos. After a few minutes, she found the clearly marked box against the wall beneath a box of old photo albums. The framed picture on top immediately caught her eye. She lifted it and blew a light covering of dust from it, scattering it into the stale air.

It was a picture of her parents on their wedding day.

She rubbed her finger over her mother's pretty face as sadness swamped her. Her chin trembled, and she swallowed hard. God, why did she have to die? She hated losing her mom at all, but especially at such a young age. Her mother had never gotten the chance to take Preslee shopping for her first bra, see her all dressed up for prom, or watch her walk across the stage during her high school graduation.

As a teenager, she'd wished she could've experienced all of that with her mother. But now that Preslee was an adult, there were a couple of other things that were even more important to her that her mother would miss out on. That they would *both* miss out on. Not only would her mom never be able to help her get ready to walk down the aisle on her wedding day, but she would also never have the pleasure of holding any grandchildren in her arms.

Preslee hung her head as sorrow wrapped around her heart like an angry fist. One that squeezed so hard that it physically hurt. While marriage and babies weren't in her immediate future, it didn't make the thought of her mom not being there any less crushing. But there was nothing she could do about it.

Although she'd convinced herself over the years that it was her own fault that everyone had always left her, she knew deep down that her mother would've never left had she been given a choice. Adam had been right about that. So had her dad.

Placing the photo of her adoptive parents back in the box, Preslee sat back and sighed heavily. She still wasn't sure what to do about Adam, but she was going to take the time to consider whether or not she could get past the hurt feelings and his betrayal. Maybe she would eventually be able to forgive him, but right now the wound was too fresh, too raw.

But where did that leave her when it came to her fitness plan? Going back to the Body Shop was no longer an option. Not unless she wanted to run into Adam...which she didn't. That would only screw with her emotions. Yet she didn't want to give up exercising either. Nor did she want to gain back all the pounds she'd already lost. She was more than halfway to reaching her goal and only had fifteen pounds to go. She couldn't quit now.

In the past, she would've given up without a second thought and gone back to her old ways in a heartbeat. It had been all too easy to do. But she was different now. She felt good. Stronger even. She wasn't the same woman who had started this fitness journey. That idealistic woman had wanted to find a man to settle down with because she was scared of being alone. But maybe being alone was exactly what she needed. She could spend some time getting to know this newer, stronger version of herself that had been hiding somewhere inside of her all along.

Because that woman wasn't a quitter.

Sure, it would be hard to continue her exercise regimen without Adam's guidance or the use of his gym, but she could do it. As he'd said before, he was only a tool. But she had shown up and put in the hard work.

So, beginning tomorrow, she was going to focus her energy into finishing what she'd started. She was going to have to do it without his help, but she needed to make it to her goal. Just to prove to herself that she could.

℮

Preslee sat patiently in the waiting room until the nurse called her back and took her vitals. Afterward, she was left in a small room alone, sitting on the crinkly white paper that made a ton of sound whenever she so much as shifted an eyeball in a different direction.

A few days ago, she'd undergone another new round of blood work, and this was her follow-up visit where she would receive her latest test results. For some strange reason, Dr. Fowler had wanted to see her in person this time, whereas last time he had given the results to her directly over the phone.

Normally, they wouldn't have repeated the blood work again

so soon, but Dr. Fowler insisted that they reorder the tests after a couple months since he would be retiring and wanted to wrap up any cases before passing them over to the new doctor in town.

And that had been one of the reasons Preslee had wanted to avoid coming in to Dr. Fowler's office. The last thing she wanted to do was run into Adam's brother, Michael . . . er, Dr. Caldwell. While she didn't think he was the type to treat her poorly just because she had dumped his brother a few weeks ago, she also didn't want to chance an awkward conversation with him either. Thankfully, he hadn't been around when she had arrived.

A knock sounded on the door, and Dr. Fowler opened it and stepped inside. He dropped down on the short stool and rolled himself closer to her. He smiled. "How have you been, Preslee?"

"Doing great. How are you?"

He gave his usual reply when asked that question. "Old and grumpy." Then he leafed through her file, pulled out some paperwork, and began reading over it. "These are your test results," he stated. "Do you know what they say?"

How the heck would she know that? "Um, no. Is it good news or bad news?"

"Both."

She wasn't sure how it could possibly be both unless she'd fixed one problem while something else had gotten out of whack. "Which one are you giving me first?"

He gazed at her. "Here's the good news. You are officially no longer in the prediabetic range. Congratulations."

"Really? Wow, that's great to hear. Thank you," she said, her mouth curving into a smile.

Holy cow. She had actually done it. When she'd first started working out and eating healthier, she hadn't thought it possible. Who knew accountability and consistency would work so well?

Adam did, that's who.

"Shut up," she whispered to herself.

"What was that?" Dr. Fowler asked, not able to hear as well as he used to.

"Nothing. Sorry, I had a tickle in my throat."

"Do I need to take a look?"

She shook her head. "No, that's okay. I'm fine. But if you could, I would like to know what the bad news is." She still needed to know what else she was dealing with.

He smiled. "The bad news is that I won't be your doctor anymore. Dr. Caldwell is taking over all of my cases, and from now on, you will have to make all your appointments with him."

"That's right. I heard you were retiring."

He nodded. "Dr. Caldwell is a fine doctor, and you won't be disappointed. In fact, I'd like to introduce you to him before you go."

Panic shot through her. "Uh, that's okay. I've actually already met him. So there's no need."

"I see. All right, then we are done here. You are free to leave."

"Thank you again. I'm sure I'll be seeing you around town, but just in case, good luck with your retirement. I hope you enjoy it."

He nodded and left the room, leaving the door wide open. So Preslee grabbed her purse and strolled out the door toward the front desk. As she was checking out, she noticed Michael coming out of the back room, so she ducked her head. The moment they gave her the visit summary and her debit card back, she shot out the door and ran to her car.

When she'd first met Michael, she hadn't thought anything of the resemblance between him and his brother. Probably because it was common for siblings to have similar features. But now that she'd seen him again, she couldn't believe how much he looked like Adam. And that only made her want to cry.

CHAPTER TWENTY-TWO

Adam settled his bulk in a chair and shoved papers away from him. The last thing he felt like doing right now was paperwork.

Kurt reached for the papers and pulled them over in front of him. "Still grouchy, I see."

"Yeah, so what?"

"Come on, man. I've never seen you like this before. It's been a month. You can't keep moping around. I know it sucks, but you have to move on. You can't keep hoping that she'll come around."

"I can't let her go," Adam said, rubbing a hand through his unruly hair. "I love her."

Kurt's eyes softened. "I get it, man. I really do. But do yourself a favor and get past this. You can't keep this up. You haven't shaved, your hair looks like you stuck your finger in a light socket, and you've put on probably a good twenty pounds. Dude, this isn't at all like you."

"Who cares?"

"I do," Kurt stated.

"Well, I don't."

"Oh, I know. You've made that perfectly clear. But maybe you should since I've been the one picking up all your slack. I've been making excuses for you to your clients for the past few weeks, and I'm tired of it. I've already killed off all four of your grandparents as well as your stepmother and stepfather."

Adam lifted his head and quirked a brow. "All four of my grandparents have been dead for years, and I don't have stepparents. My mom and dad are still married, you nimrod. You know that."

"Yeah, but your clients don't. Unfortunately, I've run out of dead or fictional family members of yours to kill. The next funeral is going to belong to either your mom or your dad. Who do you want me to kill off first?"

Adam stared at his best friend in disbelief before a small chuckle slipped past his lips. "You're crazy, you know that?"

Kurt smiled. "Yeah, but I got you to laugh, didn't I? It's nice to know that there are signs of life still in you. Especially since business has been more lucrative than ever. If you were here more often, you'd know that. In fact, why are you here? It can't be to actually work. You haven't done that in a while. You've been pretty much useless since Preslee walked out on you last month."

"Gee, thanks for the reminder," Adam said sarcastically. "As if I wasn't depressed enough already."

"Sorry," Kurt said, wincing. He leaned back against the counter and crossed his arms. "So why are you here anyway? To spread more joy and cheer?"

Adam picked up a large white envelope and passed it to his friend. "No, I came by to give you this."

"What is it?" Kurt asked, looking at it warily. "More paper-work for me to fill out?"

"Actually, I've already filled the forms out. It only requires your signature at the bottom."

Confusion warped Kurt's expression as he slid out the paper-work. Then his eyes widened. "What the hell? Is this what I think it is?"

"Yeah. You've put as much work into this place as I have. So I thought I'd make this official. Therefore, I'm signing half of the business over to you and making you co-owner of the Body Shop."

"You've got to be kidding me."

"No, you deserve it."

"Yeah, I do." Kurt smirked. "As I've pointed out, you have been pretty useless lately."

Adam grinned. "You've been helping me make this business a success from the beginning, and I appreciate it."

Kurt squeezed his shoulder. "Thanks, Adam. I can't tell you how much this means to me."

"You're welcome," Adam said with a nod. "And honestly, I know I need to pull myself together. I can't make Preslee forgive me. I know that. I don't want to lose her, but it doesn't look like I have much of a choice in the matter. It's something I'm going to have to deal with. It's not going to be easy, but it's not fair for me to lay everything at your feet and shut down like I've been doing. I'll try to be better, okay?"

Adam was telling the truth. He couldn't keep doing this. It was just tough though. He missed Preslee. Her smile. Her sense of humor. Her playfulness. Every day, he was held captive by memories of her. Or of them together. There wasn't a place in town he could go that didn't somehow remind him of her. His apartment. The gym. The park. Hell, even the bar. That was how he knew he'd never get her out of his head...or his heart.

She had been it for him. The one. And he'd let her slip away.

Preslee didn't want anything to do with him. He'd given her space for the first few weeks, but the moment he felt like she might be slipping away for good, he'd immediately renewed his efforts in getting her back. But she'd never returned any of his calls, and every time he'd gone by the antique store, her dad had covered for her by saying she wasn't available.

It didn't matter though. Adam didn't have any other option but to go along with Preslee's decision not to see him anymore. Even if it did suck. She didn't want anything to do with him, and it hurt on levels that he hadn't been emotionally prepared to deal with. Which was why he looked like a bum at the moment.

He'd been so depressed about losing her that he hadn't had it in him to do anything other than mope around on a daily basis. A full month of not exercising while lying around and eating unhealthy comfort foods had not done good things to his body. Or his mindset. And that only made him feel worse.

So did the fact that Preslee was no longer working out all because of him. She had come so far, and he didn't want her to let it all go for nothing. Nor did he want her to feel as though she wasn't worth meeting her goal. She was. God, she was worth so much more than that. Especially to him. But now she would never know that, and he would never have another chance with her.

Served him right.

Kurt must've picked up on his train of thought because he said, "I'm sorry, Adam. I feel like it's my fault that you lost Preslee. I never should've dragged you into another one of my bets. If I hadn't done that, you wouldn't be in this situation."

"No," Adam said, shaking his head. "Preslee was right. I'm a big boy and have to take responsibility for my own actions. You didn't drag me into anything. I could've said no to you, but I didn't. I went along with the bet willingly. That was my own fault."

"We're idiots."

Adam nodded, agreeing with his friend. "Yeah."

A comfortable silence settled between them as the front entrance door chimed. Glancing up, Kurt cleared his throat. Loudly. "Um, Adam? I think you might want to take a look at this. You're not going to believe what I'm seeing."

Head still hung, Adam continued to lean forward with his elbows on his knees. "What is it?"

Kurt grinned. "It's Preslee."

"What about her?"

"No, I mean it's her. She just walked through the front door."

Surging upward, Adam lurched to his feet. "What? Where?" Sure enough, Preslee had entered the building and was crossing the room, heading in the direction of the bathrooms. And she looked better than ever. "Shit," Adam said, running a hand over the scruff on his face. "What do I do?"

"Well, first of all, you get the constipated look off your face. Then you go over and talk to her."

"I can't do that."

"Why not?"

Adam cringed. "Look at me, man. I look like crap."

Kurt laughed. "I told you so. But you don't have a choice. You might not get another chance to talk to her. Now get over there."

Adam hesitated. "Wish me luck."

"You know I do," Kurt said, offering him a fist bump. "Go get your woman back."

Gazing down at his wrinkled T-shirt, Adam sighed. Get his woman? As bad as he looked right now, he'd be lucky if he could get some spare change. But Kurt was right. It was the first time Adam had seen her since she'd walked out on him, and it might be the only shot he got. He wasn't going to waste it. If there was the slightest chance that he could get her to hear him out, he had to give it a go.

He headed in the same direction that Preslee had gone. He wasn't sure what she was doing at the gym, but she clearly had an agenda. He'd never seen her looking so determined before.

Not only that, but she looked great. And it had nothing to do with her body. Instead, there was a newfound confidence in the way she moved. She held her head up high. Shoulders back. Arms swinging at her sides.

Adam found her standing in the locker room hallway, staring at the large scale he kept in the corner. Not only did she look like she had lost more weight since the last time he'd seen her, but she also looked...happy? Great. So things were probably not going to go the way he hoped they would.

Had she thought he wouldn't be here? Or had she come to say goodbye for the last time?

Sighing, Adam said, "Preslee."

Her head spun in his direction, and she bunched her fist onto her hip. "It's about time you got over here. I thought I was going to have to come and get you."

"You knew I was here?"

"Of course. It wasn't hard to figure out. Your truck is parked directly out front."

Okay, then. "So you aren't avoiding me? Anymore, I mean?"

"No. Actually, I wasn't really avoiding you to begin with. I just wasn't coming into the gym anymore after we broke things off. But it's not like I've been hiding out from you."

He lifted one brow. "First off, we didn't break things off. *You* did. I didn't want things to end between us. Still don't. But every time I went by the antique shop, your dad was always the one behind the counter, and you were nowhere to be found. He kept saying you weren't available and giving me the runaround. I'm pretty sure he enjoyed every bit of it too."

She smiled wide. "That's my dad for you. I have no doubt he probably did enjoy it. He's a bit overprotective when it comes to his only daughter. But he wasn't lying to you, Adam. I wasn't there any of the times you stopped by. I've been doing a lot of traveling with Josh recently, which has kept me pretty busy. That's why you haven't seen me around."

Anger was like a flash flood flowing rapidly through his veins as it grew in strength. "I see," he told her, his voice bordering on hostility. But then he stopped and shook it off. There was no point in getting upset with her since this was all his own fault. If he hadn't lied to her, he wouldn't have all but shoved her into Josh's arms.

Damn if it didn't sting though.

"Well, I hope Josh makes you happy. That's all I ever wanted for you. To be happy. And if Josh is the one who does that for you, then—"

"Goodness no," she said, shaking her head and giggling. "Josh and I are just friends. Well, that and technically I'm also his new boss. We've been traveling together around the local area, visiting different estate sales and auction sites, looking for antiques. Josh has a vast knowledge that comes in handy, and I've been learning a lot from him. But there's absolutely nothing going on between us."

The sound of relief was evident in his sigh, but he didn't care. Hope had filled him once more. No wonder he hadn't seen Josh in the gym lately. "Sorry. I just assumed that there was something more between the two of you. I'm glad there's not." Then he paused, realizing what she'd actually said. "Wait a minute. Isn't traveling to the auction sites your dad's job?"

"It used to be. Now it's mine. When my dad finally came back to work, he said he was impressed with the way I'd handled the business while he was away and decided he liked having all the extra free time on his hands. So now he's planning to retire within the year and is allowing me to take over the business."

Adam beamed a proud smile at her. "That's great, Preslee. Congratulations. I know you wanted that, and you deserve it."

"Thanks," she said, returning his smile.

"So why are you here?" God, that sounded rude. Maybe he should've softened it a little. "I mean, I haven't seen you in four weeks, and then you suddenly pop up. I guess I'm just wondering why." Yeah, not better.

She nodded toward the large metal scale that Adam kept in

the bathroom hallway for his clients and gym members to use. "It's weigh-in day."

He shook his head. "Preslee, you don't have to weigh in anymore. I forfeited the bet to Kurt, remember? I can tell you've lost more weight since I've last seen you, but you didn't have to hit the goal to prove anything to me."

"I didn't. I hit it for *me*."

Preslee smiled wide at the confused expression on Adam's face. God, she missed him. But those sentiments would have to wait. Right now, she needed to finish what she started. "Sorry, Adam. But it was my goal. Not yours."

He nodded. "You're right. It was yours, and you deserve to wear that badge of honor. How much weight have you lost?"

She shrugged. "I don't really know. I haven't weighed myself at all in the past month. I could just tell I was losing weight from the fit of my clothes."

"How did you do it? Lose the weight, I mean. Did you join a different gym?"

"No, I actually took up trail running. It's sort of like a mud run, but without all the mud," she said with a grin.

He chuckled. "Well, that's good to hear. I'm glad you found an activity that you enjoy while burning calories. That's half the battle when it comes to staying fit."

"I agree. That's why I've since reached out to the other girls and started a hiking group. All of us women now meet up a couple of times a week to hit the trails together. It's been fun, and I've really gotten to know them so much better. I should've done that a long time ago. That's how I was able to lose even more weight on my own. I have an awesome support system. Who knew?"

He smiled. "Well, you look amazing. I can tell how hard you've worked. You should be proud of yourself."

A maelstrom of emotions overtook her. Happiness. Joy. Pride. She was so dang proud of herself. Deservedly so. "I am. It wasn't easy."

Adam nodded. "It never is. But you're killing it, and that's all that matters."

"Thanks."

"So I guess you're ready for your final weigh-in."

Preslee shook her head. "Nope. I don't need a final weigh-in."

He blinked. "But I thought you said..."

"I said it was weigh-in day. Not that I was going to weigh in. Sorry, Adam, but I'm not getting on that scale this time. I don't need to."

A smile spread across his face. "You sure? Because no matter what number pops up on the scale, it doesn't change the fact that you should celebrate."

"I'm positive," she said confidently. "In the past, I've always quit before giving myself any real chance of being successful at losing weight. But now that I've been sticking to a healthy life-style, I've already seen exactly what I've been able to accomplish. I feel great. I'm stronger than I was before. Mind, body, and soul." Then she grinned. "I only came by because I need to finish what I started. What *we* started."

He scowled. "Look, I'm sorry. Kurt and I should've never made that stupid bet in the first place, and we both regret hurting you. It was never our intention."

"I know that. I do," she said, licking her dry lips. "And

I'm willing to forgive you both. *This time.* But it's your only chance to get back in my good graces, Adam. You won't get another."

"I won't need another." He reached for her and pulled her into his arms, hugging her to him.

She buried her face into his warm male chest and sank into his arms, enjoying the sensation of him touching her once again. When she finally forced herself to pull back, their eyes met, and his gaze instantly heated, lingering on her lips. It sent a thrill coursing through her. The man still wanted her as much as ever. She could see it written all over his face.

His eyes softened, and he swallowed hard. "I'm sorry I screwed everything up between us. I . . . I've missed you."

Her heart squeezed. The uncertainty in his voice bothered her though, and she decided it was time to put him out of his misery and let him know exactly how she felt. "I missed you too. That was my other reason for showing up here today. I have something I need to say to you."

His body tensed, as if he was bracing himself. "Okay. Go ahead. Lord knows I deserve it."

She smiled. "I want to pursue this thing between us."

Adam stared fixedly at her, as if he didn't know what to say. Clearly her words had taken him by surprise. "Do you mean it?"

"Yes."

He gazed at her warily. "Are you sure? After what I did, I wouldn't blame you if you never trusted me again."

"Yes, I'm sure. I've never been more sure about something in my life. I need you, Adam. While getting fit has made me happy, I've never been happier than when I've been with you."

His strong arm snaked around her waist and pulled her back

into his chest, his mouth a breath away from hers. "Thank God. I thought I'd lost you."

"I'm not going anywhere."

"Me neither. But you need to know one more thing. I love you."

She smiled at him. "I know. I got your messages. By the way, I love you too."

"Then marry me."

Whoa! Confusion and disbelief slammed into her so hard that her knees nearly buckled. Thankfully Adam tightened his grip on her and kept her upright. She hadn't at all seen that one coming. Had he really asked her to marry him? "Do what?" She lifted her eyes to his and realized that he was just as surprised by the unexpected proposal as she was. "Y-you don't mean that."

For a moment, there was complete silence, as if Adam was rolling the idea around in his mind. Then he grinned. "Actually, I do."

She shook her head. "No, you don't. You were just as surprised as I was about what just came out of your mouth. I saw it in your eyes."

"You're right, I was. But just because I blurted it out doesn't mean that I didn't mean it. Actually, if you think about it, people tend to only blurt out the truth."

Dear God. "No, Adam. We can't—"

He pressed his lips to hers in the softest of kisses before pulling back. "Marry me, Preslee."

"No. Stop saying that."

He lowered his forehead to hers and swallowed hard. "Look, I didn't plan this. Hell, I didn't even know I would see you today, much less that we would get back together. I don't have a ring to offer you. I'm not down on one knee. And I'm certain your father is going to kill me for not asking him for your hand in marriage first. But I want this. I want *you*. This feels right. Just say yes."

She blinked at him. "You're serious?"

His intense eyes narrowed onto her. "Absolutely."

"Adam, you don't have to propose. I've already forgiven you."

He lifted one dark brow. "Do you really think I'd play around about something like this?"

"No, but..."

"Preslee. Please say you'll marry me."

Tears filled her eyes. "Adam."

"Look, I know this is happening fast, and you probably think I'm crazy by asking you to be my wife, but I don't care. I'm laying it all on the line because I want you to know how serious I am about you. About us. Marry me."

Her voice warbled. "No."

His eyes widened slightly. "No?"

"Yes."

"Okay, you're confusing me. Is your answer yes or no?" he asked.

"The answer is no. I can't marry you."

He glanced over her face as if waiting on her to say, *Psych!* About ten seconds later, he realized she wasn't kidding and the corners of his mouth drooped. "You're serious? Your answer is no?"

Preslee shook her head. "I'm sorry, Adam. I'm not saying no to forever. I'm just saying no right now. I don't think we're ready for that kind of commitment."

"What do I have to do to prove we are—get down on my knees and beg?"

"No." She didn't want him to beg. Nor did she want pretty words. She just wanted...*him*. "There's no need. I just want to be certain about such a big decision."

"I'm sure. I've never wanted anything more. You're it for me."

"I feel the same way."

"Then why are you turning me down?"

"Because I would like to make a different proposal of sorts. One that I think better suits us right now."

"Okay, I'm listening."

"I think we should move in together."

He grinned. "Hmm. Living in sin. Okay. While I'm not sure your dad is going to like that, I love where this is going so far."

She smirked. "And I would like us to get a dog. I've been volunteering at the local shelter and there are so many that could use a good home. Then after some time, we'll reconsider your proposal."

He nodded. "Done."

Preslee stared warily at him. "That's it? You're agreeing that quickly?"

"Sweetheart, I would agree to anything as long as it means getting you back in my life permanently. While I do still want to marry you, I'm happy to wait until we're both ready. There's no hurry. Nothing is going to change the way I feel about you." He slid his hands into her hair and kissed her with everything he had. "I love you, Preslee."

"I love you too," she said, throwing her arms around his neck. Then she whispered into his ear. "I'm sorry I made you wait so long before I was ready to work things out."

"Don't be. You were worth the wait." He pulled back and kissed her forehead. "I'm just glad that we're together now, and that we have a bright future to look forward to."

"Me too."

He lifted her chin until her eyes met his. "And baby, you'll never have to worry about me leaving you. Because I'm not going anywhere. Ever."

Her heart filled with joy as tears leaked from the corners of her eyes. She wrapped her arms around his waist and rested her cheek against his hard chest, the top of her head grazing his chin. "I know."

ACKNOWLEDGMENTS

I am so grateful to everyone who worked on this book or supported and encouraged me along the way. If I forget to acknowledge you, I apologize. It wasn't intentional.

Thank you to my amazing husband, Denny, for all your love and never-ending support. And my two wonderful kids, who make me proud every day. I don't know what I'd do without you guys!

To my dad, thanks for all the love and encouragement. I can always count on you to be there for me when I need you. I love you.

Much love goes to Amanda Rushing for always being ready for another one of our long talks. I'm so glad we've grown so close over the past few years.

Bobbie Watkins, thank you for your love, support, and friendship. You are the best friend a girl could ask for. Twenty-four years and counting...

A warm thank-you goes out to the rest of my family and friends for always supporting me. In particular, Becky Lyle, Terry Bliss, Deborah McInnis, Brenda Lyle, Stacy Pyryt, Andrea Retrum, and April Jackson. Without all of you, this world would be a lonely place.

Big thank-yous go out to my wonderful and thoughtful

editor, Alex Logan, and the rest of the Forever group for all the magnificent work they did to get this book to the readers. A special thank-you goes out to Emily Andrukaitis for the great copyedits, to Bob Castillo for always being a pleasure to work with, and to the art department for their brilliance with the fantastic book cover. I love it!

As always, thank you to my agent, Andrea Somberg, for all the hard work. I can't tell you how much I appreciate everything you do.

To Rebecca Childs, thanks for all your helpful advice. It's amazing what a ten-minute brainstorming session and weekly chats can do for an author's mindset.

Big hugs go out to Crystal Wegryzonowiz and the rest of the Pure Bliss group.

Lastly, thank you to the readers and bloggers! My hope is that my humorous romances help you to forget your troubles, remind you to love, and put a smile on your faces. Because life is too short to do anything but be happy!

ABOUT THE AUTHOR

Alison Bliss is a bestselling, award-winning author of humorous, contemporary romances. A born and raised Texan, she currently resides in the Midwest with her husband and her two kids. The youngest of five girls, she has never turned down a challenge or been called by the right name. Alison believes the best way to know if someone is your soulmate is by canoeing with them because if you both make it back alive, it's obviously meant to be. She enjoys writing fun, steamy love stories with heart, heat, and laughter: something she calls "Romance...with a sense of humor."

To learn more, visit her at:
   http://authoralisonbliss.com
   Facebook/AuthorAlisonBliss
   Twitter @AlisonBliss2